A Stranger in Town

A Stranger in Town

A ROCKTON NOVEL

Kelley Armstrong

WHEELER PUBLISHING
A part of Gale, a Cengage Company

GALE
A Cengage Company

GALE
A Cengage Company

A Casey Duncan Novel, #6.
Wheeler Publishing, a part of Gale, a Cengage Company.

Wheeler Publishing Large Print Hardcover.
The text of this Large Print edition is unabridged.
Other aspects of the book may vary from the original edition.
Set in 16 pt. Plantin.

LIBRARY OF CONGRESS CIP DATA ON FILE.
CATALOGUING IN PUBLICATION FOR THIS BOOK
IS AVAILABLE FROM THE LIBRARY OF CONGRESS.

ISBN-13: 978-1-4328-8819-0 (hardcover alk. paper)

Published in 2021 by arrangement with St. Martin's Publishing

Printed in Mexico
Print Number: 01 Print Year: 2021

For Jeff

ONE

As we hitch our horses to a lodgepole pine, shouts and laughter float over on the night breeze. Teenagers partying in the forest. At their age, I'd longed to be invited to a party like the one we hear. I didn't yearn for the beer kegs or the drug buffet or the awkward couplings in the bush. What I'd wanted was something deeper: the fantasy of sitting on a log, a boy's arm casually slung over my shoulders, the warmth of his leg against mine. A crackling fire filling the air with the smell of woodsmoke as it spiraled into a star-blazed sky. Charred, sticky marshmallow on my lips. The laughter of friends, telling stories I've heard a million times, and I don't laugh because they're funny — I laugh because they are a shorthand between us, warm and comforting.

Getting back to nature is at the core of that fantasy. Leave the world behind and connect with others on a level impossible to find in busy lives. Abandon the cell phones and the laptops and the tablets, and sit around a fire, drinking and talking and feeling heard. Finally feeling heard.

As a teenager, I might have fantasized about that lifestyle, but if asked to consider it for more than an evening party, I'd have laughed. By the end of the night, I'd be scratching my bug bites and blinking smoke out of my eyes and dreaming of a hot shower to wash away the grime.

Now, at thirty-three, I have lived that life for nearly two years, with no end in sight, and I have never been happier.

As I tie up my horse, Cricket, she nickers. It's an idle complaint. They're tied to sapling pines, easily broken, meant only to convey the message that they are not to wander. We would never secure them firmly in these woods. That's staking out dinner for grizzlies.

I give Cricket an apple and one last pat. Then we're off, and I'm walking toward the sound of laughter with a guy's arm loosely over my shoulders, a mirror of that long-ago fantasy. Of course, what mattered even then wasn't the pride of having a boyfriend but this feeling, like wearing a favorite pair of jeans, a perfect fit, deeply satisfying and comfortable.

In my teen fantasy version, there would also be a dog. I was never allowed pets growing up, so if I pictured that bonfire party, I'd show up with my dog, who'd race through the forest, getting her fill of freedom before dropping in exhaustion at our feet.

I have the dog now, too, a Newfoundland gifted to me by the guy at my side. The guy who makes sure I get what my soul needs most, no matter how much I protest.

When the smell of smoke wafts over, I think my imagination is in overdrive, supplying all required elements of that adolescent fantasy. Beside me, Dalton sighs and shakes his head.

"Is the ice still thick enough for a bonfire?" I ask.

"If it's not, they're gonna find out."

The trees open to a scene that even my teen imagination would have dismissed as too fanciful. Which is silly really. The point of fantasies is to dream big, imagine things beyond our reality. Yet I'd always edited my dreams into the realm of possibility. Reach high . . . but not too high. Keep yourself safe from the inevitable disappointment of wanting too much. That was the message my parents imparted to their younger daughter.

Before me lies a bonfire on a frozen lake,

against a backdrop of evergreens and snow-topped mountains. Yet the four teens wear short sleeves as the sun beats down, though it's nearly nine at night. It makes no logical sense . . . unless you're in the middle of the Yukon wilderness, during an unseasonably warm spell in early May.

We had snow just last week, and the remains still frost the treed edges of the lake. The sunny side is thawing fast, the ice so dark it looks black. The kids stay close to the shady side as they lounge on storm-felled logs. A makeshift fish rack shows off the day's catch of Arctic grayling and lake trout. Three of the teens hold beer bottles, while the fourth sips water.

From here, they look like ordinary kids, a day of fishing serving as a fine excuse for the beer and bonfire. Obviously the fourth is abstaining to drive the group home. Yet there's no need for designated drivers here. No cars, and no roads to drive them on.

Draw closer, and something about the group seems odd. One boy wears a T-shirt, jeans, and hiking boots, with a plaid jacket around his waist for when the sun drops. One girl also wears jeans . . . paired with a hide shirt and homemade knee-high boots. The other girl is dressed in hide trousers, moccasins, and a modern sweatshirt with the sleeves pushed up. And the remaining boy is completely in homemade garb, all gorgeously tanned and decorated hides. It also becomes apparent why the second girl isn't drinking — she holds a baby on her lap.

Three of these teens have never set foot in a clothing store. Never shopped online. Never seen a computer or a cell phone or even flicked on a switch and had light fill the room. They were born out here, raised out here, and, as far as I can tell, intend to die out here.

Some people would look at these kids, happy and laughing, and credit lives free from the evils and burdens of the modern world. That's bullshit. You can walk into any park and find teens just as happy and carefree, with cell phones tucked in their back pockets. The modern age brings seemingly endless sources of anxiety, but this life has its own worries and dangers, set at the base level of "Will I survive the winter?"

We find our joy where we can, and it doesn't matter whether kids are taking a break from hunting for food or from studying for exams, they will find happiness in those moments of peace and freedom.

As for the fourth member of the group, he may have grown up with all the modern amenities, but in his way, he's as lost down south as the other three would be. At the age of eleven, Sebastian went to prison for murdering his parents. He got out when he turned eighteen.

Sebastian is a sociopath. He lacks that little thing we call a conscience. He wanted a normal life, and his solution was to poison his parents and stage it as a suicide in which they realized the emptiness of their lives and ended them, bequeathing most of their fortune to charity and leaving their son just enough to get by on.

Say what you want about the penal system, but sometimes, it does what it's supposed to: rehabilitates. Sebastian is the poster boy for that. Years of therapy — and a genuine desire to change — means he's learned tricks to overcome what he lacks.

Sebastian sees us first and comes running like an eager puppy. Bouncing at his heels is an actual puppy — year-old wolf-dog Raoul. A fitting companion for a boy who is part feral himself. Raoul spots Storm — our dog — and gallops in for a greeting.

"Is everything okay?" Sebastian asks as we head onto the ice.

"Everything's fine," I say as I scoop up the baby from Sidra.

The dogs head off to explore. As I cuddle

Abby, Dalton hoists a case of soda pop.

"We come bearing gifts," I say.

"Bribes." Dalton looks at Sidra and her husband, Baptiste. "Casey likes bacon."

"Doesn't everyone?" Sebastian says.

"Point is," Dalton continues, "that the venison variety, while perfectly serviceable, does not make our detective happy, and it is in my best interests to keep her happy. You two apparently know where to find our local herd of wild boar. So she's bribing you with soda pop."

"Oh, I have more than that, but we will start negotiations with this." I hand Abby to Dalton and tear open the case. It's a variety pack — orange and grape and root beer and cream soda — and I hold out two cans to Sidra. "An alcohol-free alternative for the nursing mother."

"Take the orange," Sebastian says.

"What does it taste like?" Sidra asks as I hand her a can.

"Oranges," he says with a grin. When none of the other three respond, he must realize they've never had citrus fruit. "It tastes sweet. Really sweet."

Sidra turns the can over, trying to figure out how to open it. I do it for her. She takes a gulp and sputters.

"It *bites,*" she says, staring into the can

with suspicion.

"It's fizzy," Sebastian says. "Carbonated water." He grabs a root beer, and they all take a can.

"This is disgusting," Felicity says, holding hers at arm's length. "Almost as bad as beer."

"Uh, you're drinking the beer," Sebastian says.

"Because you didn't bring whiskey. I like whiskey." She looks over at me. "If you want to know where those boars are, you're going to need a better offer."

Others would say this with a teasing lilt. Not Felicity. If this group has a leader, she's it. She'll negotiate for the boar location on Sidra and Baptiste's behalf, and she'll drive a hard bargain.

I reach into the backpack for a Dairy Milk bar and waggle it at her. She plucks it from my hand with a sniff and "That's a start," and everyone laughs. It's been about six months since Felicity tried chocolate for the first time, and it may be the greatest leverage I hold over her. Of course, Dalton would say the same about me.

I dump the backpack of chocolate bars and chips onto the ice. "In addition to treats, we have a box of more practical supplies in town."

Those supplies — including condoms — won't be part of the negotiation. As much as Sidra and Baptiste love their baby, they're in no hurry to have a second one. So they'll get as many condoms as they want, plus baby supplies and basic health-care products. We keep an eye on them, making sure they're okay. They spent last winter with Felicity at the First Settlement, but now that spring's here, they're moving into the bush again.

"You kids mind if we crash your party?" Dalton says as I take Abby again. "Looks like Casey needs a bit of baby time."

"She's getting so big," I say as Abby gives me her one-toothed grin.

"You just saw her last week," Sebastian says.

"As an honorary auntie, I'm allowed to say that every time I see her."

I sit on a log with the baby. Storm lumbers over and sniffs her, her black nose nearly as big as the baby's head. Abby shrieks in delight, and Raoul tears off like he's being dive-bombed by eagles. Storm stands there, the model of patience as the baby grabs handfuls of black fur and squeals, her chubby legs pedaling furiously.

"I think someone wants to ride the doggie," Dalton says and sets Abby on Storm's wide back, which makes the baby convulse in delight, heels banging the dog's sides. Storm remains as unperturbed as if a feather drifted onto her back.

"I can see why they used a Newfie in *Peter Pan,*" Sebastian says. "That dog is a freaking saint. I had nannies who weren't nearly as —"

His gaze swivels as bushes ripple at the forest's edge. Abby stops shrieking long enough for the sound to hit us — the crashing of something barreling through the trees. Baptiste snatches the baby, and Storm plants herself in front of me, growling, as Raoul races to protect Sebastian. Neither dog does more than growl, though, and Dalton and I only rest our hands on the butts of our holstered guns.

It's not a grizzly. We're making too much noise for any predator to target us. It must be a moose or a caribou, perhaps running from a winter-hungry wolf pack. That's when I remember the horses, and I stiffen, whispering, "Cricket."

A figure crashes through the last bit of brush. It's a person, staggering through and dropping to their knees before falling face-first to the ice.

Sidra lunges forward with a cry of concern. Sebastian's arm flies out like a roadblock. She smacks into it and glares at him, her dark face flushed with annoyance. He only shakes his head and keeps his arm raised.

Dalton nods my way, telling me to run point on this.

I motion for Sebastian to accompany me and then I nod for Felicity to do the same, knowing she is almost as unlikely to let empathy override common sense. I don't give Dalton orders — he's my superior officer, and he'll do what he thinks is best. As we start forward, he falls in behind, covering me with his weapon out. I let my own gun hang to my side, unthreatening, as I approach the fallen figure.

Ten paces away, I slow. The figure's shape and the long hair splayed over the ice suggest it's a woman. That doesn't hurry my steps. It's merely data to be processed.

The woman coughs, the sound racking her body. I stop and assess. The cough is too obvious a ploy.

See, hack-hack, I'm sick. No threat at all.

I watch the rise and fall of her back. Seeing it shudder on each labored exhale, I motion for Sebastian and Felicity to stay back as I move closer. Dalton follows. So does Storm, the growl in her throat dissolving into a whine and then back to a growl, as if she, too, can't decide whether to be concerned for the woman or concerned *about* her. The dog's dark eyes cut my way in search of answers I can't give.

"Are you injured?" I call.

The woman just keeps drawing raspy breaths. There's no sign of blood on the ice. We're in the shade, and I can tell only that she's dressed in dark clothing. Brown, like tanned hides. That could make her a settler or a hostile.

I glance at Felicity. She's frowning at the woman, that frown telling me she doesn't recognize her — at least not from what we can see. Pale skin. Dark blond hair. Brown clothing. I crane to see her footwear — the surest sign of a person's origin out here — but her feet are tangled in the undergrowth.

"If you understand me, nod," I say.

No answer.

I bend beside the woman's head. She's facedown on the ice. Still breathing those shallow, labored breaths, each one shuddering through her.

"I'm going to turn you over," I say. "If you can understand me, nod."

Nothing.

I glance at Dalton as I keep one eye on the woman. He shifts his weight in discomfort. Part of me screams that this poor woman could be dying, damn it, and I need to help her. The other part screams a very different message. Danger. Threat. Trap.

I slowly start to holster my gun. I hate doing that, but I can't turn her over while holding a weapon. My gun's halfway in when Dalton grunts, "Sebastian?"

"Yes, sir." Sebastian moves forward and drops to his knees. "Let me flip her."

I should have thought of this solution. Proof that, as calm as I might seem, my heart slams against my chest, my brain firing twenty instructions at once.

Sebastian crouches, and I motion for him to take hold of the woman's shoulder and carefully lift her toward him. He does . . . and her hand snaps out and grabs my wrist.

Two

The gun jerks, and I yank away, but she has my wrist in an iron grip. Dalton lunges, barking, "Raise your fucking hands!" but the woman doesn't seem to see him. She's staring at me, blue eyes impossibly wide. She hisses a harsh stream of foreign language, as if she's uttering a curse.

Storm's right there, growling, Raoul at her shoulder. I order them back. Storm retreats a few reluctant steps, and Raoul moves to Sebastian's side, still growling.

I shift my gun to my left hand, letting the woman keep hold of my right. Her fingernails dig in, blood welling up. Dalton snarls again for her to let me go, but she just stares, eyes locked with mine.

"It's okay," I say, as much for him as her.

I hand Sebastian my gun, and Dalton inhales sharply, but I ignore his disapproval. My gaze holds the woman's feverish one. I reach down and peel her fingers from my wrist, and she just keeps talking, a stream of frantic babbling that my gut identifies as Germanic.

Her babble acts like an adrenaline pause button, giving me time to pull back and assess. I'd jumped to conclusions about her clothing. Yes, it's brown — the color and texture of tanned hide — but it's modern. Expensive hiking wear. Tourist wear.

That's almost certainly what she is. A tourist on a backwoods excursion. During my time in Rockton, we haven't seen so much as an abandoned campsite, but Dalton says it happens, people pass through the area, never realizing a town of two hundred people lies a few kilometers away.

Right now the important thing is that we have a woman in distress, collapsed on the ground, her fingers digging into my hand, raspy voice telling me . . .

I have no idea what she's telling me, do I?

"Ich spreche kein Deutsch," I say. *I don't speak German.* As a cop, I learned variations on those words in a half dozen languages along with a few more, like: *"Sprechen Sie Englisch?"*

Do you speak English?

The woman doesn't even stop babbling to listen to me. I say it again, louder, and then I try *"Je parle français"* — *I speak French* —

in hopes of commonality there, but I still can't be certain she even hears me.

As cruel as it seems, I block out her words and lift her chin for a better look at her face. She doesn't fight me. If anything, her words only come faster, hoarse with excitement at this sign that I'm paying attention.

Her eyes are fever-bright, her skin hot to the touch. I don't see any blood. I run my hand over her head, and she leans into it, eyes closing, as if I'm stroking her fevered brow. Instead, my fingers palpate her skull while I watch for a flinch of pain.

My hands are all the way around the back when she shrieks, convulsing and slamming her fists into my chest. I grab her wrists, and she writhes and bares her teeth. The dogs both lunge forward, Sebastian grabbing Raoul to restrain him.

Dalton wordlessly restrains the woman's hands as he motions for Felicity to grab her flailing feet. The woman bucks and writhes and spits, as if delirious, and I part her hair but see no sign of injury.

"Blood," Sebastian says.

"What?" My head jerks up.

I realize he still has my gun, and he's training it on the woman. Letting the sociopath hold the gun may not seem like the best strategy, but he's actually the least likely to freak out and pull the trigger. When you struggle to empathize, seeing others in danger barely raises your heartbeat, and while we've been fighting with a madwoman, he's been assessing her from his vantage point. He nods at her stomach, where her shirt has pulled up in her struggles, and I see a long strip of blood-soaked cloth around her midsection.

"Shit," I mutter.

That explains why she lashed out — not from the pain of a head injury but because, in lifting her, I'd engaged her injured stomach muscles.

The woman suddenly goes still, panting, and Felicity eases back.

"Don't —" I begin.

The woman kicks, foot flying up to smack Felicity under the jaw. It's the woman who screams in pain, though, gnashing her teeth as she rasps something, her bloodshot eyes fixed on Felicity.

I glance Felicity's way, and she nods abruptly. Her eyes simmer with annoyance, half at the woman, half at herself. It's only then, as Felicity grabs the woman's legs, that I see her feet are bare. Bare and bloodied.

I motion for Dalton to take my spot, and I creep down to Felicity. I take one of the woman's ankles firmly, ignoring her kicks and howls. The soles are filthy, her feet and ankles crisscrossed with scratches.

Running through the forest. *Barefoot.*

I glance at the bloody bandage around her waist. It's crimson now, fresh blood seeping through. I move up the woman's side.

The bandage is only roughly tucked in, a haphazard job. As the others hold the woman still, I unravel the dressing, blocking out her screams and curses. I don't even have it halfway open before the smell hits me.

"What is that?" Sebastian says, hand flying to his nose.

Rotting flesh.

Infection.

I wheel to Sebastian. "Get April. *Now.*"

Sebastian is gone, Baptiste accompanying him. It's five kilometers to Rockton and the paths are too narrow for the horses to gallop. I remember running that far to school rather than wait for the bus. Twenty minutes easily. That's in the city. This is forest, where even paths aren't flat or free of trip hazards.

It'll be over an hour before April can return on an ATV. My dirt bike would be faster, and I have argued — strenuously — that my sister needs to learn to ride it, as a matter of practicality. She refuses, saying that 95 percent of her work is in town, and 4 percent in remote spots that my bike couldn't reach anyway. She accused me of playing the "emergency services" card as an excuse to "force" her to do something I consider fun.

Yes, my sister and I have very different definitions of the word "fun." Honestly, I'm not sure it's in her vocabulary. I could blame her workaholic ways, but part of that is her nature. She's brilliant and driven and almost certainly on the autism scale. Saying she doesn't know the meaning of fun is unfair. Also untrue. I bought her a new label maker on this morning's supply trip — replacing the one she wore out — and she practically vibrated with excitement.

As we wait for April, we deal with the mystery woman and her injuries. There's no doubt she's delirious, from the fever or the sepsis or both. I can only guess what she imagines us to be in her delusions. Predators, perhaps, who attacked in the forest. Or human monsters, mad scientists pinning her down to conduct horrible experiments.

I should have told Sebastian to be sure April packed a sedative. The best thing we could do for this woman would be to knock her out. It takes all our power to restrain her without injuring her more, and I'm not even sure we accomplish that.

I always carry a first-aid kit as part of my pack. Dalton also has one in his saddlebags, and he's delivered them both now, as I work on the woman.

Sidra has put Abby in her basket, and she's with Felicity bringing snow from the shady edge of the lake. I tried to get water into the woman, but most of it ended up seeping into the ground. I save the rest for cleaning her stomach wound, but even if I could harden my heart to her shrieks of agony, I wouldn't know where to begin.

The abdomen is one of the worst spots for infection susceptibility and infection leading to sepsis. The wound has been bound, but it's a makeshift bandage, presumably to stop the bleeding.

What caused the wound? I have no idea. I can't even unwrap the last layer of bandage. It's grafted to infected flesh, and the slightest tug has her howling in pain.

I need to ignore the wound and concentrate on lowering her temperature *while* keeping her warm, knowing the sepsis is far enough advanced that her body temperature could plunge at any moment.

Eventually, she calms down, which may only be exhaustion. She continues to thrash, her words so mumbled that I doubt I could understand them even if I did speak the language.

As she lies on a bed of jackets and blankets, she stares glassy-eyed at the sky, her lips moving. Storm and I sit beside her as I absently pet the dog and look at the woman.

What happened to you?

Even if she could tell me, it's almost inconsequential at this moment. Yes, it would help to know how she sustained her injuries — and I have no doubt my sister will chastise me for not getting that information — but the biggest threat is her infection, and her story doesn't affect that. I just want to know it. I desperately want to know it.

I glance at her clothing. Dalton has built another fire, rather than risk moving her closer to the first, and in the light of it I see colors in the woman's outfit. An emblem on the breast. A bit of black in the pants, as part of the design. All that, though, is hidden under a layer of dust and dirt.

It's definitely expensive. My parents were successful medical professionals, and in their world, people will drop a grand on hiking gear to join a cushy two-day guided hike along the Appalachian Trail. While some of that gear is trendy and overpriced, some is worth the money. In Rockton, I have accumulated my first rack of expensive designer footwear: hiking shoes and boots for every occasion. The newfound indulgence of a trust-fund baby who had never actually dipped into her trust fund.

I pride myself on being a sensible and informed shopper. I ignore labels and designs and do my research. I can devote an hour to weighing options as we shop high-end outfitters in Vancouver. Which gets me exactly the same results as just handing two articles of clothing to Dalton and having him declare one "a piece of shit" and the other "good enough, but that one over there is better." There is no substitute for experience. I'm gaining that, though, at least enough to look at this woman's clothing and declare it "a piece of shit."

Germanic speaker wearing overpriced outdoor gear.

My memory shuffles through images and stops at one from today's supply run. We'd been walking along the wooden sidewalks of Dawson City. It's so quiet at this time of year that it reminds me of a Wild West town at high noon, and I half expect to see tumbleweeds rolling down the dirt roads. When we did hear voices, they rang as loud as church bells. It'd been a quartet speaking in a Germanic language, all dressed in expensive outdoor wear as they prepared for a trip to Tombstone Park.

"Guess we didn't beat tourist season after all," I'd said to Dalton.

There can be a cultural component to tourism. Go to Prince Edward Island, and you'll find crowds of Japanese tourists on a pilgrimage to the birthplace of Anne of Green Gables. Come to the Yukon, and you find crowds of Germans looking to explore our fabled wilderness. Some are expert explorers . . . and some just want an adventure. From the look of this woman's outfit, she falls into the latter category.

An adventure is what she wanted. What she got, I fear, is a true taste of what it means to be dropped off in the wilderness a hundred miles from the nearest community.

This morning, Dalton and I had sat on a patio, enjoying a coffee and a pastry in what felt like summer sunshine. Another group of tourists had walked by, American weekend warriors in full gear, talking about their plans for backwoods camping up in Tombstone. Dalton had tracked their progress down the street and muttered, "Fucking climate change."

A local sitting nearby had chuckled and said, "And here we thought we had another two weeks of peace and quiet."

What Dalton meant, though, was that climate change is a trickster, luring outsiders into the wilderness before Mother Nature is ready to receive them. According to today's weather reports, by midafternoon, Dawson City would be the warmest place in Canada, which is truly insane. Yet when we left our beds predawn to hike the Ninth Avenue Trail, we'd layered up with fleece. Those hikers were about to head into the wilderness, expecting gorgeous weather, when the truth was that they could be buried under a foot of snow tomorrow. At the very least, they'd encounter frozen lakes and muddy bogs.

As we wait for my sister, I cannot help building a potential story for this woman. She's in good shape. Maybe thirty. Probably has some experience with the outdoors. Comes to the Yukon for her Canadian adventure. Dropped off in the wilderness. Then something goes wrong. The abdominal injury is almost certainly a freak accident. She slipped on mud or ice coming down the mountainside and impaled herself on a branch.

The next step should be to turn on your satellite phone and call for help. Had she underestimated the severity of her injury?

Realized how much an emergency pickup would cost and decided she'd "tough it out"? I'd love to say that no one who bought this brand of outdoorsman wear would risk their life to save a rescue charge, but people are not always rational.

There's another reason her sat phone might have failed, though I cringe to consider it. Our own radios barely work, and the council — who run our town from the safety of civilization — blame all kinds of environmental factors, but we think they employ technology that interferes with the signals, ensuring residents are truly cut off from the outside world.

Whatever the reason, this woman failed to get help, and what started as a coolheaded search for civilization would have turned into a panicked run, as fever set in. She keeps running until she loses her shoes and is too far gone to care. Finally hears voices, laughter even, and races toward the sound, only to collapse the moment she sees salvation.

It's a reasonable story, and I'm sure it bears at least a superficial resemblance to the truth. There's only one element missing. One element that tells me this is more than a woman whose adventure went horribly awry.

She is alone.

No reputable bush plane operator would drop off a solitary tourist in the forest. That means she came with at least one other person.

So how did she wind up here, injured and alone?

I'm not sure I want the answer to that.

Three

Seventy minutes after sending the boys off, we hear the roar of the ATV. It's dusk now, sliding into darkness, and the lights of the vehicle appear moments after I hear the engine. I run to meet it with Storm at my heels. The wide path ends where we left the horses, and they need to finish the journey on foot. I'm there both to direct April and to bring her up to speed.

The first person I see isn't April. Not unless my sister has turned into a guy with his sleeves pushed up to show off impressive muscles and a US Army tattoo. That would be Will Anders, our deputy, driving the ATV.

Anders leaps out as he yanks off his helmet. The woman in the passenger seat is taking her sweet time removing hers and then placing it in the back seat before climbing from the vehicle.

When Dalton first met April, he'd known instantly that she is my sister. The resemblance, obviously. Except it wasn't obvious to me. I overlook the parts we both inherited from our Filipino-Chinese mother — high cheekbones, heart-shaped face, dark straight hair. In April, I only ever see the things we don't share, the ones she inherited from our Scottish side — her pale skin, her blue eyes, her hourglass figure, all of which mean it's rare for anyone to ask where she came from, whether she speaks English, does she know any good local sushi restaurants . . .

April can pass for white, and I cannot, and this has always felt like a division that superseded all similarities. The world told us that this meant we did not look like sisters, and that made the gulf between us feel all the more impassable.

"Hey." Anders throws one arm around my shoulders. "You doing okay?"

"Better than our patient."

"Yeah, I know." He hefts the medical bag in his hand. "I'll run ahead and get started."

"Did April pack a sedative? She's going to need it."

"Sebastian warned us. We've got extra. Everything's good." He claps a hand against my back and takes off to begin triage.

Anders was premed when he enlisted in the army. He'd gotten some medic training before his superiors switched him to MP duty. He'd have made a fine medic, but he made an even better cop. When a fight breaks out in Rockton, we send Anders first. Most times, he just needs to turn up the charm, and people forget what they were arguing about. If fists do fly, he's got the muscle to subdue any resident and the equanimity not to throw any unnecessary punches doing it. He keeps up his medical training, though. In Rockton, we can always use more people who know how to set a broken bone or stitch a gash.

He's halfway down the path before my sister makes her way to me.

"Come on, April," I say. "Can we pick up the pace? This isn't a garden party."

"No, it's a bonfire party. Or it was, until this woman intruded."

I stifle a snort. "She's in septic shock, April. I think she can be forgiven for party-crashing."

"Septic shock is your diagnosis. You are a not a physician, Casey, and I will reserve judgment until I see the patient."

"At this rate, we won't need a physician. We'll need a coroner. Come *on.*"

"Running pell-mell through the forest is a sure way to end up like this woman. Sebastian says it looks as if she fell and injured herself."

"Mmm. I could speculate, but if I do, you'll remind me that I'm not a doctor."

She shoots a hard look my way as we continue toward the lake. As I tell her my theory, I leave out the "fell on a branch" part. That's where I'm most likely to be mistaken, and part of me will always be the little girl who doesn't want to look foolish in front of her big sister.

It doesn't help that April's autism means she has no problem *making* me feel foolish. I know that's not her fault, but a diagnosis thirty years late doesn't undo the damage. I grew up with parents who always made me feel not quite up to snuff, intellectually, and a sister who didn't realize that every time she "made allowances for my diminished mental capacity," I felt stupid and useless. It was hard to make anyone understand that when my IQ put me well above average. I just wasn't a genius like the rest of my family.

"Does that make sense?" she says when I finish my theory.

I tense. "Does . . . what make sense?"

"That she fell and injured her stomach."

There are a lot of things I hate my parents for, but this tops the list — that they knew April was on the spectrum and ignored it because, to them, it meant their child was broken. Yes, if I'm being charitable, I'll admit that maybe they thought this was best for April. Treat her as if she were neurotypical and refuse to allow her to be labeled or otherwise held back. In the end, though, it led to a woman who spent her life *feeling* different and blaming it on herself.

One of our residents, Kenny, has an autistic brother, and when he talks to April, I swear it's like seeing someone speak a language I never learned, a language I desperately want to master. When April questions whether my theory makes sense, it sounds combative, and my hackles rise, even as a voice inside me says that's not how she means it.

I take a deep breath and explain that, with the rough terrain and the endless slopes — foothills and mountains and valleys — one of the biggest dangers isn't falling off an edge, but losing your footing and sliding.

"One of the residents died from that in the nineties," I say. "He slipped on a muddy slope and impaled himself on a branch. Before that, a woman had to be rushed into emergency surgery for a punctured lung after falling on her own walking stick."

"I am well aware of the past cases, Casey. I'm the town doctor. I have the files."

Deep breath. "Yes, but they're very old

cases, and I wouldn't expect you to read them, much less remember them."

"Others perhaps. Not us," she says with a sniff, and I do not fail to miss that "us." One inclusive word that has the little girl inside me dancing with glee.

We reach the lake and start across it.

"My point," April continues, "is that I believe there are far more rational explanations for the abdominal injury."

That inner child sags. "Uh-huh."

"Have you considered the fact she may have been attacked by her companion?"

"Sure, that's a possibility but —"

"Shot perhaps? Or knifed?"

"Knifed?" That is not a word my sister uses. "Okay, those are possibilities, but I prefer to start with the ones that don't involve crazed companions —"

"He — or she — doesn't have to be crazed. The isolation drove them to lash out, perhaps over the last piece of chocolate." A glance my way. "I'm sure you could appreciate that."

I laugh more than the joke warrants. Attempting humor is a new thing for my sister, and we may overencourage her, rather like showering Storm with praise when she picks up a difficult scent trail. April would *love* that comparison.

Before I can answer, April continues, "It might also be a mountain man, who attacked her in her sleep. Or perhaps she was part of a group, friends who had a falling-out, and she is the lone survivor. It could have been sexual jealousy. Two friends both coveting the same lover, and when one is spurned for the other, the spurned lover —"

"— massacres the group. All except her. As we'll soon discover, though, she wasn't the lone survivor. She was the killer."

"That is a very good theory. We'll have to be careful."

I bite my lip and struggle to keep a straight face. With anyone else, I'd presume they were mocking me. My own theory sounds outlandish, so they come up with even more outlandish ones. Except mockery, like humor, is not part of my sister's DNA. Her words can cut deeper than any sword, but they are spoken in honesty. Harsh truth.

"You're enjoying those mystery novels you borrowed from the library, aren't you," I say, apropos of absolutely nothing.

"They are a much more pleasant way to pass the time than I imagined. Isabel is correct that a mental break is useful for lowering stress, but what I feared would be a frivolous waste of my time has turned into quite the mental challenge. Piecing together the clues, avoiding the trap of the red herring, identifying the killer . . ."

"A lot more fun to read about than to actually do for a living."

She waves a hand. "That's an entirely different thing."

"It is."

"The detectives in the novels always find the clues and follow a clear path to the killer. You spend far too much time dithering about, talking to the wrong people, chasing subpar leads, waiting for some vital piece of information to land in your lap. You could learn something from those books, Casey."

"Right . . ."

"I'm not saying you're a poor detective. You're actually quite adept. But there is always room for improvement."

"Oh, look," I say, raising my voice. "We've reached the patient. Finally."

Dalton takes the cue and strides over, guiding April to the injured woman, as if she could somehow miss her. Not that she'd ever snap at him for providing the obvious. To April, Dalton is competency incarnate, and there is no greater compliment she could give.

I'm heading off to speak to Felicity when April's sharp voice cuts through the quiet.

"Casey?"

I turn, slowly, trying not to cringe.

"I am about to examine the victim. Don't you need to be here, taking notes?"

"Victim?" Dalton mouths.

I shake my head, telling him not to ask, and I make my way back to my sister as she lowers herself beside the injured woman.

It's well past midnight. We're still on the ice, the two fires lighting our makeshift emergency room. Baptiste and Sidra have left with the baby, and they're camped nearby with Felicity.

The mystery woman is indeed in septic shock, as my sister grudgingly admits, while issuing another warning against me practicing medicine without a license. I say nothing about her detecting without a badge.

The woman is asleep now. At first, April had been reluctant to administer the sedative — the woman had been resting, if fitfully, and as April said, we can't question her about her injuries if she's unconscious. I could point out the "can't communicate with her even when she *is* talking" language issue, but April would probably just suggest I wasn't trying hard enough.

Fortunately, we never reached that point. As soon as April tried to look at her patient's stomach, the woman demonstrated why we needed the sedative. We wrestled her down while my sister administered it, and once that took effect, we were finally able to examine that horrific wound.

"Horrific" is no exaggeration. The flesh surrounding the wound was rotting and putrid, and April had to excise dead tissue to get a look at what lay beneath. Even then, there wasn't any sign of what caused the injury. No tree splinters. No bullet burns, either. Yes, April's wild theories amused me, but that didn't mean I was set on a diagnosis of accidental injury. It was just more dangerous to leap to the conclusion that she'd been attacked, only to have her wake up later and say "Oh, no, I just fell on a branch" after we'd spent days combing the woods for her attacker.

Crime fighting in Rockton often feels like being transported back to the world of Sherlock Holmes. April can complain about me "dithering about," but most of that is Holmesian thinking and working through the case by making endless notes.

When it comes to actual crime-scene equipment, I'm back in the Victorian age, with my fingerprint dust and rudimentary ballistics. If I need DNA testing, I can send a sample to a lab down south, but so far I haven't had a case that a modern crime-scene test would break faster than old-fashioned sleuthing.

Medicine faces similar constraints. Being off-grid means we do have power from generators and solar panels, but that goes to essentials, mostly cooking and food preservation. If April had an emergency case requiring our entire power supply, though, we'd all be eating fire-cooked food for a few days, because medical care is our priority. Yet mostly she's had to wean herself off technology the same way I have.

She works into the night using the combined light of bonfires and strong flashlights. We hold the latter as she abrades the infected wound and then assesses damage. An ultrasound may help here, and she has a portable one in Rockton, but it appears that the injury hasn't done more than nick the woman's intestines. That's what I already suspected. This woman has been alive with this wound for a few days now, which means it didn't puncture a vital organ.

The short version is that, had she gotten medical care immediately, she'd be in a hospital bed, probably arguing with the doctors to let her out of it. The issue isn't the wound as much as what happened after — days of stumbling through the Yukon wilderness, each step aggravating the injury, while infection set in.

Her feet and calves are a mess, testifying to the sheer hell of the journey that brought her to us. Two toes are frostbitten and will probably need amputation.

Besides cuts, scratches, and dehydration, there are no other obvious wounds. Or that's what April concludes. She's wrong, though, and I take no pleasure in pointing that out. Whatever our issues, proving April wrong is uncomfortable for me and always has been, even when we were children. Perhaps even then I'd realized, deep down, that she didn't point out my own flaws and mistakes to be cruel.

I glance at Anders, who's assisting April. "Can you grab me a pop? I'm getting a little dehydrated myself."

April turns a hard look on me. "If you've allowed yourself to get into that state, then I believe you can remain there a little longer, Casey."

"She's not actually asking for a soda, April," Anders says. "She's asking me to step away."

"Then she should say so."

"I was trying to be discreet," I say.

"Asking for refreshments in the middle of a medical procedure is hardly discreet. I presume you are questioning my assessment. I do not need you to correct me in private. I'm a grown woman, capable of handling criticism."

I'm opening my mouth to apologize when she adds, "However, since it's unlikely I'm mistaken, if *you* wish to be corrected in private, I understand that. Your ego is more fragile."

Off to the side, Dalton gives me a sympathetic eye roll as he holds the flashlight for us.

"I believe this scratch is significant," I say, running my finger along a shallow cut in the side of the woman's abdomen.

"She has many cuts, Casey. She was fleeing through the forest."

"This part of her body was under several layers of bandage."

April goes still and then blanches, just a little.

I continue. "It's possible that this cut is unconnected, but there's also something here." I take her forceps and point. "This looks like part of the abdominal injury, but I don't think it is. There's a deeper wound over here." I move the forceps an inch to the left. "That seems like an impalement of some sort. An object that went directly in, causing a deep wound. This part here" — I pull back — "is much shallower. The infection has made it seem like it's all one injury running together, especially after abrading the dead tissue. But if that other part is impalement, what's this?"

"Three cuts," Dalton says. "First on the side. She avoids that and gets a shallow slice. The second blow penetrates, but not deeply. Then comes the third."

April frowns. "I'm sorry, Eric, but I don't understand. Avoids what?"

I get to my feet, forceps still in hand, and walk over to Dalton. He nods, knowing what I intend. Still, when I stab at him with the forceps, April gasps, leaping up like I've gone mad.

Dalton swings sideways, avoiding the blow, and the forceps graze his side instead.

"One," he says.

I pull back for another stab, and this time, as I make contact with his stomach, he yanks away, staggering backward. He barely has time to say "Two" before I'm on him again, and this time, the forceps hit him straight in the stomach, my hand sliding up the metal, as if they're penetrating deep.

"Three," I say as I turn to April. "Three blows. Looks like you were right after all. She didn't fall. She was attacked."

Four

After that, we transport the woman to the ATV, and I drive her back to town with April, while the others bring the horses. An hour after we reach Rockton, I'm in bed, asleep.

That sounds awful. I've just realized that someone in the forest attacked this woman and left her for dead, and I'm going to drop her off at the clinic and catch up on my beauty sleep?

No, I'm not. I'm going to . . .

Well, that's the problem. What *am* I going to do at 3 A.M., with an unconscious and medically stabilized victim who doesn't speak English or French, and a crime scene somewhere in a night-dark forest? The answer is nothing. I can do nothing tonight. Which doesn't keep me from hovering over the patient until April drives me out. Or from heading to the police station until Anders physically bars the doorway. Or from returning home and pulling out my notebook until Dalton slings me over his shoulder and carries me up to bed.

They're correct in their chorus of "There's nothing you can do tonight, Casey, except get a good night's sleep." It just feels wrong. Someone tried to murder this woman and I'm heading off to my comfy bed, curled up with my partner, my dog snoring on the floor beside me.

It's not even light out yet when I bolt upright with a gasp, as if surfacing from underwater. As I hover there, Dalton murmurs, "You can't do anything tonight."

I glance down at him, lying on his back, his fingers tracing my bare side.

"The nightmare is bullshitting you," he says. "Nothing has changed. You're not forgetting anything. You're not failing to do anything."

"Nightmare?"

He gives me a hard look, as if I'm being coy. It takes a second for the dream to filter back. Me, napping in bed while shouts echoed all around me, people screaming and running for cover, a mass murderer with a knife charging from the forest, slaughtering residents as I grumble that I really wish they'd stop screaming so I could sleep.

I tell Dalton, and when he chuckles, I'm the one giving him the hard look.

"Sorry," he says, reaching up to pull me down in a tight hug. "I know it was frightening at the time." He presses his finger below my breast, where my heart beats triple-time.

"Reminds me of nightmares where I forget to study for exams," I mutter. "I haven't been in school for a decade, but I still have them." I sigh and look up at him. "You don't ever get those, do you?"

"Having never been to a class or taken an exam, oddly, I do not."

"Lucky bastard." I shift in his arms. "I bet you don't get anxiety dreams at all."

He purses his lips.

"Do you even know what those are?" I ask.

"Never heard the term, but considering what you just described, yeah, I get them. After my parents left Rockton, and I was sheriff, I used to have nightmares where no one listened to me."

I fight a sputtering laugh. "For you, that *would* be a nightmare. Did it ever happen, though? Even back then?"

"Hell, yeah. There are always people who don't listen until I show them why they really should."

"So that was the nightmare, then? You gave orders, and someone ignored you?"

"Everyone ignored me. Laughed at me, even. I'd wake up in a cold sweat. Truth was that it shocked the fuck out of me that people *did* listen. I was the youngest resident, and here I was, playing sheriff, giving orders and tossing curses and glares. I was never the biggest or toughest guy here. I just acted like it. I'd seen it work for Ty, but that's different."

"The man is the size of a grizzly."

"And I'm not. Yet residents treated me like I was the person I was pretending to be, while I kept waiting for someone to call me on my bullshit, and no one did."

"So the nightmares stopped?"

"Eventually. Now I just get the ones where you're not here, and when I go looking for you, no one knows who I'm talking about."

I wince.

"Yep, those suck," he says, kissing my cheek, "but then I wake up, and you're here, and I know you're staying, so I can shove that bullshit in the closet where it belongs."

I run a finger over his cheek, prickly with stubble, the winter beard shaved. He'll keep the stubble, though. There's something in his face that needs the scruff to keep him looking like the hard-assed sheriff. Otherwise, there's always an innocence there. A wide-eyed innocence and a wounded innocence, and a man who cannot allow the world to see either. It's only when it's the two of us that the wall comes down and that strong jaw relaxes and those gray eyes lose a little of their steel, letting me see what lies within.

What lies within is a boy who grew up in the forest, with parents who loved him and a younger brother who adored him. A harsh but also idyllic life. Then Rockton's sheriff Gene Dalton found him.

Gene took the boy home and, according to the town records, the nine-year-old was suffering from severe malnutrition and had been abandoned by neglectful parents. That was bullshit, but it gave Gene the excuse to present his wife with a son after they'd lost their own child down south in the tragedy that brought them to Rockton.

It was like those old stories of missionaries "rescuing" "heathen" children, when the truth was that they stole those children from loving parents who followed a different way of life.

What happened next is hazy in Dalton's mind, tainted by the stories Gene told him growing up. Then, a few years ago, he reconnected with his brother, Jacob, and learned that his parents weren't the negligent guardians that Gene claimed.

Yet it wasn't as if he'd been taken as a baby. Dalton had repressed nearly a decade of good memories, and he didn't know how to deal with that. So he decided not to. His birth parents were dead, and the Daltons had retired down south, so what was the point in digging up the past? What's done is done. Keep moving forward.

It obviously isn't that easy. All those questions he'd tamped down had left a smoldering keg in his soul, the rage and hurt of a boy who'd been abandoned by loving birth parents and then, as an adult, come to realize that his loving adopted parents actually kidnapped him. Little wonder he has nightmares where he wakes to find me gone, to discover I never existed at all.

It was only last winter that Dalton agreed to talk about his parents. While Jacob is more than happy to fill in the missing memories, he cannot supply the most critical answer of all. Jacob had been seven when Dalton disappeared into Rockton. He knows their parents searched frantically for his brother. He eventually came to understand that Dalton was in Rockton, where their parents assured Jacob that his brother was healthy and happy. They made it sound like having an older sibling at boarding school in a far-off place.

He's gone away to learn new things and grow up, and when he does, he'll come back to us.

From what I've heard of Steve Mulligan and Amy O'Keefe, there is no way they decided their son was better off in Rockton and left him there. So what really happened?

We have no idea. They both died fifteen years ago.

So much trauma visited on a family who only wanted peaceful lives in the forest. Further proof, as if we needed it, that the biggest danger out there isn't the animals or the landscape or the weather.

It's the people.

And here we are, reminded of that yet again with the tourist we found. A woman who came here expecting to deal with the animals and the landscape and the weather, and what put her in our clinic, fighting for her life, was another human being.

"I'm trying not to jump to conclusions," I whisper against Dalton's chest.

"Yeah, pretty sure I'm trying not to jump to the same ones." He pulls back to look down at me. "We can discuss it, if that'll help you sleep."

I shake my head. "Once I start, I won't stop. We're thinking the same thing. I know we are. It can wait. It can all wait." I glance at the clock. "At least for another couple of hours."

He pulls me to him in a kiss, and I lose myself in it, pushing the rest back, at least for now.

It's 6 A.M., the sun fully risen, and I'm in the clinic, cupping a mug of hot coffee between my hands as Dalton stokes the fire. My sister had been up all night with the patient. We've sent April to bed now, and we're sitting vigil waiting for the woman to wake. We've left Storm with Petra — the clinic is no place for any canine, but especially not one who can destroy a thousand dollars in equipment with one enthusiastic wag of her tail.

As for the patient, the sedative wore off long ago, and this is simply the deep sleep of exhaustion. She's hooked up to an IV replacing her fluids. There's a heart monitor, too. That is all we can do for her right now, that and antibiotics.

Last night, April and Anders looked after the stomach wound, sterilizing it better and using the ultrasound to get an internal look. Those images rest at my elbow, and they add nothing to the story of this woman's trauma. As predicted, the weapon pierced mostly muscle. It was intended to kill her.

I'm certain of that. The only question is whether her attacker expected her to immediately perish from her injury . . . or knew it would take time, leaving her to a slow and agonizing death alone in the forest.

I've barely taken a few sips from my coffee when a soft rap sounds on the exam room door. Dalton opens it to find a dark-haired woman hovering uncertainly.

"Hey, Maryanne," I say. "Come in."

As she does, her gaze flits to the patient and then quickly away. Anyone seeing that would dismiss Maryanne as a nervous woman. I know better. I understand that what's making her uneasy is the patient lying on that bed and what she represents.

"Kenny came by the stable this morning to take Champ for an early ride," she says, "and he mentioned you'd brought back a woman. A tourist who was attacked in the forest."

"Kenny talks too much," Dalton grumbles, but there's no rancor in it. We both know there's a reason Rockton's carpenter — and head of militia — let Maryanne know. The same reason that brought her here this morning.

Maryanne came to Rockton nearly fifteen years ago, yet no one here except Dalton had ever met her before last winter. Rockton is a town of transients. It's meant to be a way station on the journey back to an ordinary life. You come, and catch your breath and wait for the storms to pass, and then you return. Residents are guaranteed a two-year stay. After that, they may apply to extend their stay for up to five years. We do have two who've gone beyond five years — Mathias and Isabel — but they secure those extensions by blackmailing the council.

When Maryanne came to Rockton, fleeing a nightmarish marriage, she'd fallen in love. Not with a person, but with the wilderness. She's a biologist, and the child of hippies, and here she rediscovered her passion for wild places. She joined three others and set off into the forest.

That isn't an officially sanctioned choice. In reality, it depends on the sheriff. If someone wanted to go these days, Dalton would try to talk them out of it. If they weren't equipped to survive, he'd dump them in Vancouver before he'd let them walk into the wilderness. But if they could handle it and truly understood what that life entailed, then, as a child of the forest himself, he would look the other way.

Gene Dalton took a very different view, not surprisingly given that he stole Dalton from that wilderness life. Gene aggressively pursued would-be settlers, and he'd done that with Maryanne, gathering the militia for an all-out search. When they found the camp, a week later, it'd been empty, supplies ripped apart, mementos abandoned, the ruined remains of their temporary settlement telling a tragic story.

The true tragedy, though, came later.

As Maryanne leans over the mystery woman, her graying hair falls in a curtain and she reflexively starts to tuck it behind her ear. A pause, then she tucks it back anyway, and that's partly defiance, but partly, too, because she knows there's no one here who hasn't seen the frostbite. The elements don't explain the odd pattern of scarring on one cheek. Ritualized scarring. She speaks carefully, her lips hiding teeth that will get dental caps this spring to hide the damage. That damage wasn't tooth decay — it was intentional filing.

What happened in Maryanne's camp all those years ago wasn't a bear attack. It was humans. Humans that belong more in a badly researched prehistoric movie than in twenty-first-century reality.

We call them hostiles. They're former Rockton residents who have reverted to something more primal, adopting a hodgepodge of tribal elements and presenting as wild people barely capable of communication, more dangerous than any creature out here.

To the people of Rockton, hostiles have always been the bogeyman. An urban legend created by law enforcement to keep residents out of the forest. Dalton knew better. Yet to him, they were as much a part of the wilderness as the settlers and caribou, and he'd accepted the council's explanation that this was what happened when people immersed themselves too fully in the wilderness life. They lost what it means to be human.

I'm sure that can happen, but . . .

In Rockton, Dalton and Maryanne had been friends, as much as a teenage boy and a thirty-something woman could be. She'd taught him biology, and he'd taught her naturalism. Two keen and curious minds eager to discover everything the other knew. A year after she left Rockton, he met her in the forest and she attacked him. Nearly forced him to kill her to escape. She'd become a hostile. That kind of deterioration cannot naturally happen in a year.

I'd had lots of theories about how it did happen, most more outlandish than I care to admit. The key came, fittingly, with

Maryanne herself. Dalton met her again last year, and she *did* recognize him. Thus began six months of encounters in the forest, until finally, she was in a mental place to accept help. She'd spent four months living in a cave once inhabited by a friend. She had recently agreed to move into town, taking over from the stable worker who left this winter.

So what happened to Maryanne in the forest? Two words that often go together. Cult and drugs. The hostiles have two narcotic tea-like brews, which they seem to have adapted from the Second Settlement.

Rockton gave birth to two settlements out here, unoriginally known as the First and Second Settlements. Both were created by residents who didn't want to go home. The first is led by Edwin, now an old man. The second, founded in the seventies, reminds me of a commune, complete with mildly narcotic teas.

I believe the hostiles began as a small group who left the Second Settlement to pursue a more nomadic life, not unlike Maryanne and her comrades. They took the settlement's tea recipes with them, and at some point, the brew went from mild intoxicant to hardcore drug.

The Second Settlement has two teas,

referred to as the peace tea and the ritual tea. The former acts like a nice glass of wine. The latter, which they only use for rituals, induces mild hallucinations. The hostiles created stronger versions of both, brews that can no longer be called anything as benign as "tea."

The first keeps them in a state of moderate euphoria where their former life becomes a shadowy dream they no longer care about. The second whips them into the frenzied state that Dalton first encountered with Maryanne, when she tried to kill him.

What does all this mean for the woman lying in the bed? She isn't a hostile. She might look as if she's been living rough, but clear polish clings to her ragged fingernails, her hands are smooth and soft, and she was wearing contact lenses, which April removed.

Maryanne has come to see this woman because, in what we know of her story, Maryanne sees echoes of her own past: the horror that began her years as a hostile.

Her quartet had made camp a few nights after leaving Rockton. Having lost Gene Dalton and his men, they didn't post a guard. Healthy bears won't attack four sleeping humans around a smoldering fire. Fellow settlers were known to be territorial and unfriendly, but not thieves or murderers. As for the hostiles, well that was just a story, and a rather silly one at that.

That night, they learned the truth about those silly stories. The hostiles attacked while the quartet slept. They wanted the women and the supplies. They slit one man's throat before he woke. The other, though? They used a stone knife on his stomach and abandoned him to die in agony, alone.

Five

This is, of course, what both Dalton and I thought of first when we realized what happened to our mystery woman. It's what Maryanne thinks of when she hears the story. It's why she's here — to help determine whether hostiles attacked a group of tourists. Whether there might be other survivors out there, women like her who'd been given the choice between a narcotic brew and a horrible death.

When Maryanne was captured, she drank the drugs, thinking she'd play along and then escape. Her companion refused and thought Maryanne weak for giving in. For that, the other woman was bound to a tree, with someone nearby, waiting for her to surrender. A week later, Maryanne got to see what remained.

Is that the scenario playing out right now? Our mystery woman escaped and others are being held captive and given that horrible choice? Or perhaps it was the men who were captured, and the women killed. Which they chose would depend entirely on what the group needed.

What *we* need is answers from this woman sleeping in our clinic.

Who did this to you?

Did people from the forest attack you? Or was it your own companions? Or is there a chance we're misreading the evidence, and you were in a horrible accident?

Tell us something, anything, before we set off into that forest, chasing the wrong answer. Each potential solution to this mystery requires a very different tactic.

I am hoping that when the woman wakes, lucid, she will speak English. Most European tourists know at least enough to communicate. In her fevered state, she'd been unable to tell that we were speaking English and had reverted to her native tongue. That's all.

In case that's not all, though, I need a backup plan.

After Maryanne leaves, I turn to Dalton.

"Can you find me a German speaker? In the files?"

He doesn't even need to respond before I see the answer in his eyes.

"And that's a no," I say as I slump against

the counter.

"I thought of that last night," he says. "You'd think it'd be there, under useful skills, but . . ." He shrugs. "Residents must speak fluent English."

Rockton is diverse when it comes to race, religion, and sexual orientation, because none of that has any impact on your ability to survive in this environment. Otherwise, though, we're a homogeneous bunch. Sebastian is our only resident under twenty-five and Mathias is one of the oldest at fifty-five. The most serious disability is Kenny's — he wears leg braces after taking a bullet in the back.

Kenny would never have been allowed in like that, though, even if he's perfectly capable of Rockton life in his current condition. The council wants able-bodied adults. They also want English speakers, because struggling with the language would be a disability. Therefore we don't need to know if residents speak other languages, because we'll never require their skills for translating.

Resident privacy comes first. Even what does make it into the files is for Dalton's eyes only, and he can't share it with me unless it directly impacts a case.

"Any hints?" I ask.

When he hesitates, I wince. "Sorry. I shouldn't ask. If you know of any residents who lived in Germany, will you speak to them? You could conduct the witness interview to protect their privacy."

"Nah, it wouldn't come to that," Dalton says, stretching his legs. "Can't imagine language skills being top-secret personal details. But yeah, there's someone who mentioned being stationed in Germany during their entrance interview. I can see whether they speak the language. If that doesn't pan out, you can call a meeting and ask for German speakers."

"I need to call one anyway to explain the stranger in our clinic."

Dalton grumbles under his breath. Before I arrived, there would have been no announcement. Not that he could keep the woman a secret. People saw Sebastian and Baptiste race into town for the doctor. They'd be asking who got hurt, and we'd need to reassure them that it wasn't a resident, and then they'd realize the clinic is closed for a reason — because a stranger is in their midst.

As far as Dalton is concerned, that's "none of their damned business." I disagree. A stranger in town is a valid concern for people who've been promised sanctuary.

Better to explain the situation than deal with false rumors.

I'm about to say more when the door opens and a woman says, "Did I hear you say you need someone who speaks German?"

"Did I hear you knock on the goddamn door, Diana?" Dalton says.

"I'm here for my shift, *Sheriff.* I don't knock for that."

Diana walks in carrying a bag that smells like breakfast sandwiches, and my stomach grumbles. Hearing it, she laughs, walks over, and waggles it in front of me.

"Tell me what you have here, Case." She nods at the mystery woman. "And I'll give you my sandwich."

"Deal."

She hesitates and slants her gaze Dalton's way. He plucks the sandwich from her hand and passes it to me.

"You're actually going to tell me why there's a stranger in Rockton?" she says.

"Yep." I unwrap the sandwich and take a big bite, groaning softly as hot sriracha-spiked scrambled egg fills my mouth. "Because you're my friend, and I trust you."

She snorts.

"Because you're the damned nurse, Diana," he says. "April's going to need help, and you can't provide that if you don't know what happened to a patient."

"Wait, did you say I'm a nurse? You're actually admitting —"

"Health-care provider," he says. "Providing nursing."

"I'll take it. Just make sure you finally get around to officially changing my designation on the duty roster." She turns to me as I lick my fingers. "Did you even chew that sandwich, Case?"

"I skipped dinner last night," I say. "Before we went to the lake, I was called out on a problem."

"Shit," Dalton says. "I forgot all about that."

"I was counting on a late dinner of cold beer and burnt marshmallows. Instead, I got a mystery woman who doesn't speak English."

"Ah," Diana says, "so that's why you're looking for a German speaker. Well, here I am. Nurse, translator, and breakfast delivery all in one."

"Since when do you speak German?"

Diana and I have known each other for more than half our lives. She's the reason I came to Rockton . . . only to discover that she'd tricked me into it. That should have annihilated our friendship, but while we won't ever be what we were, we can manage a comfortable level of companionship.

"I took a year of German in high school," she says. "Remember?"

"Oh, right. You had a crush on that German exchange student."

"*Two* German exchange students. And it was not an unrequited crush. That summer, they taught me more than my course ever did."

"We're still talking about the language, right?"

She waggles her brows suggestively, and I can't help laughing.

"Fine," I say. "You can take a shot at translating, but since our patient shows no signs of waking, we don't need your nursing just yet. If you could grab us some breakfast with your replacement sandwich, I'd appreciate that."

Her gaze shoots to Dalton, and I want to say, *Really, Diana?*

"Fine," I say. "Please get *my* breakfast. I want two of everything."

Dalton pushes to his feet. "I'll do it."

"Oh, sit down, Eric," Diana says. "I'll bring your breakfast. I was just hassling Casey."

"No, I gotta get to work anyway. Casey doesn't need me here, and she might need a nurse. You stay. I'll bring you both a sandwich."

He's gone before she can argue. Not that she doesn't *want* the sandwich — she just doesn't want Dalton to bring it, which would mean she might actually need to say thank you. We may be fifteen years out of high school, but in many ways Diana never left.

And as soon as I think that, she proves why it's hard to cut her loose. She pours me a fresh coffee and then pulls up a chair, eagerly awaiting my story. When I'm done, she's full of questions, but none of them are challenges, none feel like subtle jabs, the way April's can. Diana is genuinely interested in my case and how she can help, and she trusts that I can solve it and keep Rockton safe from whatever lurks in the forest.

As we talk, Dalton silently delivers our breakfast, with only a squeeze on my shoulder before he's gone again. I'm unwrapping my sandwich when I catch the smell of warm chocolate chip muffins. Diana hands me one and laughs as I devour half in a bite.

"Didn't your mother teach you to eat your meal before dessert?"

"My mother didn't let me have dessert, as you may recall. Besides, muffins aren't dessert."

"Put chocolate in them and they're icing-free cupcakes."

"Then, as someone who only eats the icing, you won't mind me having yours, too."

As she passes her muffin over, I notice her hot-pink nails. "Got the care package, did you?"

"Yes, and thank you. I'll put the hair dye in later."

On yesterday's supply run, I'd bought Diana nail polish and pink dye, which she uses to streak or tip her blond hair. Cosmetics aren't a priority here, and most women — like me — are happy for the excuse to go without. But they make Diana happy, and I don't begrudge her that.

"You think it's hostiles, don't you?" she asks as we settle in again.

"I think everything is hostiles." I sigh as I nibble the muffin. "The object of my obsession."

She pulls her feet up under her. "Your brain needs puzzles. This is a good one. You've already figured out how people turn into hostiles."

"I didn't figure out anything. Maryanne told me."

"After you made it your mission to rescue her."

"*Help* her. She rescued herself. As for

figuring out what to *do* about the hostiles . . ."

I grumble under my breath. To the council, hostiles are like cult members. It doesn't matter if they're being brainwashed, we have no right to remove them. The fact that most are former Rockton residents? Irrelevant. The fact that most were kidnapped, which makes it 100 percent our jurisdiction? Also irrelevant, because they'd all chosen to leave Rockton before their "indoctrination" and therefore weren't our responsibility anymore.

The council treats our requests like we're asking to euthanize all grizzlies. Hostiles don't bother us any more often than brown bears, and so our request is unconscionable. These people chose to be out there, so leave them alone.

I take a deep breath. "Yes, I think it's possible this woman was attacked by hostiles. *Possible.* Not even probable."

"She didn't come out here alone, right? People don't do that."

"Not unless they're paranoid gold miners, which she isn't. Her clothing and —"

A gasp. Both of us swivel to see the woman's eyes open and staring at the ceiling. She blinks twice and then starts to lift her arm.

"Hold on," I say, leaping to my feet. "You're —"

Before I can get to her, she realizes she's restrained and howls in terror, thrashing. I shout at Diana for help, and we steady the bed before the woman's flailing tips it over.

"It's okay!" I shout to be heard over her screams. "You're fine. You're in a hospital —"

Diana undoes the restraints on the woman's right arm. I'm so focused on the woman's face that I don't see what Diana's doing until the woman's freed hand smacks Diana, sending her staggering backward.

"Nein!" Diana says. *"Nein!"*

Not exactly helpful. If I woke tied to a bed with strangers, I certainly wouldn't listen if they told me no. I'd only fight harder, and that's what she does.

I manage to pin the woman's free arm as I lean over her. "It's okay. You're hurt. We're helping. You're in a hospital."

I don't expect her to understand, but I'm hoping my tone will calm her.

"Hospital," Diana says. *"Krankenhaus. Klinik."* She grabs the second muffin and waves it, as if this is some kind of proof of where we are. Somehow, it works. The woman stops fighting and stares at the muffin.

I pull the eyewash kit from the wall. On the front is a red cross. The symbol for medical care. I hold it up.

"Hospital," I say. *"Krankenhaus."*

The woman pauses. Then her free hand yanks from mine, and she grabs the front of my shirt instead. Her eyes round with desperation as she begins to babble, the way she had last night, the words rushing out.

I set down the eyewash kit, wrap my hand around hers, and lean in carefully. She keeps talking, her voice barely above a whisper, words never stopping even as I glance over at Diana for a translation.

Diana's eyes widen in panic, and even before she gives a helpless shrug, I know she's not catching any of this. The woman is talking too fast. I'm considered bilingual, but when Mathias gets caught up in a subject, speaking French, I need to tell him to slow down, much to his annoyance.

"Can you tell her to speak slower?" I ask.

Relief floods Diana's eyes as she nods. *"Kannst du bitte langsamer sprechen?"* she says, several times.

The woman doesn't even glance Diana's way. She just keeps frantically trying to communicate with me.

"Do you speak any English?" I say.

No response.

"Parlez-vous français?" I try.

She stops, and I think I have it, but she's only pausing for breath, no recognition in her gaze.

"Sprechen Sie Deutsch?" I ask.

She's taking deep breaths, but there's no response.

"Did you understand anything she said?" I ask Diana.

"I . . . I think maybe . . . a word or two?"

"Are we sure it's German?"

"I . . ."

"Shit," I mutter.

The woman starts up again, frantically trying to speak as both Diana and I run through our repertoires of languages.

"Are we sure her hearing isn't damaged?" Diana says finally. "I do think she's speaking German. It sounds like it, at least."

"It's not," says a voice.

Six

I look over to see a stranger, and I give a start. With under two hundred people, Rockton is community policing at its purest, where there's no excuse for me not to know everyone's name. Okay, occasionally I'll blank, but even when I substitute "Hey, there" for "Good morning, Heather," I still recognize the person as a resident of Rockton. And here, standing in the doorway, is a stranger. Male, white, mid-thirties, light-haired, blue-eyed, taller than average, lean build. That could describe a half dozen residents, but my mind screams an alarm, telling me I don't —

Oh, shit. Yes, I do.

"Hey, Jay," I say, putting out a hand. I turn to Diana. "Diana, this is Jay. We brought him in yesterday."

I'll blame the chaos of the last twelve hours, which had me forgetting that we hadn't just been getting supplies in Dawson

City. We'd flown three residents to the airport and picked up Jay.

Residents coming and going has become routine in Rockton. Most of those who were here when I arrived are now gone. We lost one of our core militia — Sam — in this round.

As callous as it sounds, I've learned not to pay too much notice to the new arrivals until they make themselves noteworthy, for better or worse. I don't know who Jay was or what he did for a living down south, but whatever skills he possesses, they aren't critical up here, so he's been assigned to general duty, meaning I'm unlikely to have much contact with him unless he turns out to be a troublemaker. Jay's pressed clothing and quiet demeanor, though, set my threat rating at low.

Escorting them to Rockton is the extent of law enforcement's initial involvement with newcomers. With Phil — our council liaison before being exiled to Rockton last year — we have a quasi leader for the first time in over a decade. I say "quasi" because Dalton is still the guy in charge. Phil doesn't even take second place. That goes to the woman he's currently sleeping with: Isabel, whose power comes from controlling sex, alcohol, and secrets, the most potent currency in town.

"I was told to come by for a physical," he says as he turns to Diana. "You're not Dr. Butler, are you?"

"I'm her assistant. I can perform the physical basics, but I think Casey is a little more interested in what you said when you walked in."

Diana turns to the woman in the bed, who's whispering to herself. "That's not German?"

Jay offers a half smile. "No, sorry. Close, though. It's Danish."

"Please tell us you know Danish. Please, please, please . . ."

Jay's smile widens, and in that moment, with this champagne-bubbly blonde pleading with him to know Danish, I think if he didn't, he'd promise to run out and learn it for her.

He gives an awkward chuckle. "You're in luck. I'm not fluent, but my mom is Danish, and she taught me enough to carry on a conversation. I'm presuming she" — a nod toward the woman — "doesn't speak English. That's unusual for a Dane."

"Her injury led to some mental confusion," I say.

If he interprets this to mean she's a resident who temporarily lost a language,

I'm okay with that. I'm not eager to tell Jay that the place where he was promised privacy and security has admitted an outsider.

I continue, "We're trying to figure out exactly what happened, and she's eager to tell us but . . ."

"You need a translator. Guess I came by at the right time." He looks at the patient. "She seems to be asking about someone. I can't quite make it out though."

I turn to the woman. She's whispering under her breath, eyelids sagging, as if her violent outburst sapped her energy.

"Hey," I say, clasping her hand. "We have someone who can talk to you."

"Jeg snakker dansk," Jay says, walking over.

The woman levers up, her still-bound left hand snapping against the restraint. Jay jumps back, but she grabs his sleeve and hauls him to her, fever-bright eyes burning.

I catch her hand, but Jay shakes his head. "It's okay. She just startled me. I'm guessing those . . ." He looks at the restraints and gives a soft, strained laugh. "No violent criminals in Rockton, right? That's what the brochure said." His laugh turns awkward again as he adds, "Not that there *was* a brochure," as if we might not get the joke.

"I totally got the brochure," Diana says.

"Full-color. Glossy. It promised a hot tub." She turns to me. "You know anything about a hot tub here, Case?"

I lift my middle finger, and she laughs and says, "There is a hot tub, but it belongs to the sheriff. He catches you in it without permission?" She draws a line across her throat. "It's a real tease, having it here. I don't know *who* would have gotten it for him. Some sadist."

Her gaze shoots my way, and Jay laughs louder than the joke deserves. I tell him that the patient is fine — she just had an episode of delirium — and he nods and turns to her, having forgotten his question about violent criminals in Rockton.

Thank you, Diana.

Jay clasps the woman's shoulder and murmurs something soothing in Danish. She leans toward him, her lips parted, enrapt. She's in a strange place with people who don't speak her language and now finally someone does. She listens until he's finished, and then I expect a fresh stream of frantic Danish, but she only pauses.

"Can you ask her name?" I say.

His voice rises in what is obviously a question.

"Sophie," she says.

"Good," I murmur. "Can you ask her

what happened to her? She was injured outside Rockton."

He turns to Sophie, who hangs there, patiently waiting for the next question. Yet as soon as he asks, her agitation returns as she white-knuckles his hand, gaze locked on his, her words spilling out.

As he listens, his brow furrows. Finally, he lifts a finger to his lips and says something calming, reassuring. Then he turns to me.

"I think you might need to wait until she feels better," he says. "She's not making much sense."

"What's she saying?"

His gaze darts to the woman. "It seems to be some kind of nightmare."

"Even if what she's saying is obviously confused, I might be able to get something useful from her."

"Okay, well, she says she was attacked by a man in the forest. A man who . . ."

"Go on," I say.

"She's saying it was some kind of wild man."

"There are settlers in the forest, and the occasional miner wanders through. They can seem a little . . . wild."

Diana snorts. "You should see the former sheriff."

I nod. "As much as they might want to

stay clean, they can't live up to the standards of people with twenty-four-hour access to hot showers and razors and Laundromats. Then there are some who don't care to try. Consider it human repellent. Most people out there are very private. You need to be, to live that life."

"Understood, but . . ." He takes a deep breath. "She says it was a man with long matted hair and a beard, and mud on his face. Only the mud . . ."

He says something to her, and she shakes her head and then speaks in rapid Danish.

"I asked if his face might have just been dirty," Jay says. "She says no, the mud was put on intentionally, in whirls, like a pattern. He also had scars across his forehead — parallel lines that looked intentional, too."

"Well, we do get all kinds up here," Diana says.

"He was dressed in hides."

"Most people out there are," I say. "They don't have anything else."

"No online shopping," Diana quips. "Even in Rockton, we don't get much selection. Make sure whatever you brought lasts as long as possible or you'll end up in this." She plucks at her T-shirt and shudders.

Because this is police business, I should

ask Diana to leave, but she's doing a fine job of keeping Jay from pursuing questions I don't want to answer.

"Just tell me what she's saying," I say. "Don't filter it. Don't try to figure out what she actually means. That's my job."

"Sorry."

"That's fine. It's frustrating for me not being able to speak to a witness directly, so the best thing you can do is give me unedited translations. Can she describe the man more? Coloring? Age? Size?"

He asks, and Sophie hurries on with a stream of Danish that perks up my hopes, only to have Jay shake his head. "She says she was so focused on what he looked like — the strangeness of it — that she didn't really notice anything more."

"Hmm. Well, we do have an artist in town."

"Comic-book artist," Diana mutters.

"We have an artist," I repeat, firmer. "I can bring her if that would help."

Jay speaks to Sophie. She pauses, her gaze slanting my way, and then she rushes on and Jay shakes his head again.

"She can tell you all about the mud and scars, and she seems to think that should be enough, but . . ."

"It would be if she was talking about a

man who attacked her in downtown Vancouver."

"Exactly. Sorry."

"Ask whether there were others with her. Are they hurt? Are they still out there?"

He nods and asks, and as she answers, his frown deepens. After she stops, he pauses.

"Jay?"

"I . . . I think she's really confused, and I don't know how much good any of this will do." He clears his throat. "Rockton is for victims, right? I'm guessing there are women here running from men. My sister . . ." Another throat-clearing as his gaze ducks to the side. "My sister died at the hands of an abusive ex-boyfriend. It didn't matter how many times she reported him, no one listened. We did, too — her family — but . . ." He shifts in discomfort. "It wasn't enough."

"The system, frankly, sucks, and yes, obviously there are women here to escape what happened to your sister."

"Right, so what I'm saying is that I think we might be dealing with a past trauma here, one that's returned after a head injury. If there's any chance it involved an attack in the forest, that might be what we're hearing here."

"Can you just tell me what she's saying? Please? Unfiltered. Unedited."

Color touches his cheeks. "Sorry. I'm interpreting data. That's what I do for a living. Occupational hazard. She's saying that she and her partner were hiking in the forest, which I know you don't allow here."

"Just tell me what she said, Jay."

I finally get the whole story, and part of me thinks I should have just cut through the bullshit and told him the truth, which he'll probably find out soon enough. On the other hand, this gives me Sophie's words without him making the assumptions he might if he knew she really *was* a hiker who'd been attacked in the woods.

According to what he says, Sophie is indeed a tourist, one who'd come from Denmark with her partner and two friends to fulfill a lifelong dream of hiking in the Canadian north. They'd been dropped off by a bush pilot a week ago, and they'd been having the adventure they'd envisioned when she'd woken to the wild man in the forest attacking them. From there, everything is a blur. She isn't sure how long ago the attack happened. A day? Two? Three? She only recalls running for her life through the forest, and the next thing she knew, she ended up here, in a hospital bed, back in Dawson City.

That's where she presumes she is: Dawson. Which could mean either her opinion of Canadian health care was extremely low or her mind is still addled enough that she hasn't noticed she's in a wooden building, being treated by people in T-shirts and jeans. Scandinavian medicine has a reputation for being top-tier, so maybe this primitive building is what she expects in the Canadian north. I fear, however, given her lack of questions, that she's still feverish and mentally confused. Confused about the part where a wild man from the forest attacked them, though? No. Her description is impossible to mistake for anything else. Her hiking party was attacked by hostiles. And either she's the only survivor, or there are people in that forest who need our help even more than she does.

Seven

I end up telling Jay that the woman isn't from Rockton. I must. If he's going to translate, I can't keep pretending she's a local and expecting useful information. I keep it to the basics. We presume she's a tourist who seemed to have been attacked in the forest, and we're trying to help. I assure him that we'll handle all security issues arising from her being here, but he dismisses that. Helping her is the important thing, and he's happy to do that.

I'm in the police station. Dalton's sitting at the lone desk and staring at a hand-drawn map. I'm perched on the desk with Storm at my feet.

"Read it again," Dalton says as he balls up the map and pulls over fresh paper.

I could just hand over my notes, but this works better for him. I read Sophie's description of the area where they camped, and each time he draws it, he adjusts the parts she leaves out. Her description is full of landmarks that I'm sure seem as clear as signposts to her, but out here, telling us she camped near two pines growing together and a huge boulder covered in black moss is like telling a city dweller that you live on a corner lot with a basketball net and a weeping willow.

She's given us what she remembers in terms of mountains and bodies of water, as well as the unusual landscape markers, but it's a hodgepodge. "We camped in an old burn area near a lake with a mountain behind it." Was the burn area north of the lake? South? How far were those mountains? Snow-topped or tree-topped? A single peak, double, triple? I'd tried to get more, but she wasn't able to provide it.

What Dalton's doing now is taking the significant parts and rearranging them. Put the lake here and the burn site here and the mountain there. Does that look familiar? No? Okay, what if . . .

One might say we should just get off our asses and go look. And whoever said that would have zero concept of the sheer scale of land we're dealing with. This isn't a state park with three small lakes and a single mountain peak. Even "burn site" means little. Forest fires are part of the natural cycle.

"I need Jacob," Dalton says finally, pushing the paper away.

I figured he would. The problem is finding his brother. Last year, Jacob met a woman from Rockton, and that went as those things often did. Having failed to lure his brother from the forest, Dalton grumbled when Nicole managed it, but he'd been pleased. It was a lonely life, and even if nothing came of the flirtation, it portended a day when Jacob might not be alone.

Something *did* come of the flirtation, and Nicole had announced she was planning to spend the winter with Jacob, joking not to give away her apartment, because she might not last a week. She's been gone ever since.

Having a partner means Jacob isn't swinging by as often as he used to. We'll need to look for him, and that's why Dalton is trying so hard to solve the map puzzle on his own. The time we spend hunting for Jacob is time we're *not* hunting for three missing hikers.

He sets his pencil down with a snap. "Fucking tourists. They should need to pass an exam before they're allowed out there. You have to take a test to drive a car, fly a plane, do all kinds of dangerous shit. But you can just walk into the fucking wilderness dressed in your fucking fancy clothes, without a fucking satellite phone or any fucking common sense."

I let him vent. This is the guy whose cardinal rule for newcomers isn't "Don't cause trouble" or "Pull your own weight." It's "Stay out of the fucking forest."

You want to explore the wilderness? That's great. No, seriously, that is fantastic. We have ways for you to do that. Hunting teams and harvesting teams and fishing teams and logging teams.

You just want to enjoy nature? We have guided hikes and boating and even spelunking.

You know what all those things have in common? An armed guide who will take you in and bring you out and keep you safe, and if you think I'm the world's biggest asshole for not letting you go for a walk on your own? Then I'm the world's biggest asshole. Now go join a team or shut the fuck up.

"These tourists aren't our responsibility, but we need to figure out what happened," I say. "As much as I hate to say it, rescuing potential survivors isn't as important as identifying the perpetrators and convincing the council to help us resolve this."

"Yeah."

"And I *really* hate to say *this* but . . ."

"Injured tourists help our cause."

We've been looking for the spark that will light a fire under the council's ass and force them to admit the hostiles are a problem we must resolve. Having us attacked by hostiles last year didn't do it. Having Maryanne tell us her story of kidnapping and brainwashing didn't do it. Having hostiles murder a First Settlement resident last month — and their leader, Edwin, blaming Rockton for "riling them up" — didn't do it. Maybe this finally will: tourists who could report wild people in the forest and return with law enforcement and camera crews.

"I need to just get off my ass and go find Jacob," Dalton says.

"Sorry, yeah, you kinda do. And . . ." I take a deep breath.

"I need to do it alone because you've got a victim in critical condition. A victim you need to keep questioning."

"I'm not sure she can give us any more."

"She's been delirious. She might be easier to speak to later. You need to stay."

"While you run around the forest alone, after what happened to these people."

Now I'm the one venting. The hostiles have always been there, and they've always been dangerous, and if they've been worse lately, that means Dalton will be even more careful than usual, and he's already the most cautious person I know.

"I'll take Storm," he says.

"Thank you. She'll help you track Jacob, too."

"I know. I'll pack, and you go do that other thing." He quirks a smile. "The one I'm leaving town to avoid."

"Telling the council that we have a Danish tourist in our infirmary, and three more Danes — dead or alive — in the forest."

"You got it." He claps a hand on my knee. "I would love to help, but like you said, I gotta get off my ass and find my brother."

"Pretty sure *you* said that."

"Just reading your mind. Now let's go find Phil."

We don't need to find Phil. We're at the station door when it flies open, clipping me in the nose. I stumble back into Storm, and Dalton catches my arm, snapping "Can you fucking knock?"

"I believe this is a public building, Sheriff," Phil says as he walks in. "So, no, I will not knock. I will instead apologize to Casey for opening the door too abruptly."

When I came to Rockton, Phil was a disembodied voice on the radio, and I formed a very vivid picture of our council liaison. Early fifties, short and balding, supercilious and prissy, a man who'd spent his career being passed over for promotions and now had to make the most of this limited source of power.

Then he showed up here to solve a problem and turned out to be the romance-cover version of a businessman. Thirty-one. Model-handsome. Tall, fit, and trim. The kind of guy who wears glasses to be taken seriously. That doesn't mean he *isn't* fussy or supercilious or even prissy. I had the personality right. I just made the unforgivable error of stereotyping the appearance that went along with it.

Today, Phil wears business-casual attire. Considering he'd dressed in a shirt and tie for the first few months, this is progress. He isn't wearing his glasses, and I'd take that as a sign of progress, too . . . if not for the misbuttoned shirt and sleep-tousled hair that suggests he's forgotten his glasses because he's been roused from Isabel's bed.

"We have a problem," he says.

"Yes," I say, "and I'm sorry you weren't notified. I went by your house around two this morning, but you weren't there. I can't inform you if you're not where we expect you to be."

Actually, he was exactly where we expect him to be, but as long as he continues to pretend he isn't sleeping with Isabel, then I'm justified in rapping on his door and moving on.

"I . . . have a feeling we are not discussing the same urgent situation," he says. "I also have a feeling that, after you tell me what happened at two in the morning, my situation will suddenly be far less urgent."

I wave for Phil to come in and sit. Dalton hesitates, and I tap his arm, saying, "Go find Jacob. I have this."

"Jacob?" Phil turns to me. "If you are leaving again, Sheriff, you need to run that past me."

"Never did before. Not starting now." Dalton opens the door and motions for Storm to follow.

"You didn't with my predecessors, an oversight I am attempting to rectify —"

The door closes behind Dalton and Storm. When Phil reaches for it, I deftly slide in the way.

"It *is* urgent," I say. "He's distracted by that, not ignoring you."

And certainly not telling you to back the hell up because if you think he's ever going to ask permission to leave town, you have a very overinflated opinion of your position here.

"I merely wish he would inform me —"

"That's what I'm doing. Which I should have done last night. If you would just say 'I'm staying with Isabel,' then I could call on you at her place without risking the wrath of the woman who fills my tequila order. I'm very fond of my monthly bottle, and I don't dare cross the dragon who provides it. Now tell me your emergency first and —"

The door bangs open with enough force to make us both jump. In walks a woman in her late thirties, average — even pleasant — looking. It'd taken me about an hour in Rockton to discover that "pleasant" isn't a word anyone should ever apply to Jen.

"You two having a little celebration on my account?" she says as she stalks over. "Don't mind if I join, then. Since I'm the cause of the festivities."

"What are we celebrating?" I ask.

"My departure from Rockton."

I frown. "You still have another month, don't you?"

"This is fun for you, isn't it, Detective?" She stops close enough for me to smell coffee on her breath. "Any more jabs you want to take? Or do you need me to turn around so you can stab me properly?"

I turn to Phil. "I'm guessing this is related

to your urgent situation."

He glances over at Jen.

"Oh, don't look at me like that, pretty boy," she says. "I don't bite. Though, considering who you're banging, I get the feeling you like that. I might be a little young for you, though. You like them old enough to play momma and give you a spanking."

To his credit, Phil only meets Jen's gaze with a level stare, and after a moment, she shifts in discomfort.

"You're the one who's embarrassed to be banging her," Jen mutters.

"Or perhaps I am aware of the dynamic it suggests, given our respective positions in town."

"Her being the local whoremistress, you mean."

That level stare again, and under the weight of it, Jen mutters and glances away. Yes, Isabel runs the brothel, and for all my initial issues with that, I have come to agree with her "my body, my choice" stance and she has been completely receptive to all of my suggestions for negotiating this difficult ground.

The brothel is also the reason Jen despises Isabel. Not because she has a moral objection to it, but because she's freelanced in that area herself, which is strictly against town policy. We keep the sex trade tightly regulated for the women's safety; Jen sees it as an unfair monopoly.

"Yes, this is what I wanted to speak to you about," Phil says. "Jennifer requested an extension. It was rejected. To the surprise of everyone, I'm certain, but mostly you, Casey, who has had to deal with her extensive criminal activity and complete inability to cohabit with other residents, particularly those in authority."

"Fuck you, pretty boy."

"I rest my case."

"I'm part of the goddamn militia," Jen says. "Sherlock here hasn't pinned a crime on me in almost a year . . . because I haven't committed any. Even those so-called crimes were bullshit. I got hungry and grabbed some extra food. I got cold and grabbed some extra wood. Which I paid back."

"Only after you were caught," I say.

"I was framed."

"We found your fingerprints."

Her jaw sets. "They were planted. You think I wouldn't know enough to wear gloves?"

"No, I think you couldn't bother wearing gloves, because it's so much more fun to get caught and have the excuse to tell everyone how incompetent the new detective is."

"That's what this is about, then. You vetoed my extension. Or you got that sheriff of yours —"

"Jennifer?" Phil cut in. "Please stop before you embarrass yourself further. Neither Casey nor Eric knew of your request for an extension. If they had, Casey would likely recommend it be granted, as she was the one who argued to allow you on the militia. Your continued attempts to paint her as your oppressor really do only embarrass yourself."

Jen turns on him, but I step between them. "And as much fun as this conversation is, I'm going to need to bring it to a close. Jen? I'm sorry if you didn't get an extension. The last time I heard, though, you were counting the days until you could leave. If you legitimately want an extension, I can provide a reference — I'm sure Will would, too — but the council didn't grant Sam's, either, and we all argued to keep him."

"Sam didn't request an extension." She looks from me to Phil. "He told us he'd changed his mind."

"The point is —" I begin.

"They refused *Sam*?"

"He'd been here four years," Phil says. "The council felt that was enough."

"I want an extension," Jen says. "I've earned it. You know I have."

She's keeping the defensive set to her face, but genuine panic shadows her eyes.

"I will talk to the council," I say.

Her eyes narrow. Before she can speak, I say, enunciating firmly, "If I say I will, then I will. You still have another month, and right now, I have a bigger problem. You want to help? Go over to the clinic and see what you can do. Tell Diana I sent you and that I said 'Thanks for breakfast.' "

"I need a code word?"

I don't bother to answer. If she walked in without saying it, Diana would figure she was poking about, causing trouble, and send her packing.

I open the door. "You will see our situation at the clinic. If Diana doesn't need anything, then your job is to find out how many people in town know about that situation. Track it. See what's being said. Get back to me."

"You want me to be your spy?"

"I want to know how much I can trust you."

She scowls but leaves without another word.

Once she's gone, I say to Phil, "That's the sixth request for an extension the council has turned down since fall."

"Actually —" He shuts his mouth. "Yes, you are correct."

"There are more, aren't there?"

He hesitates.

"Yes, there are," I say when he doesn't reply. "They just haven't mentioned it publicly. Like Sam telling the other militia that he didn't ask for an extension. Those who asked didn't admit they'd been rejected. Has *anyone* gotten one since you've been here?"

"Mathias."

"Yeah," I say as I sit on the desk edge. "Mathias is special, in so many ways."

"There were several granted after I arrived last spring."

"When did they stop?"

He pauses. Then he says, "Late summer, I believe. However, no one who has requested it was truly essential services, which is the definition required for an extension. Sam qualified, and I was surprised his request was denied, but it *was* his third extension."

Fewer extensions being granted. Fewer residents being admitted. I should be okay with that. Dalton has said that, ideally, he'd like to see a town of about one hundred and fifty. He's done the math and calculated that fewer than one-thirty would risk essential services, but more than one-seventy means less choice in living quarters, fewer jobs, and lower overall resident satisfaction. Maybe this suggests the council is actually listening to him, rather than overpopulating Rockton to fill their own pockets.

"I'll talk to Jen later," I say. "Get a feel for whether she's honestly looking for an extension or just being a pain in the ass. For now, we have a Danish tourist in the clinic."

"What?"

I start at the beginning.

Eight

It's a good thing Dalton had to head into the forest in search of Jacob. It's much easier to deal with the council's bullshit without also having to mediate between them and our sheriff.

I understand Dalton's frustration. He has a town to run, and his focus is on the people in it. He is the shepherd, and he needs to make sure every one of his flock returns home healthy and whole. To the council, though, the residents are widgets in two-year storage, and what counts is how much they pay for that privilege.

If Rockton were a country, the council would be the corporate interests and Dalton would be in charge of social services. That leaves me playing politician and negotiating between the two.

Fortunately, I have a budding ally in Phil. When he was first exiled to Rockton, he'd been like the junior exec sent onto the work floor, supposedly to get a better understanding of the business from the ground up, but really all sides knew it was a punishment. In his case, a punishment for failing to protect a very wealthy client . . . who was also a serial-killing psychopath.

Phil had reacted like most junior execs sent to work among the masses — he'd waited for his bosses to realize that it was all a big mistake and that they couldn't live without him. When that didn't happen, he made the best of it. They wanted him managing the town from the inside? Then that was what he'd do.

The thing about being on the inside, though, is that your perspective shifts. If I'd told him about Sophie a year ago, he'd have scolded me like a child bringing home a stray — and potentially rabid — animal. He'd lecture me on all the ways my actions had endangered the town and then trot off to tattle to the council.

When I tell him now, he just sags, one hand going to his forehead. I push the lone chair from behind the desk and let him sink into it. I make coffee and, while it's only 10 A.M., I add a generous shot of Irish whiskey. Tasting that, he hesitates, before his face fixes in a "fuck it" look and he downs the rest.

Phil's equanimity restored, we discuss the matter. Never once does he chastise us for bringing Sophie in. He can be an ass, but he's not an asshole. Not a monster. Not a sociopath. Living in Rockton, I've learned more about all three than I ever cared to.

Phil doesn't suggest, even for a second, that we should have left Sophie on that lakeshore. Even in the beginning, he wouldn't have done that, but he'd probably have suggested we pop a tent outside town and care for her there. Now he sees the ridiculousness of that. It will be far easier — and less suspicious — to feed her a story once she's awake enough to ask questions.

The problem is that any story we devise still needs a helluva lot of explanation. Maybe not to Sophie herself. *You were found by people in a small fly-in community.* That makes sense. Or it does until we fly her back to civilization and she tells people about this town of two hundred souls that everyone knows does not exist.

The council, not surprisingly, freaks out. We have a new liaison on that end. A woman named Tamara who, to be bluntly honest, sounds like the female version of Phil. She does exactly what I'd have expected of him a year ago, and it's Phil himself who gets the worst of her patronizing "disappointment." He's the council representative here; we're just the dumb cops.

Tamara takes the information, and an hour later, returns to convey more "deep disappointment" from the council. As they've reminded me before, Rockton is for Rockton residents, who pay for their safety and privacy, and it is our duty to provide that. We should have stabilized Sophie at the scene and then notified them to pick her up and discreetly deposit her outside Dawson.

I'm sure this makes sense to them. It would in a city or even a rural countryside. Here, though? The council wouldn't *need* to send a plane because she'd be scavenger-chow before morning. I'm not sure they *would* send a plane. Just let the scavengers do their work for them.

Chiding us about resident safety is bullshit. Every resident who goes home is a security risk. Sure, they might not know our GPS coordinates, but like Sophie, they could provide a general distance from Dawson plus directional cues if they understand the basics of the "sun rises in the east and sets in the west."

But there are ways around this, too. We can tell Sophie that this is a secret scientific facility devoted to climate change research, and she'd almost certainly keep our secret, given that outdoor enthusiasts tend to be more concerned about the environment than the average person.

I suffer the council's condescending bullshit in silence. I don't just sit there and listen, though. The lack of a visual screen means it's like being on a telephone conference where my input is not required. I take out my notebook and start writing down questions to ask Sophie, along with avenues of investigation. When Phil glances over, I'm tempted to pretend I'm taking notes from the meeting. Then I decide "screw it" and let him see.

Phil glances at my notes and then snatches the pen from my hand. I'm reaching to take it back when he draws the beginning of a hangman game. I stifle a laugh and guess a letter, and we proceed, with random verbalizations of "uh-huh," "right," and "I understand" as we play our game.

Dalton couldn't do this. He couldn't make notes for his day. He couldn't play hangman. He definitely could not manage those meaningless verbalizations. He'd need to argue and debate, his blood pressure rising until he stalked off, requiring a good hour of forest prowling before he was fit company.

After the hour-long reminder of why I hate the council, I return to the clinic to find Sophie unconscious. She'd woken and flown into a panic. Before they could find me, April sedated her again, since she'd been in danger of ripping open her stomach with her flailing.

That's where my day hits a brick wall. Dalton has gone looking for Jacob, whom we need to find the missing tourists. The missing tourist we *have* is unconscious, and I'm not sure I'll ever get more out of her. I'm not even sure she has more to give.

I spend the afternoon and early evening doing regular police work. There isn't really enough in Rockton for a full-time detective. The last case I worked was a sexual assault: guy expects sex after a date, woman says no, he tries to change her mind by demonstrating his skill with a nonconsensual make-out session behind the Red Lion. All it took was a cry to bring someone running, and by then, she'd escaped. Dalton sentenced the guy to two months of literal shit duty, emptying toilets. Curfew from 9 P.M. until 7 A.M. One-drink limit. No access to the brothel.

I check in on both parties today. Is she okay? Is he still grumbling that we overreacted? We're fine on both sides. She's had no further contact with him, and he's embarrassed and contrite. All good.

Then I follow up on a complaint between neighbors and a workplace-harassment charge. I also take a militia shift patrolling town, and finally I join Anders doing community policing — wandering about, chit-chatting with folks heading out for the evening.

The community service part is not Dalton's forte, which is one reason Anders is such a critical part of our force. Everyone likes Will Anders. Everyone's happy to talk to him. Today, our socializing has a purpose — seeing how many people know we have a stranger in town. According to Jen's spy research, a few know there was an emergency, and many realize the clinic is closed except for emergencies, but their curiosity is purely the gossip-fodder kind. Rumors are currency here, and they want tidbits to share.

After dinner, I'm in the station doing that most dreaded of law enforcement duties: paperwork. We have less than 5 percent of what I did down south. There's zero council day-to-day oversight, so there's no need to keep records beyond Anders jotting down something like "Jen is in the cell overnight for Jen crap." Case notes are only for ourselves. There are no trials. Dalton is judge, with us playing jury as needed, and our idea of court proceedings is having a beer on the back deck to discuss what to do with an offender.

At first, I'd been horrified. This is *not* due process. But . . . well, if we are completely sure we have the right person, and they did what they are accused of, then I've realized I'm okay with skipping the formalities. As I discovered, in Rockton, we are always sure. The old Mountie motto has never held truer: We always get our man . . . or woman. It's too small a community to steal something, assault someone, or break any law without leaving proof or witnesses.

That night, my paperwork is just jotting notes in the logbook for the two complaints I followed up on. I'm finishing when night-chilled hands slide around my waist, and I jump as Dalton lifts me from my chair. I twist in his grip, and before I can give him shit, he kisses me, deep and hungry, backing me onto the desk and easing between my knees.

When he breaks the kiss, he nuzzles my neck with, "Missed you."

"I see that. Long day?"

"Very long."

I try not to tense. "And unproductive?"

"Nope. Very productive, which is why I return to you in a very good mood."

I wrap my legs around him, pulling him closer. "I see that. Also feel it."

He chuckles. "I return bearing excellent news, which is going to make you very happy and that makes me very happy. Like returning with a stag over my shoulder. Only cleaner."

I wriggle closer, hands entwined at the back of his neck. "You found Jacob."

"I found Jacob, who told me exactly where we need to look. Also, you're going to be an auntie."

I blink up at him. "What?"

"Yep. April just told me she's —" He sputters a laugh. "And I can't even finish that sentence."

"So no baby?"

"Yes, baby. No, April."

I pause. Then I gasp. "Nicole and Jacob?"

Dalton nods.

I let out a whoop and kiss him, only breaking away to say, "Is Nicole here? She needs to see April. She —"

Dalton cuts me off with a kiss. "She'll be here next week. They're in a good hunting spot, and she feels fine. They're already planning to spend the summer closer to Rockton, and they've agreed to overwinter here so they aren't in the bush for the birth."

I kiss him again, pouring all my joy into that kiss and getting all his back. A year ago, this might not have been such cause for celebration. We'd have been happy for them, of course, but it would have brought up the question of babies for us — a difficult subject in light of my medical history. But now we can be genuinely, unabashedly thrilled at the prospect of a baby in our lives, having come to realize that it's possible to love kids and not be ready to have one ourselves just yet.

"So . . ." Dalton says, tracing his fingers down my cheek. "Make my day complete and tell me how the council congratulated us for our compassionate choice and careful handling of the situation."

He sees my expression and winces with, "Shit. Sorry," and a quick hug. "I was kidding. While I'm sorry you had to deal with that shit, I'm not sorry I got to skip it, which is probably part of my good mood."

"They were pissy. I handled it. Phil did his part, too. He's really stepping up."

"I want to say I'm glad, but part of me wonders if it might not be better if . . ." He shakes his head. "I'm overthinking it. I'm glad he's stepped up, too. You can tell me all about it later. For now . . ." His lips lower to my ear. "I think Storm is really eager to get home."

I glance at the dog, who'd followed Dalton in and collapsed by the fire. Storm sees me looking, lifts one furry brow and sighs.

"She really wants to go home," Dalton says.

"Or *someone* does."

"Someone who had a very good day."

"And wants a very good ending to it?"

"Seems fitting, don't you think?"

I kiss his cheek and turn to Storm. "Come on, girl. Time to head out."

We get to bed early, and even if it's awhile before we actually sleep, it still counts as rest, and we're up at dawn to head out. While Dalton grabs food, I pop into the clinic. Diana is on night duty and reports no change with Sophie. I pack an extra-large medical bag — we have no idea what we'll find out there.

We take the smaller ATV and my dirt bike. Storm happily lopes behind us. It's a good thing she's young and in excellent shape, because it's a long run, which can be particularly hard on a large breed. We stop regularly to give her water and a rest. Normally, going so far on motorized transport, I'd have left her behind, but we'll need her tracking nose once we're there. After a couple of hours, the forest is too thick to continue with the vehicles, and we're off and walking.

We don't need to go far on foot. Even before we find the spot, Storm whines and presses against my legs, nearly toppling me into the underbrush. When I bend, she gives an apologetic look, but only crowds closer, anxiety strumming through her.

"Shit," Dalton mutters.

There is very little that scares our dog. Less than I would like, if I'm being honest. The only wolf she's encountered tried to mate with her . . . and still occasionally sneaks around, a would-be suitor whose behavior borders on stalker but doesn't quite cross the line. She has a wary respect for caribou and moose after catching a hoof in the ribs. Black bears confuse her, and she's never seen a grizzly. Settlers get a happy bark if she knows them and wary caution if she doesn't.

There is only one situation where Storm reacts like this, seeking not protection but comfort. I crouch and hug her and assure her everything is fine, even if it's not. Once she's settled, I say "Wait?" with a questioning inflection. Her answer is the withering look of a police cadet who's been given the option of staying outside a crime scene.

Yes, she's uncomfortable, but this is her job.

As I rise, Dalton slips his hand into mine for a quick squeeze. I'm never really sure who is reassuring whom. Mutual comfort, I guess. Mutual understanding that this is never easy, and the moment it became easy, we'd need to take a long look inside ourselves and find the path back to the empathy we need to do the job right.

Hoarse croaks lead us in. We arrive to see two ravens diving at a weasel, which zooms our way before spotting Storm and nearly backflipping as it races off in another direction. Storm glances toward the weasel and sighs, seeing a potential distraction she cannot accept.

"I know," I say as I pat her head.

I take a deep breath . . . which is a mistake. I cough, Dalton thumping my back as I shake my head, face screwed up.

He takes another step and then lunges, his sudden cry scattering the ravens. Storm happily accepts this distraction, joining him with a deep baying *woof.* The ravens are gone in a blink, and we are alone with the scene they've left behind.

I see the campfire first. The remains of a long-dead fire, logs pulled over, a tent still standing. Like any other camp . . . until you see that the tent lists to one side, slashed fabric fluttering in the breeze.

I walk to where the ravens had been, in a tangle of winter-bare brush behind the fire. From the brush protrudes what had once been a human arm. It's the humerus only, the radius and ulna and hand having been taken by something larger than a raven.

I start to take another deep breath before the smell reminds me why I don't want to make that mistake again.

Dalton is already at the edge of the clearing, looking my way. He isn't hesitating to get closer. As the child of doctors, I was raised to have an iron stomach, yet he far surpasses my comfort with internal views of the human body. He grew up hunting and butchering, and to him, what lies in the brush is nothing more than human remains. The person who once inhabited those remains is long gone. Dalton will be respectful, but "squeamish" isn't part of his vocabulary. He waits because I'm the homicide detective and this is a murder.

I walk to him and survey the rest of the scene. Initial assessment: at least two adult human bodies in advanced stages of predation. I see two heads, both attached to torsos, and a minimum of two separated limbs. That's the way my brain assesses. "Separated limbs." It's a cold and clinical wording, as if these are mannequins. The alternative is to see at least two horribly mutilated corpses and start thinking about what happened here, how much they suffered, whether their bodies will ever lie in graves that their loved ones can visit . . .

Keep it cold and clinical. Watching my footing, I take three more steps. A third limb appears, attached to one of the torsos, the arm having been hidden by the thick brush. Before I can say a word, Dalton is handing me a sturdy branch, which I take and use to push through the brush, searching for more parts without moving from my spot.

I clear my throat. "At least two victims. Both adult, between the ages of twenty and fifty. Both Caucasian with light hair. Eye color will be impossible to assess."

"Fucking ravens."

I nod and continue. "One torso has retained a partial leg and an arm which appears tucked under the body. The other has a partial humerus. There is an unattached humerus and an unattached femur. That appears to be the total — Oh, strike that. I see a partial foot over here."

"Two torsos, five limbs and a foot. So predators hauled off three complete limbs and several partials."

"If we presume two victims. Sophie was with three companions. We could have detached limbs from a missing torso."

"Fuck."

"Yep. Given the advanced state of predation, it's not a simple matter of putting the pieces back together. We may need to resort to DNA."

"Fuck."

"Hopefully not. The problem right now is knowing whether we have the remains of three people to transport back to Rockton or the remains of two . . . plus a survivor in need of rescue."

Nine

It's two hours later, and I don't have my primary answer. I have answers to other questions, but not that all-important one, and I am well aware that I might be fussing with dead bodies . . . while a survivor is dying somewhere in the forest. On the other hand, I could race off into the woods hunting for a survivor, only to later discover that I have the remains of three people here. Better to see what I can assess first.

I definitely have two victims. One man and one woman. I'd been generous in my age estimates, but I'd peg them both close to Sophie's age.

All she told us about her group is that it'd been four people — two heterosexual couples. Am I looking at one couple? Or Sophie's lover and Sophie's female friend? Getting more information had been on my to-do list, but it's really not important at this moment. It's just the romantic in me who wants to believe this is the other couple, and Sophie's partner is out there, alive, and I can return him to her when she wakes.

I'm guessing all four are Danish or at least Scandinavian, and while there are certainly people of color in Denmark, all the body parts I have come from the stereotypical Scandinavian light-haired, light-skinned Caucasian. That makes body-part matching tougher.

I attempt to separate limbs based on muscle mass and body-hair density. The torsos suggest that both were the same body type as Sophie — average height and lean-muscled. Even that is tough to judge when, well, the limbs are no longer whole.

What I'm looking for is a male limb that doesn't fit. One that's too thin or too muscular to belong to the dead man before me. Perhaps one with a different color or density of body hair or a different skin tone. In the end, I can reasonably identify one humerus as belonging to the woman, judging by bone size, and the femur matches up with the dead man. That leaves a humerus that cannot belong to the woman . . . because she now has both of hers. I can't tell if it belongs to the man. The foot, though? That's definitely male, still encased in a hiking boot. The hair on it seems darker than the other dead man's remaining limbs.

Does this mean I'm holding the foot of the missing man? I imagine taking it back to town for Sophie and having her fly into a flurry of excitement, certain it means her lover is out there somewhere, only missing a foot. No, sadly, he is not, and I hope I don't need to delve into the gruesome realities of that foot and the torn flesh and the gnawed bone, all of which leave zero doubt of what happened to the second man.

No, I'm sorry. The wild men of the forest did not hack off his foot before he escaped. No, he did not hack off his own foot to escape. This is scavenging. A predator found his body and chewed on his leg, and when they hauled him away, this was left behind.

No one needs that much detail on a loved one's final moments, even if I can assure Sophie that he was dead when it happened. Also, the fact that I don't have a body means I can't assure her of anything. I would lie, of course, but if Sophie is a smart woman, she'll figure it out and spend a lifetime imagining her lover's final moments as a grizzly ripped into his living body.

It might not be her lover.

It might not even be the second man's foot.

Even if this *isn't* his foot, judging by the remains, the degree of decomposition tells me the attack happened at least three days ago. Sophie was extremely lucky to survive. The missing man — even if he has both feet intact — probably wasn't as lucky. If he was, he'd have been with her, right? They'd have fled together or found each other afterward. Still, we will search, just in case.

As for what else the bodies tell us, the short answer is "nothing new." I'm hoping to get more from the autopsy, but at this point, I see evidence of stabbing on both torsos. While that isn't easy to determine, given the degree of predation, there are stab wounds through the man's back, preserved because he fell onto them, leaving the scavengers to work on his chest instead. As for the woman, her throat has been slit. Yes, ripping out the throat is a common method of killing prey, but there's a huge difference between ripping and slitting, and I don't need an autopsy to see the clean edges on the wound.

Two tourists, murdered by what seems to be hostiles. I hate jumping to that conclusion, but from what Sophie said, I can't imagine she mistook "settlers in desperate need of a shower" for wild men of the forest.

I try sending Dalton into the forest with Storm to search for a potential survivor. That goes about as well as one might expect, complete with profanity and pointed comments about the dead people on the ground, who should serve as a Klaxon-loud warning against separating. I let him talk me into postponing further crime-scene investigation while we search for our potentially missing man.

Storm takes the lead there, joyfully, as we give her a reason to leave the death tableau behind. She always struggles with a search ending in people she cannot wake with a lick and a bounce. I have to wonder, though, if this scene upset her even more because, well, what's lying on the ground isn't so much people as meat. Either way, she can hardly contain her delight at being asked to do a proper task and leave this place.

I don't have anything for her to sniff — the tent had been cleared of all belongings. Still she understands she's looking for a person. We don't use her to hunt, so work means finding people, preferably alive. She snuffles the scene, and then she's ready to go.

Newfoundland dogs are not trackers. However, they are used in search-and-rescue, and they have an excellent sense of smell, which are the excuses Dalton used to get me the dog breed of my dreams. I never handled a tracking dog down south. Never even owned a pet. So, despite my deep-dive studies, I am quite certain that the fact that Storm has become a very fine tracking dog is entirely owing to her innate intelligence and eagerness to please. If she is not quite on par with a bloodhound, well, that isn't her fault. We both try our damnedest, and at the risk of bragging, we make a good team.

Storm takes a quick sniff of the torso, knowing that's not who she'll need to find, which helps her weed them out from the scents around the campsite. I'd also brought her Sophie's jacket to exclude her scent, but I swear Storm gives me a look when I hold it out.

Umm, I met that woman last night, Mom, and she's in town — why would I think she'd be out here?

Like I said, smart dog, one who does indeed find a scent leaving the campsite. But something about it bothers her. She doesn't whine anxiously. She just seems . . . This is one of those million times when I wish we could communicate. Something is amiss with this trail, and she cannot tell me what it is, and I cannot ask.

When she follows it, I see the problem. It leads to the remains of another camp. There's a firepit ring and logs pulled over for sitting, and when Dalton digs through the ashes, he finds tinfoil, suggesting a cooked meal. He also finds evidence that the fire was extinguished properly.

So, someone made camp here. Someone from down south, judging by the tinfoil and matches. There's also evidence of a tent — rope fibers where it'd been strung between trees.

This might seem perfectly logical. Storm followed the missing Dane's trail from their most recent camp to their previous one. Except that the two are maybe an hour's walk apart. No one is going to pull up stakes and make a new camp that close by.

This could be someone else's former campsite. The Danish quartet found it and considered making camp there to take advantage of the preexisting firepit, but ultimately they chose another site. There, anomaly explained.

Except for one problem. The firepits are identical: a double ring of stones with a log-cabin-style fire built within. The similarities extend beyond that — enough that I know the same people constructed both camps. The Danes, I presume. So why the hell are they a mere hour's walk apart?

"Maybe one came after the attack," Dalton says. "Guy's injured and, as he's recuperating, he builds —" He stops short. "Well, that makes no fucking sense, does it?"

It does . . . until you work it through. If you've just seen two of your companions brutally murdered and the third stabbed in the stomach, you are not going to flee and build yourself a nice campsite while you recuperate.

Even if your brain was somehow addled enough for you to merrily construct a new camp a kilometer from the murder site, where would the tent come from? The tinfoil-wrapped meals? The matches? The rope? The attackers took their supplies. That's presumably *why* they attacked.

I crouch in front of Storm. "Can you find his trail again?" I repeat "trail" with the appropriate gestures, but she is unsure. I understand now what bothered her earlier. The sequence of events. Trails have an age, based on strength, and she's had enough training and experience to know that the trail between this campsite and the murder scene seemed older than others. She'd been backtracking along a trail. That means this is the earlier site.

She snuffles around and indicates the entrance trail to this site by walking down it a bit and then pointing. *He came from that direction, Mom, and I can follow it if you'd like, but I don't think that's what you're looking for.*

No, it is not.

I do a thorough examination of this campsite as I tell Dalton my thoughts. He doesn't have a solution to this particular mystery. There's nothing left here but signs of habitation. No marks in the dirt or the vegetation to suggest a struggle. A campsite used and cleared as they moved on.

We return to the crime scene, and I resume my investigation. Here we do find those signs of violence, and not just in the bodies left behind. There's blood in the dirt, more spattered on the tent and the campfire rocks. Scuffle marks in the soft ground. Footprints, too. I take pictures of them — I have a digital camera, and there's a screen in Rockton for me to enlarge them on, a reasonable use of our limited solar power.

I have the one hiking boot. That's it — Sophie came to us barefoot. I match this boot to some of the prints. I also see ones with a similar tread but smaller. I measure what remains of the dead woman's foot and roughly size it at a seven or eight. I'd sized Sophie's earlier, so I could locate her prints, and she'd been an eight. Two women with similar shoe sizes and likely similar footwear. The boot I'm holding matches Dalton's size ten. In other words, average for a man.

Two men and two women, wearing the same brand of hiking boots, all with average-size feet. Useless.

What's more important, though, is that I don't see any significantly *different* treads. I do, however, spot prints from footwear without treads. Different treaded boots would mean other hikers or miners or trappers. Some settlers also traded for modern boots, and everyone in Rockton has them. These, however, are the soft-soled outlines of the homemade footwear worn by most settlers . . . and all hostiles.

As I've already noted, the supplies are gone. That's not surprising. It doesn't matter if they were attacked by settlers or hostiles or fellow hikers — their gear wouldn't be left behind. There is only the tent, which appears to have been slashed in the attack. It's nylon and lightweight, perfect for camping, but too flimsy for settlers or hostiles.

The tent . . .

Something about the tent . . .

I contemplate it for a moment before turning back to the bodies. My gaze goes straight to that lone hiking boot with the foot inside.

An image flashes. Dalton and Kenny and me in a clearing, not unlike this. Surrounded by hostiles. The leader telling Dalton to undress. For a moment, I thought it was about humiliating our leader. Then I realized the truth. They were going to kill him, and they didn't want his clothing ruined.

I shiver at the memory. Dalton steps behind me, fingers going to my elbow.

"Okay?" he murmurs.

I turn and hug him — a fierce, quick hug. He kisses the top of my head as I pull away, and I pause a second before regaining my composure.

"I'm trying to determine whether they took the clothing," I say. "The packs, yes, and there'd be clothing in them, but what they were wearing . . ."

"Ah." One arm goes around me in a quick embrace as he understands that sudden hug. "May I speculate?"

"Please."

"What we encountered last spring was a hunting party in what Maryanne described as a 'down' phase."

"Lucid," I say. "Thinking clearly enough not to want to ruin our clothing."

"Yep. In the 'up' phase — the manic one — they wouldn't have thought of that, she'd said. It'd be a frenzied killing."

"Which this could be, except they *did* take all the hikers' pack goods. What happened to us was a clear-thinking ambush. They tracked and cornered us. Which should be the same here. They saw the camp and orchestrated an attack, like they did on Maryanne's group. When they attacked Maryanne's group, it was at night, and they didn't order them to undress first. The goods weren't as important as the captives. Except I'm not sure they took a captive here and . . ."

I exhale and rub my temples.

"Yeah," Dalton says. "It's not quite adding up."

"Maybe it is. We only have one boot. Both bodies are wearing shirts, which were damaged, like the tent. Both are wearing only underwear. No jackets for either of them. The lack of jackets could suggest either those were taken or it was a daytime attack and they'd discarded their warm outerwear. But the lack of pants . . . I'm going to speculate that this happened at night. That's what Sophie said."

"The killers caught them asleep, wearing T-shirts and underwear. Someone manages to pull on a boot, and afterward, when the killers are gathering the goods, they don't realize there's a missing boot."

I nod. "We thought Sophie lost her shoes. She was probably never wearing them. Surprised at night, like Maryanne's group. Bodies left in what they were wearing. The rest of the goods taken."

I turn to the tent and stare at it. What's bothering me . . .

"Shit," I say.

"Yeah. One tent."

I turn to him and arch a brow. "When did you figure that out?"

Dalton shrugs. "At the other site. Just waiting on you."

That wasn't a test. He hasn't done that since our earliest days. Instead, he was being respectful and trusting my process. It's like when I'd been a newly minted detective. On my first crime scene, I'd been poking around, rattling off observations, until my partner handed me a notebook and pen, and said, "Write it down. Time-stamp it if that helps."

He'd understood that I wanted to prove I deserved my detective shield, but my machine-gun observation patter disrupted his own musings. If I needed to show that I'd noticed clues before he did, the time stamp would do that. I got the hint and mentally stored up my observations until he would inevitably turn to me with "Whatcha got, kid?" and I could show him.

Dalton has identified the problem that niggled at me earlier, back-burnered while I concentrated on other observations.

There's only one tent. Only *signs* of one tent. I check all the nearby trees, and I inspect the ground, and there's nothing to suggest another shelter occupied this clearing.

"How about the other site?" I say. "I only recall evidence of a single tent there, too. Did I miss something?"

He considers and then shakes his head. "I didn't think to look closer, but I only recall rope marks for one."

I walk to the ruined tent and consider it. Open the flap and peer inside. It's definitely a two-person tent.

When I say that, I add, "Unless the four of them liked getting real cuddly, and if they did, no judgment."

Dalton chuckles.

"However," I continue, "whatever their living arrangements at home, they aren't going to be squeezing four people into a two-person tent after a long day of hiking. Even the two-person one doesn't leave much stretching room."

"Yeah."

"What we're seeing, then, isn't two couples who like a lot of together time, but the opposite. Two couples who've had quite enough together time, thank you very much."

He glances over and then shakes his head. "Shit. Of course. Two tents. Two campsites. They wanted a break from each other."

"Could have been a fight. Could have just been a privacy issue. They'd been traveling together for days, and they didn't particularly want to 'keep it quiet' for another night. I believe we know the feeling."

"Hell, yeah."

"That's a theory, then. They separated for the night to get some private time. But there are no signs of attack at the other camp, and Sophie clearly *was* attacked." I rub my temples. "No point speculating when I can — hopefully — ask her for more details tomorrow. For now . . ."

I look at the remains of the two victims. "Do we transport them back to Rockton? Or bury them? I'm not sure we'll get anything from them in an autopsy, but I hate to lose a chance. If we bring these bodies back, though, and anyone sees them, no 'it was scavengers' explanation is going to keep people from freaking out."

"Mobile autopsy. Cover the remains. Bring April out."

I nod, and we set to work.

Ten

The autopsy is hard. Holy shit, is it hard.

The day I arrived in Rockton, Dalton and Anders brought in a corpse from the woods, one who was missing his lower legs. This, though? This is the most disturbing crime scene I've ever come across, and dealing with it is not even the worst part of my day. The worst is having to show it to my sister.

I commit an unforgivable sin here. The sin of misunderstanding April and her neurological condition. I have grown up with a sister who is coldly competent, and in my head, I have substituted "unfeeling" for "emotionally detached."

Even knowing her condition and researching the hell out of it, I cannot move the monolith in my head that is "my sister, April." When April looked askance at my own displays of emotion, I saw judgment instead of confusion. So I expected I would warn her about the crime scene, and she'd brush off my concerns and snap that she's a doctor and suggest that I lacked the fortitude to handle such things.

The real April? She does all of that, and I'm sure when she says I'm overreacting, she thinks I truly am. That doesn't mean she is prepared. It means she cannot comprehend being unprepared. She's spent her life slicing into the human body, and it has never bothered her, so why should this?

Why indeed?

April has been working on the woman's torso for twenty minutes now, and she has to keep stopping, balling her hands to stop the faint tremor, her breath rasping against the surgical mask I insisted she wear to stifle the smell. Every few moments, her gaze moves to the side, accidentally catching a severed limb, and she closes her eyes, steeling herself to start again.

Another hand flex, and she murmurs, "I believe I overindulged in coffee this morning."

"It's okay to say you find this difficult, April."

"I do not. It is simply . . ." A furtive glimpse around. "It is outside my experience, and I am adjusting."

"I'm sorry."

"Please stop saying that."

"I can't. I'm just . . . I'm so, so sorry."

"You warned me. I failed to comprehend the situation fully."

I nod.

She glances over. "Are you crying, Casey?"

I blink back tears. "N-no. It's just . . ."

"Allergies to a substance in the vicinity that you have somehow never encountered before?" Her brows arch. "You are crying."

"I'm sorry."

"Stop. The apologies, I mean. You are permitted to cry, even if you do not need to feel bad on my account. I will adjust."

Silence. Then her fingers tentatively rest on my arm.

"I am fine, Casey."

I nod, tears flowing freely. "I'm just. I'm —" I instinctively throw out my arms to hug her and then stop, horror seizing me as I mumble yet another apology.

"You wanted to hug me?" She eases back on her haunches. "You haven't done that since you were a toddler."

I manage a weak smile. "I learned it wasn't your favorite thing."

"It is not. However, you may hug me now, if it helps."

I throw my arms around her in a quick embrace. As I pull away, she grips my shoulder, leans in, and whispers, "Yes, it is difficult. I will be fine. I would not, however, object to a very strong drink when we return to Rockton."

I pass her a wry smile. "Sounds like a plan."

"Excellent. Now let's finish this."

I put April through the hell of that scene, and we learn absolutely nothing new for it. As she points out, though, I needed her to confirm my suspicions, and without that, I'd be running a constant mental loop of doubt, kicking myself for burying the bodies before I was sure.

With the state of the corpses, an autopsy isn't 100 percent conclusive either. Yet April feels confident saying that both victims died of knife wounds. The condition of the wounds says they were alive at the time — their hearts were still pumping blood. The woman's neck slice bisects the carotid artery and would have been fatal. One of the man's stab wounds perforated his heart. Also fatal.

Both injuries are consistent with blades. April may specialize in neuroscience, but she spent years in emergency wards, and she knows the difference between a knife wound and an animal bite. Plenty of the latter here, but the killing blows are not among them.

She also confirms that the severing of the limbs was postmortem and appears to have been the result of animal predation. There are no marks on the bones to suggest cutting.

There'd been a time when Dalton speculated that the hostiles may have practiced cannibalism. Looking back, I think he'd been genuinely confused by our horror. Killing humans as prey would be abhorrent to him. Eating those who'd already died would be repugnant. But in a desperate situation, lost in the winter wilderness with no way to catch game, it would be a necessary evil.

There is absolutely nothing about this crime scene that suggests cannibalism. Nor any solution other than the one we'd already theorized. Sophie's group had been set upon by hostiles, who'd killed at least two people, left the bodies, and raided the camp.

The second campsite complicates the situation slightly — were they all hanging out together at the first one when the hostiles attacked? If so, why weren't they fully dressed? It's not a theory-breaking complication. Just something to address with Sophie once she's lucid.

The biggest question remains: Do we have

another survivor? Without DNA, April agrees we cannot confirm or refute the possibility that the foot belongs to the male corpse here. By the time we got that DNA processed, any survivor would be dead from exposure. We'll take the foot and a tissue sample from the male corpse. In the meantime, Dalton and I must search for a potential survivor.

April returns to Rockton with Anders. We'd left him with Storm and the vehicles. And no, he didn't accept that without complaint. Anders has been to war. He's seen friends blown up by IEDs. There was no way in hell we were letting him near that crime scene when it was completely unnecessary. So he waited and then handed over our camping gear before he took April back to town.

Dalton, Storm, and I set out on our search. It is meticulously slow work. We take Storm on wider circles around the crime scene, in case that helps her pick up a trail. At one point, I suspect she's following the killers. Their trail soon breaks up, and while it might seem that we'd try harder to hunt them down, they aren't our priority. I'm not even sure what to do about them. The obvious answer should be that they're murderers, and we need to bring them to trial.

Which is kind of like tracking a grizzly and bringing it to trial.

Catching the hostiles responsible doesn't solve the problem. The situation must be resolved in a permanent manner, preferably by the council stepping up and following Maryanne's recommendation to begin the process of capture, assessment, deprogramming, and reintegration.

For now, I want to focus on finding the potential survivor. Of course, he may be *with* his hostile captors. If so, then I hope he'll play along until we can rescue him. He will be safe enough if he does that. My bigger concern is that he's alone in the forest, without supplies, possibly wounded.

We return to the second campsite in search of anything we overlooked. A clue or, perhaps better, a piece of clothing we could use to ensure Storm has the right scent. We only confirm that there did indeed seem to be only one tent here, which is now gone, the entire camp cleared as thoroughly as if it'd been packed up.

Are we misinterpreting the evidence? If this camp looks like it was properly dismantled, then maybe the two couples hadn't decided to sleep apart.

"Or they did and then didn't," Dalton says.

I nod slowly, processing. "They plan to sleep apart, and then have second thoughts. Maybe it was a fight, and they resolved the issue. Maybe they had dinner together at the other camp, and couple number two decided to just stay and sleep on the ground. No, wait. That wouldn't explain the packed camp. They must have made up and reunited but it was too late to set up the second tent. Warm night. They have their sleeping bags. Set those up outside."

"That would explain how Sophie escaped. She was in the tent with her partner. Hostiles attack the two outside and kill them quickly. Go after Sophie and her partner next."

"They kill him, and Sophie escapes. Or he makes a run for it, and she's injured, and he doesn't come back to check. Presumes she's dead."

Dalton snorts. "Asshole."

That's harsh. Yes, I would come back to check. So would Dalton. Of course, we wouldn't run in the first place, not unless we could escape together. I'm sure most people would say the same. Only a coward runs. Only a coward doesn't return. But until you're in that situation, it's impossible to judge it.

I only know that we'd both stay because

we *can* fight. If Sophie's lover didn't have those skills? If he'd been sleep-groggy and panicked? If he'd been so certain she was dead that he never considered returning? I won't judge. I just want to find him.

We do not find him. Nor do we find any sign that he survived. The more we search the more certain I am that his body was dragged off by a predator. Maybe our local cougar or one of her full-grown cubs. Take the body. Cache it in a tree. We've seen her do it with a settler.

When the sun begins to drop, we declare it a day and declare our searching at an end. If he's out here, he's not close by, and we could hunt for weeks and never find him. At the very least, we can get more information from Sophie. And we can take that DNA test to Dawson and ship it south for testing.

We debate going back to Rockton. It's barely dark, but it's 11 P.M., and we've been awake since four. We're exhausted, fueled for nineteen hours by water and energy bars, and too little of both. We have our camping gear. We have food packed by Anders, and when we open the box to find both dinner and breakfast, that seals the deal. We'll head back first thing tomorrow.

Eleven

It's not yet six the next morning, and I'm cuddled on a campfire log with Dalton as he roasts breakfast sausages. The smell of venison brings a red fox, who watches Storm from the forest, as if the dog is the only thing preventing the small canine from stealing our breakfast.

Storm glances at us, checking whether we want it scared off. There's a cross fox that lives behind my old house in Rockton, and the vixen has made peace with Storm, realizing that the larger canine provides an excellent deterrent to any predator who'd bother her annual litter of cubs. Storm and the fox certainly aren't friends, but they tolerate each other, and when I give Storm the signal that chasing off this fox is optional, I'm not surprised when she only settles in to watch the beast.

We're dining with both a dog and a fox nearby, yet it's Dalton who senses trouble first. Storm's on her feet then, staring to the left, hackles rising in a warning growl that makes the fox decide it's time to disappear.

Dalton tilts his head, nostrils flaring. He takes a few steps and sniffs again, sampling the breeze. This isn't something he'd do with others around. He's well aware of how it looks, and even if few people in Rockton know his past, he will forever feel like that "savage" child, brought back and taught civilized manners, which include not sniffing the air.

Dalton's sense of smell isn't any better than mine. He's just more accustomed to using it, and when I do the same, I catch what he does. Campfire smoke. Not surprising, given that there's a campfire crackling right behind us. But this smell wafts over on the breeze. Someone else has a fire close by.

There are approximately as many settlers in this region as Rockton residents. If I'd known that before I arrived, I'd have imagined those settlers fighting for hunting territory and fresh water. Having experienced the reality, though, I've discovered that thought is laughable. Dalton estimates one settler for every three square kilometers. That's nearly a thousand acres for each person, and most share their land by choice

— they live in one of the two settlements or with a family group. If you don't want to be social, you need never encounter another person. So this fire is too close to be a coincidence.

I motion for Storm to stay where she is. She grumbles, but she's accustomed to this indignity. We cannot sneak up on anyone with a Newfoundland lumbering after us.

Dalton sets out, and I fall in behind, covering him. He places each step with care, and I follow in his literal footsteps. When we're close enough to see the fire — and two figures sitting by it — the smell of cooking meat wafts over, along with . . . Is that coffee?

Dalton tilts his head and inhales as he considers. He peers into the bush, and we both look for other figures. There appear to be none except the two at the fire.

He gestures for me to circle while he takes the straight-on approach. I keep my eye on him as we creep toward the campfire. Halfway there, I pause and motion to Dalton. He hesitates and then nods.

Unnecessary risks are not my thing, but in this case, I'm compelled to make an exception.

I take it slow, easing through the forest until I'm directly behind the two. A man and a woman, pressed as close as Dalton and I had been, sharing a log and body heat in the chill morning.

The woman talks as the man eats. While she's speaking, I step from the forest. Five paces separate us. I eye the rifle at the woman's side. Another rests within the man's reach.

I pause when the woman stops talking to sip from a tin mug. Then she resumes the one-sided conversation about plans for a trip into Dawson next month.

Two more steps. One . . .

I press my gun to the woman's blond hair. "Hello, Cherise."

Her partner, Owen, gives a start.

Cherise doesn't even flinch. "Hey, girl. Wondering when you'd join us. Coffee?"

Owen and Cherise. Or, more accurately, Cherise and Owen, because in this relationship, there's no question of who is in charge. Also no question that Owen likes it that way.

Owen is a former Rockton resident who took off after one too many clashes with Dalton. He went into the woods and met Cherise, the oldest daughter in a family of traders. Her mother died last year, and she took over the clan, despite being younger than me.

When I first heard about this family, I'd

had a very clear idea of what they would be. Downtrodden women enslaved by a patriarch. After all, they were best known for their particular goods — three pretty blond daughters who'd been available for rent soon after they passed puberty.

What I found was . . . I'm not even quite sure what I found. Dad was clearly not in charge. Mom had been, and now Cherise is, and she's a viper of a woman, whip-smart and deadly. The middle sister clearly aspires to Cherise-hood, but lacks the intelligence. The youngest is the only one who seems in need of rescue, but when I quietly offered it, she was insulted. She accepts her lot until she can find a settler to marry and start her own trading clan. I don't know what to do with that. I really don't.

I lower the gun and step back. Cherise only sips her coffee. She's mid-twenties, and model-pretty in a cool, Nordic way. Her partner is my age, dark-haired and dark-eyed, with a scar across his nose.

Dalton strides from the forest, gun still in hand.

"Hello, Sheriff," Cherise says. "Coffee?"

"What are you two doing here?" I say.

"Waiting for you. I knew you'd smell the smoke eventually. Or the coffee. I should thank you for the coffee. It puts him in a much better morning mood." She hooks a thumb at Owen.

"Why are you here?" I say again.

"Hoping to hook up with you guys."

Owen waggles his brows. "You must be getting tired of this stick-up-his-ass by now."

Dalton tenses. Owen is a sexual predator. Oh, I'm sure he doesn't see himself that way. His type never do. Good-looking former frat boy known to slip a little something extra into a girl's drink to ensure his evening ends with a bang. Owen came to Rockton claiming to be a victim and very clearly was the perpetrator. It doesn't help that I'm apparently Owen's type.

What *would* help is if Cherise took offense and shut him down. She couldn't care less. If it'd help foster a valuable trade relation, she'd gladly loan me her partner. Yet that same shark instinct means she doesn't fail to miss Dalton's reaction, which *does* jeopardize this trade connection.

"Casey has made it abundantly clear she is not interested, Owen." She pats him on the back, like a friend offering sympathy for a strikeout. "Now stop embarrassing yourself."

His mouth opens.

"Stop embarrassing *me,*" she says, meeting his gaze.

He nods. "Sure, babe. I ain't trying to cause trouble. Just goofing around."

Cherise rises as I whistle for Storm. The dog's there in seconds. When she sees who we've met, she growls.

"Yeah, I know," Dalton says. "We'd have preferred hostiles."

"Now, now, don't be rude," Cherise says. "I think I might be able to help with that."

"With what?" I ask.

"Your hostile problem."

"If there's a hostile problem, it's yours, too. Everyone out here is affected."

"We can deal with the wild people. You're the ones who riled them up by killing their leader."

"Because their leader attacked us and —" I stop myself. "I'm not here to argue. If you have information, let's talk trade. It won't be worth much, though. The hostiles have been quiet lately."

Her burst of laughter has me cursing my misstep.

"They left two people in pieces," Cherise says.

I try not to give anything away in my expression as I say, calmly, "Two people were left in that condition by animal predation."

"Oh, don't mince words, Casey. The wild

people killed them. Animals just ate the remains. We heard you two yesterday and got a look. We also overheard you talking to your sister. You believe it was a hostile attack. On outsiders."

I glance at Dalton. He lifts one shoulder, telling me he doesn't see any point in holding back.

"What do you have for us?" I say, in lieu of confirmation.

"Something you'll want."

"Eric? Could you take Storm to the stream for a drink? I think Owen wants to go, too."

Owen snorts and leans back on his log bench. "I'm good."

"No," Cherise says. "You stink, and unless you plan on sleeping alone tonight, you'll wash up."

He chuckles. "That punishment would last until about midnight, when you remembered why you keep me around." He kisses her cheek but rises to follow Dalton out.

Once they're gone, Cherise says, "If you think I'll go easier on you with him gone, you're mistaken, Casey. I don't need to prove to Owen that I'm a tough negotiator. He doesn't actually care, as long as he has a roof over his head, food in his belly, and me in his bed."

She pauses and eyes me. "But it's not him

you're worried about, is it? You don't want to break too easily in front of *your* man."

"Eric trusts me to negotiate. I just want them gone so we can drop the bullshit and do that. Without posturing."

Her lips tighten at the unfamiliar word. Then a sniff as she figures it out in context. She doesn't argue, though. She might not need to prove herself to Owen, but she's still the alpha here, and this is more easily done without her pack as an audience. Also, perhaps more importantly, I don't want Owen here as a witness to the admissions I'm about to make.

"Yes, we have a hostile problem," I say. "It isn't just the deaths. It's the fact that one of their women left them, and they may know she's in Rockton. I want to resolve this problem permanently."

As I realize what I said, and how it can be interpreted, I expect her lips to curve in a smile. Which proves that I don't know Cherise as well as I think I do.

Instead, she just eyes me, assessing.

"I don't mean exterminate them," I say, and when her gaze shows no comprehension, I amend it to, "Kill them all."

"That would resolve the problem, though, would it not? My father has suggested it for years. My mother called him a fool. She said it was like killing all the grizzlies. Yes, we'd be safer if they were gone, but we'd also be safer if the wolves and the mountain lions were gone. Then perhaps we could also be rid of the winters. Oh, and the cliffs we can tumble off or the vines that can trip us. All are part of the forest. We have even done minor trade with the wild people. Not enough to wish them to remain, but there are too many of them to 'exterminate,' as you put it."

"Agreed, and we wouldn't do that."

"Because they're human?" Her lip curls slightly. "This is where you prove yourself unfit for our forest, Casey. You are tough and you are strong, but you are softhearted, and that makes you weak."

"Maybe, but imagine if we did kill the hostiles. Wouldn't you begin wondering who we'd target next? The settlers? The traders? You?" I shake my head. "Extermination isn't the solution. We have access to resources that can remove the hostiles and treat them."

Her brows crease whenever I mention an unfamiliar concept or term, as when I say "access to resources." It's the barest line between her brows, smoothed quickly. It slows her comprehension down just enough that there's a beat pause before she catches my last words and snorts a laugh.

"Treat them? Why?"

"That isn't your concern. What I need from you is an understanding that this goal benefits us both. Whatever trade you have with the hostiles, as you say, it's not worth the threat they pose. To get them out of here, though, I need to convince Rockton's leaders that we're dealing with a serious threat."

"Then show them those bodies. That should be explanation enough."

"The council doesn't live in town."

One brow arches. "You allow yourselves to be ruled by outsiders?"

"Ask Owen how Rockton is run. He'll explain. For now, yes, those with the money and the resources to solve this aren't in Rockton. Of course I'm going to tell them about the bodies. I can even send photos. I'm hoping the fact that the victims are outsiders will help. The last thing anyone needs is a team from Dawson combing the forest for lost tourists." I pause. "People visiting from outside the Yukon."

She gives me a withering look. "We travel into Dawson, Casey. I know what a tourist is. That's why I'm hoping to make a trip before summer, when they invade like mosquitoes. I can't imagine how fewer of *them* would be cause for concern, but I will take your word on that."

She leans back. "Now, I suppose I'm supposed to tell you that I understand and will provide my information for free."

"No, you're supposed to understand that I've shared information with you, information I would rather keep to myself. Whatever you have, I expect to pay for it. I just don't expect the bullshit of posturing and negotiating and spending half my fucking morning prying it from you . . . only to realize I've paid for something I could have found out myself for free."

She refills her coffee before sitting back on her log. "Oh, you won't find it, Casey. And you are going to pay for it. Despite all this blathering that's supposed to convince me it's in my best interests to tell you everything I know."

"I would never *not* pay for information from you, Cherise, because you'd hold it over my head. I want an even accounting. All this 'blathering,' as you call it, is supposed to convince you that I'm not screwing around. If you distract me with time-wasting bullshit, you won't ever trade with Rockton again."

Her blue eyes flash. She doesn't like that. But she only says, "I want more coffee, and

I want condoms. Owen says Rockton has lots of both. I also want money. Five hundred dollars before my next trip to Dawson."

"Two pounds of coffee. Two hundred and fifty dollars. And as many condoms as you two need to keep from reproducing."

She snickers at that. "Funny girl. You're going to regret that offer, though. We need a lot."

"We get them by the caseload."

"Five pounds of coffee. Three hundred and fifty dollars. If you see what I have and you can convince me it's not worth that, I'll reopen negotiations. But I don't think you're going to be able to do that."

"Then we have a deal."

Twelve

Cherise won't tell me what she has. She needs to show me. Which means more time spent in their company, but it's quicker to endure than to argue. First, though, we need to return to our camp and dismantle it. We manage to talk Cherise into meeting us partway to her "spot," so we don't leave the ATV and dirt bike behind. We break camp quickly and ride the vehicles to the rendezvous spot where the couple are already waiting.

When Owen eyes my dirt bike, Cherise says, "No."

He glances over.

"First, you're too big for that. It's a child's toy. Fortunately for Casey, she's child-size."

I could point out that I'm not abnormally small for an adult woman — just small compared to her. That would make Cherise think she'd found a sore point, though, so I keep quiet.

"Two," she continues, "it runs on gas. Not air. Not wood. Not water. Not anything we have in abundance."

She motions for us to follow her into the woods. She's carrying one of the rifles and nothing more. Owen gets the pack. He doesn't complain. As Cherise said, he's a simple man — food, shelter, and sex, and he's good, especially if he doesn't need to bother with the logistics of attaining any of that.

Behind their backs, I motion from my pack to Dalton and lift my brows. He hooks a thumb at Storm, offering her services instead. I laugh under my breath and shake my head. I wouldn't want a guy who uncomplainingly carries my backpack when I'm perfectly capable of doing it myself. No more than I'd want one who insisted on carrying it to be chivalrous.

As we walk, we talk. Or Cherise and I do, while Dalton eyes Owen as one would a rabid wolf. I swear Dalton growls under his breath every time Owen gets within three feet of me.

In that conversation with Cherise, I learn that they didn't just happen to come across us yesterday. They'd been keeping an eye out, and hearing us yesterday, they'd abandoned the hunt in favor of more profitable prey.

They had something to show us, and it wouldn't keep forever. They knew better than to stop by Rockton, though. We've set the town off-limits, with the warning that Owen was still wanted for crimes there. A good excuse for not letting them in, where they might be able to woo residents with the promise of goods we tightly regulate — booze, cigarettes, and, of course, sex.

Cherise leads us to a mountainside. We hike up it about a hundred feet, and then she motions to Owen, who drops his pack and rolls back a rock over a small cave entrance. It reminds me of going to Easter services with a friend in elementary school, when I'd been transfixed by a painting of disciples rolling back the rock that sealed a crypt. When the smell of decomposition hits, I think it's triggered by that memory. Then Dalton scrunches his nose and turns to Cherise.

"What've you got in there?" he says.

"A gift."

"Well, we're not going in after it."

"Didn't say you had to. That service is included in the price."

Another wave at Owen. No "please." No imperious wave either. She isn't haughtily commanding him to do her bidding. She just expects it . . . and he obeys with neither grumbling hesitation nor groveling obsequence. Maybe this was what the old marriage vows meant: your husband expected obedience, and you delivered without resentment. I can't imagine being either party in that arrangement.

Owen has to drop to all fours to enter, and even then, his grunts tell me how tight the passage must be. A moment later, he backs out, boots first, pulling a long, wrapped cylinder after him, and that Sunday-school image flashes again.

Before I can comment, Owen crawls back inside.

Two more bodies follow. Three crudely wrapped corpses, the stink of decomposition still seeping out. The wrappings are partly cured skins. Rejects, from the looks of them — too damaged to make proper trade goods.

I bend to one knee beside a corpse. Gently, I peel back the wrap. The skin sticks a little, and I stop as soon as I can see the face. Male. Heavily bearded. A scar on one cheek, poorly healed, but it's not ritual scarring. The hair is roughly cut, longer than usual and not exactly clean, but showing no sign of matting.

"Too early in the year for miners and trappers," I murmur. "Settlers, then?"

I glance at the other two bodies. One is definitely female, the other taller but slighter, like an adolescent.

I wince. "A family of settlers."

"If by settlers, you mean people formerly from Rockton or descended from them, then no," Cherise says. "They came as trappers a couple of years back. Man, woman, boy." She glances at Owen, who supplies, "Teenager," and she nods.

"Teenager. They came as trappers and stayed. Built a cabin maybe . . ." Another glance at Owen.

"Ten miles," he says.

"Ten miles that way." She points west. "They didn't usually come this far, but the weather's been good."

"Cabin fever, probably," Owen says. "Long winter, early spring."

"We saw them last week and traded. They had skins. Not those ones." Cherise pauses. "Well, yes, they had those, but they were trash. We only took the good ones. Still ended up with those." She rolls her eyes. "Missy."

"Your youngest sister." I nod. "She's a good seamstress. She must have figured she could do something with them."

"No, she just wanted a romp with the boy but knows we don't give that for free." Another eye roll.

Missy had taken the damaged skins as "payment" so she could have some fun with a boy her age . . . a boy who now lies at my feet, wrapped in those same skins as a death shroud.

"Was there . . . a problem with that?" I say carefully. "An argument over it?"

Cherise's brows knit. Then she looks at the bodies and back at me and laughs. "You think we killed them because my little sister wanted sex? We aren't savages. I told Missy if he goes around telling other people how cheaply he got her, I'll tan her backside, but otherwise . . ."

She shrugs. "Missy wants a man. This boy would grow into one soon enough, and he'd be a good choice. In the meantime, I wouldn't begrudge her some fun. That took place last week. We found them like this three days ago. Owen said you'd want the bodies, and you'd want them in the best condition possible. So we wrapped them and put them in here, and then we were keeping an eye out for you."

I turn to Owen. "Why did you think we'd want them?" Even as I ask, I know the answer. I just hope I'm wrong.

"I said you'd want them because of how they died. They were attacked."

"By wild men," Cherise says. "Attacked in their camp, just like those tourists."

We're leading Storm through the forest as she pulls a makeshift stretcher with the three bodies roped onto it. While she can smell death, she seems to accept that she is performing a necessary task.

We left Cherise and Owen once I got all the pertinent information from them. While the cop in me says they tampered with a crime scene, the realist acknowledges that, given the state of the other crime scene — and the bodies — I'm grateful for their interference.

They found the corpses on a chilly morning, when the scavengers had yet to do more than nibble. The fire had still been smoldering, suggesting the family died during the night, which gives me a rough time of death. By wrapping the corpses and placing them in a sealed cave, Cherise and Owen provided me with three relatively intact bodies.

They earned their pay on this one. As for the crime scene, I'm not sure there's much point in visiting it. Cherise and Owen already stripped it of goods. As callous as that seems, the alternative would be animals ripping it apart or other settlers hauling off the usable items. Cherise described what they found, and that'll be enough.

As for what happened to this family and what it portends . . .

"No," Dalton says as we reach the ATV and dirt bike.

"No . . ."

"No to what you're thinking."

"And tell me, O Psychic One, what am I thinking?"

"That this is our fault." He pauses as he unhooks the ropes from Storm's harness. "Nah, you aren't thinking that. You're thinking it's your fault. Ours — Rockton's — but mostly yours."

"Isn't it?" I watch as he hooks the stretcher up behind his ATV. "Everyone says we riled up the hostiles, and we can bristle at that, but we kinda did. And the reason we riled them up? Because I started getting curious. Wanting to know more about them. Wanting to solve a mystery I was not hired to solve."

"Stop taking all the damned credit. If they got riled up, it's because of what Cherise said. We killed their leader . . . who'd been about to kill us. Are you saying I should have let them kill me to avoid this mess?"

"Of course not. Yes, that was unavoidable,

but it's the fallout that's the real problem."

"So when we found Maryanne after that, we should have ignored her? Better yet, tied her up and delivered her back to them?"

I sigh and check the bindings on the bodies.

"I'm exaggerating," he continues, "but I'm also making a point you can't argue. We didn't have a choice. Not if we're human. And, when you stop fretting about it, you'll do the math and realize this might not have shit to do with us. It's been a year. You think they've been stewing all this time and suddenly decided to start slaughtering tourists and settlers?"

"Something set them off recently, and that wouldn't be us."

"Exactly." He tightens the strap. "Now, unfortunately, you have three more murders to solve."

At the clinic, I help unwrap the bodies and find fatal wounds in all three — one slit throat and two chest stabs. There are more wounds, too. Brutal ones. With the other bodies, we'd ascribed damage to predation, but I'm no longer sure we didn't jump to a false conclusion there. Yes, serious predation had occurred, but it could have been nonfatal injuries that the scavengers had used as entry points to feeding.

Without this new information, we'd have reassured Sophie that her companions died quickly. Now I'm not so sure.

On these bodies I see frenzied rage of exactly the sort others have described in hostile attacks. I also see a family. I'm not sure what their story was. Cherise only knew they'd come up from Whitehorse to trap two summers ago and decided to stay.

I wondered what their son thought of that. He looks about sixteen. Had he happily embarked on this great adventure? Or resented his parents for pulling him away from a normal life? What had he thought of Missy? A bit of fun, sex between a couple of hormonal teens? Or had he seen in her the possibility of a partner?

And this is why April makes me leave the autopsy. I cannot afford those melancholy thoughts, and yet in my state of exhaustion, they seep in like ghosts. I'm sad and frustrated and overwhelmed.

My brain and my soul need a break, and so, once I've done my preliminary examination of the bodies, Anders volunteers to assist in my place, and before I can more than squeak a protest, I'm outside, with Dalton's hand between my shoulder-blades, steering me into town.

"Am I being sentenced to an afternoon nap?" I ask.

"Would you sleep? Or make notes?" He doesn't even wait for an answer. "I've got a couple hours of work. By then, April will be done, and you'll have her report, which we can go over at dinner."

I smile. "You might be the only person I know who'd suggest reading an autopsy report as dinner entertainment."

"Yeah, not exactly a break from work, is it?"

"For future reference, Eric, to most people, the problem wouldn't be working through dinner. It's reading *that* over dinner. My stomach can handle it, though, so we'll do that, and I'll take a break now instead. I have a few outstanding issues to follow up on —"

"Your definition of taking a break is as shitty as my definition of suitable mealtime conversation." His fingertips press into my back, that steering hand turning me left. "As your boss, I'm prescribing this instead."

I glance up to see we've stopped outside the Roc.

Dalton says, "Earlier April wanted a drink. She can't do that right now, but I'm going to suggest you have one for her. This is what they call 'cocktail hour' down south, isn't it?"

"Not quite. Also, the bar doesn't open until five o'clock, and even if you have the key, I'm not drinking alone."

"You won't be. Isabel's doing inventory."

"She's not going to want —"

He shoves open the door and leans in to bellow, "Iz? Casey needs a drink."

A shadowy figure leans out from the back. "Oh, so I'm playing bartender now?"

Dalton nudges me inside before I can protest. The door shuts, and I'm immersed in cool darkness, lighting only as my eyes adjust to the candles on the bar. The shutters are pulled, both to keep out the strong sunlight and to warn off anyone who might consider sneaking into the Roc for their own private happy hour.

I walk to Isabel, standing beside the bar. She wears an apron over a stylish sundress, her hair piled on her head, dust streaking one cheek.

As she reaches for a glass, I say, "You don't need to serve me a drink. I can get my own if I want one, and I don't. Eric's just fussing. I'm happy to help with inventory."

"Sit." She pours something from a condensation-stippled jug and then adds a deft shot of vodka. "You can help by sampling my new cocktail. Blackberry-infused vodka with lemonade." She puts the jug back into a basin and flips two ice cubes into the drink. "Those will cost extra."

"Naturally." I take a sip. "Nice. Very refreshing. Is this what I'll actually get if I order it? Or will the official version be a little lighter on the vodka and heavier on the lemonade?"

"It's getting warm out, and alcohol dehydrates."

I settle onto a barstool. "You know, you look good back there, Iz. No need to hire a new bartender. You can just do the job yourself."

She extends a middle finger as she rearranges the bottles.

"Why not?" I say. "You were a shrink. You're used to having people tell you their problems."

"I got paid for it."

"So? Make a new policy. Telling the bartender your woes is free. Getting advice, though? That'll cost you."

She snorts and starts wiping the counter. "Obviously you haven't ever been to therapy, Casey, or you'd know that'd be the worst moneymaking scheme ever. Most people don't need advice. They just need someone who'll listen to them."

"I actually have had therapy." I sip my spiked lemonade. "And you are one-hundred percent correct. I wanted someone to listen to me talk."

"Listen to you confess, more like," she says, slanting a look my way.

"True enough. Now I have Eric for that. Problem is, he also gives advice. *So much advice.*"

She chuckles. "Our sheriff is quite certain he knows what everyone needs. Sometimes he's even correct. As in this case. I need a bartender, and I am ready to hire one."

"Mmm, pretty sure you've been hiring them. And firing them. And hiring more."

"Well, I'm ready to hire a proper one now."

I nod and say nothing as she pours herself a lemonade even stiffer than mine. Isabel hasn't had a real bartender since Mick died, eighteen months ago. Mick, former cop, expert bartender . . . and Isabel's lover.

When her glass is full, I clink mine to hers.

"Guess it's working out with Phil, huh?" I say as we toast.

She flinches, just a little. I consider, and then sip my drink, saying as casually as I can, "Should we switch spots? Let me play bartender while you talk?"

I expect an eye roll. Instead, she says, "Have you ever been in a relationship that scared you, Casey?"

I tense.

She shakes her head. "Not like that. I had a man lift a hand to me once, and I showed him the door." She takes a drink. "A strategy that always works so much better in our heads. And in advice columns. He didn't go quietly. Once he was gone, he didn't stay gone. Old story. Women can say they won't put up with that shit, but that presumes the men listen. Most don't. Phil, however, is not remotely a problem in that way. The issue is . . ."

She sets down her glass. "I almost screwed up the other night, Casey. The new guy. The one who just arrived. James?"

"Jay."

"See? I don't even know his name, but when he flirted with me, there was a moment where I considered taking him home for the night. I certainly flirted back long enough to give him hope."

"Are you and Phil exclusive?"

"It hasn't come up, but it's clear that Phil considers it so, and unless I've said otherwise, that would be a poor excuse. The unforgivable part is that before Phil, I wouldn't have flirted with James. He isn't my type."

I start to ask why she did, then I remember what she said. "Ah, when you asked about relationships that scared me, you meant emotionally. You flirted back with Jay to convince yourself you aren't serious with Phil."

She gives me a hard look. "A therapist isn't supposed to offer interpretations."

"Then it's a good thing I'm a detective, where it's my job to interpret."

Isabel takes two bottles from the shelf and disappears into the back. I don't take offense at her sudden departure. Where I would simply go quiet, she signals that she doesn't want to discuss it by removing herself from the conversation.

Bottles click and shuffle in the back. I'm halfway done with my drink before she returns.

"Do you consider me a soft touch, Casey?" she says.

I choke on my lemonade. She picks up her cloth to wipe away the spatter.

"Perhaps I worded that wrong," she says.

"Unless that was extreme sarcasm, yes, you did. No one would ever mistake you for a soft touch, Iz."

"I do have my vulnerabilities, though. After Mick . . ." She keeps cleaning, although my mess is long gone. "He was the pursuer."

"He told me that. He chased, and you resisted."

"Not just at the beginning, either. I *always* resisted. He let me know exactly how he felt, and I . . . did not reciprocate. I hope he knew —" She clears her throat. "I trust he knew. Some women might see dating a significantly younger man as a point of pride. Smug self-satisfaction. To me, it was like revealing a weakness. Uncovering a place where others could poke me. I fought back by acting as if Mick was just a plaything. Not in private but . . ."

Another throat-clearing. "I was less respectful than I ought to have been, and I regret that. When Mick was gone, I realized just how much I'd cared for him. It's one thing for a successful man to have a hot young thing to show off. It's quite another if he's fool enough to fall for her. I worry that Phil . . ." She downs a gulp of her drink. "I worry he saw my weakness, and he's taking advantage."

"Of you?"

"Of my position here. My power in the community. I worry that he sees me as an easy mark. Get me in bed, and I'm just an older woman making a fool of herself."

"I don't see that *at all,* Isabel. If Phil was using you, he'd be flaunting the relationship, which he is not."

"Because he's embarrassed."

"Uh, no. Jen accused him of that yesterday. He said he's being circumspect because of your mutual positions in town. Also . . ." I run my finger down my glass. "I get the impression he's being quiet about the relationship because *you* are. You might not be the only one who's worrying about where you stand, Iz."

She takes another sip and says, "I don't want it happening again."

I pause, processing her meaning. Then I nod. "You think he'll betray us, like his predecessor. That he's insinuating himself with you in hopes of winning you to the council's side. Or, at the very least, stripping you of your power as an ally to Eric."

She doesn't answer, which tells me I'm right.

"Have you seen any sign of that?" I ask.

"No, which means I'm being a fool. Coming up with excuses for keeping yet another man at arm's length."

"So this is serious, then."

She dries her hands on her apron, gaze down. "God knows, it wasn't supposed to be. Phil was my horse. I'd fallen off, and I was getting back on again."

"Taking him for a ride," I say with a smile.

"A much-needed ride. As many rides as I could get. A fling with a man I would never fall for. Too young. Too pretty. Wound too tight. I wanted a shot at unwinding him."

I grin. "Which you did."

"I certainly did, and that man is . . ." She exhales. "There's a brain behind that pretty face. A fascinating brain, along with the kind of ambition I don't see anyplace but in the mirror."

"It's easier to think he'll betray you than to admit you've fallen for him."

"*Much* easier. I also don't want to be played for a fool, Casey. I worry about that."

I lean on the bar. "If you're truly worried, then test him. See if he bites. If not . . ." I shrug. "Then you're going to need to figure out where you stand, and whether he's standing in the same spot."

"You know, that James seems like a lovely fellow. Quite handsome."

"*Jay* is indeed handsome, and completely not your type. He hasn't been coming on strong, has he?"

"No. He flirted. I flirted back and then wised up and sent him on his way. I don't think I was ever in danger of inviting him home. I realized I wouldn't do that to Phil."

She finishes her drink. "I need to test him."

"Or you could just trust —"

The bar door creaks open, Anders peeking in.

"Eric said you were in here," he says. "We found something you need to see, Casey."

THIRTEEN

Anders and I are halfway to the clinic when Jay jogs up to us, and I tense, thinking of Isabel. She'd said he had readily taken no for an answer, but earlier today, I'd been reflecting on the trouble Owen caused in Rockton. The woman he'd stalked had been Isabel. She attracts admirers. Some are nice guys like Mick, who pursue ardently but respectfully. Others are like Owen, assholes who hear "no" as a challenge. I have to wonder what would have happened if Cherise hadn't said yes. Or what will happen if she stops saying it.

As for Jay, though, Isabel said it was fine. I'm just being overprotective.

Jay falls in step with us because he's heading in the same direction . . . apparently with the same destination.

"I heard Sophie's stirring," he says as we walk. "I was going to try talking to her again."

"Thank you. I'm sorry I haven't been around."

"You went looking for her friends," he says. "Someone said they thought they saw bodies being brought in the back way. I'm guessing you found them?"

Anders cuts in. "Jay has been stopping by the clinic every time Sophie wakes. She hasn't said much, but he's been taking notes."

Jay nods. "It really isn't much. I wrote it all down, though." He holds out a notebook. "She seems to be more lucid today. Is there anything you want me to ask her?"

"There is. We found two campsites about a kilometer apart. It looked as if the group split up. Can you ask about that?"

"Sure."

We reach the clinic, and Diana's waiting on the front porch. She takes Jay into the storage closet. That's where we've put Sophie. It's big enough for a bed, though I always feel guilty when someone needs to sleep in it. The clinic doesn't have a room for overnight stays, and right now, there are three corpses in the main examination area.

I head into the exam room, where April is jotting notes. There's a body on the table. The other two are stacked, still in their rudimentary shrouds. Yes, they're on a tarp, but it still feels a whole lot like stacking bodies in the corner.

"Ever get the feeling Rockton needs a proper morgue?" I say to Anders as I enter.

"Only since you got here."

April doesn't look up from her note-taking. "If you are suggesting there are more murders since Casey arrived in Rockton, that is logistically impossible. She would need to be creating them herself, and I doubt she is."

" 'Doubt,' " I murmur. "Thanks for the vote of confidence, sis."

She looks up then, frowning. "Since I am not a mind reader, I cannot exonerate you completely. However, I do not believe you murdered these people. Isn't that proper sisterly support?"

I shake my head and walk to the exam table. The body on it belongs to the son. The boy, his beard patchy with youth.

A beard that will never get the chance to grow in properly.

I hesitate. Anders reaches to pull up the sheet, but I wave him off as April says, "Casey does not require that. She is simply pausing in reflection. You knew this young man?"

I shake my head. "I know the girl he was seeing. That just makes it . . . more real."

"Shit," Anders murmurs. "Felicity?"

"No, one of Cherise's sisters." I cover the last step to the table. "So what do we have?"

He walks to the counter and lifts a small jar. When he shakes it, a bullet clinks against the glass.

"Hunting accident?" I say. "A bullet from an old wound?"

"It was lodged in his aorta."

"Aorta? You mean . . ." I turn toward the body. "He was *killed* by a bullet?"

A crash sounds from the next room. Everyone turns, and April starts toward it, saying, "If they have knocked over the IV, we do not have a backup —"

Diana screams, and I charge into the room. She's alone with Jay and an unconscious woman, leaving no doubt as to which one is making her scream.

I throw open the door and —

The bed is empty. That's the first thing I see. An empty bed with the restraint straps dangling. Diana stands at the foot of the bed, hands to her mouth. There's no one else in the room.

How the hell can there be no one else — ?

I follow her wide eyes. She's looking down at the other side of the bed. There's a strangled cry, and I race around to see Jay and Sophie on the floor.

Sometimes, the brain jumps ahead of the eyes and fills in a false picture. It's a phenomenon I know well from witness interviews. They see what they expect, and that image can leave an impression even when the truth contradicts it.

I heard a crash. I see Diana frozen in horror. I spot Sophie and Jay on the floor, and I think that Jay has . . .

Well, I have no idea what he's done, but clearly he's the aggressor here when the other person involved is the semi-sedated victim of a murder attempt.

Yet that is not what I'm seeing. Jay is facedown on the floor, and Sophie is on top of him with her hands wrapped in his hair, her face twisted in rage.

She jerks his head back as if she's going to slam it into the floor, I shout at her to stop, and she has the mental awareness to look up and see the gun pointed at her.

She snarls something in Danish, and I know, beyond doubt, that she wasn't fighting off Jay. She's tried to attack us before. She's not in her right mind. Yet I somehow still imagined Jay instigated the attack, because that's the usual narrative.

Jay's face is pure terror, his eyes rolling, blood streaming from his nose. More blood on the floor, where she's already bashed his face.

His mouth works, but nothing comes out.

"She — she just went nuts," Diana whispers. "She was talking to him, and he undid her restraints, and I said not to, but he did, and then she just . . . sprang."

"Sophie," I say. "Can you understand me?"

"She's still not speaking English," Diana says.

"April? I need a sedative."

"She's already getting it," Anders murmurs beside me. He has his gun out, too, aimed over the bed.

Sophie barks something in a voice that makes me jump. It's a definite bark. A command.

"Sophie," I say. "I need you to —"

"Back," she says in English. "Back." She jerks her chin down at Jay. "Kill."

Get back or I kill him.

Seems she knows a little English after all.

"Jay?" I say. "I know you're scared right now, but I really need you to translate. Is there any chance you can do that?"

He makes a gurgling noise. It comes out on a gasp. He's too frightened to help. *Shit.*

"Back!" Sophie says. "Back!"

I assess the situation. She's got him

facedown on the floor, as she kneels on him. Her hands rest at the base of his neck. She's pinned him so he can't lift his arms.

How serious is her threat to kill him? She could bash his face against the floor, but I'm right here, with a gun trained on her. I can shoot her before she can do that.

Still, is there any reason *not* to do as she asks? If I can defuse the situation, I will, even if that means surrendering ground.

I glance at Anders. He nods, telling me to go ahead and ease back. April appears in the doorway, syringe in hand, and I motion for her to lay it on the bed. She does, so carefully that Sophie doesn't see it.

Something's wrong here.

Uh, yes, your survivor freaked out and attacked her translator.

No, something . . .

Jay's eyes bug, and he gets a hand free. Even as it shoots to his neck, the answer flashes. The way his eyes bulge. The way he gasps and can't speak despite having his face off the floor. The way Sophie's hand rests oddly at the back of his neck.

That's why he can't talk.

She has something around his throat.

She's choking him.

I back up fast, my hands rising, gun pointing toward the ceiling. Anders shifts, and his gaze shunts my way, but then he sees the problem and his lips part in a curse. He lifts his gun and steps back.

"Sophie?" I say. "Let him go. We can't speak to you without his help."

I pantomime my words. She only snorts, her nostrils flaring. I can't see what she has around his throat. It's thin, whatever it is.

"Diana?" I say. "What does she have?"

"W-what?"

"What's she choking him with?"

"Ch-choking?"

"Sophie?" I say, louder now, firmer. "Let him go."

Sophie looks straight at me. She holds my gaze as Jay gasps, and a chill slithers down my spine.

"Let him go!" I point the gun at her again. "You want me to back off? I'm not going to do it while you're *killing* him."

She continues holding my gaze.

"You know what I'm saying," I hiss. "You know enough English to understand."

Jay gasps, and his head falls forward as he draws in rapid breaths. I see then what she's using. It's her IV tube, wrapped around his neck, just slack enough now to let him breathe.

"Dead," she says. "Malthe and Liva. Dead. Saw killed."

"You saw your friends Malthe and Liva die. I'm sorry. That wasn't us, though. I can explain —"

"Victor," she says. "Want Victor."

"Victor?" I repeat it. "Is that your partner? Your lover? Your husband?" I rattle off synonyms, waiting for the recognition in her eyes. There is none, though. Her hooded eyes give nothing away.

"April," I say. "Get the hiking boot."

She withdraws, her shoes tapping across the wooden floor. When she returns, I glance up just in time to see her holding the boot . . . with the severed foot still inside.

I open my mouth, but Anders beats me to it, waving wildly at the boot and shaking his head. It takes a split second before his meaning penetrates. April disappears.

"Victor!" Sophie snaps again. She didn't see the foot, thankfully — she's too low behind the bed. She tightens the tubing again, and Jay's eyes bulge.

"Stop that!" I snap. "If you want to talk to us, you need him."

She looks me in the eye. "Liar."

I blink. Did she just call me a liar? Or is that a Danish word? "I am not lying to you. He's the only one who can speak Danish, so unless your English vocabulary suddenly improves —"

Anders catches my eye. I understand the message.

Take it down a notch. Remember she's not herself. She's woken in a strange place with strange people. She's not thinking straight and not fully understanding the language.

"I need you to let him go," I say, motioning with my hand. "Please. We can talk about Victor. Just let him go."

"Liar."

I struggle against my frustration. Pretend she's high on drugs. Don't expect logic. Just talk her down.

April returns with the boot, sans foot. I grab it in my free hand and hold it up.

"Vic — ?" I begin.

She sees the boot, screams and yanks on the tubing, and Jay thrashes in fresh panic.

"Sophie!" I shout. "Sophie!"

She's not listening. I holster my gun and dive for the needle on the bed. Snatch it, drop onto her just as she grabs Jay's hair and smashes his face into the floor. I jab the needle in, but she bucks before I can depress the syringe. Then she's on me. Before I can blink, I'm flat on my back, sprawled half across Jay, with Sophie on top of me.

Diana screams. Anders shouts at Sophie. I feign contorting my face in panic, and that relaxes her just enough that she doesn't notice when I go for my gun. In another blink, it's pointing at her as she lays one hand over my throat.

"Let her go," Anders says as he comes around the bed. "Or she will pull that trigger."

"She will," Diana says quickly behind him. With shaking hands, she pantomimes shooting a gun.

"Shoot her."

At the last voice, I give a start. It's eerily calm, and it comes from over my head. Out of the corner of my eye, April appears. Her expression . . .

I have never seen this look on her face. Her words are cold and calm and clear, but her face is taut with fear, eyes showing whites all around the blue irises.

When she speaks again, there's a tremor under that calm. "Shoot her, Casey. Please, just shoot her." April swallows, the sound as loud as a gunshot. "She has her thumb on your Adam's apple, and I need you to shoot her now."

It is indeed on my Adam's apple. Yes, an open-handed strike at that spot is famous as a killing blow, but Sophie's thumb just happens to rest there as she presses her hand into my throat.

I lift the gun to Sophie's face. Then, beside

me, Jay gurgles.

"Casey . . ." Anders says, and I follow his gaze to Sophie's other hand, wrapped in the tubing again. I glance at Jay. The tubing digs into his throat, blood tricking down.

"Syringe," I whisper.

Anders shakes his head. "The needle's snapped. April, can you please draw up —"

"Shoot her, Will, for God's sake," April hisses. "She's going to kill Casey."

"For once, I'm with April," Diana says, voice shaky. "Will? Casey's not going to do this. Can you please — ?"

Sophie's thumb digs in. Then she yanks on the tubing, so hard her face twists with effort, and she smiles. Dear God, she smiles down at me as she yanks and —

I fire, and she twists sideways, my bullet hitting her in the shoulder as another passes through the side of her head. As she topples, I scramble up to wrench the tubing from her hand. Jay's face hits the floor.

Anders yanks Sophie's body aside. There's no help for her. I know that. Grief darts through me, grief for a woman we'd tried so hard to save. Anders had been right shooting to kill, though. He didn't know whether I would actually pull the trigger, and he couldn't risk aiming for her shoulder.

With Sophie gone, we both scramble for

Jay. He's facedown on the floor, unmoving. I flip him over. His eyes are closed, and that damned tubing is still embedded in his neck. I go to pull it free, and Anders says "No!" just in time.

"Move!" a voice says. "Both of you. Move, now!"

We part for April as my sister shoulders her way in.

"The tubing —" I begin.

"I see it."

"He's not breathing. He's —"

"Casey." Her eyes meet mine. "Let me do my job."

"What do you need?" Anders asks.

April tells him, and we all scramble to obey.

Fourteen

Jay is alive. That is all I can say. Alive, for now.

He stopped breathing, and it wasn't a simple matter of CPR to bring him back. Adrenaline can give ordinary people the strength to overturn cars to free their trapped children. It can also, when fueled by madness and rage, give them the strength to yank plastic tubing through a windpipe. Getting Jay breathing again took all my sister's emergency-ward experience. Without her, he would have died. Even with her . . .

Jay did not leap up, gasping, when his heart started again. His brain has been deprived of oxygen for too long. He's in a coma, and even if he recovers . . .

For now, we will not speculate on his mental condition if he recovers. Our focus is on making sure he *does* recover.

Ten seconds.

That's what I keep thinking. Ten seconds. Maybe even five. Yes, I'm quite certain it's five.

If I'd pulled that trigger five seconds faster, Jay would be dealing with a sore throat and nightmares. Traumatized, but alive.

Five seconds faster and Anders would have seen me shoot Sophie and stayed his own finger, and she'd be alive.

Five seconds. A blip so fast we barely register its passing. How can I possibly be judged for missing such a narrow window?

Because it is not the blink of an eye. After Jay is stable, I measure time in five-second intervals. That's how long it takes Anders to cross the room and retrieve gloves from a drawer. That's how long it takes April to tell Diana she should leave, and Diana to protest. That's how long it takes for Dalton to burst in, frantic because he'd been in the forest and returned to hear I'd been attacked by a patient. That's how long it takes for me to go outside and ask Kenny to reassure people that the situation is under control.

Five seconds.

I might have saved two lives if I pulled that trigger five seconds earlier.

Yet I couldn't. I know that. I made a

mistake fourteen years ago, let anger and outrage pull a trigger for me, and a man died for it. A man who deserved to be punished for what he did, but who did not deserve to die.

Too fast. Too slow. When it comes to this, it will forever be one or the other. There is no time I have ever fired a gun and later rested confident that I did exactly the right thing, even when, in the back of my mind, I know I did the *only* thing.

I will question it.

Anders will, too.

There will be late nights, the two of us, huddled in some quiet place, nursing drinks, whispering our doubts to the only person who truly understands them. I love Dalton with all my soul, and he has done things he regrets, but only Anders and I share this in our past — the shame of pulling a trigger when we shouldn't have.

Now we are locked together in a new regret. I will tell him that he did the right thing and saved my life, and he will not believe it. He will tell me that I did the right thing in trying to save Sophie, and I will not believe it.

I saw the plastic tubing around Jay's neck. I saw blood. I should have shot Sophie right then. But I misjudged. I thought I had the situation under control, and it was only when she yanked that tubing that I realized my mistake.

Five seconds.

"I would like to speak to my sister alone now," April announces.

I jump. I think we all do as her voice cuts through the tiny room. Dalton's grip tightens on my hand — I hadn't even realized he was holding it until now.

"Eric," April says, "you may have Casey back in ten minutes. I need to speak to her alone."

Anders nods and waves Dalton to the door. They go out back. April waits until they're gone and then walks to the door, her head tilting.

"They aren't going to eavesdrop, April," I say.

"Not intentionally, no." She pauses and then, satisfied, returns to me. "I have a dilemma, and I wish to consult with you."

Her words make my stomach flip in a sensation so alien that it takes a moment for me to identify it.

My sister is admitting she has a problem.

She wants to talk to me about it.

She may even need my advice.

I have been waiting for this moment all my life. How many times did I want to ask for her advice, but I couldn't because we didn't have that kind of relationship? If she had opened the door, though, I'd have leaped through. Even just the proof that my perfect sister *had* problems, *needed* advice, would have meant so much. I grew up feeling like the screwup, the girl who never quite got her shit together, because April did everything effortlessly.

"Okay," I say. "What is it?"

"I want to say that I am unable to properly care for this patient in his condition."

I nod. "I would disagree, but I understand if you feel you can't —"

"No." The word comes out sharp. "I do not wish you to understand, Casey. I *can* care for him. In his current state, a hospital could do nothing for him that I cannot. Moreover, here, he can receive the undivided attention of staff at all hours, and if he comes to require more than we can offer, I can personally arrange a discreet transfer to a Vancouver facility."

"Okay . . ."

"The problem is that I don't want that."

I lean against the counter. "You don't want the burden of his care. You have enough to do here, so we'd understand —"

"*No.* It is not a burden. It's that I do not want the *responsibility* for his care. I wish to transfer it to someone else. My expectations for a full recovery are low, and I wish to make that someone else's responsibility. I want to spare myself the guilt of feeling as if I could have done more."

"Ah. Well, I'd rather have spared myself the guilt of not acting fast enough to save Jay. Or not figuring out how to save Sophie."

"This isn't about you, Casey."

"No, it's not. I'm making a point. We are all going to second-guess here. What if Diana had alerted us when Jay first removed the restraints? What if we'd sedated Sophie right away? What if I didn't break the damn needle injecting it? What if I'd shot her before she strangled Jay?"

"Yes, you should have shot —"

I lift a hand. "Really not what I need right now, April."

She hesitates and then nods. "I apologize. I would have preferred you'd shot her sooner, but I understand that you made the choice you thought was correct."

I try not to stiffen at that. She doesn't mean an insult. I just hear "you thought" more emphatically than she says it.

"However," April continues, "I'm not sure what this has to do with my situation."

"I'm questioning what I did. You're questioning what you will do — and leaning toward the path of least resistance."

She snaps upright, her eyes narrowing. I meet her gaze with a level stare and, after a moment, she gives a sharp nod.

"All right," she says. "I accept that assessment. That is why I'm consulting with you. I needed to know whether my fears were justified."

"I think you've already answered that."

"I am attempting, Casey, to admit that my assessment of my abilities can be overly confident, and therefore I'm seeking your advice."

I walk to Jay and look down at his unconscious form. "This man is alive because of you. Saving him would have been well beyond my medical skill set and Will's. Yes, you have an ego, but you've earned it. Male surgeons have plenty of it. We just aren't as accustomed to seeing it from women."

"Why?" she asks, and it's a genuine question.

I shrug. "Confidence is attractive in men. Humility is attractive in women. Not saying that's right — it just seems to be how it is. If there is nothing more that a hospital could do for him, then I will tell the council you've offered to care for him. Ultimately, the choice is theirs."

She nods. "Then I am offering."

"And I will let you know what they say. For now . . ." I look from Jay to the three bodies on the floor to the open storage room door. "We need to look after Sophie. She deserves that much."

There will be no autopsy for Sophie. Possibly no grave either, beyond the one we will place her in once the ground thaws. Sometimes it is possible to return people to their loved ones. Sometimes it is not.

When residents come, they must answer that question in advance. If you die before your release, do you want us to attempt to return your body? Most say no. I suspect their loved ones would be appalled, but that's really who a grave is for, isn't it? Those who loved us and wish to have a place they can visit, knowing we are there. Except we aren't. We are dust and earth, and it would make more sense to visit us through photographs and letters and memories.

Returning a body isn't easy. Before residents leave for Rockton, they can only tell friends and relatives that they're "going away." That means we can't ship the family a covered casket and expect them to accept it without question. When residents insist on their body going home, it's "found" in another location, through an anonymous tip. I apologize to any police department that has to deal with that particular mystery.

Fortunately, that hasn't happened since I've been here. We've had only one natural death, an older woman with no remaining family . . . because she'd murdered her husband. As for the victims of violence? There's no way to send them home even if they wished it. I would never inflict that on a family . . . or a police department.

The most we can do for Sophie is return her to where her companions lie. That's partly consideration — at least she'll rest among friends — but it's practicality, too. When people come searching, if they do somehow find the grave, at least the bodies will be together.

I'll need to interview Diana and try to figure out what set Sophie off. I don't expect to get anything. From Diana's frantic babbling, Jay hadn't even gotten to my question about the dual camps. He'd been easing her in by reminding her where she was and promising that we were looking after her. She'd seemed to understand. She'd been calm, a little teary-eyed. Then she'd realized she was restrained and panicked, and Jay made the mistake of being a compassionate human being. He'd started to untie her, just as Diana had that first morning. Diana wanted to check with me, but Jay said we were busy, and he'd take responsibility. He untied Sophie and then . . .

We will never know what went through Sophie's mind at the moment she attacked. I can guess, though. As hard as Jay had tried to reassure her, she hadn't been reassured. Her mind still conjured the demons of her delirium, and she couldn't help thinking she was a captive. After all, she was tied down, wasn't she?

She'd played tearful victim to relax Jay's guard. It was the smart thing to do. It's what I'd tell someone in her place to do. Play up your "feminine passivity" to get the guy to untie you. Once he does? Attack. Which she did, and with the language barrier, we couldn't explain well enough to convince her she hadn't been captured by monsters.

She apparently *did* know English. Just enough to call me a liar. Lying about taking care of her. Lying about being a hospital. Lying about trying to help her friends.

I'm not the one she'd attacked, though. That was the person she could communicate with. The one person who could have helped explain what was happening.

Jay.

If not for this, I think he might have passed his time in Rockton under our radar. Another quiet resident, here to take advantage of the sanctuary we offered. A decent guy who'd poked his head above the parapet to help.

Did I take advantage of that?

Did I properly explain the risks?

I should have made sure Jay was protected. Despite Sophie's outbursts, though, I considered her a low threat. Restraints and sedative, and she'd be fine. We just had to wait until she was lucid enough to understand the situation and stop fighting. Jay thought we'd reached that point, so he'd set her free.

The blame ultimately lies with me for being too busy chasing corpses and killers to properly assess the danger Jay faced. Now he's in a coma, possibly brain-damaged, because he tried to be helpful.

When Dalton returns, I'm moving blindly through the exam room, tidying and straightening. He murmurs something to April, and the next thing I know, I'm walking through the forest to our backyard.

He opens the door and nudges me through. I stop in the doorway, my heels digging in.

"I need to speak to the council," I say.

"It can wait."

"It can't. I need to talk to them and finish autopsying the settlers and move Sophie's body and figure out what the hell I'm going to tell the residents and —"

I stumble and grab the doorway, straightening as Dalton catches me. He says something. I don't hear it.

I need to get out of here.

Out of Rockton.

It's like a horrible anxiety dream where every choice I make gets someone killed, and nobody else sees that. Nobody takes me aside and says, "You need to stop."

You need to get out of here.

You're only making things worse.

Dalton rubs my arms, and I wheel to see him there, frozen in worry and rising panic.

In his face, I see the problem.

Dalton lets me do what I like, trusts me to make choices, because he loves me, and he's terrified of losing me.

What if I worked in the general store? Could I do that? Please?

The words hover over my tongue. I taste hope in them, and I imagine saying them and —

And what the fuck am I doing?

Am I serious?

Please, Eric, let me work in the store, so I

don't have to make the hard choices. So I'm spared the guilt of making another mistake. You can handle it all instead, okay?

I take a deep breath. Then I lift one finger and gather my wits enough to walk into the kitchen, take the tequila bottle, and down a shot. Then I stand there, holding the counter as the alcohol burns through me.

Storm slips in, and I jump. She must have followed us to the house. I somehow missed a giant black dog at my side until she sneaks in, sensing my mood and trying to be as unobtrusive as possible. Just like someone else . . .

Dalton stands in the doorway, his expression saying he's trying very, very hard not to hover.

"I was about to ask if there were any openings at the general store," I say.

His gaze searches mine. It sounds like a joke, but he checks first and sees the truth. He walks over, fills the shot glass, and downs it, coughing slightly.

"Yeah," he says. "I was wondering whether Isabel's still looking for help."

"You'd make a lousy bartender. Everyone would get exactly one chance to tell you their problems. Then you'd offer solutions, and if they came back complaining about the same shit, having done nothing to solve the problem, you'd send them packing. The Roc would go out of business in a month."

"Truth."

I push my shot glass toward him.

He glances down at it. "You know if I fill that, I gotta dispense my unsolicited advice, too."

"That's what I'm hoping."

He tipples a little into the glass.

"Half a shot?" I say.

"For half-assed advice."

I chuckle and down it.

"This job sucks," he says. "Yours and mine both suck, but especially yours. You have a fucking awesome knack for being right there whenever shit goes down. You made choices. Will made choices. Diana made choices. So did Jay. So did Sophie, and maybe she wasn't in a mental state to make good ones, but her mistakes started when she chose to go out in the forest without a sat phone."

"Someone else in her group might have had one."

"Then she chose not to go back and get it."

"That isn't fair."

He leans against the counter. "Yep, it's not. Just like it isn't fair to blame Will for taking a headshot to save you and Jay. Like it isn't fair to blame Jay for trying to help out. Like it isn't fair to blame you for holding off on your shot, hoping it wouldn't be needed."

"I notice you left Diana out there."

"That's 'cause I totally blame Diana for being a fucking idiot." He catches my gaze and exhales. "Fine. Diana did warn Jay not to untie Sophie, and she'd been about to come and tell you when Sophie leaped up. However, I'm still blaming Diana for doing nothing after that except scream her fool head off."

I shake my head. He reaches into the cupboard and pulls out a bag of miniature chocolate bars. I'm about to joke that he's ramping up his bribes to keep me here when I remember what I was just thinking a few moments ago.

That hadn't been fair. If I sucked at my job, Dalton *would* find me a new position. He wanted me here, but never at the expense of endangering others. Thinking that had been a moment of weakness and self-pity, and I'm glad I hadn't said anything.

"These are new," I say as he hands me a couple of tiny bars.

He shrugs. "Saw them in Dawson. Figured I'd hide them until you pulled out that electronic book reader you bought me."

"Uh . . ."

He unwraps a bar as he gives me a sidelong look. "You saving it for a special occasion?"

Another pause. "I was about to joke that I was saving it for a break between dead bodies, but that'd be in poor taste."

I try to smile, but my fingers tremble as I unwrap the bar. I keep seeing those corpses stacked like cordwood in the clinic.

"You can make that joke," he says. "As long as you don't make the one about the increase in dead bodies since you arrived. That shit's not funny."

"True, though."

"Bullshit." He pauses, chocolate halfway to his lips. "Actually, no. You're right. If not for you, we wouldn't have any bodies in the clinic right now. They'd all be rotting in the forest, including Sophie."

"You *never* would have left her out there."

"Yeah, but in an alternate reality where you never came to Rockton, Sebastian and the other kids wouldn't have been having a party on the lake, because even if he'd somehow still met them, I'd never have allowed them to hang together. I certainly wouldn't have been there myself. So Sophie would have died in the forest. If somehow I was there without you, then there'd be no

April and thus no one to save her. Even if another doctor *did* manage that, I'd have shipped Sophie south, trusting the council to look after her, and we both know how that would work out. So, no, without you, there'd be no bodies in Rockton right now. They'd all be rotting in the forest, with no one to investigate and make sure it doesn't happen again. You figured out what's going on with the hostiles. We're going to stop this because of the work you did. These tourists and settlers aren't the first people they've killed."

"Hostiles didn't kill the settlers."

He frowns.

"That's why I was in the clinic. A bullet killed the boy." I sigh. "And as much as I appreciate you bringing me back here for a break, I really do need to return to the clinic so we can autopsy his parents."

"Shit."

"Yep." I waggle the bottle. "I have a feeling I'll want more of this at the end of the night, but for now . . ." I cap it. "My pity party is over. Thank you for attending. However —"

Storm scrabbles to her feet, nails clicking against the hardwood as Dalton's head shoots up, eyes narrowing.

"What the fuck?" he murmurs.

I catch the sound then. The unmistakable drone of a low-flying plane.

FIFTEEN

Rockton isn't on any commercial flight routes or any local ones — the founders chose our location well. That doesn't mean it's impossible for a small plane to randomly choose a path that takes them over us, which is why all of our buildings are constructed with structural camouflage. The council also invests in the latest technology for keeping us off radar, which is partly what interferes with the radios.

Even with all that, it would only take a stray plane passing low enough to see people and buildings.

Like a plane searching for a quartet of missing tourists who aren't at their pickup point.

Dalton and I are out the door in a shot, Storm racing past. We're barely outside when Anders shouts, and we look to see the deputy running our way as others scan the skies.

We stride to Anders.

"No one's seen it yet," he says.

"Hasn't passed close enough," Dalton says. "We'd all hear that."

Dalton turns, face upturned. He doesn't shade his eyes. He's listening, not looking. He pinpoints the sound and takes off at a lope.

"Everyone inside!" Anders calls as I run after Dalton. "Sebastian? Maryanne? Jen?"

He calls out names of people in sight and tells them to order people into their homes. Residents will obey. No one's going to risk their security. By the time I'm running, the entire town is scattering, like mice seeing a hawk glide overhead.

Dalton's already in the forest. The plane's engine roars, as if turning for a second pass. Not just idly crossing our airspace. Searching for something.

Searching for four hikers.

We are so unprepared for this. We —

The plane banks, and I whisper "Shit!" as I see where it's heading.

To our airstrip.

I kick up my pace as Dalton slows. He's holding out a ball cap that I didn't see him grab. I tug it on and pull my ponytail through the back. The hat is navy blue with a militaryesque emblem on the front. Rockton has multiple cover stories, in the event someone stumbles on it. One is "military facility." That's easy for me and Dalton to pull off. We're physically fit and clean-cut, Dalton's hair clipped to his summer crew cut. The advantage to the military story is that it's not one the average person will question . . . nor does it inspire people to want a closer look.

You've got an armed military compound out here? Er, okay, I'll just keep moving, thanks.

I'm thinking that when —

"Shit!" I hiss again and grab Dalton's arm. "We can't do military."

He glances at me.

"It's a search party," I say. "Foreign tourists missing in the wilderness. The first thing they're going to expect is for us to help them. That's part of the military's job."

"*Fuck.* Rangers, then?"

Park rangers is another option, but it's the same problem. Any military or quasimilitary organization will be expected to join in the search. We'd happily do that — and steer them in the wrong direction — but they'll also expect to set up base camp in Rockton.

Ahead, the plane is coming in for a landing.

"Just roll with it," I murmur, pulling off

my hat. "Follow my lead. We'll . . . figure something out."

I have no idea what that even means. Maybe we can be scientists? Pretend we're a research facility, privately run.

We haven't seen any hikers, sorry, but we really need to get back to our work.

We reach the landing strip as the tiny plane rolls to a stop. It's a Cessna TTx, which makes me blink and Dalton murmur "What the hell?" under his breath. The TTx is the Mercedes of small planes — a luxury puddle jumper for wealthy city dwellers with oceanfront summer homes.

My parents had died in a plane like this. That'd been the sort of circle they traveled in after April and I had moved out. They'd eased back enough on the overtime to have a social life, with friends who'd owned small planes and used them where others might have summoned a car service. The independent and the adventurous upper middle class.

The door opens and out steps . . .

I don't have grandparents. Okay, that's a lie. Technically, I do. I don't know them, though. I think my paternal grandmother is still alive, but the story goes that they'd disowned my dad for marrying a girl who wasn't white. Then along came April, and they welcomed Dad back into the fold. I followed five years later and . . . Well, their reaction made it obvious that they'd only reunited with my dad because he'd given them a pale-skinned granddaughter they could proudly push around in a pram. I was a different story.

There are many things I wish I could tell my parents, now that I've found my footing in life and found the courage to say what needs to be said. I'd tell them how badly they fucked up, but I'd also tell them the things they did right, and this is one of them. My parents made me feel inferior to my sister in many ways, but the color of my skin was never one of them, and Dad gave up a relationship with his family to protect me from that.

The situation with Mom's parents was equally complicated. She left China for university and never went back. As an adult, I realize how unusual that is for someone of her heritage. Mom rejected her family and her culture with a ferocity that now speaks to me of deep pain.

So I have no grandparents in the sense that I've never had someone to call by that name. If I imagined one, though, my fantasy grandmother would be the woman who steps out of the pilot's door. Not the soft-lapped grandma with sweets and smiles and a comfy recliner. My fantasy grandmother was, ironically, the sort of woman my own mother could have grown into. The active granny, embracing adventure after adventure, sometimes scooping up her grandkids to take along. A grandmother living her twilight years to the fullest, fit and nimble and endlessly curious.

That's the woman who hops from the plane. She's at least seventy, trim and slight, with silver hair cut short and stylish. Her outfit reminds me of Sophie's, and a pang of panic runs through me, as if this could be *her* grandmother, the source of her own adventurous genes. Yet this woman's outfit is the real thing — expensive because it's quality. In fact, given the fit of the button-down shirt and khakis, I'm guessing they're tailor made.

She pushes oversize sunglasses up over her forehead, and dark eyes twinkle as she strides toward us.

"Casey and Eric," she says. "Exactly who I was hoping would come meet me." She bends in front of the dog. "And this must be Storm."

I falter, but only for a second, as her voice twinges something familiar.

She extends a hand. "I'm Émilie."

■ ■ ■ ■

Émilie was one of Rockton's first inhabitants. She and her husband had been sent here by his parents when their college political activism got them in trouble. After they returned south, Émilie's husband took over the very lucrative family business, and when Rockton faltered, they stepped up as investors.

At one time Émilie *was* the council — along with her husband and another couple they'd met here. Two of those four have passed on, and the third suffers from dementia, so only Émilie remains, a holdover from Rockton's past, when those who ran it were more interested in philanthropy than profitability.

Émilie positions herself as our ally on the council, and we accept her assistance, while knowing she may be playing the good cop. I don't think she is, but even if she's really on our side, I fear she doesn't have the power we need to effect change.

In the beginning, Phil was quick to credit Émilie's power, but as he's lowered his guard, he's admitted that the council sees her the way corporations can view the old guard on a board of directors: furniture that came with the room and is too heavy to move. They work around Émilie as they await the day when her health wanes enough for her to release her tenuous grip on the reins.

"Welcome," I say as I shake her hand. "We . . . weren't expecting you."

"You didn't get my message?"

My expression makes her laugh.

"Sorry," she says. "I was teasing. There wasn't a message. Intentionally so. If I told the council what I was doing, they'd have stopped me, even if it meant putting sugar in my fuel tank. What would *you* have said if I told you I was visiting?"

"We . . . are more than happy to host you," I say. "This just . . ."

"It isn't a good time, to put it mildly? You're already hosting a Danish tourist who was attacked by hostiles. Hostiles who killed three other tourists, while the settlers are already grumbling that you've set the wild people off."

I hesitate, but she's already turned away, glancing at Dalton, who has taken her bags from the plane.

"Thank you, Eric. Now, I know this seems very poor timing, but I didn't just happen to show up at the most inconvenient moment. I'm here to help. This mess with the hostiles is spinning out of control, and you need someone on the ground to mediate with the council. First, I want to see this woman you're caring for. While I'm not fluent in Danish, I did spend a year in Copenhagen, which is one reason I jumped in my plane when I heard you had a Danish tourist. We'll begin my visit there."

Émilie stands over the exam table, looking down at Sophie's body. I explained the situation as we walked. Dalton took her bag to Petra's place, and I'm now in the clinic, alone with Émilie, having sent April on a break.

"I'm not sure whether this complicates matters or . . ." She taps her chin. "No, at the risk of sounding like a complete monster, it does help our situation."

"I know. I hate admitting it, but now we don't need to worry about how to get her back and what she'll tell the authorities. However, it doesn't solve the underlying problem. It just means that we've lost our sole witness to multiple homicides."

"We know the hostiles are responsible."

When I hesitate, she looks over sharply. "I understood that conclusion wasn't in question."

I walk to where a sheet has been drawn

over the three settlers. When I lift it, Émilie inhales sharply and says, "Those aren't her fellow tourists, are they."

"A settler family. No connection to Rockton. They appear to have been killed by hostiles. The wound patterns suggest makeshift knives, and they're similar to what we saw with Sophie's companions. However, when April autopsied the boy, she found that he'd been killed by a bullet."

Émilie frowns. "Do we have any evidence of the hostiles using firearms?"

"None. Maryanne's group didn't. Even if the others somehow got one, they wouldn't be using a nine-millimeter."

"A handgun? That . . ."

"Makes no sense? Agreed. April needs to autopsy the other two bodies so we can get a fuller picture of the situation. She was about to do that when Sophie was killed."

"And then I showed up, further delaying her investigation. I'll remedy that last part by getting out of your way. This is definitely not my area of expertise. I'll go settle in with Petra while you and April handle this, and then we'll discuss how to present the updated situation to the council."

"Thank you."

April has completed the autopsies. She did

not find another bullet. However, knowing that a bullet killed the son, she paid more careful attention to the parents' internal injuries. While we can't say conclusively that all three settlers died of bullet wounds, we find evidence of several through-and-through shots and of another bullet that had been removed. *Intentionally* removed.

This family didn't die from a hostile attack. Someone shot them, and the killer removed any embedded bullets except the one they missed. Then they exacerbated the wounds with a knife to cover the entry and exit holes and simulate a frenzied knife strike.

Staged to look like a hostile attack.

I don't know what to make of that.

It casts doubt on the events surrounding the deaths of the hikers. *Were* they attacked by hostiles? Or by someone pretending to be hostiles, who then ravaged the bodies to simulate a hostile attack? They'd disguised themselves as hostiles, in case someone survived, as Sophie did. Maybe they even left her alive as a witness — she would describe her attackers, which would leave no doubt they were hostiles.

The problem, though, is that we found zero evidence that the hikers *weren't* killed by hostiles. Also, at no point did Sophie mention gunfire.

I believe that Sophie and her companions were attacked by hostiles. I also believe that the settler family was attacked by someone pretending to be hostiles.

And as I say those words, curled up at home with Storm, explaining to Dalton and Anders, I stop myself and curse.

"Damn it, don't do that," I mutter.

"Do what?" Anders asks, taking another slug of beer.

"Conflate the evidence," I say. "I know the settlers were not killed by hostiles. I know their bodies make it appear that they were. I'm ramming those two things together and presuming a link."

"Uh . . ." Anders glances at Dalton. "That makes sense to you, doesn't it?"

"She means that just because the settlers appear to have been killed by hostiles doesn't mean that their *killers* staged it."

"Ah. Okay, I get it." Anders pauses. "Shit, yeah. Especially considering who turned those bodies over to you."

I nod. "Cherise. Being terribly helpful, wrapping them up and storing them away from the elements."

"And away from predators that might mess up their handiwork," Dalton mutters.

Anders leans forward. "So you think

Cherise and Owen found this family, who'd been killed by someone else, and they made it look like hostiles so they could trade the bodies. That's cold."

"That's Cherise," I say.

"Any chance they're the killers?" Anders says. "They shoot the settlers and then stage it to look like hostiles? You did say they took the settlers' goods. They could also get their hands on a nine-mil in Dawson."

"They could. They may even have one already. I don't want to jump to that conclusion, though. Who else out here would have a nine-mil?"

"Besides us?" Anders takes out a key and dangles it. "All weapons present and accounted for. I will check the logbook, though, and see whether anyone had the nine-mil out for target practice."

I motion toward my own gun, the holster slung over a chair. "As the only one of us with that caliber, I'll run a ballistics test to confirm the bullet wasn't from my gun."

"You do realize that really isn't necessary, right?" Anders says.

"Don't bother," Dalton says. "She'll insist, because otherwise, we'd all be whispering, 'You know, I think I saw Casey sneak into the forest to kill some settlers last week.' "

"I carry the same caliber of gun used in a

murder. I will test it for exclusionary purposes. I will do the same with the one in the locker, whether it was signed out or not."

"So who in the forest would have a nine-mil?" Anders says, lacing his fingers around his bottle. "No one, right? It's a handgun, not a hunting rifle."

"That doesn't mean shit," Dalton says. "Anyone with access to the outside world can get a gun, and everyone has access, if they're willing to walk far enough."

I nod. "A nine-mil is the most common weapon in Canadian law enforcement, which makes it easy to come by, if you want it badly enough. I'm also sure there are people up here who got one legally."

"It's not exactly an AR-fifteen," Anders says.

"You can get those legally, too, if you follow the rules. You just can't legally modify it to hold more rounds. There wouldn't be any use for an AR-fifteen up here. A nine-mil, though?" I shrug. "It'd be shit for hunting, but it's fine protection against anything smaller than a grizzly."

"It'll even kill that if you aim it right," Dalton says.

I lean back and rub Storm's ear. "Speaking of protection, I wonder if the hikers could have brought it."

"Ah," Anders says. "They bring a handgun for protection. The hostiles kill them and then use it . . . No, the settlers died first, right? Or around the same time? Close enough that the hostiles didn't have time to figure out how to use guns, let alone become crack shots."

"You're meeting Cherise tomorrow, right?" I say to Dalton. "To give her the trade goods."

"I am."

"I'd like to come along."

"I figured you would."

Sixteen

Next I need to talk to Émilie. I'd said that I'd get to her right after the autopsy. I can argue that I wanted to run my theories past my fellow law enforcement officers first, and that's partly true, but it's also me being territorial and obstinate. Émilie wants to be the bridge between us and the council, just as Phil does. Everyone wants to smooth things over so we can all work together, put our differences aside to focus on Rockton and its residents.

In theory, that is good. In theory, it is excellent, and at one time, I'd have led the charge for unity. Yet the council has screwed us so often that the push for cooperation has started to feel like victim-blaming — if we'd just stop causing trouble, they'd stop punishing us.

I do believe there are elements in the council — like Émilie — that we can work with. I also believe there are elements we can't, and since we only speak to Tamara, we can't mentally sort the good from the bad from the indifferent. Other than Émilie, they are a homogeneous blob of negative experiences that I cannot trust. So in talking to Dalton and Anders first, I am saying these people are my priority. Protecting Rockton means communicating with my proven allies before anyone else.

When I go to talk to Émilie, I take Storm. She serves vital law enforcement purposes beyond guarding and tracking. She's a comfort animal when needed and, in this case, she's distraction and diversion. Nothing says "this is just a pleasant conversation" like bringing along your dog.

I'm halfway to Petra's place when Storm gives a happy bark and races forward to meet Petra herself, out walking.

This winter, Petra took an arrow to the chest, and while she seems fine, I'm not sure how much of that is a true full recovery and how much is just Petra toughing it out. When we draw near, Petra drops to one knee and spreads her arms, a sign that allows Storm to embrace her, paws over Petra's shoulders as they hug. Petra pats Storm and then rises, making an exaggerated show of spitting fur from her mouth.

"I do believe your puppy needs a brushing," she says as I walk over.

"Weirdly, it hasn't been high on my priority list this week."

"Which is why I'm offering to do it for you."

"Are you sure? Looks like you'll be busy entertaining a guest."

"Yeah. About that, I didn't know she was coming. Not that I'd have been able to talk her out of it, but I'd have warned you."

"I know."

Less than a year ago, I'd thought how wonderful it was to have such an uncomplicated friendship. Then I learned that the smart, stable, drama-free comic-book artist I'd befriended was a former special ops agent.

As Petra argued, that was just one aspect of her, an aspect unrelated to our friendship, and what I saw was the real her. I've come to accept that — not only about Petra but about pretty much everyone in Rockton.

I use the analogy of the internet. On it, you can present whatever version of yourself you choose. While you can be a better person online — kinder and wittier and more open-minded than you are in real life — it's easier to be your worst self, freed from expectations. An acquaintance who knows not to joke about cats in Chinese food when he's near me may feel perfectly comfortable sharing those jokes online . . . or sharing Asian fetish porn with my face attached. Yes, I had that happen, from a colleague I'd thought was a decent guy.

Rockton is the internet in real life. Be the person you want to be, with no fear of long-term consequences. You can reinvent yourself, like Kenny, the high-school math teacher who decided to hone his carpentry skills while pumping weights as if it were his job. He became the buff, tough head of Rockton's militia. Except . . . well, "tough" is a word I'd only apply to Kenny in the most positive sense. He doesn't back down from trouble. He's never complained about his injury, and he worked his ass off to get back on the militia legitimately, not as a pity post. Yet underneath the new exterior, he's still the sweet and somewhat awkward guy I suspect he's always been.

That's the thing about Rockton. We can pretend to be someone new, but truth still outs. We are our real selves, for better or worse, because anything else is exhausting and pointless. The Petra before me is still the Petra I knew a year ago, even if it's uncomfortable to admit that after her lies.

I continue, "Your grandmother's arrival is

a surprise all around. Phil is going to have a conniption."

She snickers. " 'Conniption' is exactly the right word. Poor guy."

"Any chance I can get some advice?" I ask. "For dealing with her."

"That's why I'm here. I was watching to see when you started heading toward my place so I could intercept. I told Émilie I'm grabbing a snack at the bakery before it closes. Join me?"

"Yes, please."

"We can skip the part where you tell me I can trust your grandmother," I say. "I already expect to hear that."

When she doesn't answer, I look over to see her mouth set with concern.

"Are you actually going to warn me that I *can't* trust her?" I say.

"No, but . . ." She shoves her hands into her jean pockets. "You can trust that Émilie only does what she perceives to be in Rockton's best interests."

"Uh-huh. Everything the *council* does is apparently in Rockton's best interests."

"The difference is that they're feeding you a line of bullshit. They *are* concerned with the town's well-being insofar as that keeps it financially stable. Émilie doesn't give a shit about that. She has more money than she can spend. Every one of her children, grandchildren, and great-grandchildren has a trust fund. We still have to work for a living, but we can take whatever job we like, without concern for income. That's her gift to us. My grandmother genuinely cares about Rockton as an ideal. I only mean that you two may disagree on how to best achieve that goal."

"So trust that she *thinks* she's doing what's best for Rockton."

"And for Eric."

I glance over sharply. "Eric?"

Petra shrugs and lowers her voice as we enter a busier part of town. "I don't know his full story. Only that something happened when he was a child, and she was concerned for his well-being and fought for him."

She means Gene bringing Dalton into Rockton. Émilie disagreed with allowing Gene to keep him — she'd been uncomfortable with Gene's story that the boy was neglected and abandoned.

Petra continues, "Do you remember those ads on TV for 'fostering' kids in Africa? You were assigned a child and sent money for their schooling and health care?"

"I knew someone who did that."

"My parents always did. Now it has a

whiff of the white-savior complex, but at the time, it was cool getting updates. My parents were so proud when 'their' kids grew up and graduated high school and went to college or learned a trade. As if they'd played a role beyond sending checks. That's a bit like Émilie with Eric. She's very proud of him, and she definitely has a soft spot for him. You can use that to your advantage."

"Got it."

"Otherwise? Don't underestimate her. She's old. She's a woman. She isn't physically intimidating. She uses all that to her advantage." Petra slides a glance my way. "As someone who meets those last two criteria, though, I suspect you're prepared for that."

"She flew a plane out here on her own. I would not make the mistake of underestimating her."

"Good."

We change the subject once we reach the bakery. It's almost closing time, meaning pastries are half-price, and there's a line. I feel gazes on me, people wanting to ask questions, but Petra keeps up a running patter that no one dares interrupt.

Once we reach the counter, I know I need to say something. Devon is watching me.

He's a baker and one of the town . . . I won't say "gossips." To me, that implies malicious intent. Devon fills the role of news source in a town without public media. His partner — Brian — bakes in the back, and Devon interacts with people. Conversation will naturally turn to current events, and he's happy to discuss them. So when he watches me with that look, I know he's waiting to see whether I have anything to pass on.

"Lots of talk, I'm guessing," I say.

"Talk and speculation."

"Mmm."

The latter is the problem. The less we say, the more people make shit up to fill in the blanks. Let it go too long, and there's no point correcting them. What they'll remember is the speculation.

"Tell people I'll call a meeting first thing tomorrow," I say. "We have someone here from the council, and I can't speak until I've run it by her."

"A woman from the council?" Devon says.

I nod. "Petra is taking her in."

"What about Phil?"

He means why not have her stay with Phil, but as soon as he says the name, I mentally smack myself. Émilie is here, and no one has told Phil.

Shit.

Earlier, I'd had a mini-meltdown, overwhelmed by everything after Sophie attacked Jay. Now I'm tempted to have another. Not so much a meltdown as a short-circuiting, my brain pulled in too many directions at once. So many things to do, and it's already dinner hour, and I'm torn between needing more hours in my day and feeling like it should be midnight already.

Instead of ticking items off a to-do list on this endless day, I seem to be adding a dozen an hour. Juggling more and more balls only to be reminded, every now and then, of the ones I've dropped. Like telling Phil about Émilie.

I'm halfway across town when I see the man himself . . . walking with Dalton in the direction of Petra's house. Dalton catches my eye and gestures something between a shrug and an exhausted shake of his head. He's picked up this particular dropped ball then, having told Phil about Émilie, and now Phil is insisting on speaking to her and Dalton doesn't have the energy to argue.

We reach Petra's house at the same time. Phil marches straight inside, door banging in his wake.

"He's taking it well," I murmur as we follow.

"This is unacceptable," Phil says as he strides into the living room, where Émilie sips tea.

"Hello, Phil. You look good. The fresh air obviously agrees with you."

He stops in the middle of the room. "All visits by board members must be sanctioned by the council, with ample time provided to prepare for such a visit."

Émilie frowns. "Are you certain? I don't recall such a rule. Of course, at my age, my memory can be —"

"Do not even attempt that with me. Your memory is fine." He glances back at us, his face hard. "The council insisted on a full psychological exam last year, when they had reason to doubt her faculties. She passed with flying colors."

"Reason to doubt my faculties?" Émilie snorts. "They *wanted* to doubt my faculties. When Bruce was diagnosed with dementia, it gave them an idea. They hoped I would fail so they would have reason to oust me."

"I thought you two had never met," I say. "That's what you told us last year, Phil."

"We have since spoken, and I have launched inquiries. Her mental faculties are in perfect working order."

"Excellent," Émilie says. "Then you will have no excuse to ignore my advice."

"And you have no excuse for being here."

"Well, I could say that I came to help translate, but I don't actually need an excuse. I am an original board member, and my husband and I were the largest early contributors to Rockton's financial health. As such, we are grandfathered from all restrictions later placed on the board, which is why I was able to contact you last year without fear of censure." She meets Phil's gaze. "Section 9.3.2.1 of the policies and procedures manual."

"I will check that. I have a copy in my lodgings."

"I'm just surprised you haven't memorized it."

Phil rocks back on his heels. "I did not foresee the need before my tenure here, but I have been working on it."

"That was a joke, Phil. Sit down. Have a tea. Try to relax. Whatever rules I have or have not broken, no one will blame you."

"That is not my primary concern."

"Then it seems Rockton has worked her magic on you, too. I'm glad to see it."

Their eyes lock, and Phil stiffly lowers himself onto a seat. Dalton and I sit on the floor — unless you have one of the chalets, your place isn't big enough for group entertaining, and Petra's job at the general store doesn't qualify her for better. I'm sure she could get top-notch accommodations with Émilie pulling the strings, but Émilie doesn't seem the type to do that, and Petra certainly isn't the type to accept it. Their privilege is the sort that only greases wheels that undeniably need greasing.

Petra sets out a platter of cookies. As I reach for one, she pulls it away with, "Everyone else, take yours fast, or they'll be gone once Casey gets her hands on them. I've never seen a woman eat so many cookies without an extra ounce to show for it."

"We work it off," Dalton says as he takes a cookie.

Both Émilie and Petra sputter laughs.

"I bet you're very helpful that way, Eric," Émilie says. "Keeping Casey in shape."

He hesitates, cookie to his mouth, and spots of color bloom on his cheeks. "I meant the job. It keeps us busy, which is the reason for this meeting." He glances over, his eyes begging me to change the subject.

Before I can, Petra pushes the plate my way and looks at her grandmother. "If you want to get in Casey's good graces, these are the key. Cookies. Preferably with chocolate. Chocolate chip, peanut butter with chocolate, oatmeal with chocolate . . . The bakers have learned to incorporate chocolate into at least one batch of every cookie they make. They know Casey's weakness."

"Nah," Dalton says. "It's not a weakness. It's a trick. People think they can get on her good side with cookies and chocolate, and she lets them believe that so she gets all the cookies and chocolate she wants. No one actually benefits from it except Casey. And me. I'm the exception, right?"

He looks my way.

"Absolutely," I say. "Just keep telling yourself that, and keep the chocolate coming." I glance at Phil, who has finally relaxed.

"So, to bring everyone up to date . . ." I say, and I explain what happened this afternoon, for Petra and Phil, who'd only known the basics.

"Unfortunately, you're going to need to throw Jay to the wolves," Petra says.

When we all look at her, she wipes a crumb from her mouth and says, "I should be careful. Up here, that could be taken literally. What I mean is that I know Casey's first impulse will be to downplay his responsibility. The poor guy is in a coma. No one wants to suggest it's his own damn fault but . . ." She looks at me. "It is."

"I'm not convinced he was aware of the risks —"

Dalton cuts me off. "He was, Casey. I know that. Diana knows it. April knows it. He knew Sophie was an outsider. He knew her companions had been killed. He knew her head injury and infection left her confused and periodically violent. What the hell was he thinking untying her?"

"He was being kind."

"Yep, and it may have gotten him killed. Petra's right. Blaming the poor bastard is shitty, but it's not a lie. We're telling the true story, one everyone involved can verify. Sophie seemed calm but was distraught over the restraints. Jay went to remove them. Diana told him not to, but before she could call you in, Sophie had Jay on the floor. In the ensuing struggle, he was strangled with the IV cord, and you and Will were forced to shoot Sophie to save him. He is currently in a coma. That's the story for the town, too. The truth. If you want me to tell it, I will."

I shake my head. "It should come from me — and Will if he wants. I just struggle with telling people that we let a brand-new resident become involved in a dangerous situation."

"Because he offered. He offered because

he had a unique skill you needed. It was not a dangerous situation until he removed the damned restraints."

"I barely knew the guy. I don't want to eulogize him. I just . . ." I glance at Dalton. "Does he have anyone at home? Family?" I pause. "Sorry. I shouldn't ask that."

Émilie shakes her head. "Under the circumstances, I think you should have that information, as we may have some difficult decisions to make. Phil and Eric already have it, and I can get it easily enough."

Petra rises. "But I don't need to hear it. I'll take Storm for a walk."

No one stops her from leaving. When it comes to resident background, nobody tries to overhear anything they shouldn't. If they were the subject of the discussion, they'd want equal care to be taken.

Once Petra's gone, Dalton looks to Phil, letting him take the lead. Also covering his ass against any charges that he shared privileged information. Phil takes it as a sign of trust, possibly even a ceding of authority, straightens, and pulls out his cell phone.

"You have a cell phone?" Émilie says.

"To be used as a secured PDA rather than a communication device. The council has allowed me the use of the generators to charge it in return for access to my files on request." Phil taps icons. "Jay came to us as a professor of Nordic studies from a Canadian university. The name of the university is, I believe, unnecessary. His credentials were validated."

"Nordic studies," I murmur. "He claimed his mother was Danish, but I guess his specialty explains the real reason he knows the language."

"Yes, he is fluent in several Nordic languages. He volunteered that information and offered any necessary translation services, though at the time, we assured him everyone admitted to Rockton spoke English."

"I hate to say it, but that helps our case. The council knows he was willing to translate."

"As for family, he has an ex-wife and no children. He did not list his ex as an emergency contact. His mother is deceased. His father is not in the picture."

"Again, I hate to say this, too, but please tell me that means he's essentially on his own."

"He is. A lack of close family ties is not unusual for our residents, and Jay fit that pattern. There is no wife or long-term girlfriend or child or parent waiting for his return. If he must be moved to a hospital, though, he has sufficient funds to cover any care over and above his provincial health insurance."

"Anyone else who might come looking for him? Something to explain that healthy bank account? I'm not asking why he came here, but if he cheated someone out of money . . ."

Phil shakes his head. "His bank account is healthy due to a tenured position and presumably frugal habits. He is here due to issues with a female student."

"Ah."

"He was briefly involved with a graduate student from a different department. When the relationship dissolved, she reported him. He claimed a consensual relationship and says she targeted him in retribution. Whatever the truth, the university granted him a two-year sabbatical, which he wished to take in Rockton to distance himself from the young woman. He paid the higher entrance fee required for nonvital cases, and so he was granted access as a low-risk, high-return resident."

It's good that he doesn't have close family, in case he doesn't survive his coma. It's good that he has a nest egg, in case of long-term brain damage. It's very good that he offered to act as a translator. Otherwise, Jay is exactly what he seemed — an ordinary man who otherwise would have passed through his two years without a ripple.

"That's Jay," I say. "Now, though, we have another problem."

I tell them about the bullet.

Seventeen

Émilie has a plan. And, by this point, I'm really only in the proper mental state to process step one, which fortunately is the only step that matters right now. Her suggestion? That we take no further steps tonight.

It's too late to contact the council. They're on eastern time, and it's midnight for them. Insisting on notifying them at this hour suggests an emergency. Well, I suppose a dead body and a comatose resident does qualify as an emergency, but there's nothing they can do. Sophie isn't a resident, and the resident is stable. Notification can wait, and if anyone questions that, it was Émilie's decision and her authority supersedes ours.

I try going to check on Jay, but Dalton threatens to physically block the clinic door. April will notify us of any change in his condition. The next step is dinner. He sends one of the militia to fetch us a hot meal and deliver it to our home, one of the perks of being the guy in charge. We curl up on the sofa to wait for it and . . .

And the next thing I know, I'm waking on the floor, under a blanket, still curled up with Dalton, who's asleep. Storm dozes on my other side. It's dark outside, and I can faintly smell dinner, but there's no sign of it. Just me, my guy, and my dog, napping by a smoldering fire.

Dalton has stripped down to his boxers — raised up here, the man is not good with heat — and I slide the blanket off his shoulder to admire the view, the hard curve of lean muscle, the smooth skin with only a few faint scars, so much different from my own marred canvas. I touch his chest, too lightly to wake him, and run my hand up to the bristle of his stubble.

I trace a finger along his jaw as my gaze traces the curve of his lips, and heat sparks deep inside me, the urge to kiss those lips and run my hands down his body and —

And the poor guy is getting some much-needed sleep, which I will not disturb even if, come morning, I'll confess this urge and he'll assure me he never needs sleep that badly. I chuckle under my breath and press my lips to his with just enough pressure that

I hope the touch wends its way through his dreams.

When one gray eye opens, I smile and murmur, "Sorry."

"Looking for your dinner?" he murmurs back.

"Not . . . exactly."

His lips curve in a sleepy smile. "Hungry for something else?"

"You could say that."

The smile grows, and he rolls onto his back, arms folded behind his head, blanket pushed down over his hips.

"All yours," he says.

I pause a moment to enjoy the view. Then I roll onto him.

Sex and then dinner, which we eat on the floor, naked in front of the fire. We don't talk. Talking right now would be police work, so we eat in companionable silence. When we're done, Dalton shifts closer, leg hooking over mine, both of us on our stomachs.

"How are you doing?" he asks.

"Scared," I say, and the word comes with a jolt, as if someone has pushed it out of me. I shake it off with a ragged laugh. "I don't know where that came from."

He looks over, his expression calling me a liar.

I shift uncomfortably and shrug. "I'm feeling overwhelmed right now, but I'll be fine."

"You sure?"

"I can manage this, Eric."

"Not doubting that. I mean are you sure it's just feeling overwhelmed? Not feeling like there's a boulder over our heads, rocking there, ready to fall? 'Cause that's how I'm feeling."

"I hoped it was just me."

"Nah, sorry."

He flips onto his back and puts an arm out, and I slide onto it, letting him tug me half onto him.

He continues. "I just feel like all this . . ."

"Might be the last straw? With the council? That, at the very least, this mess with the hostiles makes a good excuse for clamping down? And by clamping down I mean doing something drastic."

"Like firing me? Sending you away? Separating us so we can't cause more trouble?"

I nod.

He exhales, a long hiss of breath. "I was really hoping it was just me being paranoid."

"It's probably both of us being paranoid. Separation is our biggest fear, and it makes sense from their point of view. You were always a thorn in their side, but put the two of us together and . . ."

"Double the pain in their asses?"

"More than double, I think. I provide you with the justification you need to push harder. They can no longer blame your lack of formal education or your lack of experience in the world. Likewise, you give me the nerve to fight harder. I feel you at my back, and I don't waver the way I did on the force, always worried about my job security, worried about coming off like a bitch."

I shift. "It's like in school, sometimes two kids who were only mild troublemakers before get into the same class and they play off each other. First thing the teachers will do is separate them."

"But we have a plan. We always have a plan."

I try not to hesitate before I nod, but he catches that extra split second.

"You don't think we could pull it off?" he says. "Starting a new Rockton? That was your suggestion."

When I'm slow to answer, he tugs me on top of him.

"Seems tougher now, doesn't it?" he murmurs. "Easy to say when you were new here, when you didn't really see how much it takes to run a place like this. The work, the resources . . . You're having second thoughts."

"No." I meet his eyes so he'll know I'm telling the truth. "But you are right. It wouldn't be as easy as I once thought. That's what scares me. In the beginning, it was like . . ." I consider and then say, "Kids often threaten to run away from home. It seems easy, until you're older and you realize exactly how difficult that would be."

"You realize that things need to be really, really bad before you'd attempt it."

I nod. "But we could do it. If we had to."

"We just hope we never have to."

I nod again and snuggle down against his chest as his arms close around me.

The next morning starts with a town meeting. Yesterday, Brian had offered to start work early to "cater" the event, which really just meant that I could start as early as I liked, without hearing grumbles that I was trying to avoid a crowd by holding it before people even had their first coffee.

I took him up on that, and he passed on the news. Town meeting, 6 A.M., coffee and pastries provided credit-free, in acknowledgment that it was hellishly early but the local police were busy and had to squeeze it in where they could. And, yes, it also means that half the town doesn't show up. They might have intended to, but then the alarm goes off at five thirty and damn, that's early. Hit snooze a few times and soon you just give up and reset it for seven. Someone will tell you what's said at the meeting.

I explain the situation exactly as Dalton suggested. A simplified form of the truth.

We found a woman injured in the forest. We're still investigating the cause of those injuries. She didn't speak English, and Jay offered to help with translation. Her mental state meant she was restrained, but he thought she might communicate more freely if he removed those restraints. She attacked, her fevered mind mistaking us for captors. In the ensuing standoff, Anders and I were both forced to shoot her to save Jay — our resident's safety coming first. The fact that we shot simultaneously proved that it had been absolutely necessary. Jay is unconscious but stable. As we continue to investigate the cause of the woman's injuries, we're suspending forest work details and doubling town patrols.

I also introduce Émilie, as a member of the board of directors — and former Rockton resident — who came to ensure the woman we found doesn't present a security risk. Émilie takes over and greets everyone and plays up the sweet little old lady routine, which serves the dual purpose of distracting people from Jay's situation and alleviating any concern over council intervention. If the council sent someone her age, obviously they don't really see a problem here.

When I open it to questions, almost all are about the restrictions. Will that affect next week's bonfire party? Will there be any wood rationing? What about harvests? We need to collect spring greens before it's not spring anymore.

This might make our residents seem self-centered — forget the deaths, how does this impact me? — but it really is a sign of trust. They acknowledge there's a problem, but trust us to resolve it so everything can go back to normal. It helps that Jay had only been here a few days. I had to explain who he was, and then watch people turn to their neighbors, whispering, "Did you know him?" Few did.

Post-meeting, Anders and I load up coffee and leftover pastries and head to the station. Phil, Dalton, and Émilie join us there, where we discuss the itinerary.

Anders's job is simple. He's the police force again today while Dalton and I are gone.

As for the big to-do on our list — speaking to the council — I have agreed to cede it to Émilie. That wasn't easy. Dalton and I spent an hour talking about it last night. She offered, and my first reaction was "hell, no." But as Dalton argued, we had things to do, namely his meeting with Cherise, which I wanted to attend.

The question wasn't whether we trusted Émilie. We don't. Not yet. The real question was whether we trusted Phil, who'd be there, too. The answer was "not entirely." Yet at some point we need to test that. He wants us to trust him. Here was his chance. He'd facilitate the call between Émilie and the council, and if we find out he misreported anything, we'll have our answer.

By eight, we were walking to our meeting with Cherise, three kilometers from Rockton. The distance conveyed a message: This is as close as we want you to our town.

When we arrive, I greet Cherise while Dalton assesses their reactions. Her attention will be on me — it always is, as if she knows no other dynamic than a female-led relationship. Owen's is also on me, though I never know whether that's genuine interest or him just goading Dalton. Meanwhile, Dalton studies them for signs of apprehension. Do they seem nervous? Concerned by what we might have found in examining those bodies?

I pull out the coffee and a bulk box of condoms. She lifts the latter and peers at the item count with a smirk. "That'll keep us going for a month or two."

"I couldn't get the money just yet," I say. "We don't keep much cash in town. Eric uses the bank machine in Dawson."

That's a lie. There's a safe filled in town so we don't leave an ATM paper trail. They don't need to know that.

When Cherise opens her mouth to protest, I take five twenties from my pocket. "Here's a hundred. And we have something to offer in potential trade for the rest."

From the bag, I pull out a gun case and two boxes of ammunition. I open the case to reveal the spare 9 mm from our locker.

"Holy shit, yes," Owen says, reaching for the case. "Come to Daddy, baby."

Cherise smacks his hand, as if he's a misbehaving child.

"Oh, come on, babe," Owen whines. "That sweet piece of steel would make me a very happy man."

"And what will you use it for? Strutting around like him?" She waves at Dalton. "If you want to play sheriff, I'll buy you a hat."

"His gun is a revolver," Owen says. "Like

something out of the fucking Wild West. Antique piece of shit. That" — he points at the box — "is a fine piece of modern weaponry."

He's right on one out of four here. Yes, Dalton carries a revolver, but it's hardly an antique and certainly not what they'd have used in the Old West. As for the Smith & Wesson I'm pretending to offer, if Owen thinks it's the latest in handgun technology, he's been up here far too long . . . or knows very little about guns. From the way he's salivating, I'm going with option two. I've seen that look on far too many guys down south when they saw my service weapon.

"Again, I ask, what the hell would you use it for?" Cherise says.

"Hunting?"

The inflection at the end makes her snort.

"The only thing these hunt is people," she says. "You just want one because you want it, and the answer is no. The deal was for two hundred and fifty dollars more, not a gun we can't use, with ammunition we don't stock."

I hold up the boxes of ammo.

Cherise shakes her head. "Sure, let me take that gun. Owen can go shoot some birds and bunnies, and when he's out of bullets, you can find something else to trade for more, overcharging me so my husband can amuse himself with a toy."

She turns to Owen. "Remember that knife you liked in Dawson? With the fancy handle? I said no because it's just a knife, and I can get them a whole lot cheaper. It's yours on the next trip."

His eyes light up. "Seriously?"

"You aren't a child, Owen. I don't promise you things to quiet you down and hope you'll forget later. You found the bodies." She hands him the hundred dollars. "Yours. For that knife or whatever else you want . . . as long as it doesn't require special ammunition. I'll give you fifty more after Casey pays it."

She shoves the gun back at me. "Because Casey *is* going to pay it, with ten dollars interest for every week she delays."

"You'll get it after our next trip to Dawson," I say.

I try not to glance at Dalton as I put away the gun. Our first question has been answered. They don't have a handgun, meaning they didn't kill the settlers, which is a relief. There's manageable trouble, and there's the kind of trouble I don't want to get near.

"So *you* found the bodies," I say, turning to Owen.

"Yep," he says as he pockets the money, the gleam still in his eye.

"Tell me about that," I say.

He shrugs. "Not much to tell. I was out hunting. Shot a bird, went to fetch it, and the bodies were there. Cherise wasn't far off, so I called her over."

"The family was in their camp?"

He nods. "Looked as if they'd been eating when they were attacked."

I take a pad of paper and pencil from my bag. "Since the scene no longer exists, I need to draw it from your memory. I'll put the campfire here, and this arrow points north. Now, tell me where the tent was."

"Uh . . ."

Cherise snatches the pad and pencil and a few minutes later passes the pad back with a complete drawing of the crime scene.

"She's good, ain't she?" Owen says with pride. "Could be a real artist."

Cherise huffs and shakes her head, but I can tell she's pleased even as she says "It's a sketch, not a work of art."

True, but it's hardly an X for a tent and stick figures for bodies, which is pretty much what I'd have done. In a few deft strokes, she's depicted the scene as well as any crime-scene artist. Basic figures, all clearly identifiable.

While I examine it, she fingers the pencil. It's only as I look up that she seems to realize she's still holding it and thrusts it back at me. I reach out, but Owen lifts a hand, blocking her from returning it. Then he pulls a twenty from his pocket.

"We need the pencil," he says. "And the book after you've taken the page. I'll give you this for it."

Cherise opens her mouth in protest, but he cuts her off with a firm "We need it."

They don't "need" it. He noticed her reluctance to part with that pencil, and he's buying it for her, along with paper to draw on.

I don't understand their relationship. I'm not sure I want to. But with this, I realize I should not mistake it for a purely functional partnership. There is genuine affection here.

Giving Owen money to buy a knife wasn't a sop to shut him up about the gun. It was, in its way, an apology. *I cannot let you have that thing you want, so I will give you a different thing instead.*

I think of the kind of life Cherise has led, where paper and pencils are luxuries she cannot afford. No, she *can* afford them — the family is wealthy, in settler terms — but she cannot justify the expense, however small, for something as frivolous as a hobby.

"It's a cheap pad of paper and a pencil," I say. "Five bucks, tops. I'll take it out of what I owe you."

He shakes his head. "Take the twenty and bring more. She'll need a sharpener, too."

This time, when Cherise starts to protest, I accept the money and hold out the sketch, saying, "Is this to scale?" I pause. "Are the distances —"

"I know what 'to scale' means. I can read a map. It's not perfect, but it's proportionally correct." She looks at me. "Would you like me to define 'proportionally'?"

"No, thanks." I look at Owen. "Did you move anything before Cherise arrived?"

"Hell, no. There were three hacked-up people on the ground. You think I wanted her walking over to see my hands covered in blood?"

"So they were lying just like this?" I show him the sketch. "Around the fire?"

"Yep. Like I said, looked as if they'd been attacked during their dinner. Coals were still hot."

He's wrong. Not lying, just not playing through the scenario enough to understand that his conclusion is inaccurate. Dalton glances at the sketch and grunts, telling me he sees the problem. Not so much a problem, really, as confirmation of our original theory.

Owen says they were attacked over dinner. Technically correct, but he means someone set on them with a knife while they ate. If that happened, at least one would have had time to rise and fight, moving the action — and their corpses — away from the fire.

The placement of the bodies means all three were shot quickly, not giving the victims time to do more than rise from their seat on seeing their loved one fall.

"Tell me about the blood," I say.

Cherise's brows shoot up, but Owen nods.

"You mean the blood patterns." He looks at Cherise. "Cops can tell how people were killed by the way the blood falls." He looks back at me. "There was a lot of blood, but they must not have fought very hard, because it was all under them, soaked into the ground. It wasn't, like, dripping from the trees or anything."

"Did you notice any blood spatter?"

" 'Spatter,' that's the word. No, their stuff was clean. It must have happened fast."

Again, Owen's mistaken here. Blood doesn't spatter because people fight. It can, but most of it would be arterial spray. The family fell from the gunshots and were stabbed where they lay.

If Cherise and Owen caused the damage themselves after they found the bodies, they'd have noticed a lack of blood flow. Rather like butchering after the blood has settled. Without a crime scene — and no way to contest their story — they'd make up something consistent with what you'd expect in a frenzied attack, with blood dripping from trees, as Owen said.

I ask more questions, poking their story from every angle. Owen happily answers. This is all very interesting to him. Cherise is mildly intrigued and doesn't complain when I backtrack over old ground. Their story has just enough consistency to give it the seal of truth. Sometimes they disagree. Sometimes they admit they aren't sure. Not a rehearsed recital. An honest witness account.

They didn't shoot the settlers, because they don't have a handgun. And they didn't stab the bodies to trade as hostile kills, because if they had, they'd do a better job of selling it as a frenzied knife attack.

They did exactly what they said. Found three bodies that they presume were killed by hostiles, wrapped them up, and stored them for us. Nothing more.

Eighteen

Dalton, Storm, and I are heading back to Rockton. Am I relieved Cherise and Owen aren't the perpetrators? The last thing we need is to have to confront Cherise with murder. But if they'd been guilty of staging the hostile attack on otherwise dead settlers? It would mean I could never trust them again, but I'm already uncomfortable with them. Maybe I'd have appreciated the excuse. I do feel as if we need an excuse.

It's like when I'd been on the force, my first partner retiring, and it looked like I'd be set up with a guy I knew was dirty. I absolutely did not want that. Yet what could I do? Make vague excuses about his racism and sexism, which were, let's be honest, only garden-variety? I'd breathed a huge sigh of relief when he was paired up with someone else. Likewise, I think I'd have been happy to discover Cherise and Owen did the damage, giving me an excuse not to work with them.

The problem with that, though, is that they did me a favor here. Okay, so maybe "dumping more dead bodies at my feet" doesn't seem like a favor, but it is something we needed to know about. They preserved the bodies and, sure, they sold them to us, but it proved they could be the sort of eyes and ears Rockton needs in the forest.

I'll cross them off our suspect list and not think too much on whether I'm disappointed by that. It does put us back to the original question. Well, beyond "Who the hell did this?" The question of whether we're looking at one situation or two. Did someone shoot the settlers and then stage a hostile attack? Or one party did the shooting and another did the staging? Without the crime scene, I can only go by Owen and Cherise's account, which suggests enough blood that the two events happened in a tight time frame. Murder and then staging. Most likely by the same people.

Yep, that gets me pretty much nowhere.

When Dalton changes the subject, I don't think much of it. We've talked this one to death — last night, on the walk out, on the walk back . . .

Then Storm makes a noise, and he pats her head. I figure it's an animal — caribou or moose — and he's thanking her for the warning. Mid-conversation, he says, "Hello, Felicity. If you've come to take us to Edwin, you can turn around right now. Casey isn't in the mood for a fucking summons."

"This isn't a summons, Eric," a voice says. A voice that is not Felicity's, though when I glance over, I do see her standing just off the path.

"Oh for fuck's sake," Dalton mutters.

"You know, Eric, if you used less profanity, people might have a higher opinion of your intelligence."

"Why the fuck would I want that?" Dalton stops in front of Edwin, towering over the old man by nearly a foot. "Now turn your wrinkly ass around and toddle back to your settlement."

"My, my, you are in a mood. You usually manage a veneer of respect."

"Yeah, I did, before you started haranguing my detective, kicking her ass like she's sitting on it, twiddling her thumbs. Now your granddaughter here has told you about the woman we found, and you gave us a few days to swing by and talk to you. When we didn't — because we're too fucking busy solving the problem — you came to hassle Casey in person."

I lay a hand on Dalton's arm. "It's okay.

I'm happy to talk to him. Saves me a trip."

Dalton's brows rise only a fraction before he catches my expression and nods with a gruff "Fine, but he'd better not make this a habit." He turns to Edwin. "You ever show up again unannounced, and your granddaughter won't be welcomed back."

Felicity stiffens. That's not fair, but the message is for Edwin. This isn't like an Amish community, where a youngster slipping off to hang out with the English may be cause for concern. Edwin knows she isn't enviously eyeing our lifestyle. She's forming a valuable relationship that benefits the entire First Settlement. A relationship he wouldn't want to jeopardize.

That doesn't mean Edwin appreciates the threat, and his gaze hardens as he says, "Understood," and then turns to me and says, "May we speak somewhere private?" in Mandarin. That makes Dalton's lips twitch in amusement. It's an obvious brush-off, clumsily done, which proves Dalton's annoyance hit its mark. Edwin knows he's overstepped by showing up. Good.

We've only gotten a few steps when Kenny appears on the path ahead. Despite the leg braces, he moves steadily, but I don't fail to notice the way Edwin's gaze sweeps over him, landing on the rifle under Kenny's arm.

"Your militia, I presume?" Edwin murmurs. "The situation has indeed declined."

"Grandfather," Felicity says under her breath. It's a warning. Telling him he's embarrassing. I have to smile slightly when his face tightens at the rebuke. Felicity may act the dutiful granddaughter, but she knows how to herd him, just a little.

"Everything okay?" Kenny says, nodding at the newcomers. "I saw them out here an hour ago, and we've been keeping watch. I know Felicity is allowed in, but I've never seen him."

"It's fine," I say. "Thank you."

Despite Edwin's sarcasm, this is the militia Rockton needs. Someone who recognized that the two people hovering on our outskirts did not pose a threat and therefore did not need to be confronted.

"Kenny?" I say. "I'm going to take Edwin and Felicity to the station. Could you ask Phil to join us? And Petra's roommate, please?"

At that Dalton nods, his eyes glinting. He wondered why I'd let Edwin off so easily. Now he has his answer.

"I'll stop by Petra's," Dalton says. "Kenny, you can grab Phil."

They head off together down another path as Storm and I lead Felicity and Edwin into town.

One advantage to the rapid turnover in Rockton is that most people don't notice when the status quo changes. If we started allowing more picnics and hikes, they'd presume there'd been a reason why we hadn't during their first year. It also means we can walk into town with a stranger and people only glance over in curiosity. As the only witness to twenty years of town history, Dalton tells me he can count on one hand the number of times a stranger passed the town borders. It's not exactly a regular stream now, but people do come, and the council isn't saying much about it, so we see no reason to sneak Edwin in the back door.

People have seen Felicity before, and so they only glance over with nods, their gazes resting on Edwin, thinking perhaps that if not for his clothing, he would no more match their idea of a forest dweller than she does. He's small but straight-backed and still strong, a gray-haired second-generation Chinese-Canadian who'd been a lawyer before coming to Rockton.

I don't know Edwin's exact history with

the First Settlement. There are no records from that time — Rockton has always been cagey about its backstory. Edwin is cagier still — if I asked how he came to the First Settlement, he'd wonder what I hoped to gain from the information and, with the lack of records, how he could tailor his story to suit.

I know he's been in the First Settlement since near its inception. I've heard a couple of variations on the story, the prevailing one being that he founded it, though Dalton's grumbled that it seems more likely Edwin slid in and took over after the hard work was done.

With Émilie's arrival, I have a way to get the truth. If Dalton is the witness to Rockton's recent past, she is the archives. Of course, I could just ask her about Edwin. I have a feeling, though, that this will be much more interesting.

I take Edwin and Felicity to the police station and start coffee. As I make it, I tell him what happened to the tourists. I don't see any point in dissembling. The information I wish to temporarily withhold is the death of the settlers. Obviously, I don't care to give him more ammunition for his "riling up the hostiles" rhetoric, but more than that, well, someone staged their deaths to look like hostiles did it. That someone had a reason, and I suspect it was less about hiding murder than about laying a crime at the feet of the hostiles.

Look at these savages. They're running wild, slaughtering hunters and tourists and settlers. Someone needs to do something about them.

Who's bellowing that demand the loudest? The old man sitting in our police station. He has the most reason to stage a hostile attack. Stack a few more logs on the fire he's already set blazing under our asses.

I hold out a cup of coffee. Edwin only looks at it disdainfully.

"I do not drink that," he says.

Felicity reaches for the mug, but Edwin's hand shoots out to block her reach. "Neither does she."

She reaches past him and takes it.

"Do you prefer tea, Edwin?" I say. "I have a special blend here we got from the Second Settlement."

His eyes narrow. "Is that your idea of a joke, Casey?"

I shrug. "I just thought you could use a cup. I hear it's very relaxing."

"Humor does not become you. For a woman, jests mean you will not be taken seriously."

"Or it means I'll be underestimated," I

say as I settle in with my coffee. "I can tell a few jokes if you like. Perhaps the one about the old lawyer who walks into an armed camp confident he has the upper hand."

"You're in far too fine a mood today," Edwin grumbles. "That, too, is unbecoming. It tells others they can take advantage of you."

"Nah, it just means that I am, at heart, a nasty bitch who takes far too much pleasure in the discomfort of those who've pissed her off."

"If I seem uncomfortable to you, then I might suggest —"

The door swings open, and in walks Émilie. Her gaze goes first to Felicity, eyebrows knitting in only the briefest flash of confusion before she smiles and gives a queenly nod. Then she turns to Edwin. She stops, and I hold my breath.

"Sheriff Dalton?" Émilie says, her voice ice. "Please remove this man from Rockton. He is contravening the terms of his banishment."

Nineteen

"Banishment?" My brows shoot up in mock horror. "You never told us you were banished, Edwin. Well, this is awkward."

His look warns that I have lost ground here. I meet it with a level stare that tells him he already lost that ground when he decided to treat us like incompetent children. I have a feeling that's the way he's accustomed to treating law enforcement. Some lawyers are. Some *people* are.

Yes, we're public servants, but that doesn't mean you can insult and pester us to the point of interfering with the job your taxes pay us to do. Also? Edwin isn't paying taxes. We aren't *his* law enforcement team to kick around.

"Be careful on your way home, Edwin," I say. "It's windy today. I remember when I was a kid and a windstorm blew down a huge tree in our backyard. It fell partly into the neighbor's yard. Dad hired a company to clean it up, but they were busy after the windstorm. The neighbor wouldn't stop pestering, so my dad hired another company, at a higher price, and sent the neighbor a bill for the difference."

Felicity frowns, wondering why I'm telling this story. Then she realizes and pulls back with a nod. Edwin gets it right away and only sniffs, "Did your parents take an ax to the tree before it fell?"

"No," I say. "But it had been leaning precariously. They were trying to figure out a way to remove it safely. One could argue they waited too long, but when they discussed the matter with the neighbors, they offered no help. Just told us that, however we handled it, the tree better not fall on their side of the fence."

"As charming as this analogy is, Casey, I don't believe it actually fits our situation."

"Mmm, no. I believe it does. You've never offered to help us deal with the hostiles, Edwin. They aren't a new threat. We've been trying to figure this out, and you just sit there and warn us they'd better not attack your people. Which they never did before we 'set them off' by refusing to let them murder us, right?"

I lean forward. "Tell me that you've never lost people to the hostiles before."

"I am here to help," Edwin says through his teeth.

"Yes," Émilie says. "I believe we've heard that one before. Shall we tell them why you were banished, Edwin?"

Dalton turns on her. "Are you sure, Émilie? Maybe you should wait. It's not like we need this information. Not like the council wasn't very aware that we were in communication with Edwin and didn't bother to mention that he had been *banished.*"

Dalton walks to his desk. "You can both leave. Felicity? If your grandfather had something to tell us, you're welcome to stay behind and speak for him. But Casey and I have work to do, figuring out what the fuck is happening in the forest, and what to do about it to keep our residents safe." He meets Edwin's gaze. "*Our* residents. They're the ones who pay our wages. You're just the old man who sits on his porch banging his cane."

"What's going on here?" asks a voice from the door. Phil enters carefully, his gaze sweeping those assembled. Kenny wisely lifts a hand in farewell and retreats.

"Edwin and Émilie would like to speak to you, Phil," I say. "While you do that, we'll be at the clinic, talking to April."

"Casey," Émilie says. "I understand you

and Eric are both upset at being caught in the middle —"

" 'Upset' isn't the word," I say.

"Fucking fed up with everyone's fucking bullshit," Dalton says.

"I feel as if I've missed something," Phil murmurs.

I turn to him. "Did you know that Edwin was banished from Rockton? That he was forbidden to set foot in it again?"

"No, but I'm sure . . ." His gaze travels across us, and he clears his throat. "I was about to say that I'm sure, whatever his crime, the council now considers him harmless, or they would not allow you to have contact with him. I will, however, amend that to the sincere *hope* that whatever he's done is moot, given that they have allowed communication."

No one answers . . . which is an answer in itself.

Dalton growls under his breath, and when a voice says, "Sedition," everyone is caught off guard, turning toward the last person in the room we expect to speak.

Felicity.

"My grandfather was accused of sedition," she says. "Inciting the residents of Rockton to rebel against the authority of those in charge."

"Ah, sedition." Émilie crosses the room and stands in front of Edwin. "Your chair, sir."

His brows shoot up.

"Give me your chair. I'm tired of standing."

He snorts. "We are of an age, Émilie. I am certainly not ceding the only chair to you."

"Really? I am the weaker sex, am I not? That's what you always told me. You were very clear about that."

Felicity's gaze swings on her grandfather, who deftly ducks it.

"My opinion has changed —" he begins.

"Has it? Truly? Then you will cede the chair out of deference to my *authority.*"

Edwin glowers at her. Then he slowly rises . . . and she takes the chair, shoves it behind the desk, and sits on the front.

"Gather 'round, children," she says. "Let me tell you a story of sedition. Such a lovely word. Such a noble cause." She turns to Felicity. "Did your grandfather tell you the nature of his rebellion?"

Felicity nods. "When residents founded the First Settlement, they wished to trade with Rockton. The town refused to allow it — they didn't want anyone living in the forest. My grandfather arrived during the dispute. He saw the First Settlement's point and attempted to help them. For that, he was exiled. The First Settlement took him in and made him their leader."

Émilie's lips twitch in a humorless smile. "Seems you left out a few details, old man. Or, should I say, a few bodies?"

"What?" I turn to Edwin.

Émilie continues. "Our lawyer friend here did not intervene in the dispute by arguing eloquently in favor of trade. You see, at that time, Rockton had a far more trusting nature. We kept our hunting rifles in a communal chest, for anyone who cared to hunt. Edwin emptied that chest and gave the guns to the settlers, who invaded Rockton, took the residents hostage, and made their demands. When Rockton's leaders refused, they were both shot. Murdered."

"What?" I say, wheeling on Edwin. "You *killed* —"

"Not me," Edwin says. "You know that, Émilie. You were there. You and your husband. The three of us negotiated a peaceful settlement."

"Negotiated? You have such a charming way with words." She looks at us. "Edwin held a rifle to my husband's head. I had a handgun that Robert bought me after the first death threat over our political views. Edwin didn't expect that gun, and he sure as hell didn't expect a woman to pull it on him. He laughed at me. I put a hole through the wall, singeing off a few of his hairs, and he decided perhaps we really should talk after all."

"I was *trying* to talk all along, Émilie. No one was listening until I pointed a gun at your husband." He glances at us. "The deaths were a mistake. *My* mistake, because I put guns in the hands of idiots. Yet Rockton refused to talk to us, and we grew desperate."

His gaze shoots Dalton's way, waiting for sarcasm. Dalton says nothing. He's trying very hard not to look at me. Dalton knows exactly what's going through my head. I want to sneer at Edwin, to give him the reaction he expects, but I cannot. Because once upon a time, I took a gun to persuade someone that I was serious, to force him to listen to me. And then, when he didn't, I pulled the trigger, and I will never stop regretting that. Bringing that gun had been a stupid, immature move from a stupid, immature kid.

A kid who would have only been a few years younger than Edwin and Émilie at the time.

"Émilie?" I say, as evenly as I can. "How close is that to the truth?"

She doesn't answer.

"If it was not the truth," Edwin says, "would I still be here? Would they have settled for banishing me? Left me in charge of the First Settlement, where I could plan my next assault on Rockton?"

Émilie says nothing.

"We were not in charge here," Edwin says. "Émilie, Robert, myself . . . Back then, we were considered children, errant youths who'd stumbled into trouble at home and now needed the protection of responsible adults. We chafed at that. We were idealists, and we thought we could do better. I attempted to do better by helping the settlers, which was something we *all* wanted." A meaningful look at Émilie.

"Yes," she says. "The three of us wanted that. However, only one of us put guns in the hands of people who didn't want peace. They wanted Rockton."

Edwin nods. "I underestimated their capacity for violence and overestimated their intelligence. The result was a tragedy. I do not deny that. No more than I deny the fairness of my sentence." He looks at us. "Robert argued my case, despite . . ."

Another look at Émilie.

"You held my husband at gunpoint," she says, each word coming slow, old fury igniting in her eyes. "I don't care if you didn't plan to pull that trigger. All I saw was a friend holding a gun on my husband, threatening to shoot if he didn't get his way. I will never forget what that felt like. I will never forgive you for that moment."

"I understand," Edwin says. "I hope you and Robert had many years together —"

"Don't." She spits the word, glaring at him.

"Whatever you think I'm doing —"

"You're subtly reminding me that Robert did *not* die, and that we went on to a happy and long life together. You're suggesting that my reaction was merely a moment of panic. A moment that I have lived a thousand times in nightmare, and if you want to see that as feminine weakness — hysteria or the vapors, perhaps — then you do that, but do not patronize me."

"All right. Then I apologize sincerely, Émilie, for the pain I caused you."

Dalton glances at me. We're both uncomfortable here. So is Phil. Felicity just looks confused. She's watching her grandfather the way one might watch a loved one displaying characteristics that suggest a mental break . . . or alien possession. Edwin is apologizing. He is admitting to mistakes. For her, I suspect, this is a first, and it is unsettling.

Does Edwin even remember that Felicity is here? I don't think so. Not Felicity, not Dalton, not Phil, and not me. Neither does Émilie. We are witness to a private conversation, and the only thing that kept me from slipping out earlier was the understanding that they need to have this talk, and even a subtle departure might disrupt that.

Also, I want to understand what happened here. What happened between them, and what Edwin did. Whether I can trust either of them. What sort of people they really are.

I have cleared a peephole into their psyches, and I see something far too uncomfortably close to a mirror, at least in their past selves. Idealistic, impulsive, reckless, overconfident, convinced that they're doing the right thing . . . and making a horrible, tragic mess of it.

Edwin is right. If the past leaders considered him a serious threat, they'd never have allowed him to retreat into the forest. They set him up to be the leader there, because they trusted he'd learned a lesson and also that he hadn't intended for his "revolution" to leave bodies in its wake.

"Is Émilie right?" I ask after a moment of awkward silence. "Did the settlers want to take over Rockton?"

Edwin sighs. Felicity pulls out the chair, and he sinks into it.

"That is the problem with supporting a group you are not part of," Edwin says. "You aren't privy to its secrets. When I arrived in Rockton, it was during a time of rising political idealism, especially among the young. I'm certain you can't see it now, but I was right in there, supporting causes and championing the underdog. We wanted to save people, particularly those less fortunate than ourselves."

Émilie makes a face. "Our hearts were in the right place, but there was a definite air of privilege. Taking it upon ourselves to save the downtrodden, whether they wanted our help or not."

Edwin nods. "We wanted to help the settlers. Three of us, plus a couple of the other younger residents. We argued for open trade. That's what the settlers said they wanted: the ability to trade with Rockton. It seemed obvious to us that Rockton should allow it."

"But Rockton's leaders had a touch of savior complex themselves," Émilie says. "Living in the forest was wrong, and if they could force the settlers back to Rockton by refusing trade, then that was for their own good."

"The settlers disagreed," I say. "And when they had the chance — and the guns — they decided trade wasn't enough. They wanted the town. The infrastructure. The supplies. The plane."

"Some of them did," Edwin says. "Yet even those who supported the leader were appalled by the murders. They turned the perpetrators over as part of the negotiations. What happened to them after that . . ." He shrugs.

"They were sent home," Émilie says firmly. "In later times, a harsher justice might have prevailed, but those in charge of Rockton back then were not killers."

"Back then?" I say.

"Those in charge have never been sociopaths, Casey," she says, meeting my gaze. "I think you and Eric know that, or you would never allow anyone to be sent south for their crimes. That would make you complicit in their deaths."

Phil looks over sharply. "Did you honestly believe — ?"

"They worried," Émilie cuts in.

I turn to Edwin. "You said you came with information. To impart it, not to demand it, correct? You wanted to tell me something useful. Give it to me now. Then you will go home and wait while I solve this damned problem."

TWENTY

"I think we both know Edwin is physically incapable of sharing his information and walking away," Émilie says. "The man is not a giver. Unless you have guns. He'll be quick to give those away."

"That is beneath you, Émilie," Edwin says, the formality returning to his voice.

"Nothing is beneath me. Especially when it's true. That's the deal then, Edwin. You tell Casey what you came to tell her, and then you leave and trust her to update you once the crime is solved."

"Or?"

She looks him in the eye. "The terms of your banishment stated that if you ever set foot in Rockton, you would be shipped home. I suppose you thought no one was left to remember that."

"Hostiles murdered a group of tourists," he says. "That was vital information that Casey failed to impart."

I turn to Felicity. "Is that true?"

Her look warns me against putting her on the spot, but I'm only making a point here, and Edwin gets it with the tightening of his lips.

I turn back to him. "Felicity was here when the woman found us. She knew what we suspected — that she'd been attacked by hostiles. Your granddaughter would not have failed to convey that to you. We presumed you'd take the threat seriously, though I'm not sure what difference it would make, since your settlement is already on high alert."

I allow a two-second pause. Then I say, "There were three other deaths. Settlers. We discovered them yesterday and haven't had a chance to alert you."

"The hostiles murdered *seven* —"

"The settlers weren't killed by hostiles. Someone just wanted it to look that way."

Phil eases back, almost imperceptibly. He thinks I'm bluffing, and guilt prickles at that.

I watch Edwin for a flicker that says he knows I'm telling the truth . . . because he played a role in the deaths. I don't see it, though. I do, however, notice Felicity's gaze slide her grandfather's way. She's wondering whether he knew this. She's wondering whether he's involved. His own features, though, only gather in irritable confusion.

"Is this a joke, Casey?" he says.

I let my expression answer. He meets my gaze. Studies it. Narrows his eyes.

"Explain," he says.

I arch my brows. I could remind him that I'm not *his* public servant, but I won't be petty. My expression says enough.

"I'm not sure what you want me to explain," I say. "We found three settlers. They appeared to be the victim of hostile attacks. The classic signs were there, with frenzied slashes plus evidence of blunt force trauma. But then April discovered a bullet lodged behind bone. We found evidence of other bullet wounds, with the projectiles either passing through or being removed. That remaining one, I believe, was missed. The stab wounds were then used to disguise the entry and exit paths. Decent work, and without that bullet, I'd have bought it. April would have figured it out, though, through internal tissue damage."

Phil stares at me. He realizes now that I'm not making this up. That we once again excluded him from the "need to know" roster.

I'll need to convince him it wasn't a lack of trust but, rather, that we'd been too busy dealing with everything else and weren't ready to inform the council. And, yes, perhaps that last bit *is* trust. We don't trust him not to tell the council, but we also don't wish to put him in that position.

"You think *we* did this thing," Edwin says.

I shrug. "Makes sense. You have guns. You also have a reason to prove that the hostiles are a wildly escalating threat."

"We are not killers," he says, enunciating each word.

"Then someone from your settlement found these settlers, already dead, and you decided to make use of their bodies. Give meaning to senseless deaths. You'd use that to convince us — and through us, the council — that the hostiles must be stopped. Relocated or otherwise removed."

Edwin watches me for a moment. Then he says, "Were you good at your job down south, Casey? Or did you achieve your position based on your sex and ethnicity? The elevation of an underwhelming officer to fulfill some bureaucratically determined quota?"

Dalton rocks forward, eyes flashing as his mouth opens. Before he can say anything, though, Felicity walks past him. Strides to the door. Opens it.

"Felic —" her grandfather begins. The

shutting door cuts him short. She doesn't stomp out and slam it. Just wordlessly leaves, letting the door close behind her.

"Nicely done, Edwin," Émilie murmurs. "I see your attitudes haven't changed, even with a granddaughter you are obviously grooming to succeed you. Didn't have any grandsons, did you? Such a shame."

"Casey is —" Dalton begins.

"Casey is well qualified for her position," Phil cuts in, his voice cool and smooth, his gaze equally cool as it lands on me. He's furious with my perceived betrayal but rising above it to defend me, which adds iodine to the sting. "Her performance ratings and clearance scores placed her in the top tenth percentile and —"

"And none of that matters," I say. "Because Edwin isn't really questioning my skill or my ability. He's *seen* how effective I am. He's just playing a very old and very tattered card. Do you think that's a new one, Counselor? Insinuate that a woman got her job because of her sex? That a minority got it because they tick a box? I'm sure you heard that yourself, back in the day. Or is your memory really fading that fast?"

"I was simply —"

"Being an asshole. Being an asshole *defense lawyer,* to be precise. I laid out my case against you, and you deflected by pretending my theory only proves I'm clearly a lousy detective."

"We neither killed nor mutilated these settlers," he says. "I don't see the point of such a sham. You already know the hostiles are dangerous. Even if we mutilated the corpses, would we not ensure you found them?"

"I believe we were supposed to find them. Eventually. Scavenging would only add to the damage, as it did with the tourists. The bodies would be left for a couple of days, and then we'd be alerted to their presence. However, before that could happen, they disappeared from the scene. Those responsible for the deaths pondered that, uncertain how to handle the unexpected twist. Then . . ."

I shrug. "Perhaps the person responsible decided that the best way to handle it was to come to Rockton himself. Come and tell me that a hunting party happened upon these poor murdered settlers and returned to tell him, but in the meantime, the bodies disappeared. So he proceeded to Rockton to inform me personally, despite his banishment, proving that the situation was indeed dire."

Edwin's face darkens for a split second before he leans back in his chair, hands folded on his lap. "That is quite a tortuous piece of speculation, Detective Butler. Reminds me of all the times I had to explain away a bit of irrefutable evidence against a client. Come up with a preposterous story and pray the jury was filled with gullible idiots. Apparently, now I'm the gullible idiot."

"No," Dalton says, "you're the very old lawyer who's forgotten how to ply his trade. Even I can see what you're doing, Edwin. Discrediting the witness. Isn't that what they call it? Don't provide any proof that you didn't do this. Just deny it and insult the detective and her theories."

"What *are* you here for, Edwin?" I say. "I have work to do. You know what I found. You know you're a suspect. Now please convey this critical information that brought you here, so you may return to your village and let me solve the six goddamn murders currently on my plate."

Edwin straightens. "I came to inform you that there has been increased evidence of hostile activity. Another hunting party was confronted. Fortunately, the situation was resolved without bloodshed."

Silence, broken when Dalton says, "What?"

"I said —"

"We all heard what you said," Dalton says, "and we're waiting for the punch line. Casey just suggested you came to tell us about the settlers, not knowing we'd found them. Now you're revealing that your 'critical information' is bullshit. Either that's your idea of a joke or you might as well put up your hands and say 'you got me.' "

"I hardly consider an attack on my people 'bullshit,' Eric."

"It sure as hell isn't a reason for you to come all the way here personally."

"Is that really all you have to tell me, Edwin?" I ask.

"I consider an unprovoked attack on my people an egregious —"

"I have no further questions for this witness." I walk to the door, open it, and turn to Edwin. "You are free to go. You will be escorted from town. Please do not see this as a lifting of your banishment. You are not welcome back. Nor is your granddaughter until I have cleared your settlement in this matter. If you decide you have further information for me, you may send Felicity to the edge of our patrol area, where she will wait for a militia member to bring her message to me."

"We had nothing to do with the deaths of those settlers, Casey."

"Maybe not, but you're playing a game I don't have time to join. I will not forget your *assistance* in this matter. Now please leave."

He rises stiffly and says, "May I at least see the bodies of the deceased settlers? We have had members of our community leave over the years, and I may be able to identify them."

"They have already been identified. They're not from your settlement or Rockton. They were a married couple and a teenage boy, trappers who came north a few years ago."

His chin drops in a slow nod. "We did know them, then. Thank you."

I wait to see whether he'll still find a reason to view the bodies, proof that his "excuse" was just that. He doesn't. As I hold the door, Dalton glances at me, that glance questioning my decision to let Edwin leave. It's a mild question, though. If he felt strongly about it, he'd interfere.

I lead Edwin outside and flag down Kenny, who hasn't gone far. I tell him to escort Edwin to the main path. I'm about to ask whether he's seen Felicity when I spot her sitting with Sebastian.

Edwin doesn't notice Felicity and Sebastian. He's keeping his gaze forward, avoiding any hint of curiosity about the town. I murmur that I'll find his granddaughter and send him on ahead with Kenny.

Once Kenny and Edwin are gone, I make my way toward the young couple. They're on the edge of town, sitting on a bench, Felicity gripping the edge of her seat, hunched forward as Sebastian leans in, talking to her.

I contrast that with the first time I'd seen them together. Felicity had come to town, and Sebastian took it upon himself to play host. Not being creepy, just considerate. He'd regaled her with amusing stories, and she'd sat there, both mesmerized and terrified. He'd fascinated her, this first glimpse of a "regular" boy, one from down south, but I know it'd be uncomfortable, too, wondering how she looked through his eyes.

As the "kids" — Sebastian, Felicity, Sidra, and Baptiste — began hanging out, I'd felt compelled to tell Sebastian about a First Settlement resident who murdered three people, and who almost certainly shared his diagnosis. How did Sebastian handle it? Promptly told Felicity what he was and what he'd done.

If I feared that would end the friendship, then I misjudged them both. Sebastian wanted her to know what he was and how he was coping with it, and Felicity appreciated the opportunity to make her own informed decision.

Then, last winter, Felicity herself killed someone. In my gut, I call it justified, but a court wouldn't agree. There is no provision in our legal system for what Felicity did. We've been working on her feelings around that. I think I've helped, but Sebastian has helped more.

Now, seeing her leaning toward him, pouring out her thoughts about the meeting with her grandfather, Sebastian listening intently, my heart lifts for them, finding each other in this corner of the world.

"Hey," I say softly when I reach them. "You need to go, Felicity. I'm sorry. I also need to ask you to stay out of Rockton until this is settled. It's not you . . ."

"I know." She rises. "I apologize for my grandfather's behavior. It was inconsiderate."

Inconsiderate on all levels. An insult not just to me, but to his granddaughter. Émilie needled him about not having grandsons. It's true, though. I wonder whether Felicity feels that if there'd been a male heir, he'd have only needed to be half as capable as her.

"You make him uneasy," she says, as if

reading my mind. "He likes that you are Chinese. He would like it better if you were a man."

I quirk a smile. "He can't have everything. I don't think he minds me being a woman — he just wishes that meant I was easier to handle."

She returns a ghost-mirror of my smile. "That is true. But if you were easier to handle, he would not respect you. He tells me I am too headstrong. Yet if I were not . . ." She shrugs.

"You wouldn't be his heir."

"As you said, he cannot have everything. Sometimes, I am not convinced he even knows what he *does* want. I can tell you, however, that I know nothing of these dead settlers. If my grandfather played any role in their deaths or the treatment of their bodies, I heard nothing about it." She pauses. "I would add that I do not think he did, but you would expect me to say that, so you can put little weight in it."

"Thank you anyway. I am sorry about the recent encounter with the hostiles. I'm glad no one was hurt."

Confusion flickers over her face. It's a millisecond long, followed by a millisecond of anger as she realizes she's given something away. Then that vanishes, and she shakes her head. I can interpret that, too, a rueful acknowledgment that I played my hand well, and she cannot fault me for the trick.

"Your grandfather is waiting on the main path," I say.

She murmurs a farewell to Sebastian, who has stood in silence. He leans in and whispers something before she goes and she nods, lips twitching in a wry smile.

Once she's out of earshot, he says, "So, Edwin claims some of his people were attacked and they weren't, because Felicity knows nothing about it. Right?"

"Uh-huh. I hate playing her against him but . . ."

"You gotta do what you gotta do. She understands that."

"Speaking of unfairly playing people against each other, I don't suppose she told you why they came."

He shakes his head. "Nah. Just that Edwin needed to speak to you, and then he played some power game, and it pissed her off. He's always telling her to hide her cards better, learn a few tricks of her own, and she doesn't see the point."

"She prefers blunt honesty."

"Yep. She's more like Sheriff Dalton. Her granddad's more like you."

I arch my brows.

"Hey, you just admitted to playing people against each other. The difference is that you aren't an arrogant asshole about it. Edwin's been in charge too long. Spent too long being the smartest person in the room. He only likes games when they're rigged in his favor."

"Speaking of the smartest person in the room . . ." I say, giving him a meaningful look.

He laughs. "Oh, I'm not the smartest." He smiles. "Just the most dangerous."

He winks at me, and then jogs off with a nod. I watch him go, and a thought flits through my head, but before I can pursue it, Phil appears, striding through town, and I jog to catch up.

Twenty-One

"Phil?" I call.

He keeps walking, moving fast toward his house, and once he reaches it, he'll be home free. I break into a run and swing into his path.

"Phil, please," I say. "Five minutes."

He stops, his jaw twitching as his gaze slides past me. "I do not have time —"

"Five minutes. That's it. I swear."

An abrupt nod, and he waves toward his house. We walk there in silence. Once we're inside, he closes the door.

"I really am busy," he says.

I nod and stay in the hallway. "We need to discuss how to handle things in the future."

Cool blue eyes rest on me. "Do we? My position in this town tells you how to handle matters. I should have been apprised of the new information. You didn't trust me not to run to the council with it."

"It isn't about trust —"

"Eric is in charge here. You and I support his efforts. That makes you a colleague, not an underling. However, it means I am not *your* underling either. I am management level. I need to know everything that affects the management of this town."

"Do you?" I say.

His jaw twitches again. Before he can answer, I continue, "Is that what you want? I'm not being facetious, Phil. Eric and I need you to take a long and hard look at your position and what is expected of you and whether you actually want what you're requesting. You're right. You and I are management level supporting Eric. But we're not in charge of the same department. You actually *don't* need to know new developments in a criminal case. It isn't your department."

"It is if it affects town security."

"Does it?" I ease back. "Does it make an actual difference whether these settlers were murdered by hostiles or not? We're keeping residents out of the forest. That covers all bases. And while Eric may be our CEO, he's not on Rockton's board. He works for them. We work for them. If Eric and I decide not to keep them abreast of every new development, that's our choice. They expect it from us, to be honest. Do you want them to expect it of you?"

When he says nothing, I continue, "That's what you need to decide, Phil. Where do you serve Rockton better? As the guy they can trust to pass on all new information? Or do you want to risk them finding out that you've jumped sides?"

I meet his gaze. "Have you jumped sides? Or is this your exit strategy?"

He blinks. "What?"

"Your exit strategy. Your way out of Rockton."

"I know what an exit strategy is, Casey. I just don't understand how it applies . . ." He trails off and then says, "You think I want the council to realize they cannot trust me. They'll recall me and send someone else in my place. The problem with that is what they'll do when they recall me." He lifts a hand.

"And, no, I don't fear being buried in a shallow grave. What I fear, Casey, is the loss of my career. I was headhunted to the organization before I graduated from university. I interned there and immediately went to work for them upon my graduation. I have exactly one position on my résumé. A position I cannot use if they fire me."

"You can always use them on a résumé. You just can't use them as a reference."

"They would deny ever having employed me, and a future employer would not find any record of such an organization. They've paid me very well for accepting this 'quirk' of my employment. Should I ever leave, they've promised to provide a proper reference from one of the board members' corporations. That presumes, obviously, that we part on good terms. Otherwise . . . ?" He shrugs. "I believe Eric would say they have me by the balls. In an iron grip."

"Okay, then you need to decide how to handle that. Do you want us only to tell you things you can pass along? Or tell you everything and let you handle the fallout if they realize you withheld information? Take time to think about that, please, Phil. I will apologize for not letting you know about the bullet, but in my defense, we were still working through the implications."

He nods. "Understood. I'm sorry if I overreacted."

"You didn't. It was a shitty way for you to find out."

"You were putting Edwin on the spot. I realize that. And I will let you return to your investigation and decide, with Émilie's input, how to handle this with the council."

"Or, since she's technically your boss, you could just let her handle it. If she decides not to pass the information along . . ."

A smile touches his lips. "I will consider that. Thank you."

When I get to the station, it's empty. I'm about to retreat when Dalton calls, "Back here," from the rear deck.

I find him in his chair, boots braced on the railing. He's wearing the hat I bought him for sun protection, which bears more than a passing resemblance to a Stetson. He has it pulled down to shade his eyes, and as I walk out, I have to smile.

"You should be on the front porch with that pose," I say. "Put a shotgun across your lap, and you'd be the perfect Wild West sheriff."

He tilts up the hat. "Nah, the perfect Wild West sheriff doesn't need a shotgun. Just a steely-eyed glare." He narrows his eyes. "How am I doing?"

"I'm thoroughly intimidated."

I hop onto the railing next to his propped-up feet. Behind me, a raven croaks, and I toss her a piece of bread. She'll gobble it down and retreat, knowing she only gets one each time she spots me. A moment later, Storm appears from wherever she's been wandering. The dog climbs onto the porch and thumps down between us.

"Edwin lied about a standoff with a hunting party," I say.

Dalton grunts.

"You figured that?"

He lifts one shoulder. "About as much as you did. Felicity confirmed?"

"Unwittingly."

"So what do you think Edwin's up to?"

"You first."

Dalton reaches down to pat Storm. "I think he came for exactly the reason I said. To give you shit about the hostiles. Kick your ass for not moving fast enough. Bitch about you not personally informing him of the tourist attack. Showing up in person only meant he was serious. When I chewed him out for it, he had to regroup. Made up some bullshit about having information. Probably hoped after that memory-lane trip with Émilie, we'd forget to press him on his purpose."

When I don't reply, his boot brushes my hip. "You disagree?"

"No. I don't think Edwin had anything to do with the death of those hostiles or the staging. Unless the First Settlement got a handgun in the last few months, we know they only have rifles." Last winter, one of Felicity's friends tried to buy a handgun from us, and the discussion made it clear they had none and, like Cherise, saw no point in them.

I continue, "He's right about the staging. He'd be subtler and, yes, the problem with the staging is that we were unlikely to find it . . . . Back to that in a moment. Felicity knows nothing about the settler deaths, and I don't think he did either. That doesn't, however, mean that no one from the First Settlement was involved."

"Without Edwin's knowledge." Dalton pauses to rub Storm's ear. "You think that's why he let you send him packing so easily. He wanted to hightail it home and see if his people had anything to do with this."

"He certainly didn't leave because he felt bad realizing he'd been an asshole."

Dalton snorts and then puts out a hand, a gesture for me to come over and sit with him.

"I do believe we're on the clock, boss," I say.

"We are indeed, meaning if I say" — he motions me toward his lap — "you gotta obey."

"Pretty sure that's a harassment suit waiting to happen."

"Write out a report. I'll make sure it gets to the proper authorities."

I slide from the railing and step over

Storm. Dalton eases back in his chair, tugging the hat down again as his eyes half close, arms open for me to slide into them. Instead, I veer to the door, his alarmed "Casey?" following me. I return with two bottles of beer from the icebox.

"Since we're apparently on a work break," I say.

He smiles and takes one, his hand sliding over it to flick off the layer of condensation. I lower myself onto his lap, and icy fingers glide down the back of my neck, making me yelp and nearly drop my own bottle.

"Payback," he says.

"For getting you a beer?"

"For encouraging me to drink on the job."

"You don't need to drink it," I say.

"I succumb to peer pressure far too easily."

He flips the cap into the rusted can by his chair. I remember the first time I saw him drinking during a shift. I'd been appalled. Exactly the sort of behavior I expected from this redneck bully of a sheriff.

It hadn't taken long to realize just how old those caps in the can were. He did have the occasional beer midafternoon, but considering how many hours he put in, no one could fault him for that.

I lean back against him. It's a brief respite.

We both know that, and after a pull from my beer, I say, "I messed up with my theory."

"Ah." His arms tighten around me. "Confession time. All right, Detective, tell me the very minor error that you made and then self-corrected before anyone caught it."

"Edwin caught it." I lay my head against his shoulder. "I kept thinking that whoever killed the settlers meant for us to mistake it for a hostile kill. Add to their body count and intensify the situation. But that doesn't make sense."

"Only if you presume the people responsible have the forethought to realize the flaw in their plans. That's presuming a lot, Casey."

He's not being sarcastic here. Most crimes aren't masterful acts of forethought and calculation. It is very possible that someone stumbled over the dead settlers, saw an opportunity, mutilated the corpses, and then said, "Shit, how do we show these hostile kills to Rockton without them realizing we did it?"

That'd been the strongest argument against Cherise's culpability. She's far too smart to stage a crime scene and then lead us to it.

"You're right," I say. "Someone could have

done this, seen the flaw, and backed off to think it through. In the meantime, Cherise and Owen moved the bodies. If people from Edwin's settlement are responsible, that's the answer. But it's also possible that this has nothing to do with us. That the killers were just covering their tracks by making it look like a wild-animal attack."

"Which we then mistook for hostiles."

I nod. "We can tell the bodies were slashed with a knife, but to the average person, with no forensic knowledge?" I shrug. "Knives and claws both tear."

"That would make this an unrelated crime. It's equally likely that someone found bodies, had a brilliant idea, and then realized it was stupid. Two potential theories."

"Yes. I'm just kicking myself for not realizing the second one."

"It's been less than twenty-four hours since April discovered that bullet. It's not like we've executed a suspect." He rests his chin on my shoulder. "You aren't down south anymore, Casey. None of your colleagues are going to question your handling of the case, and there's no jury of public opinion to pillory you with ridiculous expectations." He pauses. "Except Edwin, but he doesn't count."

He's right. Down south, I learned to fall

on my sword before anyone pushed me onto it. Make a mistake, however small? Be the first to mention it or else someone will use it as proof I didn't deserve my position, like Edwin did. As Dalton has pointed out, such defensive tactics can backfire. Be too quick to say "mea culpa," and no one misses any mistake, making it seem as if you screw up more often than others.

"Let's work on this," he says. "In the future, the correct response is not 'Oh my God, I screwed up so badly,' but 'Hey, Eric, I've considered another possibility.' Save the blame-taking for when *I* screw up. Then you can have it all."

"Thank you." I sip my beer. "What Émilie said about the First Settlement revolt, had you heard anything like that?"

"The version I got was that there'd been some trade trouble shortly after the First Settlement separated, and that's why we avoided contact. The fact that guns were involved? Two residents killed? Edwin being the asshole who gave them the guns? No, somehow that didn't get passed along."

Which is the problem with an oral history in a transient population. If the council wanted to hide the specifics, they only needed to wait ten years or so for the story to fade into half-formed rumor.

"Do we stop dealing with Edwin?" I ask.

"Nah. The council has let him stay in the area. It's been almost fifty years, and he's never posed a threat. Hasn't let his people pose one either. Right now, he's a nuisance. I won't put up with that shit. If he searches his settlement for potential perpetrators — and brings any back to us — then we can talk. If he protects them? Whole other situation."

We drink in silence. Then he says, "Good call, by the way. Putting Edwin and Émilie together."

I laugh, sputtering a mouthful of beer. "I did not foresee *that,* let me tell you. I figured they're roughly of an age, and both mentioned they weren't Rockton founders but came shortly after. So I thought there was a reasonable chance they knew each other — and with two strong personalities, that they had probably clashed."

"Oh, they clashed all right. You expected sparks and got fireworks."

"Yeah, somehow my mental scenarios did not include 'Edwin and Émilie were friends and idealistic collaborators until Edwin held Émilie's husband at gunpoint.' " I shake my head. "I always suspected relations with the First Settlement were volatile, but I had no idea. At least they don't seem to have had trouble with the other settlement."

"Different time, different reason for leaving. The Second Settlement just wanted to get back to nature. Hippies."

"And the tea helped, I'm sure," I say with a chuckle.

"Yeah. The tea definitely would have helped."

I stop with my bottle halfway to my lips. Then I push to my feet, startling Storm.

"Lightbulb just flashed, didn't it?" Dalton says.

I set my beer on the railing and head into the station. On the desk is the sample of tea I'd needled Edwin about earlier. We'd gotten it from the Second Settlement, along with the recipe, which we'd re-created and compared to an analysis of the sample to prove it was the same.

The Second Settlement arose during the late hippie era, when a group of Rockton residents decided they wanted to renew their bond with nature. That sounds very New Age — and naive — but they'd had experts in their group, and they'd been a lot like the quartet Maryanne had headed out with. The difference was that there hadn't been any hostiles to contend with . . . probably because, if my theory is right, they accidentally spawned the hostiles themselves.

Yes, I'm well aware of the irony there — the most peaceful settlement gave birth to the most dangerous people in the forest.

It was the Second Settlement that discovered the tea. I don't know how. They'd been vague on that. I presumed a botanist in their midst. The percentage of people in Rockton with degrees and advanced degrees far exceeds the general population. Dalton used to joke about that with the nonvictim residents — you'd think being so educated, they'd be less likely to get caught if they commit crimes. After I arrived, he realized it applied to me and stopped joking.

The truth is that the higher your education, the more likely you are to have the networks and the means to get to Rockton. Less likely to have dependents. More likely to have cash flow. Also, let's be bluntly honest, more likely to have your application accepted. It's easier to take a former dentist and assign him shop-clerk duty than to take someone in retail and occasionally ask him to perform dental surgery.

So my presumption is that among those early Second Settlement residents was a botanist or a pharmacist or a scientist with an interest in "pharmaceutical recreation." That's what's in this jar on my desk. A natural intoxicant, mixed with dried berries and rose hips. As for what provides the intoxicating effect, I have that information under lock and key, literally. We don't need residents coming across it and searching the woods for a natural high, especially when they're more likely to end up brewing a lovely tea of deadly water hemlock. Even knowing the ingredients, it's the proportions that matter. Whoever created this tea knew what they were doing.

A Second Settlement resident concocts a tea that provides a mild narcotic effect, similar to marijuana. It calms nerves and, well, makes for very happy and peaceful settlers, the stereotype of the hippie with a joint in their mouth. It's enjoyed the same way we enjoy our beer — at the end of a long day, a much-needed break in the daily grind of survival. A treat, not a staple.

I have a second jar of tea, too. It's used for rituals, and it produces an added state of mild hallucinations. The Second Settlement reveres nature, and they hold rituals where they imbibe this tea to connect with the elemental spirits. I make no judgment call on that. It is their faith, and like most faiths, it both enhances their lives and, occasionally, impedes them.

Two teas. Two purposes. Both as tightly regulated as our liquor. I've seen nothing in the Second Settlement that would lead me to argue against either version. I believe what happened with the hostiles is an unintended consequence, impossible to foresee.

I know from Maryanne that the hostiles also drink two forms of narcotic. The first produces results similar to what the Second Settlement calls their peace tea. The second brew is much more dangerous, heightening awareness and aggression and lowering inhibitions while causing a hallucinatory state similar to LSD.

I've shown Maryanne ingredients from both Second Settlement teas. Only the hostiles' shaman knows the exact ingredients of theirs, but Maryanne was able to confirm these were among the items she was told to gather. She has also sampled the peace tea and confirmed it seems similar to the hostiles' daily intoxicant brew, though the hostiles' was far more potent.

I believe, then, that the original hostiles were from the Second Settlement. They leave to pursue their own community. They brew the tea they're accustomed to and then, well, it's the age-old question for intoxicants, right? If a 5 percent beer gives me a buzz, what does an 8 percent beer do? An eighty-proof shot of whiskey? A hundred-proof?

I believe human nature led them to experiment, and the result was a drug that made people placid and easy to control. An invaluable bonus for the right leader. Turn your followers into drone workers, contentedly gathering berries and chopping wood all day.

Continue down that experimental path with the Second Settlement's ritual tea, and eventually you might get something that lowers inhibitions, increases aggression, and induces a hallucinogenic state. Again, the right kind of leader — or, more accurately, the wrong kind — would see true Yukon gold there. Between the two narcotics, the leader and shaman could control their followers, making them both complacent worker bees and the aggressive hunter-warriors that terrified everyone around.

Dalton, Maryanne, and April agree this is the most likely scenario. It makes far more sense than hypothesizing that a group of people in the forest just happened to concoct a narcotic with many of the exact same ingredients as the Second Settlement's teas.

Where does that take us? Nowhere really. We can't blame the Second Settlement and ask them to clean up "their" mess. My hypothesis only answers the question of how hostiles were created.

But now, holding a jar of the tea, I have another question.

How was *this* created? My hypothesis about a botanist or pharmacist or natural-drug enthusiast works, but are there other possibilities? There's another answer, one only raised now, during our discussion on the back porch.

I look at Dalton as he comes inside. "The last time we spoke to Tomas and Nancy, they said they were going to camp by Lynx Lake when the weather got warmer."

He nods. The couple had asked our permission, the lake being a few kilometers from Rockton.

"Do you think it's warm enough for them to be there now?" I ask.

"It is. I'm guessing you want to take a hike?"

"Please."

Twenty-Two

Lynx Lake is an hour's walk from Rockton. It's not the same lake where we found Sophie. There are several bodies of water within what we consider easy walking distance, and Lynx Lake has nothing to recommend it over the closer ones. Not unless you're looking for more privacy or, well, lynx. That doesn't mean you can expect to see the felines. The Yukon isn't a zoo. That can be hard for southerners to understand. I've seen maybe a dozen lynx since I arrived, and ten of those I would have missed altogether if Dalton hadn't pointed out a brown shape moving against a brown backdrop.

We walk to the lake and find three tents of varying sizes, along with fish racks and a food-storage system rigged up in the trees. Food left on ground level is a sure way to get an unwanted wildlife sighting, particularly of bears. You especially don't want to attract them if you have young children, as Nancy and Tomas do.

This afternoon, the kids are up and out. Miles and Becky, ages seven and five, both have their fishing poles in the lake. They're at the edge where the ice has receded. Tomas is out on the ice itself, fishing through a hole. Nancy sits on a log bench, working her embroidery magic on a new garment. There's another woman with her, maybe in her early fifties. That gives me pause until I remember Nancy mentioned that her aunt wanted to come with them to help with the kids. To support Nancy and Tomas, I suspect, with the childcare being an excuse.

Nancy and Tomas are breaking away from the Second Settlement. It's as amicable as a divorce can be, which means that while it's friendly enough to maintain trade ties, the settlement isn't exactly thrilled with their decision. The reason for that parting? While we think of the Second Settlement as the more liberal one, it still prohibits homosexual relationships.

At eighteen, Nancy was caught with another girl and forced to marry a man. She chose Tomas over her intended groom. He knew about the girl and decided if he was a good husband, he'd be enough for her. He's since seen his mistake, but they have children and Nancy loves him. She wants them to be a family, and they'll work out the rest. Part of working it out is leaving the settlement to spend the summer on their own before deciding their next move.

As we approach, we hail Nancy and her aunt, Josie. The Second Settlement practices communal living, so the "aunt" honorific is given to all women who helped raise you.

Josie is a tall woman, strikingly beautiful, her dark skin glistening with sweat under the strong sun. She's Dalton's height and towers over me as she rises. I clasp her hand between mine and bow my head, the proper greeting for an elder. Tyrone Cypher calls the Second Settlement a cult. I wouldn't go that far. There's no charismatic leader. No slavish devotion to dogma. To me, they resemble a faith-based back-to-nature commune. I obviously don't agree with all their customs, but I will grant them the respect of a proper greeting, especially Josie, who has been Nancy's staunchest supporter.

Dalton goes to join Tomas on the ice, pausing first by the kids to chat. When he leaves, a gesture grants Storm permission to stay with the children, and she does, lapping up their hugs and pets.

"Tomas wants to get them a dog," Nancy

says as I settle in. "I don't suppose you're thinking of breeding her."

"We are, actually. Not this year, though. A litter next spring would be nice. You're welcome to one if you're still around."

She smiles. "Tell the kids that, and we may need to stay."

She sets aside her needlework and rises to make tea. While I settle on the log, I look out at Dalton and Tomas.

"Is it different now down south?" Josie asks.

When I glance over, she laughs softly. "Oh, I'm sure it's very different, in very many ways. But you were thinking of our division of labor, weren't you? The man out fishing while the women sew."

I try not to look startled. "Actually, yes."

"Chores are less gender-based down south, I presume. I hope so. It had been changing when I left, but it moves so slowly." Her bone needle glides through leather. "For myself, this is fine. I would rather sew than fish. It's good to have choices, though. That is what I want for them." She nods at the children. "Let Becky choose to sew or fish. Let Miles choose, too. The old ways can be just as hard on the boys, if it is not what they want."

"True. It's easy to see what choices the

girls lack, but sometimes it's tougher to see that the boys lack some, too."

Nancy brings me a cup of tea. It's regular herbal tea from ingredients found in nature, the bitterness of the brew cut by dried berries. Unlike the hostiles, the Second Settlement doesn't drink their narcotic brew regularly. This cup does, however, provide the perfect segue into the subject that brought me here.

"We've had some potential activity by the wild people," I say.

I'm about to tell them what has happened when I stop. Tell them seven people are dead? That would be national headline news in Canada. It is shocking in a way I haven't fully allowed myself to process.

This might be the biggest crime committed in the Yukon since the gold rush. And for these women, still reeling from a single murder in their community, to have me nonchalantly inform them that seven people were attacked nearby just last week?

They need to know about the danger, of course. That's what Dalton is speaking to Tomas about. I suspect, though, that he'll also realize the enormity of what he's saying before he numbers the dead. So I do the same. I tell the women that there was an attack on a group of tourists.

"And you think it is the wild people?" Josie asks.

"It seems to be, but we're investigating all possibilities. Right now, we're warning everyone to be careful. We came by today to do that, but also because I have more questions about your ritual tea. I realize I didn't get enough information the last time I spoke to your settlement about it. Specifically, I'm interested in the person who created the tea."

"The tea man, hmm?" A smile twitches the corners of Nancy's mouth. "You don't know anything about him, do you, Auntie?"

Josie sighs and shakes her head.

"He was a handsome tea man, wasn't he?" Nancy elbows Josie. "That's what I heard. Did you hear that, Auntie?"

"Are you done, child? I can wait if you aren't."

Nancy's eyes dance. "I think Josie can tell you a bit about the tea man."

"I got that impression," I murmur.

"Yes," Josie says. "I knew the . . ." She cuts a look at Nancy. "Tea man. As you can probably guess by Nancy's tittering, I had a relationship with him. A fling. I'd been in the settlement for a year, and the other men all had wives, so he was a welcome arrival."

Nancy snickers.

Josie only shakes her head and continues. "It was no great love affair. I was young. He was young enough. When he left a year later, I was sad to see him go, but not heartbroken. I could tell the settlement had only been temporary for him."

"Did he become a settler?" My mind leapfrogs forward, thinking of my theory.

"No, no. He returned to Rockton and requested passage south."

"So he was from Rockton?"

She nods.

"How long had he been there?" I ask.

"A month or two? It didn't suit him. After a year, he decided this wasn't quite what he wanted either and went home."

"That was . . . okay? With Rockton and your settlement?" She shrugs. "It was a different time. He wanted to try life out here. Rockton suggested us, and we allowed him in. After he returned, I found a pair of his boots and took them to Rockton, but he'd already left."

I double-check the times with her, confirming that he'd been in the Yukon for less than his two-year minimum before they allowed him to return down south. Is that significant? Maybe. But also, as she says, it was a different time. Rockton certainly wouldn't be recommending the settlements to residents now, no more than Josie would feel comfortable walking in with those boots.

"Can you tell me more about how he created the tea?" I ask.

She can and does. He'd spent a lot of time in the forest. He'd often be gone for days, and when he returned, he'd brew teas for himself.

"He was the only one who drank them?" I ask.

"He would allow a few others, after he'd tested the brew. Most of our teas come from him." She points at the cup in my hand. "Including that one. That's why he's known as the tea man. He didn't just invent the peace and ritual teas."

He *did* invent those, though, through a trial-and-error methodology, until he had the right blend with ingredients found close by. There'd been other formulations, according to Josie, but he'd wanted one with easily accessible components.

"Did he have any obvious expertise in botany or medicine?" I ask.

"Hendricks was obviously very well educated." She gives a gentle smile, dark eyes softening with old affection. "He reminded me of a college professor, and I would worry when he went so far into the bush. But he knew what he was doing, both out there and with his teas."

"Did you get a sense of *why* he was developing teas with . . . medicinal effects? Was it a . . . hobby?"

She looks at me and then bursts out laughing. "You mean was he the kind of guy who grew weed in his backyard and mushrooms in his basement?" Her dark eyes glitter. "I wasn't born in the settlement, Casey. I did my share of pharmaceutical experimentation down south." She catches her niece's confusion and pats her back. "You missed out on many things, child. For better and worse, and I'm not sure which *that* is. A little of both, I suspect."

Josie turns to me. "You're asking whether Hendricks was a hobby grower. Maybe even a small-time entrepreneur. My laugh may have answered the question. He was as far as I can imagine from the type. Like I said, he reminded me of a professor. A hot professor." Her brows waggle. "But a professor nonetheless. Science major with a liberal arts minor. Serious and academic. He would drink the tea to relax, but only sparingly. So why create it? Boredom."

She settles back and sips her own tea. "He had a mind that needed constant stimulation. While he insisted that he'd been an office worker, I suspect he was a scientist. I have a couple of degrees myself." She shrugs. "I was restless, couldn't figure out what I wanted to do. So I know the type, and I know the feeling. He was looking for something he didn't find in Rockton and didn't find here. He bored easily and creating teas became his pet project."

"You said he created most of your teas — the regular brews and the narcotic ones. Did you feel as if the peace tea and ritual tea were his goal? That he was looking for something more than a soothing afternoon brew? Or did he stumble on them by accident, and it was the community who wanted those perfected?"

"Hard to say. We might have shared a bed, but Hendricks was not an easy man to read. Nor was he one to share his thoughts. We argued about that. I took offense. Accused him of thinking the color of my skin meant I wasn't smart enough or educated enough to converse on his level. That wasn't it, though. We talked about many things, big ideas and esoteric trivia. Just nothing personal."

Another sip of her tea before she continues. "I'm not sure whether he intended to create the peace tea, but he seemed happy with it. We had a few residents who wanted to ban it. They worried about reefer madness — the fear that marijuana would turn people into lunatics. He argued against that, with enough facts that told me if he *wasn't* a practicing scientist, he definitely had the education for it. The other tea, though? He wasn't as happy with that."

"The ritual tea? The hallucinogenic one?"

She makes a face, and I hurry on with, "I mean the tea that induces visions."

Josie laughs. "My expression didn't mean I was offended by the use of the word 'hallucinogen.' When it comes to our faith . . . Well, down south, I went to church for the picnics and the luncheons and the singing. The sense of community. My church wasn't fire and brimstone. It was love and peace and mercy. That's what I wanted, and it's what I have here. If there is a force in the world that I think deserves our respect, it's nature, so I'm good with that. I'm just not . . . as wrapped up in the specifics of our faith."

Nancy nods, and Josie leans against her briefly, murmuring a word or two I don't catch. A shared moment of understanding.

Then Josie continues. "Hendricks didn't like the ritual tea. I don't think he'd have shared it with us except . . . Well, the original formulation didn't affect him in that way. It only caused a stronger euphoria. Others experienced mild hallucinations, so he tried to rescind it, but people already knew the recipe. After he was gone, they strengthened the hallucinogenic qualities."

"How strongly did he argue against it?"

"It concerned him, but not enough to do more than impart educational warnings about the dangers of hallucinogens."

"How soon after that did he leave?"

"Quite soon. He perfected the first tea, tinkering a bit, mostly with the taste. Once it was done . . ." She shrugs. "He lost purpose. He'd given us several drinking teas and the ritual one, and after that, he seemed at loose ends. Within a month, he was gone."

Twenty-Three

I ask more questions about Hendricks. I presumed that was a surname, but it seems to have been the only one he divulged. I get a physical description, too. That part confuses Josie. It's been over thirty years. Am I hoping to find him? No. I just want all the details I can get.

I have another question after that. One designed to zero in on the genesis of the hostiles. When the "wild people" first appeared, were any of them recognizable former members of the Second Settlement? This is not the first time I've asked. The elders avoided my questions with platitudes about how everyone has a right to choose their own path in life.

This is how their commune views hostiles. These aren't savage settlers lurking on their borders. They're just "wild people" with a different belief system and traditions, and we are in no position to judge them for it.

It's a lofty ideological goal. A bit hypocritical, I'd argue, considering their views on homosexuality, but people often argue equality for one group while failing to see how they're denying it for another.

In this case, there's a weird blinkered vibe to it, too. Like knowing your neighbor beats his wife and kids, but not reporting the abuse with the excuse that it may be a "cultural difference." The settlement adopted a "live and let live" attitude while failing to admit that the hostiles are dangerous and growing their ranks through kidnapping and brainwashing.

So I ask the question while knowing there's nothing I can do if they block me. Nancy and Tomas have a more realistic view of the hostiles — having befriended a former one — but that doesn't mean Nancy can overcome her background to speak where the elders wished silence.

Nancy looks at her aunt with obvious discomfort. Josie sips her tea, her gaze fixed in the distance, and I think this is my answer. Then she says, slowly, "Some of the early wild people were former members of our settlement. I realize the elders object to you knowing that, but they haven't forbidden it. Nancy has spoken to me about her friend, pushing me to see that the wild people may be in need of help in a way we didn't realize. In a way that makes the other elders uncomfortable."

Josie sips her tea again before continuing. "Down south, I had a cousin who took his own life, and my family insisted it was heart failure. To admit the problem would be to face our own failure to help him. The same principle applies here. If we are reluctant to admit a link between our settlement and the wild people, it is because we fear we are responsible, if not for creating them, then for treating them as fellow settlers, composed only of willing members, and turning a blind eye to anything that would suggest otherwise."

Josie wraps her hands around her cup. "They began as a group of settlers. Three of our own had left peacefully, and we traded with them. Others joined them. From Rockton, I believe. We expected the group would become a third settlement, and that seemed to be their intention. Then . . ."

"Things changed?" I say. "*They* changed?"

"If I hesitate, it is uncertainty, not evasion. They disappeared. At first, we assumed they'd gone hunting. It was summer, and they'd mentioned traveling farther afield. When we didn't hear from them by winter, we grew concerned, but by then, if they'd died — as we feared — it would be too late to help. We could only fret and grieve. It was two years later before we saw them again, and by then . . ."

She shifts on the log. "By then they were not the people we remembered. Only one was still from our settlement and she was . . . not open to communication. The elders met. I wasn't one of them at the time, so I can't speak to the specifics. I only know that after two days of meetings, the elders decreed that our brethren had 'rejoined nature,' shedding the restraints of civilization to live closer to the divine. We needed to understand they had undergone a spiritual transformation, and we had to respect their 'otherness.' Respect their obvious wishes, too. Don't communicate with them. Don't interfere with them. Allow them to live their lives as they see fit."

"You never had any violent encounters with them?"

"Yes, but that came much later, and by then, the doctrine regarding the wild people was entrenched. They were like wolves or bears, and if we had a negative encounter with them, the fault was ours, for stumbling onto their territory."

She folds her hands around her teacup. "The fault was always ours."

■ ■ ■ ■

On our hike home, I tell Dalton what I learned. When I finish, he says, "Fuck," and doesn't speak for a few minutes, as we walk in thoughtful silence. On the way here, I'd told him my theory. That's something we've had a problem with in the past. When I'm considering a new direction or a possible link in a case, I'm much more comfortable saying, "Hey, Eric. Do you mind if we go chat with some people from the Second Settlement. Why? Just . . . because."

Hold my cards to my chest until I can confirm — or refute — a potential theory, and if I'm wrong, well, there's no reason to tell him what I'd been thinking, right? Save myself the embarrassment. Which is a shitty way to treat a law enforcement partner, and if mine had acted like that, I'd have been looking for a new one.

But Dalton isn't just my partner. He's my boss, so I want to impress him. He's also my lover and my friend, and both of those also mean I want to impress him. Except he's my *junior* investigative partner. My mentee. I'm supposed to be teaching him detective skills.

It's unconscionable for me to make him

follow blindly so I can pull a rabbit from the hat and look brilliant. I'm only lucky that when he did call me on it, he was gentle, and he knows me well enough to realize it arose from my fear of looking stupid rather than deliberately cutting him out of the process.

So before we'd reached Lynx Lake, I'd shared my wild theory, and he'd added his thoughts, which helped me solidify the idea in my mind.

"You were right, then," he says when he speaks again.

"There's no proof —"

He lifts a hand. "Let me rephrase that. You did not disprove your theory. You accumulated additional evidence to suggest you may be looking in the right direction. Is that equivocal enough for you?"

I squeeze his arm. "Thank you. Yes, this does suggest I'm not as far off base as I feared. It also means . . . Shit. I'm not even sure where to go with this right now."

"Then let's talk."

We do that, walking with Storm and talking. As for my theory?

It goes back to being in the station, jokingly offering tea to Edwin. He said they don't drink it, which I knew. But then later, after hearing his story, I'd thought that the council was probably glad the Second Settlement had the tea. They were the peaceful settlement, the hippie commune, its people happily bonding with nature and drinking tea that kept them calm and content with their lot.

What if the Second Settlement didn't just randomly invent that tea? What if someone took advantage of their New Age ways and gave it to them to keep them docile?

Yes, it was a wild idea, and it made me feel even more like a conspiracy theorist. First, I think the council is responsible for the hostiles. When I'm proven wrong, I can't just admit that I was mistaken. I need to concoct a new theory that implicates them.

It's the tea that ultimately created the hostiles? Well, then, the council must be responsible for the tea.

Even if they are, that doesn't mean the council knowingly "created" hostiles. They gave the Second Settlement a mildly narcotic tea that it uses recreationally. The ritual tea was an accidental formula that Hendricks cautioned them about and, again, the settlers have been responsible with it.

The problem is that a splinter group left the Second Settlement, exactly as I'd hypothesized. They took the tea recipe and tinkered with it, and that led to a dangerous increase in potency. Yes, that's speculation, but it's also a logical extension of the facts.

What does all this mean for the crimes I'm investigating? On the surface, nothing. I suspect hostiles attacked the tourists. No answer to the evolution issue would change that. This doesn't shed any light on who killed the settlers, either. It may, however, help resolve the problem of the hostiles in general.

The council refuses to do anything about them. Not their problem. If I'm right, though, it *is* their problem. They gave the commune settlement the tea. That tea, in turn, brought about the hostiles. So, in attempting to ensure that the Second Settlement remained peaceful, they actually created people who posed a greater threat than Edwin's settlement. I'd see the irony in that, if I didn't also see the tragedy.

Hendricks seems to be a plant. His story is too odd otherwise — he stays in Rockton only a couple of months, gets introduced to the commune by Rockton's leadership, and then stays there just long enough to create the tea before being allowed to return home, far short of his two years.

The council sent Hendricks to the Second Settlement to formulate a tea from local ingredients. The question is whether the entire council was involved or . . .

Wait. There hadn't been a council at the time. There'd only been a few administrators and the board of directors.

The board of directors. Which had been Émilie and her husband and their two friends. Were they involved? Or was this something the administrators dreamed up . . .

A memory slams into my head. Last winter, when Petra had been shot by an arrow, I'd sat with her in the clinic for days while she recovered. We'd talked endlessly, and one piece rises now.

It was a conversation about Émilie. About her work with Rockton and the amount of time and money the family had devoted to the town. I'd been saying that was how Rockton should be funded. If residents had money — like me — they should pay for their stay, but the town should also seek donations from wealthy former residents, the way schools do. Émilie was the perfect example of that.

"Well, I wouldn't say 'perfect,' " Petra said with a smile. "It's not entirely altruism."

"She can't claim it as a charitable donation, though."

"Oh, I'm sure part of it becomes a write-off. But while she's definitely grateful for what Rockton provided . . ." She shrugged. "There's guilt there, too. No one donates like big pharma."

I must have looked confused, because she continued, "That's where our money comes from. Profits from the drug trade." She winked. "The legal kind."

Her family's money came from pharmaceuticals. We talked about that, including her own discomfort with it. Afterward, I realized she shouldn't have told me this. It was personal information that could identify Émilie and Petra, and for what? A self-conscious joke about the guilt of earning your fortune overcharging for medicine?

I thought medicine itself had been the reason she overshared. She'd been on painkillers for her injury. It made her loopy, and she'd inadvertently revealed more than she intended. When we never spoke of it again, I hoped that meant she didn't realize what she'd given away.

Which underestimated Petra entirely.

She knew exactly what she'd given me. If called on it, though, she could blame the pain meds.

Three days before that, she'd been lying on the ground with an arrow in her chest. We'd had no idea how deeply it had penetrated, only that she'd been shot near the heart, and she was bleeding in the snow as I knelt beside her, panicking, trying to assess the damage.

"Émilie," she'd whispered. "The . . . the hostiles . . . Your . . . your theory."

At the time, I thought she'd wanted me to tell Émilie about my theory. Clearly, Petra had been in shock, not quite making sense, her brain seizing on this meaningless bit of unfinished business as her last words.

Tell my grandmother about your hostile theory. She can help.

No, that wasn't what she'd been saying at all, was it?

That's where our money comes from. Profits from the drug trade. The legal kind.

She hadn't been telling me to work with Émilie. She'd been saying that my theory might be right . . . and her grandmother could be responsible.

Petra had been trying to give me one last gift, in case she didn't survive. Words she couldn't say while she lived, not when they implicated her beloved grandmother.

Don't give up on that theory of yours.

Look into my family. Into my grandmother.

Later, she couldn't go back and explain her meaning. But she could nudge, couldn't she? Give me another tidbit, in case I made the connection between the hostile narcotic brews and Rockton.

If I'm right, I need to confront Petra. First, though, I need to be sure I'm making the right connections.

I turn to Dalton, who has been walking in silence while I retreated into my memories. Now he slants a look my way, one that isn't quite convinced that I'll share my thoughts. I take a moment, running my hand over Storm's back as I consider how to word it. A distant shout makes me jump, but when I look up, I realize we're only about ten minutes from Rockton.

"How much do you know about big pharma?" I ask.

His brow creases in confusion, and then his face tightens in a look I know well. Like when residents make pop-culture references. It doesn't annoy him, even if his expression might convey annoyance. It's pride snapping the shutters closed before anyone mocks his ignorance.

"Pharmaceutical companies," I say quickly. "The really big corporations that manufacture prescription drugs."

"Ah," he says. "I know what they are. We've had people with that in their background."

He relaxes. "Before Beth came, we were

looking for someone with medical experience, and we had a person who'd worked for a pharmaceutical company. I made the mistake of confusing that for 'working for a pharmacy.' The council set me straight. That resident didn't know anything about drugs except how to sell them. Which I thought was an odd occupation but . . ." He shrugs.

"Some of the richest people in the world made their money off drug manufacturing."

He frowns. "There's money in that? Sure, I don't figure they give them away, but Canada has free health care. Drugs are covered by taxes."

"Health care, yes. Drugs, no."

"You mean optional medication. The ones you *need* are free, though."

I shake my head. "There are programs if you can't afford them, but medication is never free, and the drug companies are definitely in it for profit. Lifesaving drugs can cost a thousand times the manufacturing cost."

"That's fucked up."

"Yep. And that's where Émilie's money comes from."

"You think so?"

"I know so. Petra told me. Seemingly out of the blue. Big-pharma families are among the world's greatest philanthropists, and she was joking about it being guilt money. Except I don't think it was really joking. She said it a few days after she'd been shot. When she had *just* been shot, she said something about my hostile theory and Émilie, and I thought she was just going into shock."

He says nothing, just walking, his distant gaze telling me he's searching for connections, rather than asking me to supply them.

I continue. "This Hendricks guy came from Rockton, and I'm speculating that he was *sent* to the Second Settlement to create the tea from local ingredients."

"To keep them calm. Reduce the risk they'd set their sights on Rockton, like the First Settlement did."

"Right. He clearly had some idea what he was doing, and Josie figured he was a professor . . . or a scientist."

Dalton's hand tightens on mine. "Like someone who'd work for a drug company. Not selling them but making them."

"Exactly. It —"

Another shout comes, and we both stop. Storm halts, too, her ears perked as she turns toward the source. A few minutes ago, I'd heard what sounded like a neutral shout. Not anger or excitement but surprise mingled with a mild warning. Like realizing someone is about to walk straight into a tree.

We were close enough to Rockton that I'd presumed it came from there and only made a mental note to warn people against being so loud when a search party could be looking for the Danish tourists.

This shout is different. Rockton is to our left, and the only people allowed in the forest right now are the militia on patrol, who wouldn't be that far from town.

We strain to listen, but nothing else comes. I'm about to ask Dalton what we should do when another sound rips through the forest. A bellow that only comes from one creature out here.

"Bear," I whisper.

Another shout then, clearly human, spiked with panic. A young voice, and in it I hear an accent I recognize from Edwin's settlement. There's a recognizable note in the voice, too. One of Felicity's friends.

Twenty-Four

We make our way carefully toward the voices. It seems to be two men, their voices coming through as we draw near. They're shouting at a bear to scare it off. It is not scared. It is angry, and the more they shout, the angrier it gets.

I put Storm behind us. She doesn't like that, but we have no idea what we're walking into. Well, yes, we have some idea. Bear versus human. It's the specifics that elude us, and so we'll keep Storm at our rear, lest the bear spot her first and attack.

We soon see one of the settlers. A third man, perhaps in his thirties, this one not making a sound as he stands with his empty hands raised. Dalton grumbles under his breath. Your hands should never be empty out here. Even if a bear surprises you, you should have time to at least pull a knife. But this man has clearly been caught unawares, with no weapon within reach. As soon as I think that, I spot a bow propped against a tree. Why the hell didn't he grab it as soon as he saw —

"Fuck," Dalton breathes, and I see the answer to my question as I get past the tree that partly blocks my view.

At first, I'm not sure what I'm seeing. My gaze is level with the man's shoulders, and there is something right in front of him. It is a wall of brown fur, and I have to look up at least a foot above the man's head to see the muzzle of the beast.

A grizzly. Brown bears, as they're more rightly known. Alaskan brown bears, a head taller than their southern brethren. I've caught sight of them fishing. I've spotted them in the distance, decimating a berry patch. I've seen them making their way along a mountainside. I've even encountered one up close. I'd been goofing off with Dalton and darting around a fallen tree to find a grizzly rooting out grubs. In each case, the bear had been on all fours, and while I'd thought *Holy shit, that beast is big,* nothing compares to seeing a brown bear on its hind legs, towering over a grown man. . . .

Something inside me gibbers in panic, a tiny voice telling me to get the hell out of here now. Grab my man. Grab my dog.

Push them ahead of me if I have to. Just get out.

This unarmed stranger has made a fatal error, and if his companions have any sense, they will run. Let their companion's death buy them time to escape.

It is a horrible, cruel thought, a primal terror that lasts only a second before I feel the reassuring weight of the gun in my hands. My mind taps images of my bear spray and knife, tiny pats of reassurance. I am fully armed. So is Dalton. As for Storm, she has seen what we do, and thank God, she does not leap at the beast. Does not even growl. She just slips forward enough so her head brushes my leg. She recognizes that we are not in danger. Just this other man. This stranger.

As the man's companions shout instructions, Dalton says, "Shut the fuck up."

He doesn't yell it. The words still reverberate through the clearing. The only one who doesn't turn our way is the bear itself. To it, Dalton is just more noise.

"Everyone, just shut the fuck up and stay calm," Dalton says. "You're only pissing it off, and it already seems plenty —"

A growl sounds, and Dalton's head snaps up. That growl doesn't come from Storm. It doesn't come from the grizzly. It comes from behind the man . . . and I follow it to see a second bear. A juvenile, probably a yearling, already bigger than Storm.

With that we see the problem. The very big problem.

Last summer, I came between a black bear and her cub. That'd given everyone near heart failure, but we'd avoided bloodshed by getting that cub back to its mother. Also, black bears are only modestly protective of their cubs around humans. Grizzlies are a whole other situation.

The settler found himself between the two, and before he could rectify that, the mother reacted. It's pure luck that she hasn't attacked already, maybe because her cub isn't a baby. She's ready to do it, though. Just waiting for this settler to give her an excuse. Which means he can't go for a weapon, can't step aside, can't do anything except wait for her next move.

"Fucking settlers," Dalton mutters, loud enough for them to hear. "You're as bad as our residents, and at least they have the excuse that we don't let them into the forest. Hell, even most of them know you don't shout and wave your arms at a grizzly. That's for black bears, who might actually be intimidated. Does she look intimidated?"

"Eric?" I murmur. "Maybe this isn't the

time for the bear-aware lecture?"

His grunt says it's never *not* the time to teach idiots how to behave in the wild. I glance at the mother grizzly. She's fixed in place, huffing and popping her jaw. Signs of stress. She's aware that her baby isn't in immediate danger, but it isn't safe either.

"She's in a holding pattern," he says. "Hasn't made up her mind yet, and you're damned lucky there."

"I don't think he feels lucky right now," I whisper, my gaze shifting to the poor man, who doesn't dare even open his mouth to respond.

"Well, he is, especially with all that racket these other morons were making."

I look at the other two men. One is twenty, dark-haired and bearded. It's Felicity's friend, and it takes me a moment to name him. Angus. He's holding a hunting knife. The third man is older, maybe in his late forties. He looks similar enough to Angus for me to suspect this is his father. He holds a hunting rifle aimed at the bear. It's a .308 — I don't need to look closer to know that. Edwin's settlement only has .308s, so their guns will all use the same ammo.

"We were trying to distract her," Angus says.

"Moses is between the mother and her

cub," the third man says. "We hoped that by getting her attention, he'd have a chance to move."

Dalton grunts, granting them a point. "Could work. Could also just piss her off. Please tell me he has a weapon on him."

"No," the third man says. "He put down his bow and pack, and his knife is in that."

"Fuck."

"You have a gun," Angus says. "Shoot her."

"Yeah, you get a look at that baby bear? Not such a baby. If I shoot his momma, he'll attack. Also? This isn't a guaranteed grizzly-killing gun. I'd need to hit her just right."

"Then maybe you should have a bigger gun."

"I should say the same to you." Dalton nods toward the rifle. While it might make sense to carry bigger-caliber guns for just this situation, that would mean lugging around a larger gun everywhere we went on the very off chance we'd need it.

Anders actually does carry a .45, which would do the job. He's terrified of a grizzly encounter. Yet in his four years in Rockton, he's only seen two and didn't come within a hundred feet of either. For him, the gun is comfort and reassurance. For us, it'd be dead weight.

"Should I take out the spray?" I ask.

I've used bear spray against smaller predators. Getting it, however, means holstering my gun.

Dalton considers and then shakes his head. "Same problem. Maybe even worse. Spray Momma Bear, and she'll start screaming, and that'll set off Junior. Shooting would be better." He pauses. "For us, at least."

Because a clean shot in the right spot would drop the mother bear dead. That could make the youngster attack, but it could also make him run instead. If she starts bellowing in pain, though, it'll set him off for sure.

"Okay, here's what we'll do," Dalton says.

"Excuse me?" Angus says. "You aren't sheriff here."

"Oh, I'm sorry. Would you like us to leave?"

Dalton lowers his gun, and my heart thuds. I know he's making a point, but I'd really rather he did it without, you know, disarming himself in front of a *grizzly.*

"Come on, Casey," he says. "These guys have this under —"

"No." The sound comes as an almost inaudible squeak. It's the man trapped by the bear. Moses. His eyes slide our way, round with fear. "Please."

"Ignore my son," the third man says. "We appreciate your assistance, Eric. Your suggestion is . . . ?"

"You aren't going to like it," Dalton says, gun going up.

"Eric," I murmur. "Less talking, more acting."

The third man gives a ragged chuckle. "Just tell us what to do."

"Angus? That's your name, right, boy?" Dalton says.

Angus bristles, but only says, "Yes."

"On my signal, you will come over with us. Your dad will stay where he is, rifle aimed at Momma Bear. Casey? You're going to step about three paces right until you have a clear shot at her face. Let Storm do whatever she wants."

My breath catches at that.

"I know," Dalton murmurs. "But trust her, okay?" He raises his voice. "Casey and Angus's dad —"

"Leon."

"Casey and Leon? Momma is your primary target, but only if she attacks. Junior is the secondary target."

"What will you be doing?" I say.

"This is the part you won't like," he murmurs under his breath. "Moses? On our signal, you will dodge my way. Toward me and Angus. Stand with us."

"What?" I say.

He continues. "Do not run. That goes for you, too, Angus. If we run, she'll charge, and one of us is going down, and Casey will make sure it's not me. We stand together. United front. Hopefully, a bigger threat than she cares to tackle once no one's between her and her baby."

He's right. I don't like it. He may be armed, but his focus will be on Moses. It's the best option, though. This isn't a case of trying to save the bear's life. It's trying to save human ones. Miss that shot, and we have two enraged grizzlies to deal with, and at that point, it might really become that nightmare scenario of "grab my guy and my dog and run," leaving the settlers to their fate.

"Okay," I say. "Do you want me in position first?"

"Please."

I move and then Leon does. The younger bear notices. Stepping to the right means I have a better shot at the mother bear's face, but it also brings me parallel to the cub.

When the young bear eyes me, Dalton says, "Can you adjust?" while struggling to cover the strain in his voice. I do. It isn't easy. Move farther to his right and I risk getting behind the cub, who won't like that. Move farther away and I risk my shot. I edge in both directions as much as I dare. That puts me waist-high in foliage, and Dalton seems to appreciate that partial blind. He nods in satisfaction and has Angus move toward him, which the mother bear allows.

"Okay," Dalton says. "Casey, you ready?"

"I am." My gun is aimed at the mother bear's nose, for an upward shot into her brain.

"Leon?"

"Yes, sir."

It's Moses's turn. Dalton tells us that he will count down from three. I take one split second to adjust my grip. Out of the corner of my eye, I can see the younger bear. It stands on all fours, watching. Curious and a little anxious, sensing its mother's stress, but trusting that if she's not attacking, everything is okay.

Dalton counts down. When he hits one, Moses darts toward Dalton, and the mother bear roars and lunges. My finger twitches on the trigger, but my brain processes her trajectory in a split second. She's not lunging at Moses, she's lunging into the spot he's vacated, toward her baby.

She hits the ground on all fours, and the earth vibrates with four hundred pounds of force. My insides quiver, sweat dripping onto my cheek. I don't blink, though. I keep my gun aimed at the mother bear, my side gaze aimed at her youngster as they reunite, the cub bleating with joy.

I take a deep breath and slowly exhale. Storm nudges my leg, and I absently reach down to pat her head and . . .

I know my dog's fur. It's long, and it's soft. What my hand touches is coarse, thick and bristly, like Raoul's wolf fur. Hot breath exhales on my leg as I pivot my torso, keeping my legs planted. There is Storm, between me and Dalton, her gaze fixed on the reuniting bears. And beside me? A beast the size of my dog, hidden in the waist-high brush. A beast with golden-brown fur and the unmistakable rounded ears of a grizzly.

"Eric?" I say, his name coming as a squeak just as Storm turns, catching the new scent.

Storm lunges, and I yelp, "Stay!" Moses leaps to grab her even as she halts, bristling and growling. Dalton looks over, frowning in confusion, seeing nothing at first and then . . .

And then he lets out a sound, almost inaudible, a gasp and a hiss as his eyes go wide and his gun rises.

"Don't move," he says, his voice nearly as squeaky as mine.

"I'm fine," I manage. "I'm aiming." I am, too, my gun pointed down at the head. Two cubs. There'd been two yearlings, one safely hidden in the brush until I walked over, and it ambled my way. Now it's on all fours, snuffling my leg. Curious, as bears are. Trying to figure out what I am. Prey or predator? Dinner or danger?

"Eric?" I say.

"Right here. You've got this."

"I know, which is why I need you to turn that gun away."

He hesitates, and in the silence, I swear I hear him swallow.

"You can't get a good shot at this one," I say. "I need you aiming at the mother while I get out of this."

"She's right," one of the men murmurs. I don't know who it is — I don't dare look over. "She's got this, like you said, Eric. But if she shoots, that mother bear is going to charge."

"Right now this one's curious," I say. "Tell me how to let it know I'm not dinner. How to let it realize I'm a threat . . . without alerting its mother."

Silence. He's thinking fast. The question isn't fair, though, because I don't think there's an answer here. Anything I do is going to put me in the same situation Moses just escaped — trapped between mother and cub.

"I'm going to start toward you," I say. "Is that okay?"

A pause. Then, "Yes."

"I will move sideways. I will do it now. I can't wait, or Mom will figure out what's happening."

"Okay."

I take one very careful sideways step. The young bear huffs, and my heart stops, everything in me saying to run, that the mother will have heard that and —

Another step. A third. I am about to step out of the long grass when —

A massive paw swipes at my leg. It's not even a hard smack. Just a curious bat, but it hits behind my knee and catches me off guard and my legs fly out from under me.

Twenty-Five

A shout. A shot. Two shots. A snarl.

All that passes as if through a soundproofed wall, muffled and indistinct, as I grit my teeth against the urge to twist and break my fall. I wrap both hands around my gun just as I crash onto the ground, arms flying up with the jolt, gun still gripped tight and . . .

And I'm flat on my back. My head must have slammed down, because there's a moment of black and then confusion, muffled shouts and —

"Casey?" Dalton's voice, shakier than I've ever heard it. "Casey? Do not move. I have this. I swear I have this."

Something blocks the sun. I blink, brain muzzy, registering only that someone's bending over me.

Everything's okay. Dalton is bending —

A face lowers over mine. A brown-furred face. Broad nose. Tiny eyes. Rounded ears.

"Casey?" Dalton says. "I have this."

There is a bear standing over my head, looking down, face barely a foot over mine. Not the juvenile who'd knocked me down. Its mother.

A growl off to my side. One that has the mother bear's head jerking up, and a moment of sheer relief that vanishes when I see what she's looking at. Storm facing off with the young bear that tripped me.

"Eric?" I say, just loud enough for him to hear. "Call her back. Please."

He hesitates, and I know what he's thinking. Storm has the mother bear distracted as she faces off against the cub. Let the dog draw her away, and he'll protect her once I'm safe.

Shoot the bears. Save Storm. Save me.

Wait, I heard two shots, and I don't see any blood, don't hear a whimper of pain. The shots were mine. I realize that now. When I fell, I'd fired, and neither bullet hit, because as easy as it is to say "I've got this," there is a split second between pulling the trigger and the bullet hitting a target, and if that target is no longer where you aimed . . .

"Storm," I say, louder, my voice firm. "Storm, back. *Back.*"

She retreats toward Dalton. The young bear only leans forward, nose working, still curious but not approaching as Storm retreats. The mother bear turns her attention back to me.

I've used the distraction to raise my gun as high as I dare, but it's not quite right. She looks down at me. Her jaws open, and I see teeth as long as my fingers. Saliva drips onto my face. Her breath is hot, stinking of raw meat.

"Casey?" Dalton says. "I'm going to shoot."

"No."

"Yes, damn it. Now on the count of three, bring your gun up —"

"Wait."

He swears, a ragged stream of profanity.

"I'm okay," I say, and my voice is oddly calm. Am I in shock? If I am, then I might be making a terrible mistake.

"I'm okay right now," I say. "I'm going to aim my gun. If she attacks, shoot."

His laugh is almost shrill. "Yeah, that's pretty much a given, Butler. She moves another millimeter toward you, and I'm pulling this fucking trigger."

"Remember there are still two other bears. Is someone watching them?"

"I've got the first cub in my sights," Leon says. "It's staying back."

"And I'm keeping an eye on this one,"

Moses says. "Your dog is, too."

"Thank you," I say. "Now let me raise my gun."

Again, I move it millimeter by millimeter. The bear doesn't even blink. Her face is upside down over mine, jaws open just enough for me to see teeth that could rend flesh and crunch bone. I don't think of that, though. I channel Dalton, and I force myself to *see* her, really see her. The gleaming thick fur and bright, intelligent eyes. She's barely out of hibernation and thinner than she'll be later this year, but she glows with health, a far cry from any bear I've seen in captivity. I listen to the sound of her breathing. I inhale the musky scent of her. I feel her hot breath on my face.

I will never be this close to a grizzly again, and so I will frame this moment in memory because I *will* survive to remember it. My gun is now high enough that one pull of the trigger will end the threat. I will survive, and I will look back with wonder and awe, and so I force myself to experience that now, slowing my heart rate and sharpening my focus.

If she wanted to kill me, I'd already be dead. Same as Moses. I've seen bear attacks in movies, where you get between a mother and her cubs and she attacks like an avenging angel. That isn't what's happening here.

Her cubs are not babies. She is not starving. She's not at full weight or energy yet either, and she is intelligent enough to know that this will be no easy kill. Five humans and a dog. The odds are not strongly enough in her favor. So she is thinking. Considering. Assessing. And all we need to do is make one wrong move, one wrong noise, and she will attack. But for now . . . Breathe. Just breathe.

Her eyes lock on mine. As for the gun, it is a mere extension of my puny, clawless hands. It's my eyes that she watches, as if knowing that's the key to dealing with humans. Watch the eyes. Their true weapon lies behind it.

I keep my eyes wide and clear and calm, even when a string of drool hits my brow.

"Casey?" Dalton says.

"I've got this."

"I don't like —"

"I know. Has she moved?"

Hesitation. Then a reluctant "No."

"Am I on target?"

A grunt now, frustrated that I'm being calm and logical when everything in him itches to pull his trigger. I know that because it's what I'd be doing if he were the one lying here.

Just let me shoot, damn it. Forget the other bears. This is the one with her jaws a foot above your face. Let me shoot.

"It's okay," I murmur, as much to the bear as to him. "Everything is okay."

The bear huffs. It's a soft sound, though. Discomfort and mild stress.

"You want this to be done as much as I do, don't you?" I say. "You want to walk away with your family, and I want to walk away with mine, and we don't quite know how to do that."

Her eyes flick, but she doesn't move.

"Casey?" Dalton says. "This is a stalemate."

"I know."

"We need to end it."

"Not yet."

I swallow as carefully as I can. As hard as I'm struggling to stay calm, anxiety strums through me. Focus. Just focus and stay in the moment.

"Do the cubs have an escape route?"

"Yes. The first is to your left. No one's near it. Storm's watching this one, and he's still too fucking curious but . . ."

"He's calm?"

"Yeah."

"Then let's wait."

Dalton grumbles under his breath, but he

knows that if he were lying here, he'd say the same. The situation is temporarily under control.

"You can go," I murmur to the bear. "No one will stop you. Take your babies and go."

Of course she can't understand, but I'm hoping the tone of my voice will tell her I'm not a threat. I continue talking, just as I would to a suspect holding a weapon on me. She stays right where she is, hot breath streaming down on me, jaws closing and then cracking open, drool dripping. I think I see a change in her eyes, a gradual easing of tension. Then, just when I'm sure I'm imagining it, she huffs and swings her gaze on Dalton.

My heart stops. My finger tenses on the trigger. I've had it there the whole time. This isn't a situation like with Sophie where my finger stays clear until I decide to shoot. I might not get that extra moment if she attacks.

When she looks at Dalton, my finger tenses reflexively, but she only eyes him. Storm comes next, the bear's gaze assessing the canine. Then she checks the first cub, the one safely on my other side. Out of the corner of my eye, I see it clawing at a dead log. It's grown bored of the situation and started digging for a grub snack. Its sibling shows signs of the same boredom, having sat down to scratch its ear.

The mother bear huffs one more time before letting out a grunt that almost has me pulling the trigger before I realize she's calling to her cubs. Then she lumbers to my left, so close her hairs brush my leg as she passes. Another grunt to get their attention, and she continues into the forest, the cubs falling in line behind.

I don't move. I don't even think I breathe. I lie on my back, gun aimed at the spot where I last saw them. Everyone stays perfectly still, listening as the bears lumber through the forest. It is only when the sound fades to the softest rustle of distant foliage that I sit up, and then Dalton's there, lifting me up into a hug so tight I can't breathe and I don't want to. I collapse against him, my entire body quivering, and he just keeps murmuring "Okay, okay, okay," like a mantra, as much for himself as for me.

You're okay. We're okay. Everything's okay.

I take a deep shuddering breath, and he does the same, our exhales in perfect syncopation. Storm nudges my leg, whining, and I reach down to pat her head while Dalton keeps his arms locked around me. At least a few minutes pass before he sets me on the ground, and we both holster our weapons.

"I got to see a grizzly up close," I say. "Really, really close."

He lets out a shaky laugh and smiles, arms going around my shoulders in a squeeze. "You did."

"It was awesome."

"Not quite the word I'd use."

Another hug, and then I catch a glimpse of Angus and remember we aren't actually alone here. I straighten, and Dalton takes my hand and turns toward the settlers —

There is a gun pointed at us.

Leon's rifle, pointed right at us, Moses beside him, arrow nocked and aimed at Dalton.

TWENTY-SIX

I spin fast, hand going for my gun, certain the bears are emerging from the forest, but Moses says, "Miss Casey? Please don't do that," and my hand stops and I see no sign of any bears behind us.

"What the fuck?" Dalton says. "What the actual fuck?"

"Please lift your hands," Moses says.

"You're shitting me," Dalton says. "Tell me you're shitting me, because if you are actually holding a gun on my wife after she just risked her life —"

"Calm down, Eric," Moses says. "Please calm down."

Dalton sputters, unable to even respond beyond a few half-formed profanities as his face purples with rage.

"What's going on here?" I ask slowly.

"We need your help," Moses says.

"Our help?" Dalton's voice rises, booming through the forest. "You want our fucking help? Pretty goddamn sure we did just help you. Saved your fucking life and Casey nearly got killed doing it. I don't know what this is about, and I don't actually give a fuck. You have five seconds to lower those weapons and *apologize,* or as far as I'm concerned, the First Settlement is as much a threat as the fucking hostiles. Do you understand me?"

"We aren't going to hurt you, Eric. Not you. Not Casey."

"Then lower your fucking — !"

"We need one of you to come with us. As our guest."

An unintelligible string of profanity from Dalton.

I lift a hand to stop his tirade. "We have been through this bullshit before with Edwin, when he wanted a hostage to ensure our help finding a killer . . . a killer who, I will point out . . ."

I turn and look straight at Leon. I don't need to say another word. The look on his face — the guilt and pain — almost makes me regret bringing it up. Almost.

"This is not how you get our assistance," I say. "We allowed it that one time, only because someone volunteered. Apparently, that set a dangerous precedent. I understand Edwin wants this problem with the hostiles resolved, but we do not need the incentive of a hostage. Tell him —"

"You tell him," Angus cuts in. "Better yet, give him back and give Felicity back, and we won't need to take any hostages."

"What?" I say.

"Fuck," Dalton mutters. "Let me guess. Edwin and Felicity haven't returned from Rockton, and you think we're holding them hostage."

Moses shoots a look at Angus. "We are not accusing anyone. All we know is that my daughter and my father-in-law went to Rockton and didn't return."

"Daughter . . ." Dalton breathes. A quick glance at me. "Fuck."

"Okay," I say. "Everyone's freaking out and we all need to calm down. Yes, Edwin and Felicity came to Rockton. We spoke to them, and they left." I lift my watch. "Almost four hours ago — half a day." I look up at Moses. "I understand that you're worried, but think about it. What possible reason would we have for taking them hostage?"

"Yeah," Dalton says. "Best way to deal with complaints is to lock the person up. Then go investigate the case they came to complain about. Makes perfect sense." His hard gaze sweeps the trio. "Edwin is an asshole, and I don't want him around a minute longer than necessary."

"Then you've hurt them," Angus says. "You're a very angry man, and you lost your temper and hurt them and now you're holding them captive."

"A very angry man," Dalton mutters. "Nah, kid. Right now I'm a fucking *furious* man. Because the assholes we just saved turned their weapons on my wife — two minutes after she escaped a grizzly bear."

"Nobody in Rockton hurt Edwin or Felicity. I think you two" — I nod to the men — "know that. You realize they left town of their own free will. The problem is that they've gone missing, and if you return home and say so, people will presume we took them. You need to be able to say you crossed that off the list first, by coming home with me in tow as a hostage."

"Except you *don't* actually need to do any of that," Dalton says. "You could just thank us for saving your asses and then tell us what happened, and let us help you figure out a solution. All that works a helluva lot better when you aren't holding a gun to our heads."

"We need leverage," Moses says. "Whether you have Edwin and Felicity or know something about their disappearance or can help us find them. You will do none of those things without cause."

"Interesting hypothesis," Dalton says. "You know the problem with a theory? It remains theoretical until you actually fucking test it. You refuse to collect the empirical evidence required to make this one anything more than a goddamn *theory.*"

A look passes behind Moses's eyes. It's the same one Dalton gets on hearing unfamiliar words — that mingling of confusion, shame, and anger — and I'm about to cut in when Dalton says, "Test your damn hypothesis. Ask us for our help. See what you get."

"Make him stop talking," Angus says. "This is what he does. He talks and he talks and he talks, with big words to make us feel small." He steps forward, knife raised. "Stop talking."

"Or what?" Dalton says, meeting his gaze.

"I'll make you stop. By cutting your tongue from your head."

Dalton's gray eyes chill. "So your sister wasn't the only —"

Angus lunges, knife flashing. Dalton's fist slams out, hitting him in the arm, knocking the knife aside, and then, in a blink, he has Angus in a choke hold and I have my gun out, and there is a moment of chaos —

everyone shouting — and then silence. Utter silence as everyone freezes into place.

Dalton has Angus on his knees, arm around his neck. Leon points the rifle at Dalton. I point my gun at Leon. Moses's bowstring is taut, weapon aiming first at Dalton and then at me and then back. It is as Moses pivots, trying to choose a target, that he stops, shoulders tensing, a sharp hiss of breath whistling through his teeth as he spots something. He pivots his bow —

"Don't," Anders says.

"Hey, Will," I say. "Nice timing."

He stands behind Leon, his gun to the back of the man's head. His gaze darts my way, a smile chasing it. "It's all about the timing, Case. And knowing when you're shit at sneaking up on people, so you wait for a bit of noise to cover your advance."

A throat-clearing to my left reveals Sebastian pointing a rifle at Moses. I look at the gun, and then I look at Anders, who shrugs. While Dalton had agreed to let Sebastian try militia duty, I'd suggested not being too quick to give him a weapon. Apparently, not knowing the boy's background, Anders had decided to ignore that advice. We'll have to talk about this later.

For now, though, I must admit that Sebastian is doing exactly what I'd expect.

He's calm and collected, pointing that rifle at the correct person, finger off the trigger, the barrel steady, no sign of nerves. I'm not sure Sebastian *has* nerves, though he can fake them when it's in his best interests. His true self is this — terrifyingly coolheaded.

"I decided to take the kid on patrol," Anders says. "We heard shots earlier and came running to find these guys holding you at gunpoint."

"We're fine. Just shaken."

"Well, you're lucky, because we spotted grizzlies. Three of them. They were off in the distance, though."

My lips twitch, but I say nothing.

Dalton looks at his deputy. "You almost done? Or do you want to chat about the weather before you get this asshole to point his rifle away from my fucking head?"

"It is nice weather, isn't it? Bit cooler today, but the sunshine makes up for it."

Dalton glares at him.

Anders only grins and shrugs. "I'm the deputy, boss. It isn't my place to give orders while the sheriff is right here and not physically inhibited from giving them himself."

Dalton grunts and shakes his head. "Leon? Aim that fucking gun somewhere else."

Moses lowers his bow, but Leon only tenses.

"Yeah, that's a bad idea," Dalton says. "You've now got a third gun trained on you, Leon, one held by a young man without a whole lot of experience in trigger control."

Leon's gaze swings left, and he gives a start, seeing Sebastian for the first time. He doesn't lower his rifle, though, just says, "I'd appreciate it if you release my boy first, Eric."

Dalton grunts. "Not actually how this works when you're outgunned, but I'm gonna let you have this as a sign of good faith."

He kicks Angus's knife to his father's feet and then gives the young man a shove in the same direction. Angus scrambles up and spins on Sebastian.

"You," Angus says. "This — this is the boy I told you about." He swings on Moses. "The one who's been wooing your daughter."

"Wooing?" Sebastian's brows shoot up as he lowers the rifle. "Is that like flirting? Or more like dating?"

Angus's face purples, and amusement dances in Sebastian's eyes. I shoot Sebastian a warning look, but he only grins my way.

"Either way," Sebastian says, "it's incorrect. Felicity and I are friends. You just don't like that because you're the one who wants to go a-courting . . . and she's not interested." He slings the rifle over his shoulder and holds out a hand to Moses. "You're Felicity's dad, then? Nice to meet you. I'm Sebastian."

Moses shakes his hand. There's a wariness in his eyes. Veiled curiosity rather than hostility. Maybe a hint of trepidation. Felicity has mentioned Sebastian, then, and Moses isn't quite sure what to make of the blossoming relationship. His expression reminds me of the mother grizzly's when she'd been staring down at me.

Are you a threat to my baby?

I don't think so, but I'm not sure, and I need to be sure.

I do not doubt for one instant that Sebastian spots and correctly analyzes Moses's reaction. Sebastian is an alien placed on Earth, knowing he must emulate humans if he is to survive. I consider myself skilled in the interpretation of body language, but when I'm with Sebastian, I feel like I do when I watch Dalton navigate the forest — witnessing a skill level I will never reach, because for me, it will always be a matter of interest, never one of survival.

"My name is Moses," Moses says after a moment. "This is Leon and his son, Angus, who I believe you've met."

"Briefly." Sebastian eases back with his most disarming smile. "He doesn't come around much. Shame, really. As much as I like Rockton, it's nice to hang out with people my own age."

Sebastian turns to Dalton. "Did I hear something about Felicity and her grandpa?"

A smooth segue, punting the ball in the direction it needs to go. And then, with a look, Dalton lobs the serve my way. Yes, Sebastian was correct to send it to him first — as the sheriff — but Dalton recognizes that he might not be the best person for this conversation, not when he's still seething.

"Felicity and Edwin are missing," I say.

Sebastian's eyes widen, and I can't tell whether he'd already overheard that or not. "After they left Rockton?"

I nod. "Did she say anything to you?"

He shakes his head and looks over at Moses. "Felicity and I were hanging out while Edwin talked to Eric and Casey. I did make some comment about whether her grandfather was okay with the long walk. She said they stopped to rest, and that's where they left the villagers who'd accompanied them. They planned to do the same on the walk back. I'd guess that's where they are — resting — except that I'm also guessing you guys are the ones they were meeting."

"We are."

"Where were you meeting?" I ask.

They tell me, and it's roughly three-quarters of the way from their settlement to Rockton. They'd been hunting there while they waited. Edwin had arrived in Rockton around eleven this morning. He'd left a couple of hours later. He should have reached his escort by midafternoon.

At that time, we'd been at Lynx Lake. Moses, Leon, and Angus had headed toward Rockton. They made it almost to the town with no sign of their leader. As they'd been deciding their next move, they'd heard Dalton and me talking, our voices carrying in the quiet. They'd headed out to intercept us. Moses decided he still had time to pee, stepped away to do that, setting down his bow . . . and found himself between the mother grizzly and her cub.

I glance at Anders. "When were you last in town?"

"An hour ago. The kid and I were patrolling maybe a hundred feet in when we heard the shots. We'd been close to town up until then. So, no, Edwin and Felicity didn't come back, presuming that's what you're asking."

"It is, thanks."

I don't ask whether there's a chance Edwin left the path for a bit of hunting. He was an old man with a very long walk ahead of him. He wasn't adding any extra activity to his day.

So now, on top of everything else, we had two people lost in the forest.

Except there was zero chance they actually were lost. Even if they stepped off the path for a rest, they'd find their way back to it easily.

They've been taken. I don't say that. I just exchange a look with Dalton and then turn to the men.

"We'll help you find them," I say. "Storm here is trained for tracking. While we are busy handling the hostile problem, we recognize that this is an emergency, and so we'll divert our resources temporarily. As a gesture of goodwill between our communities."

"We still need one of your people to come with us," Leon says.

"Oh, for fuck's sake!" Dalton explodes. "Really? Are we back to this?"

"If it was your wife missing, Eric, and we promised to help, you'd want some assurance of that."

"No, actually, I wouldn't. I'd appreciate

the offer, but I'd understand you don't owe me shit."

"You do owe us. Edwin and Felicity were taken because of you. Because of the trouble you've stirred up with the hostiles."

"I didn't drag Edwin's wrinkled ass —"

Moses cuts him off. "You are wrong, Eric, when you say you wouldn't require assurances if the situation were reversed. If it was the best way to get your wife back, our promises would not be enough."

Dalton starts to argue, but Moses shakes his head. "Whoever we take will be treated as an honored guest. We promise that."

"The more time we argue, the colder the trail gets," Anders says. "Casey needs to work with Storm, and Eric's our human tracker. So . . ." He turns to the men. "You get me."

Their gazes slide up and down him, taking in his height and the size of his biceps.

"I . . . believe we can come to another arrangement," Moses murmurs.

Anders chuckles, but Dalton only advances on Moses. "You're right. We can. And that other arrangement is that you turn around and go look for your leader and hope — just hope — that we don't say 'fuck you' and continue investigating our case, leaving your leader and your daughter in the goddamn forest."

"Take me," Sebastian says.

Dalton spins on him. "No. Just no. Stop this shit. First him" — a finger jab Anders's way — "and now you. We are the ones in charge here. We have the guns. We have the dog. They don't have jack shit, and they need to remember that."

"But I'd *like* to go with them," Sebastian says softly. "As their guest. Think of me that way. Not a hostage you need to worry about, but a line of communication between the communities as they sort this out. I'll take Casey's dirt bike if she'll let me. I can ferry messages back and forth. And . . ." A sheepish look Moses's way. "It's a chance to get to know Felicity's people. As her friend."

"What?" Angus squawks. "You *are* wooing her." He spins on Moses. "You see that, don't you? He wants you to get to know him better so he can ask for Felicity's hand."

Sebastian shrugs. "I'm not looking for a wife. I just want to get to know her family."

It's impossible to fake a blush. That's a physiological reaction no one can force. But there are ways to emulate the same look without the actual coloring, and Sebastian does an Oscar-worthy job of it. His eyes drop, his gaze slipping just a bit to the side.

It's not just that. His brows lower, and his

expression would do a blushing maiden proud, demure and just a little coquettish. His stance, though, is far from maidenly. He holds himself straight and tall, head turned to his best advantage, muscles flexed.

Sebastian's appearance is so average that, on a college campus, he'd be one of those guys whose name you never remember. Blandly innocuous. But he's pleasant-looking, with a lean build that's been putting on muscle since he arrived in Rockton. The outdoors agrees with him, too; he's like a plant kept indoors far too long, bursting into glowing good health in the sun and fresh air.

That's what he's putting on display here. Youth and health. A young bull in the cattle market. Healthy and strong. No signs of deformity or breeding issues. Good, viable stock. Because that's how Moses is looking at him, and Sebastian knows it. A potential suitor for his daughter. A potential mate for his daughter.

If the settlements have one problem, it's a lack of external bloodlines. That's the reason Edwin finally relented when Sidra brought Baptiste home. He might not like her husband being from the other settlement, but at least there was no question of inbreeding. That's what Moses is thinking here. A healthy, strong, intelligent young man who cannot possibly be related to his daughter.

Sebastian is setting him up.

"Sebastian?" I say. "May I speak to you a moment?"

He follows me off to the side. He doesn't jog after me with his usual puppylike enthusiasm. He strides purposefully. A strong-willed young man who recognizes authority but retains his self-assurance in the face of a possible reprimand. Keeping up the persona he wants to present for Moses.

"What are you up to?" I ask once we're out of earshot.

Anyone else would feign surprise, confusion, maybe even irritation at the accusation. Sebastian only grins, unperturbed.

"Nothing bad," he says. "Don't worry."

"I didn't think it was something bad," I say. "Which doesn't mean I'm not still worried."

His grin grows. "Good call. But in this case, you don't need to be. I'm defusing the situation in a mutually beneficial manner."

"Uh-huh."

"I go with them, of my own volition and against Eric's wishes, so it's clear he didn't cave to their demands. I take the bike — if that's okay — so I can leave anytime I want.

And, yes, I can run messages between you. Also, if I really am an honored guest — which I think I will be, if I play this right — then I'll get access to things you and Eric can't. Information on the settlement."

"So you're spying."

He shrugs. "If you want to call it that, sure. But also . . ." Another shrug, one shoulder lifting. "I'm worried about Felicity. The settlers are being assholes, and they're pissing off Eric. I want to shove past the stalemate."

I eye him.

"I promise not to hurt anyone unless my own safety is at stake," he says.

"It's not them I'm worried about. They might call you a guest, but you're still a hostage."

He winks. "I can look after myself."

I still hesitate.

"They didn't want Will because he's big and scary. They'll take me because I'm neither of those things. Which proves they are shitty judges of character all around, so we might as well use it to our advantage, right?"

I nod and wave Dalton over to make the final decision.

Twenty-Seven

Sebastian will go with the settlers after he gets the dirt bike. Also, the settlers may not "escort" us back to Rockton. If Sebastian really is a guest, they'll accept that.

As for Edwin and Felicity, the settlers will conduct their search, and we'll conduct ours independently, which keeps them from breathing down our necks.

Moses agrees. So does Leon. Angus is furious, but he's too young to have any say in the matter. Maybe his hostility should make me worry for Sebastian's safety but, like Sebastian said, he can take care of himself. I may feel weirdly protective of him, but he isn't a child.

We're quiet on the walk back. Anders keeps glancing at Dalton, and then over at me, his mouth tight with worry. What happened back there was a shit show, and Anders doesn't even know the half of it. I'll tell him the rest later.

We saved the settlers, and they turned on us while we'd been recovering from the shock of the bear attack. They'd demanded a hostage and, while we've been clear that's not what Sebastian will be, Dalton still feels as if he's lost ground here. It's not so much about the hostage as the fact that they won their original goal — getting our help — and there's not a damn thing we can do about it. What's our other option? Abandon Edwin and Felicity to prove a point?

See, you can't boss us around. You need to ask nicely. Otherwise . . . well, sorry for your loss.

But Felicity deserves better. If only they'd asked. That's all it would have taken to resolve this happily. We save Moses from the bears. They tell us their dilemma. We magnanimously offer to throw our resources into helping them. We come out as heroes and good neighbors, and everyone's happy.

Except everyone wouldn't be happy with that scenario, because it would place Edwin's settlement deeply in our debt. Instead, sure, we helped with the bears, but they cleverly secured our assistance afterward.

The endless balance of debt and obligation. Who owes whom. People out here will risk their own lives to keep from dipping too low on the scale. Dalton cannot abide that. Burn the damn scales and act like civilized people who recognize we're all fighting the same battle and should help each other when we can.

It doesn't work like that. It should, but it does not.

As we walk, Anders isn't the only one glancing at Dalton. Sebastian checks, too, and while his face never gives anything away, I know he's concerned. Worrying that he's made this situation worse. When we near Rockton, he asks if he can speak to Dalton while they get the dirt bike, and we let them go. Storm glances at me. She senses Dalton's mood, and she's asking permission to stay with him. I grant it with a wave, and she jogs after them, her huge paws pounding the ground.

Once they're far enough away, I tell Anders about the bears. Shock turns to outrage. Demanding a hostage to secure our help was heinous enough. Add the fact that we rescued them first, and it's the worst kind of betrayal, backing Dalton into a corner where he can only do what feels like surrender.

Speaking of betrayals . . .

I spot Petra heading back from her shift at the general store. A few hours ago, I'd been making my way to Rockton, hell-bent on confronting her with my suspicions. Now, seeing her, there's a moment of "Hey, didn't I want to talk to Petra about something?" before it all crashes back.

I take one step in her direction before checking myself.

"Everything okay?" Anders murmurs as I stop short.

No, everything is miles from okay. This particular problem, though, must wait. Spring days may be long, but they are not endless, and it's past six already. We need to find Felicity's trail, and I cannot get distracted by confronting Petra. Also, I cannot confront Petra and then walk away, leaving her with the chance to tell Émilie what we know and let Émilie — possibly both of them — fly beyond my reach before I can return.

Would they flee? That's the question. Whatever they've done, the council will undoubtedly back them. Yet the council isn't here. In their shoes, as much as I'd like to stand my ground, I'd know that the smart thing to do would be to get out of Rockton. Fast.

"Throwing Émilie in jail for the night would be a bad move, wouldn't it?" I murmur. "Politically, I mean."

Anders glances over. "Uh . . . not even

sure I want to touch that one."

"Have you seen her?"

"Not since she left the station earlier." He glances at me and lowers his voice. "If you want her locked up, we'll do that, but you might want to talk to Phil first. See how bad a move it would be. I can't believe I'm suggesting consulting him but . . ."

Anders is right, of course. We'd need to ask Dalton, too, but he'll agree without a second thought. If I think a suspect is a flight risk? In the cell they go, no matter who they are. It's Phil whose opinion I'd need. I won't ask, though, because even I know it would be a very bad idea. I'm only voicing a wish while letting Anders know we need to keep an eye on her.

I'm saying that, as quietly as possible, when Petra spots me. I tense, and Anders murmurs, "You want me to head her off?"

Will I be able to resist confronting her? Yes, with effort. Can I hide the fact that I *want* to confront her, that something is wrong? Probably not, and if I don't, then I tip my hand, and we might very well come back to find Émilie and Petra gone.

I should tell Anders yes. Run interference, please, and distract her while I escape. Yet even that could be a tip-off, however deftly handled. And there is another way. A way to divert her and make sure that, even if Émilie bolts, she won't take Petra with her.

"Hey," I say.

"Hey, yourself. Everything okay?" Her gaze trips over my clothing, and her lips twitch in a grin. "Looks like you and Eric took the opportunity for a little couple time in the woods."

I glance down to see just how dirty and rumpled my clothing is.

"Bear," I say.

She stops short, grin freezing. "What?"

I shrug. "I was tripped by a young grizzly. Landed flat on my back. It's okay, though. Momma Bear considered devouring me and decided against it."

"I . . . I think you must be joking but . . . you're not, right?"

"Nope. It's been a very long day. And now I could really use your help finding Edwin and Felicity."

Another blink, as if she's still not hearing right. "The old man and the kid? They were here, right?" She pauses. "Does this have something to do with the bears?"

"I really hope not. The more likely suspect is hostiles. Or a search party looking for the missing hikers. Or, possibly, whoever killed the settlers and the tourists, if it wasn't the hostiles."

"I . . ." She looks at Anders. "This all makes sense to you, does it?"

"Sadly, yes," he says.

"So," I continue, "what I really need is you, Petra. I'd like you to help us find Edwin and Felicity. I know you aren't a tracker, but if they've been taken hostage, I might need your particular skill set."

"Sure. When do we leave?"

"As soon as possible. I'm just going to check in with April and see how the patient is doing. Then I'll grab a takeout dinner. We want to catch as much daylight as possible." I pause, as if just now considering something else. "Wait. Émilie. Will she be okay by herself?"

Petra chuckles. "She flew here by herself. Believe me, she doesn't need me to feed her. I will pick up something for her, though. She's been resting."

"Taking it easy?"

She hesitates long enough for me to know she suspects there's more to it. Then she shrugs and says, as nonchalantly as possible, "That meeting took a lot out of her. She said it stirred up memories, and she needed some time. That's why I went into work. I had the day off, but she very clearly wanted to be alone with her thoughts, and my apartment isn't big enough for that."

"Huh. Are you sure she's okay?"

"I'll check in when I drop off dinner."

"Should I send April by later?"

"No, no —" Petra stops. A heartbeat of a pause that says so much before she forces lightness into her tone with, "Sure, that can't hurt, right? Émilie will say she doesn't need it, but she won't argue. I'll tell her April will stop by. No need for your sister to set a specific time. Émilie won't be going out."

If April could come by at any moment, Émilie must stay put. Yet Petra was fine leaving Émilie home alone, though, so maybe I'm reading too much into this.

Anders offers to pick up food for the search party, and I let him do that while I go talk to April, and Petra heads home to speak to Émilie.

There's no change in Jay's condition. He's stable and still comatose. As I'm talking to April, I notice a report on the counter. It looks like an autopsy, but the name on it is Sophie's. I pick it up, and before I can read anything more than a few words, April snatches it from my hand.

"You will receive the report when I complete my examination."

"Why are you autopsying Sophie? We know how she died."

"It is not a complete autopsy. Now that she is deceased, I am free to more thoroughly examine her wounds, which may provide greater information on the earlier attack she suffered."

"Ah. Okay, then. Thanks."

April relaxes, though her answering nod is abrupt. Did she think I'd give her shit for taking initiative? Rockton is all about initiative. If you have spare time and you want to go beyond the call of duty, by all means, go for it, even if only to satisfy idle curiosity. Staying challenged keeps the cabin fever at bay.

That's a conversation for later, though. Right now I'm just here to check on Jay and ask April to stop by later for Émilie, and then I'm zooming off to find Dalton and get our asses on the trail.

Anders has the militia mustered for extra patrols, but we don't want them going too deep into the woods. Mostly they're just listening and watching, in case an attack on Edwin and Felicity preludes an attack on Rockton.

The search party is only three people and a dog. That's for our own safety. Each of those three has a gun. Each is trained to use it. No dead weight allowed on this mission. Dalton and Storm are our searchers. I'm in charge of Storm. Petra is our guard, allowing us to focus on the hunt.

We don't have time to eat before we head out. It really is grab-and-go, the only exception being Storm, who ate and rested while we bustled about preparing.

We've asked Sebastian to walk out with us. We part ways about a half kilometer from where the settlers wait, where he hops on the bike and goes. From there, while we can't hear the conversation as he meets them, we'll hear trouble. We don't.

We set Storm on the trail right out of Rockton. She knows Edwin, and while he's never paid her much attention, she's happy to track Felicity.

We asked the settlers to wait down a side trail for Sebastian, and when we'd returned to Rockton post-bear, we'd avoided the main path. That kept the scent as pristine as possible for Storm.

Now we backtrack to that main route and have Storm pick up Edwin and Felicity again. The problem with a scent trail like this is that they walked all the way to Rockton, and then headed back on the same path. Figuring out where they stepped off the path is trickier than if they'd been diverted on the way *to* Rockton. Fortunately, Storm has been trained for this. She won't just keep her nose to the path. She'll be looking for places where a leg of the scent trail branches off.

That happens almost as soon as we rejoin the main path. Storm signals that the scent veers right. Dalton has already seen the same diversion; a freshly cracked bush branch and disturbances in the dirt tell him someone left the path. I let him take the dog as Petra and I wait. A minute later, he's back, saying, "Piss break," and we continue on.

Another hour passes. It's a quiet walk. That isn't easy for me. Petra is right beside us, and I so badly want to confront her about Émilie. Yet the more noise we make, the more we risk alerting anyone who might be around.

When I notice Dalton's gaze surveying the wider landscape, I murmur, "Everything okay?"

"Ridgeback Peak," he says, nodding to the right.

I pause two heartbeats. Then it hits. We're in the rough vicinity of where we found the dead tourists. It's also where Cherise and Owen found the settlers. I hadn't realized it because we took a different route then.

I murmur an explanation to Petra. She

hasn't asked for one. Anders jokes about being a good soldier and not questioning orders. I suspect Petra is even more accustomed to that, having been in the line of work where you complete your task without always understanding the rationale. Sometimes, she'd have been better off not knowing. Plausible deniability.

We slow our pace while Dalton studies the undergrowth. When a distant rumble sounds, our gazes swing up, and my first thought is *plane.* It's only a matter of time before someone comes looking for the missing tourists, and we feel that ticking clock. There's no plane, though. Just darkening clouds to the south.

"Please don't roll this way," I murmur.

Dalton grunts his agreement. A storm would disturb the scent trail. For now, those clouds seem to be staying in place, the rumble of thunder equally distant.

I'm turning back to the path when Storm's head snaps up. Her nose rises, sniffing the air. There are two types of scents a tracking dog can follow: ground and airborne. The former indicates a past trail — sloughed skin and hair wafting to settle on the ground. Airborne, though, means you're picking up an active scent-emitting target.

"Is it a person, Storm?" I ask. "Person?"

She knows this question. We've had to train for it, hour upon hour of presenting her with both human and animal scents, until she could reliably tell the difference. She keeps sniffing, nose raised, and lets out a tiny whimper.

Yes, human.

Dalton's scanning the undergrowth. His grunt says he doesn't see a breaking point — a spot to indicate someone left the trail here. That only means they might have gone in farther down. He paces, looking for a spot to get through the dense brush. He finds one and motions for Storm's leash. I pass it over and he takes the lead, cutting a path into the forest for us to follow.

Ahead, Storm strains at the leash. She's well enough trained that no scent will have her tearing into the forest. The leash only signals that this is work.

We've gone maybe twenty feet when a sound makes my stomach explode with panic. My knees lock and my throat dries up.

A snuffle. The low snuffle of what sounds like a bear. That panic explosion assures me that while I may seem to be coping with what happened earlier, I am not past it. My psyche has done me the favor of tucking that trauma aside so I can proceed with my day . . . until I hear this wet snuffle.

Thankfully, no one notices my overreaction. Dalton is in front of me, Petra behind, and she only bops into me before stopping. A noise in her throat says she catches the same sound. Dalton has, too, and he's stopped, gun rising. In the front of the pack, Storm has gone still. Or so it seems until I see her back quarters quivering.

Something moves twenty feet ahead, on the other side of a bush. Brown fur shimmers, and my heart thumps double time. My grip on my gun slides as my palms sweat.

Dalton scans ahead. I do the same. We won't be caught off guard this time. There's no sign of a second beast, but it's dense forest, and we can only make out that fur-shimmer of the first.

Dalton passes the leash back to me. I'm to stay where I am while he investigates. A wave tells Petra to circle wide and cover him. As I take the leash, he glances back and our eyes meet. He catches something in mine that makes him do a double take, and I cover my fear with a reassuring nod.

He returns my nod, and then his gaze is back on the bush, now shaking as the bear brushes against it, still snuffling, the occasional snort mixed in. Then a grunt that tells me it's eating.

The beast is distracted. That's good. Stay distracted.

Dalton pauses and then chooses his direction. Petra fans out farther. I wrap the leash around my hand and then take a careful step in the other direction. Another step. Another. I'm trying to get a visual on the bear's head without attracting its attention.

One more step, my gun raised, as my gaze sweeps the scene, making sure we aren't missing a second bear —

I stop, heart slamming as I catch sight of something on the ground. A brown lump. My mouth opens to get Dalton's attention, but there's no way to do that without alerting the feeding bear. I swallow hard and step to the right, ducking to peer under the foliage.

A long length of tan tops the dark brown lump. My brain tries shoving the image into bear shape, but it doesn't fit. I blink, and then I realize what I'm seeing. A boot and a leg and, above it, the dark hump of a body. Someone lying in the clearing. Lying on their back, while a bear is ten feet away, feeding —

I clamp my jaw shut against the urge to warn Dalton. My stomach twists, but I know I can't say a word. I also know, as horrifying as this is, that it doesn't actually matter what the bear is eating. Not at this moment.

I stare at the boot and I struggle to remember what Felicity and Edwin had been wearing.

With Storm on a tight lead, I step forward until I can make out the shape of the bear's head as it yanks back, a sickening wet noise as it rips into its meal, snorting and . . .

I see hair not fur. Bristly hair and upright ears and a snout longer and smaller than a bear's.

"Hie!" Dalton shouts, and I swear I jump two feet in the air. "Hie, hie!"

He rushes forward, a dark shape charging at what I now realize is a boar. The beast tears past us. Storm whines and dances in place, but I don't release her.

This isn't my first encounter with one of the wild pigs. Technically, they don't exist in the Yukon, but years ago, Rockton experimented with livestock, including a crossbreed for northern climates. The herds had escaped and gone feral.

I keep my gun aimed at the fleeing porcine as it crashes through the undergrowth.

"Hey, Casey," Petra says as she tramps toward Dalton. "You had a perfect shot there. Could have caught us some bacon."

"I don't think anyone would have wanted it," I say, cutting my gaze toward where the boar had been feeding.

"Why — ?" Another step, and she can see what I meant. "Oh God. I . . . I don't think I'm going to be eating forest-pork ever again."

A man lies on the ground. A stranger with a bloody gaping wound at his stomach where the boar had begun eating.

It's a hostile. The clothing, the rudimentary tattoos, the mud-smeared face and matted hair — they all leave no doubt. The man's face is scored with deep gouges and there's a bloody divot in his temple, where someone struck a fatal blow.

My chest tightens, and I spin toward what I'd seen earlier. The sight I'd almost forgotten.

A boot protruding from the undergrowth. Tan khakis over that boot, a leg ending in the heap of a human body. A second body.

"Fuck," Dalton exhales.

I move toward the man on the ground. It is a man. A stranger, I can see that from here. He's covered in blood and dirt.

Despite the modern clothing, he could be a hostile or settler, having stolen the clothes from the Danish tourists. His hands tell me otherwise. So does his hair — worn a little long, but fashionably so. Despite the blood and dirt, it's not the hair of someone who lives in the forest and makes their own soap.

The clincher, though, is the hands. There's blood under his nails, those nails have been manicured, and his fingers are smooth. Not the digits of a man accustomed to chopping logs or hauling water.

The man lies on his back, eyes half open, mouth agape. Staring up at the forest as he breathed his last. Blood plasters down his hair. His shirt is bloody and shredded. A knife attack.

There's also a rock clenched in one hand.

The hostile attacked with a knife. The man managed to hit him in the head with a rock and kill him, then collapsed over here and died alone in the forest. He defeated his attacker, but too late to give him more than a moment of satisfaction.

"Two feet," Dalton says.

I blink up at him.

"He's got two feet. Two boots."

That means he's not the missing fourth member of the Danish tourist party. This man is dark-haired, and the leg we'd found seemed to have lighter hair, but that wouldn't have precluded it being the same guy. This man, though, clearly has all his appendages.

He seems dressed like the Danes, but on closer inspection, I amend that. He's dressed in a *similar* manner. Khakis, hiking boots, lightweight shirt. Except the brand name is one I wear myself, the kind of good-quality outerwear worn by serious outdoors types, unswayed by trendy brands.

I tell Dalton.

"Shit." He rocks back on his heels, looking down at the dead man. "Searcher?"

"I really hope not."

I reach into the man's pocket, leaning over him to get my fingers in at the odd angle. When I touch something like an ID wallet, I tug . . . and the man jerks up, gasping.

Twenty-Eight

I yelp and scramble back, crablike. Dalton swings his gun on the man, and Petra does the same. The man is flat on his back again, his eyes half open, mouth open, exactly as he'd been a moment ago.

"We . . . all saw that, right?" Petra murmurs. "The dead guy leaped up."

"Yes."

"Like something in a horror movie?"

"Yes."

She gives a tight laugh. "And instead of jumping for joy, we all pulled our weapons on him?"

"Except me," I say, my voice still shaky. "I just shrieked."

"It was a very small shriek."

Storm approaches the motionless man and snuffles him.

"I believe the dog has a question," Dalton says. "Like why are we standing here talking when there's a dead man who isn't actually dead?"

We're all staring, as if waiting for him to lever up again, maybe give a zombie moan. Even as I crouch beside the man, Petra and Dalton keep their weapons aimed.

I pause over the man, overcome by indecision so strong I could almost laugh at the ridiculousness of it. I should be jolted into EMS mode, jumping in to evaluate his condition. I mean, he's obviously alive and in need of medical attention. But I'm weirdly unsure of how to proceed. Talk to him? Shake his shoulder? See if I can wake him? Or just start a medical examination, risking giving him another jolt of shock, maybe one strong enough to stop his heart?

"Hey," I say, tentatively, and to their credit, neither Dalton nor Petra laughs.

I lay my hand on the man's shoulder and give a soft squeeze. "I'm here to help, okay?"

Again, it's ludicrous dialogue. The guy isn't dozing. He's . . . Well, I don't know what state he's in, which is the problem. His eyes are half open, mouth ajar, and that is not the look of an unconscious man, yet he's been that way since we arrived, which made us certain he's dead.

Is he brain-damaged? In severe shock? I need my sister here. I really do. I'm looking at a man who has almost certainly undergone some sort of neurological trauma, and we have a neuroscientist in Rockton. But that doesn't help when she's a two-hour walk away, and he may be in severe medical distress.

I grip his shoulder tighter. "I'm going to examine you, okay?"

No response.

"Can you hear me?"

No response.

I adjust my position, shifting in discomfort. I'm certain I'll make the wrong move, and both Petra and Dalton are relying on me to get this right.

"Is he definitely alive?" Petra whispers.

It seems like a silly question. We saw him sit up. I'm 99.9 percent sure that can't happen as a postmortem reflex, and now that I'm up close, I can see the artery pulsing in his neck. He is alive. But there's physical death and there's brain death. Is it possible that this man's brain is only alive enough for that physical reaction to being touched?

I need April. I need her so badly, and I don't care how much side-eye she'd give me for these questions. I'll take it, if it means I don't make a mistake here and shock-kill a living victim.

"He's breathing," I say. "That's all I know."

I raise my voice, as if hearing impairment might be the problem. "I need to examine you. I'm going to start by touching your head to check for skull fractures."

That seems the most likely answer, given his mental state and the blood in his hair. With extreme care, I touch his skull, where there's a thick clot of blood. I verbalize my every move — *I'm going to touch your head, I'm going to clean this wound, I'm about to press a damp cloth to your forehead.*

He doesn't react until I wipe at the blood. Then his eyes fly open. That's it. Just those open eyes, staring at nothing as I jerk the cloth away.

We all go still, no one even seeming to breathe. The man blinks. Once. Twice. I'm opening my mouth to speak when he croaks, "Is someone there?"

I ease into his line of vision, but he doesn't react. Just that wide-eyed stare past me.

"Shit," Dalton mutters.

The man's head swings Dalton's way, and then he pushes up onto an elbow.

"Hello?" the man says.

"We're right here," I say, as calmly as I can. "My name is Casey. I'm with a camp nearby. I have two other people with me."

His head swings, following my voice. "I can't see you. It's too dark. I need a light."

I look up at the soft yellowish light of early evening. Then I take a deep breath. "I . . . I think you've suffered a head injury. You appear to be temporarily blinded."

Is it ethical to say this when I have no idea whether it's temporary? Maybe not, but it'd be a hell of a lot less ethical to panic a man when I don't know how badly he's injured.

"You're okay," I say. "We found you, and you're okay. I was just examining you before we get a doctor."

Silence.

"Can you understand me?" I ask.

He nods.

"You've suffered a head injury," I say. "Your eyes look fine. It's probably just trauma. Do you remember what happened?"

"I — I was attacked. Some guy from the forest. He looked like . . . I don't even know what." He swallows. "I've heard stories. About crazy folks. Criminals. Killers. People who escape into the woods out here, and I thought they were just stories but . . ."

"All right. I have questions, but first I need to examine you. You've been stabbed."

He shakes his head. "Not stabbed. Just sliced up." A hollow laugh. "Suddenly, that distinction seems really important."

Another swallow, and he sits upright and rubs his eyes. "Go ahead and examine me, but I suspect I'm okay other than this . . ." A wave at his eyes. "The guy clocked me in the head. With a rock, I think. Snuck up behind me. I fell, and he seemed to think I was unconscious, so he flipped me over. I jumped up, and he came at me with the knife. I'd put my pack down, so all I could do was follow his example and grab a rock. After he slashed me a few times, I managed to hit him and . . ."

His voice trails off, coming back in a whisper that is half awe and half horror. "I don't even know how I did it. Something inside me just took over. An instinct for survival, I guess. I hit him, and I just kept hitting him until he went limp. Then . . ."

He shakes his head. "It's a blank after that." He pauses, that empty gaze lifting to mine. "Is he . . . ?"

"He is."

A moment of silence. Then, "What was he?"

"We can talk about that in a minute. I know you don't think you're badly injured, but I'd like to examine you. We found you while searching for other people. If you're badly hurt, we'll abort that search to get you to a doctor. If you're okay for now, though . . ."

I look up at Dalton, who gives an abrupt nod. While getting this poor guy to April might seem like the obvious next move, if he's stable, we need to consider Felicity and Edwin.

"My injuries can wait," he says. "But go ahead and double-check."

"Thank you. If you're fine, one of us will stay with you, but we were following their trail, and we'd hate to lose it."

The man nods. "I understand."

I ask his name — Colin Berger. Then I remove his shirt. His injuries do look worse than they actually are. There's a lot of blood, but it's surface damage. I don't even see any cuts in need of stitching.

"You aren't going to ask who we're hunting for?" Dalton asks after a few minutes.

Colin's head jerks up, tracking the voice.

I don't stop Dalton from asking the question. I should have asked myself — I'd been too focused on the man's injuries to realize it's odd he didn't question us about the search.

"For the Danes, right?" Colin says. "Or, at least I certainly hope you are, and I definitely hope you did find their trail. I've been hunting for two days without a trace."

"What's your interest?" Dalton asks.

"Not sure I need an 'interest' in finding missing hikers." Colin's tone cools. "But I know folks out here can be private, so I'll respect that. I dropped them off last week. They were . . ." He rubs his chin. "I'm a pilot and I love my job, but I hate how many people like them we get."

"They were difficult?" I ask as I plaster the worst of his cuts.

"Yes and no. As customers, they were damn near perfect. Paid their deposit. Showed up on time. Didn't make any demands. The problem is inexperience. Oh, sure, they've done plenty of backwoods hiking at home. But they don't understand the sheer scope of this wilderness. Part of me always wants to refuse to fly people like them. But if I did, someone else would. As long as they have some experience and proper equipment, I can't rightly say no. Doesn't keep me from worrying they're making a huge mistake. I lost a couple of Germans about five years back. Ever since then, if they don't have a satellite phone, I bury the rental fee in my charge and insist they take it and call me every forty-eight hours. My buddies joke I'm a mother hen but . . ." He shrugs. "I haven't had so much as a scare since the Germans. Until now."

"When did the Danes stop calling?"

"I last heard from them six days ago. When they didn't make their next call, I wasn't too worried. They were late with the first call, too. I gave it forty-eight hours more. Then I called them. I hate doing that. It crosses a line, you know? Treating clients like children. Also, the last time I did it, the people complained on their online reviews. That's a lousy excuse but . . ." Another shrug. "Every little bit counts."

"So you called the Danes, and they didn't answer?"

"It went straight to the warning message. There's no voice mail, but a message will tell me if it's powered off. I told myself not to overreact. Yesterday, though, was the day they were due to be picked up, so I flew my ass out here damn quick."

"And they weren't there," I say.

"We had a midafternoon pickup. That gave me a few hours to search after I was sure they weren't just running late. I slept in the plane and headed out first thing this morning. It was maybe noon when that . . . person attacked."

Colin pauses, his gaze lifting in Dalton's general direction. "You *are* tracking my clients, right? Please tell me yes."

Dalton grunts. The guy takes that as confirmation and nods.

"We're losing our light," I say. "I'm going to stay with you while Eric picks up the trail again. Storm?"

Colin blinks. "Shit. That's right. There's a storm in the fore —"

The dog brushes against him, and he jumps.

"Sorry," I say. "There's a dog here. Storm. Our tracker."

He gives a shaky laugh. "I thought I smelled a pup, but I figured I was hallucinating."

"There's another person here, too."

"Paula," Petra says.

I nod. "I'm going to leave Paula with you for a minute while I speak to Eric."

I've been picking up the hints that Dalton wants to talk. I tell Storm to sit beside Petra, and then I slip off with Dalton, getting far enough away that we can still see them, but they can't overhear us.

"So . . ." he says. "He seems okay?"

"Physically? Or his story?"

"Story seems legit. Matches what we can see — clothing and whatnot. I'd like to check his pack . . ."

"Easy enough to do when he can't see you."

A short grunt of a laugh. "Yeah. You think the blindness is temporary?"

"Only April would know, and even then, it'd be an educated guess. I want to say it could be temporary damage to the optic nerve, but I'm not sure that's an actual thing or just me quoting a line from a novel."

Another snort as he smiles. "Yeah. I was thinking the same thing. Must have read the same book. I'll check his pack. I meant, does he seem okay physically? I know you'd say if he didn't. I'm just . . ." He rubs a hand over his beard. "I don't like leaving anyone alone in the forest, after what happened to him."

"I know. I'll remain behind, but Petra can stay with me. We also have the blind guy."

"I trust *him* more." He shakes his head. "Nah, that's not true. Petra saved you from an arrow last winter. You'll be fine. I'm just fretting."

"He *is* injured. Maybe we should take him back to April. I could be underestimating the damage. Especially with that blow to the head."

"Now you're just humoring me." He slings an arm around my neck and leans down to press his lips against my cheek. "You have Petra. I have Storm. We'll both be fine, and the longer I fret, the less daylight I'll have." He squints into the sky.

"I keep telling myself those dark clouds aren't moving closer."

"So do I." I squeeze his hand. "Go on."

Dalton quickly checks Colin's pack before he goes, but it's a cursory look. I want more. I motion to Petra to distract Colin. She does an excellent job of it, simultaneously engaging his attention and making enough noise that I'm able to slip the pack aside, go through it properly, and then return it before he even realized I'd stepped away.

I found exactly what I'd expect. Well, no, he's missing one important item — one that makes me wonder whether he's almost as inexperienced as his clients. He doesn't have a gun. No handgun. No rifle.

While I'd never set foot out here without one or the other, though, that only shows my law enforcement bias. Colin has a big hunting knife, and he likely considers that sufficient protection. It would be, too, if he'd been carrying it when he was attacked.

He also has bear spray, which I will argue is equally pointless when you leave it in a zipped knapsack. Still, wilderness experience can be measured on a continuum, and with a large knife, bear spray, food, water, and a sat phone, he does have the essentials. He's even carrying a first aid kit.

I also find ID showing him to be Colin Berger, a small-plane pilot out of Whitehorse. Before I return to Petra, I hunker down and consider what I've found. Consider the implications of it. I haven't had time to do that, and I wish now that I had before Dalton left.

The fact that Colin is blind is, in the most callous terms, a godsend. We could conceivably bring him into Rockton for treatment and then back out again without him getting a good look at the town. Just as long as he doesn't regain his sight.

That's a horrible thing to wish for, isn't it?

Oh, I certainly do hope you get your sight back, Colin. But could you hold off until we get you back to civilization? Thanks!

Even if he regains it in Rockton, we can deal with that. Once he's ready to get out of bed, we can slip him a sedative and let him wake up in a hastily erected encampment outside town, where he can recover — briefly — and then we'll escort him to his plane. And, maybe, if we can finagle it right, we'll tell him we've stumbled over the remains of the tourists in the interim, so he can take those home with him.

Off you go, Colin. So sorry about your clients. Good thing you managed to kill that crazy mountain man who murdered them!

Yep, that makes me feel like a callous bitch. Doesn't stop me from liking the plan, though. We'll take good care of Colin, and we *will* find who killed his clients. That's far from callous.

I slip back into the clearing as Petra says to Colin, "Hey, we haven't asked if you're hungry. I have a protein bar in my pack."

As I return his pack to its spot, my gaze catches the dead hostile. I hadn't forgotten him. It's just . . . well, he wasn't going anywhere.

I head over to him, saying, "I'm going to check out the guy who attacked you. Can you tell me anything more about him?"

"I was kind of hoping you guys could," Colin says. "Like what the hell he is." He shifts. "Sorry. I mean, obviously he's a man, but the way he attacked, it was . . ." He shivers. "Like he was a wild animal."

"Tell me more about that," I say as I bend beside the hostile.

Colin explains as I examine the dead man. I don't see any evidence that he isn't a hostile. Maybe that should be obvious — looks like one, acts like one, smells like one — but after what happened with that settler family, I'm extra careful.

Striking the back of Colin's head with a

rock is classic hostile modus operandi. He'd hit hard enough that he expected Colin would at least be incapacitated. When he wasn't, that caught the man off guard, and he blindly slashed with his knife.

I find the knife still clenched in the man's hand. It's a homemade weapon, as I'd expect.

There is nothing in the attack to suggest anything except a hostile. The man didn't cry out in perfect English when he realized he was in mortal danger. He isn't carrying a hidden gun in his waistband. His matted hair is real. The tattoos and ritual scarring are real. It's all real. A real hostile, and a real hostile attack.

I rise and —

And there is someone in the forest. A figure, watching me. I can make out what looks like a young man. I see a face, that's all. A smooth-cheeked male face, light brown skin, dark hair, and wide eyes, staring at me like he's just spotted a hostile. I open my mouth and take a step forward —

"Casey!" Petra shouts.

Even as she calls out, I catch a blur of motion as another figure charges from the opposite direction.

Twenty-Nine

I wheel, my gun rising as I bark "Stop!" at the same moment Petra fires. It's a warning shot, and it does what it's supposed to — halts my would-be attacker in her tracks.

It's a woman. A hostile. She looks to be in her sixties, with graying hair, but she might be as much as a decade younger. She stares at me, lip curled as her face darkens with blazing hate.

"You," she snarls.

"Stay where you are," I say.

"Or you will shoot?" she says, her voice guttural and hoarse, but her words clear. "Shoot me, too?"

"Yes, I will shoot. But I'd like to speak to you, since you seem to be able to do that."

"Able to talk?" She sneers. "You mean that I am not an animal? Will that make it harder to kill me?"

"Not if you attack me." I motion for Petra to hold her fire. "Now —"

The woman's gaze drops to the dead man at my feet. Her blue eyes widen. Then she howls and rushes at me. I kick her away before Petra decides to shoot.

"I didn't hurt him," I say as she staggers back. "That wasn't me."

Her gaze swings past Petra to Colin. A flash of recognition, telling me they must have been stalking him. In a heartbeat, she realizes who killed her companion, and she flies at Colin, screaming.

I shoot her. It's all I can do. My bullet hits her in the shoulder and whirls her around. She catches her balance to see Petra's gun and mine both aimed at her. She's lucid, and she knows what those guns mean. Her hand claps over her shoulder wound.

"I can treat that," I say. "Just —"

She backs away, growling. That sets me back. Despite the snarls and the curled lip, she has, until now, struck me as more "human" than any hostile I've met. That growl, though, is a pure animal sound. It takes me a split second to recover, and by the time I do, she's bolted into the forest.

I take off after her. Behind me, Petra shouts my name. Tells me to get the hell back there or —

A thunder boom cuts off the rest. Ahead,

the woman is running, hand to her shoulder, weaving through the forest as if she's suffered a mere scrape.

"I know you can understand me!" I shout. "Just let me —"

Movement to my left. I wheel so fast my boot slides, and I have to grab my gun with both hands to keep hold of it. I may fall, but goddamn it, I am not letting go of my weapon.

Steadied, I survey the forest. Lightning flashes across the sky. As it fades, it is as if someone flicked off the lights. Those ink-black clouds roll in, swallowing the evening sunlight and casting me into near dark. The wind whips past, my ball cap smacking up and then dangling from my ponytail. I don't reach to fix it. I don't dare. I saw movement in the forest. I know I did, and now I can see nothing but trees and shadows. I strain for the running hostile's footfalls. Everything has gone silent.

I've run straight into a trap.

No, not a trap. I might actually feel better about that. This is an ambush of my own creation. I saw from the woman's reaction that she knew both the dead man and Colin. They must have been tracking him, and she became separated from the dead man. It isn't only the woman out here, though. I'd seen a young man, and while I hadn't thought he was a hostile, I hadn't seen enough of him to be sure.

When the injured hostile ran into the forest, what did I do? Gave chase, ignoring Petra's shouts and curses. Ran into the forest even as I knew — beyond a doubt — at least one other person waited here. I'd known it . . . I just hadn't processed what it meant. That I could run straight into an entire troop of hostiles.

I breathe deeply. I don't see anyone yet. I'll start backing toward Petra, gun raised, gaze canvassing for even the slightest movement. Listening, too, for a cracking twig, for the swish of soil underfoot.

All that would be so much easier if it wasn't nearly dark out here, if the thunder wasn't rolling overhead, if drops of rain weren't splashing my face. I can look and listen all I want, but if I can't see or hear —

A sound behind me. I spin, gun pointed. No one's there. I know I heard something, though, and when I squint into the dusk, I realize it won't be Petra and Colin. I've chased my target farther than I intended.

Lightning cracks open the sky, and in that split second of illumination, I see someone to my left, crouched and watching me. A hostile between me and Petra. Waiting for me to run back toward them.

Another sound. No, not a sound. The sense of a person to my right. I turn twenty degrees that way, so I can still see where the first hostile waits, now hidden in shadow. When I spot someone to my right, I give a start.

He's right there, less than ten feet away. It's the young man. Hope leaps. Hope that he's a settler, an ally. Hope that detonates as I take in his makeshift clothing and his wild hair.

But he's so young.

God, he's so young.

That trips me up, my brain screaming that I am mistaken. This cannot be a hostile because they don't have children. Yet he's not a child. He's Sebastian's age. To me, though, all I see is a boy, one who should be in college or starting his first job, and *how the hell did you get here?*

That's the question screaming in my head, blocking rational thought.

How did you get here?

And how do I help you get out.

Those whispers of rational thought remind me he is *not* a child, not trapped, not in need of my help, no more than kids I saw in the streets when I was a cop. Still, that never stopped me from seeing them and thinking the same thing.

How do I help you get out of this?

Maybe that's basic human empathy or maybe it's projection, seeing myself at nineteen, trapped in an alley, going down under a rain of blows, waking in a hospital to be told I might never walk again and then walking out . . . and putting a bullet through the heart of the guy I held responsible. At that age, I'd been so lost and so alone. I saw those street kids, as I see this boy, a distorted reflection of who I'd been at their age, trapped in their eyes.

How do I help you get out of this?

That passes in a split second before, thankfully, I remind myself I am in the forest, during a storm, surrounded by hostiles, and this boy is one of them. I have my gun in hand, and I should point it at him. I should let him know I will use it. I will kill him. Yet my hands don't move.

The boy stares at me. There's no malice in his gaze. Certainly no rage. He's staring at me, eyes clouded with what I saw the first time we met Maryanne. The confusion that only comes with a glimmer of recognition, as if he's saying to himself, "Something about this situation is familiar, and I don't know why."

Maryanne looked that way when she saw

Dalton. The expression on this boy's face, though, isn't quite the same, and I may be misreading it entirely. Seeing what I want to see.

"I'm not —" I begin, but he slices a finger under his throat. It could be a threat. I know it isn't. It's the sign for urgent silence.

He shakes his head, eyes widening to confirm I'm not misidentifying his gesture. He is afraid the others will hear. That they will realize he's close enough to attack . . . and he has not.

He lifts his finger to his lips. Then his gaze sweeps the landscape. I know there are hostiles nearby — at least the injured woman — but they remain out of sight. The rain beats down, sky dark and rumbling, and in that moment, it is only the boy and me, standing in the rain, both on guard, every muscle tensed as water sluices over us.

He motions for me to approach. I adjust my grip on the gun and mentally tap the knife at my side, reassuring myself it's within easy reach. As I approach, though, he moves to the side. That gives me pause, and my gaze shoots past him, looking for an ambush. No, he's just getting out of my way.

I jerk my head, telling him to come closer. He doesn't even dignify that with a response. I have a gun, and I suspect even if I didn't, he wouldn't risk his companions seeing him with me. I still take a step his way, but he backs up fast, his hands rising.

Come with me, I mouth.

He shakes his head. I doubt my face is more than a blob in the pelting rain, but no matter what I'm saying, the answer is no.

"I can help," I whisper as loud as I dare.

Head shake. Hands raised. Then a finger pointed left.

Whatever you're selling, lady, I'm not buying. Not today. The door is over there. Have a lovely day.

I can't linger. I saw what happened to Colin. Whether the hostiles are responsible for the death of the Danish tourists or not, they are still dangerous as hell. This boy is offering me a safety hatch, and I need to take it. Now.

"Find me later," I say aloud. "Please."

Without answering, he slips away. Then I'm gone, moving fast through the rain, watching my feet, watching my surroundings, telling myself I am fine. As if I can see more than a couple of damn feet in front of my face as the rain slams down in torrents. As if I'll hear a twig crack over the constant rumble of thunder. As if I'll sense someone there even with my brain preoccupied, worrying about Petra, worrying about Dalton and Storm, worrying about that damned kid I just left behind.

I keep moving until I spot the pale blur of Petra's face and blond hair, and it's a good thing I do, because otherwise, I'd have walked right past, my treacherous brain insisting they were fifty feet to the right of where they actually are. I pick up speed and reach her in a few heartbeats.

She's poised over Colin, her gun raised to protect him. When she sees me, she swings that barrel my way with, "Stop right there!"

"It's me!" I call, and then add, "Casey!" as if I could be a hostile in disguise. She shifts her gun to cover my approach.

"Is she gone?" Petra says, never stopping that slow surveillance.

"Yes, but there are others."

"Huh. What a surprise."

I don't answer. She knows me well enough to realize I'm already smacking myself over my mistake.

"How many?" she says as I back into position on Colin's other side.

"I saw the woman and a kid, but the kid's not a threat."

She snorts.

"He's not an *immediate* threat," I amend. "He helped me get away. There are probably more, though."

I'm not sure how much of that she hears in the rain. I realize only then that she's moved Colin. I orient myself by the dead hostile, who is now farther to my right than when I left. Colin's sitting with his back against the biggest tree in sight.

As soon as I ran, she strategically repositioned so she could protect them both. Colin is behind a tree, with thick brush to one side, impossible to pass, allowing her a 180-degree window to watch. Now with me, we can each cover half of that while Colin sits between us.

We stay poised and silent, as the rain pelts down, thunder gradually rolling away, lightning falling farther behind, until the rain is only a steady drumbeat and the sun peeps through cloud cover.

Soon the sky brightens to twilight. One last bit of illumination before the sun will sink past the horizon.

"They're gone," I say. "If they were going to attack, they'd have done it during the storm."

Petra spins on me. "What the hell were you doing?"

That gives me a start. Apparently, her silence was only a reprieve, granted because arguing while under ambush would be stupid.

"I made a mistake," I say. "Let's drop it. Right now, I'm worried about —"

"You are always worried about someone," she snaps. "That's the problem, Casey. You're out here searching for a man you don't like and a girl you barely know."

"I know Felicity quite well," I say. "Also, they aren't the people we were looking for." I cut my gaze down at Colin, warning her against saying too much.

"Right, you were looking for total strangers. Risking your life for them, and then risking your life to help an *attacker.* Oh, I'm sorry, did I shoot you? Let me help fix that. Wait, come back!"

I say nothing. She grunts, as if in satisfaction that I'm listening, while a kernel of rage rolls in my gut, growing with each revolution.

"These people aren't worth your time," she says. "They've chosen —"

"Maryanne chose nothing," I say, my voice low.

Petra has the sense to flinch at that, but only rolls her shoulders and says, "All right, Maryanne was there under duress, but that doesn't make them *all* your problem."

"No, they're the problem of whoever gave

the Second Settlement that tea."

She blinks. It could be confusion at the seeming segue. It is not. That blink evaporates every foolish hope that I am wrong.

I am not wrong about the tea. I am not wrong about Émilie's involvement. I am not wrong that Petra knows, and that she's been watching me like I'd watch Storm when she was a clumsy puppy searching for a particularly well-hidden treat.

Petra egged me on and tossed clues my way. She patted me on the head when I got one right, all the while certain I'd never get the whole thing, but gosh, I was so adorable to watch, wasn't I?

Now, instead of pretending she has no idea what I'm talking about, she just looks at me, waiting. Waiting to see if the puppy has figured it out.

"The First Settlement revolted," I say. "Two Rockton residents died. Later, when the Second Settlement left, they seemed harmless enough — modern-day hippies — but no one dared take the chance. Not when it'd be so easy to take advantage of that hippie vibe and source them a locally grown happy tea. That's where your grandparents came in, with their big-pharma company. Send a researcher to source the brew and convince the commune to drink it. Sounds reasonable, right? No harm in that."

She still says nothing. Just listens.

"I agree," I say. "No harm in that. It's a bit patronizing, but the settlers weren't forced to drink the tea. They made a choice. And when someone breaks away from the group and tweaks the recipe and things go awry? It was an unforeseeable consequence. The fault lies in the cover-up. In turning a blind eye to what happened next. In telling every goddamn sheriff that they were imagining wild people in the forest. In hearing stories like Maryanne's and saying 'not our problem.' Worse, hearing those stories and telling us it's not our problem, that we shouldn't help. You're right, I shouldn't run into the woods after a woman who attacked me. But maybe, just maybe, I can't help it because I feel complicit."

"You aren't."

"The hell I'm not. We all are — everyone who knew and did nothing, said it wasn't our problem."

A moment's silence. Then she asks, slowly, "So what are you going to do about it?"

Is my grandmother in danger? That's what she wants to know. Am I a threat to Émilie.

I'm opening my mouth to answer when I notice the man sitting between us, and I give a start, as if he's appeared from nowhere. I'd wiped him from the scene. It's me and Petra, butting heads as he sits silent and invisible, out of our line of sight.

Colin sits quietly, like a kid overhearing something juicy when his parents have forgotten he's in the room. Keeping his mouth shut and hoping they don't remember he's there.

He's heard, and I panic until I replay my words and realize how little I've actually said. No names. No details. Just vague references to settlements and some kind of tea. I'm sure he realizes that's what I'm blaming for the wild people we just encountered, but it is indeed like overhearing a parental conversation, most of it flying past without context. Tantalizing glimmers of secrets and nothing more.

"I'm sorry, Colin," I say stiffly. "You don't need to hear any of that."

"You think you know what's wrong with these people, right?" he says. "Then you should help." An empty-eyed look toward Petra, half puzzlement, half wary concern. "I don't know why anyone would say otherwise."

"No one is," I say. "It's just an internal dispute. Now —"

A bark. My head jerks up. There's not a split second where I wonder whether that bark comes from any canine but Storm. It's not just that I know my dog, it's that a Newfoundland's bark is very distinctive, especially when they're in distress, and that's what I hear. Storm's deep woof of warning and rage and fear.

"Don't you dare," Petra says.

I turn and lift my middle finger between us. Then I walk away. I don't run — she'd only accuse me later of running blindly into the forest at every provocation. I wouldn't give a shit about what she thinks except that she has the power to get me fired, get me sent back down south.

I have never been more aware of that than in these last few minutes. Petra isn't simply a resident. She isn't just a comic-book writer or a friend. She's a spy whose grandmother might be at the top of the Rockton food chain. That last gives her a power I hadn't recognized because she hides it so well, taking on a shop clerk position in town, pulling her weight, accepting a tiny apartment. Camouflage, all of it, and I failed to see the threat hiding in the center.

So I walk from that clearing with a brisk and purposeful stride, as if I've just decided to go patrol the area. Nothing alarming, certainly not the fact that my dog is freaking out in the forest, a forest filled with angry hostiles, where she's alone with the man I love. Nope, none of that. One agonizing step after another until I'm far enough away. And then I run.

THIRTY

On that run, I imagine every horrible scenario, and I will my muscles to move faster, my damn fucked-up leg to do better, driving myself through the rain-soaked forest, slamming down each foot hard, as if that will keep me from sliding. I run, heart hammering, the sun dropping as I strain to listen in the silent forest.

The barking has stopped, and my first thought was *Good, they're fine.* Then other scenarios play, all the ways that a cessation in barking means anything but "they're fine."

I'm tearing through the woods in the direction I last heard Storm, and I'm telling myself that I'm still aware of my surroundings, despite the near darkness, despite the blood pounding in my ears. I'm certain I'm fooling myself, until a movement to the side has me spinning, gun up, and I see Dalton and Storm running toward me. I don't ease my stance until Dalton waves.

As I jog to meet them, my gaze scans both, looking for injury. The only thing I see is that they're both soaked, Storm a black mop impersonating a canine and Dalton dripping wet, his T-shirt sculpted to his body in a way that makes me temporarily forget I'd spent the last ten minutes running in abject terror. He catches me looking and laughs.

"You checking me out, Butler?"

As relief washes over me, I grin wider than the soft teasing warrants. "Looking good, Sheriff. Wet T-shirts suit you."

"I'd say the same back, except I can't see your T-shirt under that sweatshirt. You look like a bedraggled kitten. Adorably bedraggled."

He starts to put his arms around my shoulders, but I throw mine over his, hugging him tight.

"Hey, you okay?" he asks, hugging me back.

"I should be asking you that. I heard Storm freaking out. Let me guess, just a fox or a hare, right?"

His pause tells me no, and I know better anyway. That was no animal-spotting bark.

"Ran into a couple of hostiles," he says. "Well, didn't run *into* them, thankfully. A woman and a guy. I heard people moving through the forest, thought it might be Edwin or Felicity, and we surprised each other. Had a bit of a standoff. The woman was hurt, though, so she backed off fast. Storm helped convince her."

He lays a hand on the dog's head. "The woman didn't seem to know what to make of our pup and wasn't eager to find out. The guy followed her lead."

"Was he young? Maybe twenty?"

"Nah. Forty or so?" He squints down at me. "That was a bullet in her shoulder, wasn't it?"

"I didn't have a choice."

"Shit." His arms tighten around me.

"I think she came for the guy Colin killed. She saw he was dead, freaked out, saw Colin and *really* freaked out."

Dalton curses. "They must have been tracking him together."

"Exactly what I figured. Anyway, I'll explain later. Right now, if you're safe, we need to get back to Petra." I pause. "I may have gotten a little pissed off at her."

"Ah."

"Yep, I planned to confront her, but not quite like that."

"Did she deny it?"

I shake my head. "No denial. No anger. Totally calm and collected."

"Bitch," he mutters.

"Right?" I say. "Damn her for not waving a gun in my face, telling me I've got it all wrong and if I tell anyone my crazy theory, I'll be sorry." I hug him again. "Thank you for understanding that her reaction only pisses me off more."

"It hurts you," he says. "But yeah, we'll go with pisses you off, if that helps."

"It does." I kiss his cheek. "Thank you."

The place where I left Petra and Colin is empty.

Earlier, I'd almost overshot it, and then even when I reached them, I'd mentally mused at how unremarkable the spot was.

As I'd chased Storm's barks, I'd taken note of my path as best I could, so I could find my way back. All that was unnecessary. I had someone with me who could have found their way back even if we'd still been in the middle of a thunderstorm. Apologies to Storm, but it's not her.

Dalton led the way, and as we approached the place, my mind began ticking off landmarks with small nods of satisfaction. Then we reach the actual spot, and I find myself hoping Dalton has made a mistake.

He has not made a mistake. There's a dead hostile on the ground, exactly where we left him, leaving zero doubt that this is the spot.

"Paula!" I shout, my voice echoing in the night. "Paula!"

"Petra!" Dalton's shout is a snarl that cuts above mine.

It's possible the hostiles returned and kidnapped Petra and Colin. Neither of us even voices that idea, though, because if it happened, there'd be at least one more dead hostile on the ground. Petra had a gun, and she would use it.

Did she use it . . . to take Colin hostage?

I still want to believe she only retreated to Rockton. Took Colin back and left some message here that I can't see. Yet I fear the scenario I imagined earlier, where Émilie and Petra flee. Where they don't dare stand their ground and try to explain away Émilie's culpability. Where they fear that we won't let them explain — that we'll demand truth and reparations, neither of which is in their interests.

So what are you going to do about it?

I knew she'd been worried about what I planned to do with my information, how it might affect Émilie. Yet I left her here and I ran, and I can seethe at that, but if it played out again, I'd do the same thing. Dalton and Storm were in trouble.

We comb the spot they left behind. The pack — with Colin's sat phone — is gone. The dead hostile remains exactly as we left him and so does everything else. I do find signs of a scuffle in the dirt.

We follow Petra's trail, even as we realize it's pointless. She helped raise and train Storm. She knows what our dog can do, and sure enough, we haven't gone more than fifty feet before the trail ends at a stream, where she must have ordered Colin barefoot as they waded in freezing-cold water. I only hope the poor guy doesn't lose toes to frostbite.

I keep thinking about Colin. The guy who came here because he was worried about his clients. Came to save them and ended up attacked and blinded, and now kidnapped.

We don't try very hard to find the trail again. There's little point. Petra's heading to Rockton. Slip in under cover of night, warn Émilie, and the two of them will fly out in her grandmother's plane. As for why she took Colin, the angry part of me wanted to insist he's a hostage, in case she needs leverage. The calmer side admits that she likely took him because it would be wrong to abandon a blind man in a forest with hostiles who want him dead. She'll take him to Rockton and leave him there, safely.

Petra already has a head start. The creek trick, though, will have cost her time. She's only done that to ensure we don't follow her direct trail. Now she's on her way to town. The only problem? In diverting for the creek, she may stumble around in the general direction of Rockton before finding the trail. So we have an advantage, and we use it, hightailing it to the trail and proceeding along it far faster than a woman leading a blind guy.

By midnight, we are back in Rockton, and there's been no sign of Petra and Colin.

"You go check Petra's place," Dalton says. "See if Émilie's there. I'll head to the hangar and check on the plane, do a little creative mechanics to make sure it's not flying out of here tonight."

I start to jog off, and he calls, "Take Storm. Just in case."

I'm about to joke that I'm not exactly worried about an eighty-year-old woman. Then I remember who I'm talking about, and I gesture for Storm to follow.

Émilie is gone. I'm standing in Petra's living room, skeleton key in hand, looking around the dark and empty apartment. There's one bedroom, and from here I can see the bed is made. The tiny bathroom door is open, and no one is in there.

I walk into the bedroom and pause. There's a suitcase on the floor. Émilie's suitcase, the kind of high-end carry-on bag used by savvy and wealthy travelers who don't want to fuss with checked luggage when they must, ugh, fly commercial.

Did she leave the bag behind? Certainly possible. With her money, it's like me not bothering to grab my toothbrush as I flee in the night. Still . . .

I look around, as if it's not past midnight, dark and silent. I heft the bag onto the bed and unzip it. Inside are more containers, packing squares and such. There's also a leather folder tucked into a zippered pouch. I open it and find myself staring at —

Holy shit.

It's Émilie's passport.

I could say it's fake, but the surname is recognizable as one of the few big-pharma family names I know.

This is Émilie's actual passport. Alarm bells sound, the weird compulsion to warn her that she shouldn't be leaving this around, even in a locked apartment. She needs to be much more careful hiding her real name.

Of course, it's to my advantage that she

didn't see the need. It also tells me she hasn't left Rockton. She's not fleeing without her passport, especially when we're guaranteed to find it after she leaves.

I check my watch. Where the hell would she be? The Roc and the Red Lion are closed.

Storm and I step outside. There's no sign of Dalton . . . or anyone else. I'm heading to the nearest town border, intending to circle around to the hangar, when I catch a flicker of movement. My gun flies out before I realize what I'm doing. It's not a hostile, of course. It's a resident, sneaking to or from another resident's bed.

I'm sliding my gun back into the holster when the moonlight illuminates just enough of the figure to tell me it's no resident. Well, it was a resident, once, but that was a very long time ago.

It's Émilie.

Seems there's more than one secret agent in the family. Émilie's spy game may not be on par with her granddaughter's, but she's clearly not out for an evening stroll. When I mistook her for a resident sneaking from another's bed, that's because she'd been outside a resident's back door. Mathias's door, to be exact.

I stride between buildings, and when Émilie walks past, she gives a start, seeing Storm first. Then she spots me and lets out a small laugh.

"Casey," she says. "Petra always said your dog looked like a bear, and I didn't see it until I came around that corner there. Nearly gave me a heart attack."

"What are you doing out and about?" I ask.

Her silver-gray brows arch. "Is there a curfew?"

"I thought you were unwell."

"I was tired. It passed, and now I'm most decidedly not tired. That's the problem with napping, especially at my age."

"Did Mathias have something to help with that?"

She frowns.

"He's a licensed psychiatrist," I say. "He can write prescriptions for sleeping pills. You don't need one, though. April will supply them without a script. Around here . . ." I shrug. "Mathias is just the butcher." I pause. "Well, maybe a little more, but that can't be why you went to his house, can it?"

"I have no idea what you're talking about, Casey. I certainly hope you're not implying I'm carrying on some kind of illicit liaison." Her lips twitch. "I wouldn't object in theory, but there's no one here in my age bracket."

"I saw you coming from Mathias's house."

She turns and frowns. "That chalet there? Only essential services get those homes, and I can't imagine a butcher would qualify."

"Oh, Mathias is special. It's his other job that's helped him wrangle his prime real estate. He's a spy for the council. But I'm sure you know that, which is why you were visiting."

Silence. A long silence as the wheels turn and she considers her next move. Finally, she exhales and motions for me to follow. I hesitate until I see Dalton. With a wave, I ask him to join us. He does, and he keeps quiet as we walk. I think Émilie is going to take us to Petra's place, but she keeps walking.

"I believe you'll want to continue this conversation in a more private location," she says. "It may be night, but I fear the soundproofing here may not be what we might require."

She starts veering toward our house. I tense, hackles rising, and Storm gives a low growl, as if sensing my reaction. Dalton strides into the lead and turns toward the station instead.

Émilie sighs loud enough to make her displeasure known, but she says nothing.

Inside the station, the fire burns low.

Dalton stokes it as Émilie settles into the only chair.

"I might have hoped for more comfortable surroundings," she says.

"This is fine," Dalton says and heads out back, returning with the two patio chairs. We settle into them by the fire, and Storm thumps down between us.

"Enough dancing around one another," Émilie says. "Yes, I know Mathias works for the council. I would argue he's not a spy, but a mental-health monitor. He's very good at that. As a spy, though, he leaves much to be desired. The only time he's interested in information-gathering is when he can use it to his own advantage."

I keep my expression neutral. Dalton only stretches out his legs, crossing them at the ankles and crossing his arms, too. The body language is clear, and he doesn't care if she knows it.

Émilie continues. "I was not at Mathias's house. I truly was just out for a walk."

"Okay," I say.

Our gazes meet. I don't believe her, but this conversation won't proceed as long as we lock horns over this.

"Petra's gone," I say.

When her entire body goes rigid, I realize how that sounded. I should hurry on to clarify. I don't. I pause, if only for a moment, to throw her off balance.

I continue, "We found a man in the forest, injured. He'd been the one who dropped the Danes off, and he was searching for them when they missed their pickup. He was attacked by a hostile. While I tended to him, Eric and Storm returned to Edwin's trail. Petra stayed with me. We got into an argument."

Those last words are the ones that truly penetrate. Émilie's head snaps up, her eyes wide, and I know what she's thinking. That this is the end of the story. How her granddaughter died.

We got into an argument.

"I confronted Petra with a theory about the hostiles and your involvement."

This is why I am callously dragging out the ending. Because if I uttered those words "your involvement" under any other circumstances, her defenses would fly up in the proper expression of confusion. But all she's thinking about right now is Petra. She does not react, and that tells me everything.

I continue. "Eric and Storm ran into trouble in the forest. Hostiles. I heard Storm in distress, so I took off, leaving Petra with the pilot. When we came back, she was gone. They were both gone."

"The hostiles took — ?"

"No. Petra was aware they were in the area. We had an encounter ourselves, with the same group that ran into Eric. They were in retreat. But I left Petra on full alert, in a defensive position, guarding a blind man. If they'd been attacked, there would have been bodies. All we found was a trail. It headed straight for the nearest body of water, because Petra knows how to evade Storm."

"No."

"No to what? Petra wouldn't know how to confound a tracking dog?"

"No to all of this, Casey. Petra wouldn't do that. I thought you knew her better."

My face hardens, and I open my mouth to answer, but Dalton cuts in, his voice calm, breezy even.

"When Casey came to Rockton, Petra sought her out," he says. "Made a point of winning her friendship. Casey was flattered, naturally. Petra cultivated the friendship of the new detective, the sheriff's girlfriend —"

"No," Émilie says. "She cultivated a friendship with *Casey.* The person. In Petra's former job, they knew better than to send her undercover to cozy up to targets. It isn't her skill set. Her friendship with you was real, and if you felt —"

"It doesn't matter," I say quickly.

"Fuck, yes, it matters," Dalton says. "You were hurt. Anyone would be."

Émilie meets my gaze. "Endangering your friendship hurt her more than you can know, Casey, but a little part of her, I think, was glad of it. Not to lose you as a friend, but to burn away the lies. To be who she really is, at least with you. To share the parts of herself that you two have in common."

"None of that matters right now," I say. "This isn't Casey-Petra relationship therapy. It's me convincing you that she came back here. I told her my theory, and she didn't deny it. She granted me that much, and I hope you'll do the same. But knowing that the truth was out, she saw an opportunity to protect you, and she took it. I don't blame her for that."

"How does this protect me?"

I don't answer. I can't without telling her what I know, and that will come later. Soon.

When I don't respond, Émilie shakes her head. "That isn't what's happening here."

"Then what is?"

"I-I don't know."

Émilie fidgets, and in her face, I don't see the turmoil of an old woman telling herself her granddaughter wouldn't do that. When

I worked special victims, I cannot count the number of times I sat across the table from parents, telling them what their teenage son did, watching Dad explode in righteous fury as Mom retreated into sick horror and grief. I've heard the snarled cries of "Not my child," while the look in their eyes quietly whimpers, "Oh, God, what has he done?"

This is not that look. This is the look of a parent genuinely struggling to find another explanation, firm in their conviction that there must be one.

Émilie straightens. "You say this man has been blinded. You'd left to help Eric, and it was getting dark, and I'm presuming the storm had passed by then. Petra's bringing him back for medical care. She saw the sun dropping and knew you and Eric would be fine."

"And the fact she led him through a stream?"

"They had to cross it."

"We didn't cross a stream coming from Rockton, so when she reached it, she'd know they'd gone the wrong way. The water is barely above freezing. They waded in near-freezing water to *lose* Storm."

"I . . . I don't know what the answer is, Casey, but I know Petra was not running away."

"Not running. Coming to protect you. And before you keep denying it, you need to hear what I told her, Émilie."

THIRTY-ONE

As I tell my story, Dalton makes coffee, knowing there's no chance we're getting to bed tonight. I step through the full story, from Maryanne's description of the tea to the research we've done to Josie's tale. I leave nothing out, even the bits Émilie has already heard.

There'd been a time in my life when I dreamed of getting a doctorate, or at least a master's degree. Then my career took off, and I found plenty of other opportunities to expand my education. I knew people who'd gotten those higher degrees, though, and it involves defending your thesis, the culmination of your studies.

This is my thesis, the project I've been working on since I first came to Rockton. And this is me, defending my dissertation, to the person with the knowledge and experience to shoot it down.

When I finish, every muscle is tense, waiting for Émilie to do exactly that. Shoot me down. Laugh even. She won't mock me, but I will see mockery. I am the doctoral student no one expected to get this far. I'm just not smart enough, see? My parents always told me so. My sister always told me so. I don't have what it takes, and if I overreach, I'll embarrass myself.

I hold myself like there's a bomb in my gut, ready to explode at a single touch. And I'm not the only one. I see the set of Dalton's jaw, the steel in his gaze. He's a watchdog straining at his chain. Even Storm, who'd napped as I spoke, is awake and shifting, sensing the tension in the air.

Émilie does nothing. Says nothing. Just sits there, watching me as if I'm still talking. Or watching me as if there's more to come. Surely there must be more. Maybe I'll burst into laughter and tell her it's a prank. Or I'll start blaming space aliens so she can chalk my mad theory up to delusions. Too long in the bush, and I snapped.

With each passing second, I tense a little more, the bomb inside me buzzing, so close to triggering. It's coming. I know it's coming, and I want to handle it without exploding . . . and I'm not sure I can.

I know I'm right.

No, I *knew* I was right as I stood in the

forest and saw Petra's face. Now the fear creeps in again. Like marking down an answer on an exam that you're absolutely sure of, only to later second-guess.

Should I have couched my theory in question marks? Acted like it was only a hypothesis?

No. I believe in my facts, and I must stand up for them. I might have a detail or two wrong, but the overall theory is sound. I'm sure of it.

"I . . . can see you've put a lot of work into this," Émilie says, and something inside me collapses, deflates into this hard nub in my stomach.

I know what comes next. I've heard it before, in that same, careful tone. Every time my music tutor graded a test piece, her gaze would slide to my mother, standing stiff, her expressionless face radiating cold judgment. The tutor never looked at Dad, relaxed and open, smiling as if I hadn't just massacred Chopin.

That's the mistake everyone made. If someone drove me too hard, if someone could crush my self-confidence under their thumb, clearly it was my mother, right? The Chinese tiger mom? Oh, my mother definitely had high standards for me, definitely pushed me to achieve them, but the one who would lambaste me after this musical disaster? That would be the genial Scot lounging on the couch.

I can see you put a lot of work into this.

That's what my music tutor always said, and she'd been right. I'd worked my fingers off practicing, but it never mattered. I suspect she always wanted to award me an A for effort. She couldn't, though. My parents would see through that and send her packing, like they had her predecessor. Effort is not enough. The world only rewards achievement.

Now Émilie says those words, and the same pronouncement is coming. A for effort, Casey. C for achievement.

I don't speak. I won't speak. I sit as still as I had on my piano bench, chin raised, eyes hooded, inwardly raging and shamed, outwardly channeling my mother.

"You say Petra confirmed this?" Émilie continues.

"She confirmed the pieces she could. I have no idea how much she knows."

"Nothing," Émilie murmurs. "She knows nothing. But yes, she could confirm the pieces, and that would be enough. She would put them together and know that your theory is fundamentally correct."

"Right, which is why she ran —" I stop.

"Fundamentally correct?"

Her eyes are distant, as if she's only half listening, half lost in another place.

"You are correct about the Second Settlement," she says, "and the young man. What was his name?"

"Hendricks."

"Ah, yes. An alias. Henry, I believe it was. Henry Richardson? Henri Richard? I can't recall, but it hardly matters. He's dead. Car accident a few years after he left Rockton." She meets my gaze. "Yes."

"I didn't say anything."

A sad curve of her lips. "But you were thinking it. Car crash. How convenient. At the time, I thought nothing of it, other than a spot of grief for a man I only vaguely knew. My husband knew him better. Hendricks's mission in the settlement, though, was my idea. It seemed so terribly clever. Take a group of people already inclined to peace and natural intoxicants, and nudge them a little down that path. A tea to keep them happy and calm and unlikely to attack Rockton."

That wistful smile grows rueful, one corner of her mouth twitching. "It seems silly now. A tea? That's going to fix the inherent problems of dissatisfaction and envy? How naive. But part of me was still the girl who watched Edwin put a gun to my husband's head. I was obsessed with avoiding that. So I synthesized a brew based on local plants."

She glances up at me. "That's how Robert and I first met — I worked a summer term at his family's company while studying pharmacy and biomedical science. I devised the brew, and we tested it ourselves, naturally." Her eyes twinkle. "That was the fun part. Then Robert hired Henry to join the Second Settlement and continue perfecting the tea while convincing them to adopt it as part of their lifestyle."

"Which he did."

"Very successfully, yes. Now here's where your theory slips, just a little. You believe someone from the Second Settlement broke off and turned the two teas into narcotics, and that was the birth of the hostiles."

"I know that the original hostiles did come from the settlement."

"True, but your version is a little more . . . innocent than the truth, I fear." She sips her coffee and settles in. "Shortly after Henry returned, my husband's family began joint research with a European firm. They came across my Second Settlement study, and they were fascinated. They saw wider uses for the tea, beneficial uses, and they sent researchers in, posing as Rockton residents. We would have rather sent Hendricks back but . . ."

"They wanted their own people."

"And they got that, without argument, because Hendricks was conveniently dead."

"Ah."

"Yes, ah. Had he died *after* they asked to send in a researcher, we'd have seen a connection. But his accident occurred before they suggested it."

"They came prepared."

"Evidently, and as you have guessed, this European company plays the black-hat role in my story. Which you will have every reason to doubt. It's an obvious ploy, isn't it? Blame some shadowy foreign corporation."

"Just tell me the story."

She nods. "So they sent two researchers to Rockton. A man and a woman. They arrived acting as if they'd never met, and then they feigned a whirlwind romance and skipped off into the forest together. The Second Settlement fell for their story and welcomed them in. Their purpose, as far as we knew, was to study the long-term effects of the tea, and I was thrilled by that. While I saw nothing in the ingredients that raised concern, there is always the risk of unforeseen side effects. I welcomed their investigations. It eased my conscience."

"And then?"

"And there the story ends. Or so it appeared. The researchers stayed for a year. While they found no evidence of long-term effects, they also didn't find what they'd hoped for, in terms of the tea having useful applications. Other drugs did the job more efficiently and cheaper. My husband's family soon parted ways with the European firm."

"Okay . . ."

"Decades pass, and then along comes Rockton's first detective, who starts doing what she was hired to do. Detecting." She smiles at me. "Funny how that works, isn't it? Hire a detective for a town where she might have a case or two a year, which leaves all this extra time, and she finds new things to investigate. Like the wild people living in the forest. The council always dismissed those reports as obvious exaggeration. Clearly, past sheriffs had encountered the wilderness equivalent of the homeless — people suffering from mental illness or other issues. If they didn't want help, then the only course of action was to stay out of their way. Suggesting they were living in packs? Ludicrous. Residents had seen a few troubled settlers and blown it out of proportion."

"You thought the same?"

"I did. I've been here. I know this wild place preys on the imagination. Every dead tree becomes a bear. Every red-squirrel nest is a wildcat poised overhead. Even the settlers can be both frightening and dangerous."

"So what changed your mind?"

"As soon as you mentioned Maryanne's experience, I started to dig. At first, my thoughts paralleled yours. A splinter group from the Second Settlement must have altered the recipe. That made it my fault. I failed at proper scientific procedure. I introduced a new drug, and then I walked away, without monitoring it, without taking responsibility."

"Then you remembered the European group and decided they were to blame."

"That isn't how my mind works, Casey. I don't go looking for alternate targets. I accept my mistakes, and I strive to fix them. The same way you would, I think."

I say nothing.

She continues. "My way of fixing it was to support your efforts to resolve the issue. Lobbying for the council to take the problem seriously. Then it seemed as if they were considering a solution. A drastic solution."

That has Dalton's head jerking up.

"Attrition," she says.

I'm still struggling to understand what she means when Dalton says, "They're shutting us down."

"What?" I say. "No. They haven't given any signs of . . ." I trail off and Dalton murmurs what Émilie just said. *Attrition.*

I continue, "They've all but stopped sending us new residents. And they aren't extending stays past two years. That's what Jen was talking about. It's not just her. They aren't granting *any* extensions, and we weren't thinking much of it because everyone who was denied — including Jen — has other reasons for being turned down."

Dalton nods. "Our numbers fluctuate all the time. Since I've been here, we've been as low as one-fifty and as high as two-twenty. Sometimes it's budget. Other times . . ." He shrugs. "It's a natural flow. I wouldn't have really thought much about it until we dropped low enough to have trouble filling positions."

"Wait," I say. "We have a few clashes with hostiles, and we discover that some of them are former Rockton residents — our *residents,* kidnapped and brainwashed — and this is the council's solution? Not how can they rescue our people? Not how can they detox the hostiles and see what *they* want? But shut down the town?"

"Relocate, most likely," she says.

"It's an excuse," Dalton says. "We've been inconvenient. Misbehaving. You can sure as hell bet that we aren't on their hiring list for the new town. None of us will be. This isn't abandoning the house and moving the people. It's letting the fire burn it out and starting fresh. They'd tell us Rockton was permanently shutting down, and we'd never know they were starting up elsewhere."

I look at Émilie.

"I'm not privy to their plans," she says. "They insist there *are* no plans. But Eric is, I fear, correct. However, you're also right, Casey. It's entirely the wrong reaction. Think of this as a chemical spill."

I nod. "They're trying to close shop and move on without cleaning up."

"Correct. I believed there was more to it, so I began to dig, and that's when . . ." She trails off. "More on that in a moment. For now, let's just say I discovered something that drove my mind back to that collaboration with the European firm. I decided to speak to the two researchers they sent. Bribe them, that was my plan. Make them an offer they couldn't refuse."

"They're dead, aren't they?"

"No, they never returned from the Yukon."

"They decided to stay?"

There's no incredulity in my voice. People come for work or vacation, and they decide to stay. Not in the wilderness, but in Whitehorse or one of the smaller towns. As someone who's been seduced by this place myself, I understand their choice.

It's Dalton who says, "They didn't *choose* to stay, did they? Not really. They became hostiles."

"What?" I say.

No one chooses that life. Well, no, I'm sure a few have, but I cannot imagine scientists coming to work here, seeing wild and savage people in the forest, and saying, "That looks cool."

Except there hadn't been savage people in the forest before they arrived.

"They started the hostiles," I murmur. "They were the first."

"It was part of the study," she says. "That's what I uncovered. The European firm wasn't looking to create life-enhancing medication. They were making bioweapons for foreign powers. Their interest was in how the tea might subdue protesters and rebels, an exaggerated variation on my own goal. At some point, their interest shifted to the hallucinogenic tea. What if it caused more than euphoria?"

"Enhancing violence," I say. "Reducing inhibitions. Like what we see with the hostiles. They tinker with the tea and take a few people into the forest for further experimentation. At some point, it becomes Frankenstein's monster. Their creation turns on them."

"That's my theory," Émilie says. "I can't prove it. I know only that they went into the forest to change the formulation, and they never returned."

"So the hostiles are a science experiment?" I say.

"They were. Past tense. A brief foray into behavioral control that might benefit some of the shadier world powers of the day. The results weren't what the firm wanted, so they ended the study and recalled their researchers, who ignored their summons."

"The firm didn't send a search party?"

"They claim they did, but as you know, this is a very big forest."

"So the hostiles were a *failed* experiment, one the council knew nothing about?"

"I believe the majority of the council knows nothing about it. But someone does. That firm didn't walk away from Rockton as cleanly as we hoped. They have at least one influential person on the council, someone who has been keeping them abreast of recent developments."

I nod. "And that element is exerting pressure on the rest of the council to abandon ship. The European firm wants us out of here so they can . . ."

I trail off.

European firm.

I remember what Émilie said shortly after she arrived.

While I'm not fluent in Danish, I did spend a year in Copenhagen.

"Where exactly is this firm?" I ask.

Once again, her gaze meets mine. "I think you already know." Denmark.

Thirty-Two

Émilie has gone back to Petra's place. At this point I no longer really care whether she flees. I have what I need. Besides, Dalton has made sure her plane isn't going anywhere. Right now, I just need to think.

"You can go home to bed if you like," I say to Dalton.

His brows shoot up. "You really think I'd sleep after that?"

"I —"

"You need time alone before you're ready to discuss it. I'll walk Storm home — no reason for her to stay up all night."

"Actually, I'm going to go talk to Mathias," I say. "That's where I found Émilie earlier — sneaking back from his place."

"Ah-ha," he says, brows wriggling, and I laugh, tension easing from me.

"Sadly, it's going to be the less interesting option. He's working with the council, and she wanted to talk to him. Before she has a chance to speak to him again, I want to see if anything she said contradicts the story she just gave."

"You okay with us walking you over?"

"I am. Thank you."

I rap on Mathias's door. Dalton and Storm wait a few feet from the porch. When the door swings open, Mathias fixes me with a glower that makes me rethink going into his place alone. While I've never feared him, in that moment, a chill slides over me.

Still, I wave Dalton off and step inside as Mathias moves back.

"I'm sorry to disturb your sleep," I say in French.

"You disturb nothing. I was not asleep."

If he's not annoyed because I woke him . . .

He walks inside, leaving me to follow. I look around and notice another new piece of art, which must have come in the latest shipment. We often need to pick up a package or two for Mathias when we're in town. Few residents have that privilege. Dalton uses his for books. I use mine for gifts and chocolates. Mathias buys art.

"How am I to rest," he says, "when my responsibility lies beyond my reach?"

I try — and fail — to untangle that. I

presume the meaning is lost in translation, an idiomatic use that flies over my head.

"I don't under —" I begin in English.

"No." Mathias wheels, so close to me that I fight the urge to back up. "I am the one who doesn't understand. Did you not tell me he was my responsibility?"

I glance around the room, realizing I haven't seen Raoul — Mathias's wolf-dog. Normally, he'd be at the door, dancing and whining when he smelled Storm. My heart skips until I find him on the sofa, his head ducked just enough to tell me he's in hiding.

Mathias follows my gaze. "No, not the damned dog."

Mathias rubs Raoul's ears and murmurs to him, "I am not angry with you. No one has taken *you* from me without a word of warning. No one has taken you and left me wondering for hours where you've gone, until a near stranger casually mentions that you are in the forest, having offered yourself up as hostage."

I wince. "Sebastian. I'm sorry, Mathias."

"Are you?"

That tone makes me straighten. "Yes, I am, despite the fact that Sebastian is old enough to make his own choices. He's only your responsibility insomuch as I'm relying on you to help monitor his mental state and provide the therapy he needs. Also, I'd think you'd be happy to have him gone for a few days. You're always complaining about him."

He glowers at me. "That does not sound like a sincere apology."

"It was . . . until you challenged me on it."

He grumbles and sits beside Raoul, who lays his muzzle on Mathias's leg.

"I believe, Casey, that to truly understand my current sleepless state, you might consider what you just said. That I am responsible for his mental well-being. Might it not, then, have been prudent to consult me before sending him off on this mission?"

I settle into the chair across from him, and Raoul zips over to me. "I could point out that, under the very tense circumstances in which this occurred, consulting you was impossible. But after Sebastian agreed, we returned to pick up the dirt bike and we should have spoken to you then."

Mathias relaxes a little, marginally mollified.

"He wanted to do this," I say, "and they'd never hurt him."

"He would not allow them to. He can take care of himself. I simply do not like him being sent into a situation where he may need to do so."

"He really wanted to help Felicity."

Another grumble, louder now. "That girl. He is developing feelings for her, and I have told him it is unwise. He will not allow me near her for a proper assessment of her suitability."

I smile. "My parents used to do that. Tell me they weren't thrilled about a relationship and then ask to meet the boy. That warned me to keep him far, far away."

"It is not the same. I am concerned for *her.*"

"That's half your concern. The other half is for him, whether he's falling for a girl who won't fall back. And the other half is worry that they'll both fall for each other . . . when he's not going to be here forever."

"You were not good at math, were you, Casey?"

"You're a complicated man."

He waggles a finger. "Do not flatter me. Next time, I insist on being consulted. I do, however, appreciate that you came by to speak to me about it, despite the lateness of the hour."

I pause.

"That is not why you came, is it?"

"Sorry," I say. "If I'd thought of it, I would have, but I came to talk about Émilie."

"Émilie?"

"The woman —"

"I know who she is. I presume someone saw us speaking and warned you we were having a tête-à-tête?"

"Something like that."

"Well, I planned to speak to you myself about it tomorrow. When I was no longer annoyed with you." He settles in. "She came by to discuss Sebastian, or so it seemed at first. She said she'd learned of his condition and feared I hadn't been warned by the council. I told her that I was forced to make the diagnosis myself, and I was not pleased about that. She apologized, and then asked about new residents who came after Sebastian, whether I had concerns about any of them. Terribly considerate, I thought."

"Uh-huh, let me guess. She asked about each individually, not as a group."

His eyes widen in mock surprise. "As a matter of fact, she did. How ever did you guess?"

"Because you planned to talk to me about her visit, which you wouldn't do unless you saw something suspicious in her questions. She starts asking about Sebastian, knowing you'd be upset about being misled there. Then she parlays that apology into dutifully asking after each subsequent new resident, to hide the fact she's concerned about one person in particular."

"*Mon Dieu.* One would think you were a detective, Casey Butler. How astute of you."

"You know what would be a real show of astuteness? If you could hazard a guess on which resident she was interested in."

"Sadly, I am not a detective." He crosses one leg over his knee. "And our Miss Émilie is herself very astute, enough to ask after each new resident with equal concern and listen to my responses with equal interest. I know only that she wanted my assessment of each recent resident, particularly whether I feared that any, like Sebastian, weren't what they claimed to be."

I sputter a laugh. "We're a town of people who arrive under false pretenses."

"So I said, but she was looking for more."

"She suspects someone's backstory is false. Not just their *cover* story, but the one they gave the council. Huh." I lean back. "Well, that's one good thing about the council restricting the inflow so much. There are only a handful of suspects."

"And that raises another concern I wished to bring to your attention. My application for an extension has been denied."

I straighten. "What?"

"Yes, I am equally shocked. Requesting

my extensions has always been a formality. This week, I was denied."

"Shit. Émilie's right. They really are shutting us down."

He blinks in rare surprise. "Shutting down Rockton?"

"We'll deal with it. I'm close to solving this mystery, and that should resolve the issue." I rise. "I'm sorry we didn't at least tell you about Sebastian going to the First Settlement, but thank you for speaking to me. Émilie denied seeing you tonight, and I knew she had been here. Now I know why."

He frowns. "Tonight?"

"Yes, I saw her leaving your . . ." I trail off as I take in his expression. "When did she speak to you?"

"Yesterday afternoon. She has not been here since."

I mentally run through the residents who live nearby and compare it to that short list of new residents she'd been interested in.

"Holy shit," I whisper.

"The detective has solved the case?" he asks as I stand and head for the hall.

"No, she's solved a mystery she never realized was a mystery at all. I'll talk to you later."

"Tease!" he calls after me as I hurry out the door.

■ ■ ■ ■

There isn't a guard posted outside the clinic. That throws me, until I remember that we have no need of one. How often in the past has our overnight patient been a suspect or a victim? Far too often. But not tonight. Such a relief.

As I hurry inside, a figure rises from an examination table, and my gun flies up. I hit the light . . . and see my sister blinking and squinting at me.

"Casey?" she says.

I lower the gun. "What are you doing here?"

"Monitoring the patient, of course." It only takes a second for brisk efficiency to return to her voice, and she runs one hand through her hair, returning it to perfection. "I would request, though, that you please do not mention it to Kenneth. I told him that I ought to monitor the patient, and he made it quite clear I should not do so at night, for my own safety. I pointed out that Jay is currently comatose, but he still worried."

She rolls her eyes, but there's a glitter of pleasure there, too, that Kenny was concerned for her safety. Then she snaps back to herself and says, "Whatever are you doing here? At . . ." She checks her watch. "Two in the morning."

"I popped in to check on the patient. But since you're up, can I run something by you? I need your brain."

"A medical question, I presume?"

"There's a medical question included, but mostly, I just want to bounce my theory off someone smarter than me, someone who might see the holes that I'm missing."

She frowns. "Detective work is your forte, Casey, and I'm quite certain you're the expert in that regard. As for requiring someone smarter to vet your reasoning, any difference in our IQ is minimal enough, on the overall scale, that I hardly think you need my help."

She peers at me and steps closer. "Are you all right? Your eyes appear to be watery. You didn't encounter any potentially toxic substances in your search for Felicity, did you?"

I laugh, say, "Thank you," and hug her, a brief hug that she endures, even patting my back awkwardly.

"I do believe you're overtired, or else I am still half asleep, because I fail to see what I said that requires gratitude or shows of affection."

"If you'd like to rest, April, that's fine, but if you're up . . ."

"I am."

"Then I would love to bounce this theory off you. Get your take on it. Is that all right?"

That look sparks in her eyes, the dart of pleasure I'd seen when she talked about Kenny's fretting.

"Of course," she says. "Tell me everything."

I do.

Thirty-Three

As I'm talking, Dalton comes in, having tracked me down. He slides into a chair and listens as I tell my sister the whole story behind the creation of the hostiles.

When I finish, April says, "That is . . ."

I brace for the next word. "Ridiculous"? "Preposterous"? ". . . completely the wrong way to conduct scientific research," she says. "Highly irregular and unethical."

I laugh. "So it's impossible, then?"

"Nothing is impossible, particularly when it comes to drug research. People have this misguided image of scientists in a lab, chatting amicably and sharing their knowledge for the betterment of humankind. It is like any other big business. Competition is both fierce and cutthroat. This firm could certainly afford to send a few researchers into the wild, particularly for the possibility of a drug with military applications."

"My logic is sound, then?"

"With the independent corroboration of Émilie, yes, I believe you have solved your mystery, Casey. Well done." If the smile she offers holds traces of a patronizing pat on the head, I know her well enough now to take no offense.

"So our Danish tourists weren't actually tourists," I say. "We started having problems with the hostiles and that — combined with my reports about their narcotic brews — prompted the Danish pharmaceutical firm's council contact to inform them. Then they sent a team in to evaluate the situation."

April frowns. "I am uncomfortable with the nationality of the transgressors. I have always found the Danes to be a peaceful people."

"It's a private corporation working for foreign powers. Where there's money to be made, there are unethical people ready to make it, no matter what their nationality."

"True. Sophie wasn't an innocent tourist, then. That will alleviate Will's guilt."

It isn't that easy, but I only say, "It explains her sudden burst of both power and skill. I chalked it up to adrenaline, but that was her training. She knew exactly what she was doing."

"I would not go quite that far, Casey. She was obviously mentally confused at the time. She would need to be, to attack Jay."

I open my mouth and then pause. Not yet. Instead I say, "So the four Danes were sent in to evaluate, and they must have triggered the hostiles in some way and were attacked. Or they weren't attacked by hostiles at all, but by someone pretending to be hostiles, ironically killing the very people sent to help the situation."

"Are we sure the Danes were sent to *help*?" Dalton says. "Or sent to clean up the mess? Which doesn't tell us what happened to that settler family." He rubs his chin. "Unless it does. A case of mistaken identity."

"Hmm?"

"This Danish firm wouldn't send their people into the wilderness unarmed," he says. "We didn't find guns, but they sure as hell had them. What kind do you think they'd have? Hunting rifles?"

"Handguns." I pause. "Like the ones used to kill the settlers? You said mistaken . . . Oh, shit. The Danes are the ones who mistook the settler family for hostiles. The Danes came looking for wild people of the forest. They seemed to find three and carried out execution orders, only to realize they made a mistake. So they staged the scene to look like a hostile attack. That hides their crime and plants further proof that the hostiles are a dangerous element. Then they come across actual hostiles who turn the tables and slaughter them."

Dalton shakes his head. "Will definitely doesn't need to feel so bad about shooting Sophie now."

"You think it's plausible?" I ask. "The firm ordered them to *kill* all the hostiles?"

"We already suspect they staged the car accident that killed Hendricks, the original researcher," he says. "Do I think those four Danes planned to slaughter a couple dozen hostiles? No. I think they underestimated the numbers. That's been the pattern all along, right? Clearly, we're exaggerating."

He makes a face. "Maybe I've read too many spy novels. Maybe they didn't intend to kill them, but things got out of hand. Either way . . ."

"They were unprepared," April murmurs. "That much seems evident. They mistook the settlers for hostiles, and the actual hostiles then killed them." She looks my way. "Is that the medical question you had? Whether your theory fit . . . No, that was Eric's theory, newly formed. What was your question, then?"

"Is there any chance Jay is faking his coma?"

"What?" Her brows shoot up to her hairline.

"Yes, it's probably a silly question."

"His vital signs confirm he is, indeed, comatose and likely to stay that way for a while."

"That may be for the best. Otherwise, Kenny's concerns might have been valid." I look at Dalton. "Émilie did talk to Mathias. She'd asked about recent arrivals and whether any seemed suspicious. That conversation, though, took place yesterday afternoon. When I saw her creeping about, I believe she was coming from an apartment near Mathias's house. Searching a residence she knew would be empty."

"Jay's," Dalton says. "Fuck."

"Yep, convenient that he knew Danish, right?"

April frowns. "But he arrived before Sophie."

"I don't think Jay came here because of Sophie. I think he was just a second prong of the Danish mission. Send four agents into the woods to investigate the hostiles. Send Jay here to monitor us. He speaks Danish because he *is* Danish. It was pure luck for them that he was already here when Sophie arrived."

"He offered his help so he could mistranslate. Redirect your investigation if necessary."

I nod. "Then her mind cleared enough for her to realize he was mistranslating. That's why she flipped out. It's also why she targeted him. She might have still been confused, recognizing him as a fellow employee but not necessarily an ally. Or she was thinking just fine and blamed the firm for her colleagues' deaths."

"Either way, she knew he wasn't an innocent guy caught in the cross fire."

"No one was innocent here." April's gaze turns toward the other room, where we're storing the evidence. "Except those poor settlers."

"Yes," I say, "but unfortunately, while their killers are dead, this has snowballed into new problems with other innocent victims: Felicity, Edwin, and the pilot who came for the Danes."

As I rise from my chair, I look toward that room April had glanced at. The repository for our evidence. We'd need to decide what to do with Sophie and the items we'd brought from the dead settlers. Also the foot of Sophie's lover.

Or maybe Victor hadn't been her lover. Jay could have embellished their relationship to support the tourist theory and add an extra layer of pathos to the story. Victor had been something to her, though. She'd snapped when April brought in his boot.

Wait. Had she actually snapped? We'd interpreted her reaction as grief. Knowing she wasn't an innocent tourist, I replay that scene and see strategy. We bring in the boot, and she feigns a fit of grief, which throws us off guard and allows her to strangle Jay.

I tell Dalton my theory that Sophie used the boot to distract us.

"Yeah," he says. "Makes sense."

"But the whole reason we presumed that foot belonged to the fourth tourist — her lover — was her reaction. That clinched it. Without that . . ."

"Fuck."

I pause, seeing him thinking and piecing it together. Then he mutters another "Fuck."

"April?" I say. "The guy we found, the pilot. He was blind."

She blinks at me. "While I know there have been immense strides taken to improve accessibility —"

"Not when he flew. Afterward. He was blinded by the attack. No apparent damage to his eyes, but he'd been struck on the head."

"All right . . ."

"Can that cause blindness?"

"Total blindness? In both eyes?"

The incredulity in her voice answers the question. "That'd be a no, then."

"It's not impossible, but without damage to the eyes, the most likely cause of total binocular blindness would be a clot, unrelated to the attack."

Colin isn't blind, and Petra didn't take him anywhere.

He took *her* hostage.

Colin Berger is Victor, the fourth Dane.

It'll be dawn in an hour, and there's no time to waste, but we need to make one stop first. Dalton goes to fetch Storm and gather supplies while I stop in to see Maryanne. Despite the hour, she's gracious, inviting me in.

I give her the briefest rundown on our hostile encounter. As soon as I mention the young man, she shakes her head.

"That isn't my group," she says. "There was no one nearly that young. I'd have mentioned it."

"That's what I thought."

I describe the dead hostile, and there's a flicker of potential recognition, but when I describe the woman I shot, her eyes round.

"That's the shaman," she says.

"You're sure?"

"Absolutely." She shivers. "You were lucky. She's the worst of them. Brutal and smart. I always got the sense she drank less of that narcotic than the others, to keep her wits sharper."

I tell her about our brief conversation, which was clearer and more lucid than I expected.

She nods. "That is undeniably her, then. That means I *do* know the man who was killed. I wouldn't be surprised if he was her new husband, though he'd never have been the leader. Once she seized the reins, she'd hold them tight."

"Then the young man?" I say. "Either the two groups have joined or he's new."

"New . . ." she murmurs. "I didn't consider that, but it makes sense. He must have joined after I left. Perhaps recently, which explains why he isn't as indoctrinated. He could be an ally, but be careful, please. The shaman will not hesitate to use him against you."

I thank her, and she gives me more advice plus all possible details about the two groups. When I step outside, Dalton is sitting on the front step, sipping steaming coffee as Storm wanders off toward the woods to do her morning business.

I settle in beside him to await the dog's return, and he fills a tin mug from the thermos. I tell him what Maryanne said.

"That's what you figured, right?" he says. "That this woman was the shaman?"

"It is. I just wanted independent corroboration. I still don't know whether these people have Felicity and Edwin. I have no idea who does. So my focus will be on Petra, though by now I'm sure Victor has her on a plane to Whitehorse."

"Nah." He reaches into his pocket and pulls out a set of keys. "Our pilot's not going anywhere."

"Nicely done. You suspected his story, then."

He pauses, mug halfway to his lips.

"You can tell me if you did," I say. "In the future, I'd rather you shared that right away, but I've been guilty of the same thing. We need to share our hunches, even when they seem far-fetched."

"That's not it. I hesitated because I'd love to say I suspected the guy. Truth is . . ." He shrugs. "When I peeked into his pack, I just grabbed these. I figured if I found his plane, there might be first-aid supplies you could use, and with him being blind, it wasn't like he needed the keys."

"Huh. Well, good call either way. And may

I suggest, when we tell this story to the council, we say that we took the keys because we doubted his story?"

"Works for me."

"Then Victor is in the woods, trying to figure out his next move. He has Petra and his backpack, with a few days' supplies. He probably has a gun, too. That's why I didn't find one. He'd have hidden it when he heard us coming. He can also summon help. He has a . . ."

I turn to Dalton.

"Sat phone," he murmurs. "Victor has a sat phone, and so does Émilie. We may not need to go poking around the forest after all." He pushes to his feet. "Let's go see if there's any way we can broker a deal."

Thirty-Four

The problem is, of course, that we need Victor's number. We bring Émilie on board, in hopes she can obtain it. We also bring in Phil. If either of those choices is a mistake, well, right now, we're on a sinking ship hailing passing vessels. They might help . . . or they might fire another shot through our bow, and it'll only speed up the inevitable.

Émilie tells us that she flew to Rockton as soon as she heard about the "Danish tourists." Finding a newcomer whose application had been rushed through — and who conveniently speaks Danish — she had a good idea what Jay had been up to, but by that time, he was in a coma and Sophie was dead.

She'd resorted to investigating on her own, begging off time with Petra by claiming exhaustion and then talking to Mathias and, last night, searching Jay's apartment. She'd found a sat phone smuggled into a secret compartment in Jay's luggage, one that bypassed Dalton's tech-device checks. In the same place, she found notes in Danish. They were in code, but the fact that he was making notes in Danish means it wasn't just some language he knew passably well, as he'd claimed.

When we check the sat phone, we find a few preprogrammed numbers. One is to another sat phone. Victor's? We certainly hope so.

Émilie calls the number, and it goes through, but no one answers. There's voice mail, though, in Danish, and she leaves a message. We'll give it an hour, and then we'll go on foot to find Petra.

We tell Phil everything, and then we eat breakfast. Well, everyone eats except Phil, who's still processing. Not arguing. Just processing.

He doesn't confirm or deny any of it. He can't. As Émilie has warned, the Danish connection operated above his pay grade.

A few older members of the council were aware of the original drug trial and undoubtedly saw the connection to the "narcotic brew" reported by Maryanne, but they had feigned ignorance. Then there's the element that's on the Danish firm's payroll. All other council members have a justifiable claim to ignorance. I'd still say they're guilty of not taking the problem seriously. But it's understandable that Phil knew nothing . . . with one exception: the plans to close down Rockton.

"I had raised concerns," he says when he returns from a walk. "About the dwindling numbers. It was a matter of budget and long-term planning. If this was a permanent decrease, then we'd need to close buildings, and we should allow higher-contributing members to take larger quarters. I suggested a plan for reconstruction, doubling the size of some apartments. I also noted that if the decrease continued, we'd need to reevaluate our storage requirements and possibly reconfigure jobs. They insisted it was a temporary drop only — we'd had a decrease in applications and tightening of the extension guidelines."

"Yeah, I remember you mentioning that," Dalton says. "Wait. Nope. You never said anything about downsizing. Or tightened extension rules. Funny you didn't mention that last part when you brought Jen to us."

"I considered it a management issue."

Dalton just waits, gaze fixed on him.

Phil meets that gaze with an equally cool one. "There are management issues that I bring to you, and there are ones I do not, ones that seem primarily about supply and resource. I was under the impression you appreciated not being bothered with that."

Dalton grunts. It's a grudging concession. Yes, he'd been happy to turn that over to Phil, but in this case, supply and resource concerns implied something larger. It had not, admittedly though, grown to the point where anyone, including Phil, realized that.

As Dalton said, it seemed a normal fluctuation in numbers. If there are plans to shut us down, they're restricted to a very small number of people, with the general council — and Phil — knowing nothing about them.

"What if we fix this?" I ask Émilie. "If we prove the Danes were behind the hostiles and they're the ones who wanted to shut us down, then we'll be okay, right?"

She doesn't answer. She can't, and I hear my words, and I hear a child's hope in them.

I can't get a dog because they're too much work? What if I promise to look after it and, if I don't, you can take it away?

Even as a child, I'd known that denying me a dog because they were "too much work" was an excuse. Is it the same here?

Émilie opens her mouth to speak. Then the phone jangles.

She answers it on the third ring, sounding breathless, the old lady who scrambled to grab a phone.

"Hello?" Even her voice is tremulous. "Hello?"

She holds the receiver from her ear so we can listen in. She wears hearing aids, very discreet and — I'm sure — the best money can buy. She doesn't strain to hear with the receiver a few inches away.

"Is this Émilie?" a male voice says.

"Y-yes, yes it is. Please tell me you have my granddaughter."

Petra calls out, "It's me, Nan. Don't worry. I have this under control. Whatever he says . . ."

Petra's voice fades as he must be moving away. She doesn't shout to be heard. She knows we got the message, and she also knows that if Émilie called this number, then we've realized that "Colin" isn't a hapless pilot looking for his tourist clients.

Victor comes on again. "I'm guessing that detective did her detecting and figured out what happened, if you have this number."

"Actually, no." Émilie's voice comes clearer, still with a quaver, but as if the savvy businesswoman is wresting control from the fretting grandmomma. "I know what's going on. That's why I'm in Rockton. To make sure Casey doesn't dig deeper than she already has, which is quite deep enough, as

I'm sure you know. She thinks my granddaughter has taken you hostage. I knew better, and I obtained this number, which I am using to negotiate my granddaughter's release."

A humorless chuckle. "All right, then. Let's negotiate. I want one thing and only one thing. Get me out of this hellhole."

"You don't have a plane? Casey thought she saw keys."

"Yeah, well, she didn't just *see* them. She stole them. Doesn't matter. That bird is a useless hunk of metal right now. Those people got hold of it. Fucking vultures. Picked the corpse clean. What I need is your plane, which your grandgirl here says you have, and she'd better not be lying because that's the only reason I made this call. What've you got?"

Émilie tells him. He's still suspicious, particularly about the possibility Émilie flew it in herself. So he quizzes her, and meets each answer with a sniff that reminds me of when guys quizzed me on guns. Instead of nodding at my answers with grudging acceptance, they'd give this sniff, as they watched their chance to mock me plummet. Victor might be really hoping Émilie has a plane, but he can't help being annoyed, too, that she isn't fitting into his prebuilt little-old-lady box.

Finally he says, "Fine. You know how to fly and you own a plane. Doesn't mean you brought it here."

"Would you like me to fly a loop over the forest for you?"

"Can't fly loops in that."

"Then might I suggest you've never flown one?"

She doesn't say a Cessna TTx is out of his price range. She doesn't need to. He mutters in Danish as she tugs control into her corner of the mat. He'd fooled us with his unaccented and idiomatic English, but that's our fault — failing to remember that not everyone who speaks perfect English is a native English speaker.

"Fine," he says. "I'll take the plane."

"Borrow it, you mean."

"Hell, no. I need to get out of this mess, and that baby is worth a pretty penny. That's the price of your grandgirl, Miz Émilie."

"All right."

Hesitation, as if he realizes he should have asked for more.

Émilie continues. "I'll tell the sheriff that I'm flying to search for my granddaughter. If they insist I take a copilot, I'll bring the council representative. He isn't aware of the situation, but his silence would come cheap. He's been exiled here, and he's rather desperate to leave."

Victor grunts. "I know how he feels. I was brought in on this damn job by a buddy who swore the company knew the value of good employees. I have a feeling his opinion changed, but I can't ask him, since he's lying in pieces somewhere in this fucking forest."

"I would point out that I am not your employer," she says. "I have not been affiliated with your employer in thirty years. But that is hardly your point or your concern. You feel that you've been betrayed and you want out, and I am going to provide that. Tell me where you left your plane, and I will join you there in one hour."

The plane isn't within easy walking distance. The Danes must have been given an area to search for hostiles, and they've landed on the other side of it, as far as possible from Rockton. So we're taking the ATV while Émilie flies.

Phil is *not* going with Émilie. Dalton is. He's playing Phil. Yep, when I first suggested that, I got a split-second "Huh?" look from Dalton, as if I'd forgotten that he'd been there when we found Victor . . . who isn't actually blind.

"You'll be wearing shades and hearing protectors," I say. "You should fit into Phil's business clothes."

A tiny whimper from Phil, who clears his throat to cover it.

"We'll get them dry-cleaned after," I say. "Or, more likely, replaced. If Eric has to wrestle Victor down, he might break a seam or two."

"If that is a disparaging comment about my physique, I am in perfectly fine shape," Phil says. "Eric is hardly Will. He won't burst from my shirts like the Incredible Hulk."

"Damn," I say. " 'Cause that'd be hot."

A low rumble of chuckles as everyone relaxes a little.

I continue. "We'll borrow your glasses, too, Phil, in case he needs to remove his shades."

He hands them over. Dalton puts them on, and I say, "You owe me twenty bucks. Right?"

"Yeah," Dalton mutters.

Émilie's brows rise.

"We had a bet," I say. "I said they were plain glass."

Phil opens his mouth to protest, but I cut

him off with, "Let's finish playing dress-up and get going."

We take Anders. That's a risk — it leaves the town exposed. But with Petra gone and Kenny less than fully ambulatory, there's no one else I can trust to cover my back. Kenny will be in charge of Rockton, with others stepping forward to assist, and they all know that the priority today is surveillance. Watch our borders. Any trouble — from hostiles to unexpected planes — fire off a flare, and we'll abandon our mission to get back.

Another person joins us. Maryanne. She knows the shaman, and while I argue that the hostiles have nothing to do with Petra's kidnapping, they are out there, and they're pissed off, and they may have Edwin and Felicity. We haven't forgotten their plight. We just need to deal with Petra's first. We'll take the ATV, while Storm runs beside us.

We're almost at the stopping point before we hear Émilie's plane. That's still cutting it close. I make the executive decision to use the noise of the plane to drive a little farther. Soon, though, we're off the vehicle and jogging on foot. There are no paths, and I'm in the lead, finding game trails, before Maryanne softly asks if she can take over. Of course she should — she is the expert out here.

As we run, the plane circles twice, as if second-guessing its landing spot. That'd be at Dalton's command, making sure we see where to go. We do, and it helps that we're downwind, because Storm catches Petra's scent and gives a little whine of excitement. I tell her to stay on that scent, quietly, and she moves into the lead, deftly finding a path that her big body can pass through.

It's Anders who sees Victor's plane first, when a beam of sunlight strikes the metal. As Émilie's plane lands, my heart thumps. I'd wanted to be in position before they touched down. I get Anders to cover me, and I tell Storm to wait with them. Then I slip through the forest, my gun out as I stay in the shadows.

I spot Victor. I don't see Petra, but I trust she's nearby and safe. I position myself to come out behind Victor as he keeps his gaze — and a gun — trained on Émilie's plane, idling in place, doors shut.

The second plane sits ten meters away. Even from here I can see the damage, and I remember Victor saying he couldn't leave because the "vultures" had picked it clean. Hostiles taking what they could? Or intentionally disabling it?

I glance back and wave for Anders to join

me. Maryanne and Storm will stay where they are.

I don't wait for Anders to catch up. While those propellers are turning, the whoosh of them drowns out all sound, and I need to get into the best possible position to defend Dalton. Yes, Émilie and Petra are there, too, but my attention is on Dalton. I know Victor's is, too — faced with an eightysomething woman and a thirtysomething guy, he'll focus on the male part of the equation.

Victor has made a mistake, though. He's on the wrong side of the clearing, opposite the pilot's door instead of the passenger's. He takes a step toward the front of the plane, realizing his tactical error, but there's no time to correct it now.

"Get out of the plane," he shouts.

The pilot's door opens, and Émilie waves a gloved hand. "Show a little patience, young man. It takes me awhile to get anywhere these days."

She takes her time sliding from the seat, and when she's on the ground, he shouts, "Are you turning off the damned plane?"

She throws up her hands. "You told me to get out." She turns. "Phil? Please shut off the engine."

"You get out, too," Victor shouts over the engine noise.

"Before or after I turn the engine off?" Dalton calls back, and his usual drawl is clipped with Phil-like annoyance.

"Turn the fucking plane off, get out, and come around where I can see you. Hands raised. If you have a gun, I'd suggest you leave it behind because if I see it, I'm shooting."

Hesitation, and then Dalton lifts a gun and puts it aside. Even through the windows, I can tell it isn't his revolver — the barrel is too short.

See, I'm disarming. You're in control here.

"Where's my granddaughter?" Émilie says.

Victor waves toward the other plane, his gaze never leaving Dalton as he walks around to the front.

Émilie starts to hurry over and then catches herself, moving slower as she makes her way to the plane. Dalton stays in the shade with his hands raised. He is indeed dressed as Phil, in new jeans and a button-down shirt. He's taken off the shades and put on Phil's glasses instead. He's also shaved, and it gives his face a babyish look that, with the outfit, is a far cry from the wilderness sheriff Victor saw earlier.

Victor grunts, satisfied that this is the right guy. That means he's nervous — too nervous to insist Dalton come closer and too nervous to question. Dalton looks like a pencil pusher, so that must be what he is.

Gun still trained on Dalton, Victor looks over at Émilie as she yanks on the other plane's passenger door.

"Not there," Victor shouts. "The cargo hold."

She goes to the next door and pulls, grunting with the strain.

"Oh, for fuck's sake. It's open. Just pull."

Another grunting tug. Victor curses some more and stalks over. The moment he walks away, Dalton slides out his revolver. He points it at Victor, who doesn't even glance back, distracted and intent on his mission. Émilie steps aside, and Victor yanks open the cargo door.

"She's right — What the hell?"

He leans into the cargo hold. "Where the fuck — ?"

"Behind you," says a voice.

Victor backs out and slowly turns toward the tail of the plane, where Petra holds a little Beretta Pico on him. Then she sees Dalton over Victor's shoulder.

"Shit," she says. "Way to ruin my moment, Eric."

Victor looks over and spots Dalton, revolver trained on him. Victor's gun arm swings up on Émilie, but she's already five feet away, and Petra yanks her back.

"Casey?" Petra calls. "I'm guessing there's a third gun on this bastard?"

"Third and fourth," Anders calls back as I walk from the forest.

Petra shoves her tiny pistol into her pocket and makes sure Émilie is safely behind the plane before she goes after Victor. He still tries to raise his gun, but she's on him, and the gun's wrested free.

"Your turn to put your hands up," Dalton says as he tugs out a wrist tie.

Victor peers at the handcuffs and then up into Dalton's face. "Fuck."

"Yep," Dalton says. "You've seen me before, and you don't even have the excuse of blindness. You were just in too big a hurry to get your plane. Now turn around and —"

Victor staggers back, and everyone jumps, three guns training on him. Dalton barks at Victor to stop. Then we see the blood blossoming on Victor's shoulder. He thumps against the plane, metal clanging.

Blood on his shoulder, not from a bullet, but from the arrow embedded there.

Thirty-Five

"Will! Get down!" Dalton shouts as he pushes me toward the open plane hatch.

I give him a shove toward the front of the plane. Dalton nods and runs around front, leaving Petra and me at the back. Victor stumbles after us until the *thwack* of a second arrow has him slamming into the door. I glance over to see him sliding to the ground.

I get around Victor's plane and find another cargo door. It opens before we can reach for the handle. Émilie's holding it for us, and we scramble inside. Dalton's there a second later, and I pull him in.

The first thing Dalton does is look into the cockpit, as if hoping he could fly us out despite the external damage. The panels have all been smashed, though, wiring pulled out. Definitely intentional. We aren't going anywhere.

Outside, Victor whimpers. I glance

through the dirty window, but I don't see him. He's on the ground, shot twice, possibly dying. I don't care. Can't care. Anyone who helps him will risk the same.

"Will," I whisper to Dalton. "Will and Storm and Maryanne are out there."

His nod is curt. He is very aware of who we've left in the forest. I think about Felicity and Edwin, but push them from my mind. Later. They must wait for later.

Seconds pass, and then comes the thunder of running paws. Storm bursts from the forest. I lean out the far hatch, and she runs straight to me, clambering in.

"Tight quarters," Émilie says with an even tighter smile, as we rearrange ourselves in the cargo hold.

"Fish in a barrel," Petra mutters.

I shake my head. "We're fine. I'd like that other hatch closed, but as long as someone's guarding —"

"Got it," she says, turning her gun that way.

"You okay?" I murmur as I lean toward her.

"My ego is on life support, but I'm fine. Asshole." She scowls toward the hatch, and then shakes her head and inches that way.

Dalton glances at the other plane, as if wondering whether we could get to it and escape. It's too far and too dangerous for all of us to make that run, even if we would all fit, which I doubt.

I lean out the back as Dalton covers me. I listen for Victor but hear nothing. Then I listen for Anders. Still nothing. Is he lying low with Maryanne? I hope so. I pat Storm, reassuring her, and she nuzzles my hand.

"I'm coming out!" a voice shouts. "And I have a hostage. Fire at me, and I fire at him."

It's Anders. My heart thuds, and Dalton tenses, rocking toward the front hatch. Anders is coming that way, and there's nothing either of us can do to stop him. Leaping from the plane would only give our attackers a second target without protecting the first.

"You folks can see me?" Anders says. "Just stay cool, and he'll be fine."

Anders appears through my angled vision out the hatch, and when I see him, my heart does a double thud. His hostage is the young hostile. The boy isn't small, but beside Anders, he looks like a child, his face blank with terror as Anders hustles him along, positioning the boy between him and the forest. Between him and whoever is out there with bows and arrows.

Whoever? No, we know who it is now. The

shaman and her troop of hostiles.

A soft noise behind us has me spinning, gun up, cursing myself for not monitoring that open back door. But Émilie is — she has Victor's gun, which Petra must have given her, and she already has it trained on the newcomer. Or she did, until she saw it's Maryanne. That's part of Anders's ploy. Create a distraction so Maryanne can get to us.

I let Émilie help Maryanne in while I cover Anders. When Dalton eases forward, I resist snatching him back. Yes, he's moving into a more exposed position, but Anders needs that. From our vantage point, Petra and I can only survey the left side of the forest.

Dalton hesitates a split second, and then darts to the other side of the hatch. No one fires from the forest. Outside, Anders is almost to us, still using his military voice as he talks to the hidden hostiles. That voice is rock-steady, just short of a bark.

He's almost to us when the arrow comes. He must hear a *thwang* that we miss. He moves fast but the young man still lets out a hiss of pain, and we open fire. We shoot into the trees, above anyone's head, the sudden gunfire intended as both warning and cover as Anders drags the boy the last few feet, and then Maryanne and Émilie haul them both in.

Once they're inside, we stop shooting, and the forest goes silent. While Petra and Dalton stand guard, I crawl over to the boy.

Blood soaks his shirt. A hole shows the arrow's path through his side.

"They aimed at him," Anders growls as he rips off the boy's bloodied and dirt-crusted shirt. "They damn well aimed at him. Their own goddamned guy."

I get the young man lying down. Maryanne is there, crouched at his side, gripping his hand.

"You're okay," Maryanne says. "You're okay."

She smiles down at him, and it's a big smile, one that shows her teeth — her filed teeth — and that is intentional. When she says "You're okay" again, his eyes fill with tears.

"Yeah, he's fine," Anders says. "Looks like they just nicked him."

That isn't what Maryanne means. Not the injury but his ordeal.

You're safe. You'll be fine.

"If I hadn't seen it coming, though?" Anders shakes his head. "It was a chest shot. Mother*fuckers*. They were taking out their own guy."

I could say that I'm not surprised. At the time, I'd been too worried about Anders to see the danger the boy faced, but now I realize that they absolutely would have taken him out. Maryanne had warned us that the shaman wouldn't hesitate to use him.

Did they shoot him so they could get to Anders? Or to show us the futility of taking hostages? Or because the boy had been too "weak" to avoid capture?

From what Maryanne said of the shaman, I'm betting on the last two. Even with that insight, though, Anders couldn't have foreseen this. He comes from the military, where taking out your own man is unthinkable.

"You're okay," I tell the young man, and he seems to see me for the first time.

"Careful," he whispers, his voice rough with disuse. "Please, please be careful. She's . . ."

He swallows and doesn't finish, and he doesn't need to. The "bad guys" in this scenario may be a distant Danish corporation and its agents, but the real danger lies in its victims.

We want to help the hostiles — or at least those who'll accept help — but that doesn't matter. There's no opposing team to fight, so the hostiles will fight us. We still don't want to attack if there's a choice, especially when they may have Felicity and Edwin. I ask Anders, but he hasn't seen them. He did see Victor and thinks he's dead.

As Dalton and Petra and Émilie guard the exits, I talk with Anders, and the boy contributes where he can. Bennett. That's his name. First or last, I don't know. It doesn't matter yet.

Anders spotted one hostile — that's how he saw the movement that preceded the arrow fire. He'd also spotted another before he'd grabbed Bennett. Dalton and Petra check Anders's directions and find both hostiles still in place.

According to Bennett, there are five people left of the shaman's group. Two of them are watching "the old man and the girl." Felicity and Edwin are alive. Relief surges . . . until I realize this only adds to our need to resolve this peacefully. Otherwise, the hostiles may kill them for revenge.

Worse, the shaman's group has apparently joined forces with the other group, the shaman having rallied them to the fight. Only a few members of that group are here. A total of five in the woods then, including the wounded shaman. Three are armed with bows.

Dalton listens to the assessment and then

opens his mouth, but Petra beats him to it.

"Eric?" she says. "I'm going to suggest you let me and Will go after the ones we have eyes on. That's two of the three archers."

He hesitates, but only to check with Anders.

"Makes sense," Anders says. "If Petra and I can subdue them quietly, that leaves one bow, one guy armed with a knife, and the wounded leader."

They head to the back hatch. Dalton shouts out the hatch, "We want to talk to the woman in charge!"

Silence.

"We know it's a woman. Your shaman or whatever. Your leader."

Silence.

"Fucking hell. Seriously? We know your numbers. We might be holed up like cornered foxes, but that only means we've got eyes and guns on the exits, and we're feeling a little trigger-happy. There are seven fucking people crammed in this tin can. Five guns. One really big dog. You honestly want to test your odds?"

Still no answer. He shifts his gaze, making sure Anders and Petra are gone before he continues his bluster.

"So what the fuck are we doing here?" he shouts. "You sit in the forest? We sit in this plane? Wait for dark? That's a helluva long time, and I can guarantee you, the dark will be our friend, not yours. We'll shine flashlights out this hatch and see you coming."

Nothing.

Before he can react, I lean into the open hatch.

"I would like to speak to the woman I shot!" I shout. "I know you're capable of talking."

I pull back fast, even as Dalton growls.

It takes a moment. Then the shaman calls back, "I will talk to you. Not him. You. But you need to come out."

Dalton's laugh echoes through the clearing. "Fuck no."

"You can be silent," the shaman calls. "You call us savages, but you can barely speak a sentence without that word. You are ignorant and uneducated."

I glance over at Maryanne, who is staring at the side of the plane as if she can see through the metal. Her brows are knitted, as if she's not quite sure what she's hearing. When I catch her eye, I lift my brows and mouth, *Is that not her?*

"No, it is," she whispers. "I've just never heard . . ." She swallows. "She always spoke better than the rest, but not like that. Not so fluently."

I think Maryanne's hunch was right — the shaman regulated her own intake of the narcotics. She kept her mind clear and her wits sharp. Dalton hides his intelligence behind his rough language. She hid hers behind fractured speech.

"If I come out, so do you," I say. "If your people shoot at me, you'll be dead before you can get back into the forest."

"I know that."

"Do your people?"

"They will not fire unless I tell them to," she says.

"Will you come out and speak to me?"

"If there isn't a gun pointed at me."

"Well, since I can't tell whether there's an arrow pointed at me, that's a problem."

"Lower *your* weapon," she says. "That will be enough."

"Agreed."

We proceed with care. She steps to a point where Dalton can spot her through the trees, and then I ease into the hatch opening.

My gaze goes first to Victor. He lies slumped on the ground, his eyes shut. Dead? I can't say for certain, but I think so, and if not, there's nothing I can do. Nothing I particularly want to do either as the image of that dead settler family surfaces.

The shaman and I proceed step by careful step until we stand in the clearing less than three feet apart. This is the first time I've seen her in the full light of day. She's older than I thought, definitely in her sixties. Her shoulder has been patched up more expertly than I would have expected, given the substandard medical care I saw on Mary-anne.

It's one thing to lack the skills to do better; it's another to have those skills and withhold them, and my dislike for this woman solidifies into something dangerously close to hate. I rein it in. I can't afford that. I'm here to get my people to safety, and protect Edwin and Felicity, and help those hostiles who will accept it.

"You shot me," the shaman says without preamble.

"You tried to attack us."

"I tried to attack the man who murdered one of my people. You also killed my husband and two more of my people a year ago."

"Again, in self-defense. They took us captive, and they planned to kill us for our clothing and supplies."

Anger surges through my voice. I want to say more. I want to say that this is what they do at her behest. They will kill us for trespassing on their territory. They will kill us for our goods. They will take us captive and brainwash us like they did to Mary-anne. I don't know what Bennett's story is, but my gut says he wasn't with them by choice. They had lost men. They needed more, and so they took one. Because this woman told them to.

If I start down that road, I will not come back. So I say, as evenly as I can, "We are not your enemy."

She snorts.

"Your group attacked three people in the forest last week," I say. "They were with him." I nod back at Victor. "You attacked because they were hunting you. Because you had reason to believe you were in danger. Yes?"

No answer.

"Did you *not* attack them?" I press. "Are you *not* responsible?"

Still nothing, which tells me I'm correct. She just doesn't deign to answer.

"You did. Presuming it was self-defense, that's between you and them. It has nothing to do with my people in that plane or the settlers you've kidnapped."

Her face remains implacable, and my frustration rises.

"What do you want?" I say.

"To be left alone."

I gesture toward Victor again. "Considering you just killed the last of the four who came after you, it seems you've got your wish."

"More will come."

"Not if I can stop it, which I think I can. However, if you kill us, more will definitely come, because the only people who give a shit about you are here."

Her lip curls. "You'll protect us, will you?"

"Yes, Heidi," says a voice behind us. "They'll protect you."

At the name, the woman's head jerks up, her lip curling even more as her gaze lands on Émilie, sliding from the plane as Dalton grabs for her. Émilie brushes him off and steps forward.

"Hello, Heidi," Émilie says. "I always wondered where you ended up."

The woman — Heidi — lets out a sound close to a growl.

"She's . . ." I glance at Émilie. "She's one of the researchers, isn't she? One of the original Danish employees."

"Not Danish. Canadian. Heidi worked for us — worked *with* me — until she quit about a year before the Danish firm sent two researchers up here. Apparently, she got a better offer. Funny that she wouldn't just say so. Our firms were working together. Or so I thought. She obviously knew better."

"So you came to Rockton," I say to Heidi. "You and your new colleague joined the Second Settlement and quietly developed the stronger version of Hendricks's teas. Then you took settlers into the wilderness to create your own cult."

Her entire face contorts in a sneer. I knew it would. That's the point. Make up something so insulting that she'll rise to the bait.

"Cult? We were professionals. We were conducting research. Then the firm decided they were done with us. Time to come home, they said. Home? Yes, in a *casket.*"

Heidi turns to Émilie. "They did headhunt me away from you, but I thought I was just changing jobs. A new challenge. A new chance to make a name for myself. Then Georg told me the truth. If we failed, we lost our value as assets and became liabilities. They'd kill us. *Kill* us." Her voice rises.

"And you believed him?" I say.

"No, I did not. I agreed, however, to run. To be careful. Our employers came after us. Tried to kill us. There was no doubt, then."

"Georg was the other researcher," I say. "Your partner. The man who died last year."

A bitter laugh. "No, that was not Georg. We parted ways long ago. We divided our people."

"He leads the other group."

"Did. He died years ago. He was a fool. I should have known that. Only a fool would have taken that job knowing how it could end. A greedy fool."

"When your research failed, you became a threat to —"

"We did not *fail.* We did as they asked. We created what they asked, and I perfected its use. You've seen my people. Soldiers who follow my orders without question. I gave that company what it wanted, and then I was stuck living with these . . . these creatures."

It takes everything in me not to grab my gun and pistolwhip her. She *created* these "creatures," and then she kept creating them long after the study ended. Kept them as her own private cult.

She might hate that word, but it's true. She created a cult of half zombies who did her bidding, and at any time she could have stopped providing the narcotics and freed their minds. But she didn't. She may not have been drinking as much as the others, but she'd become an addict in her own way. Addicted to the power of controlling lives.

"It's all over now," Émilie says. "I had nothing to do with what happened to you, and now that I know the truth, I can help you out of this. I'll protect you. I'll take you home."

"Home?" Heidi's voice rises with that fresh edge of hysteria, and as I look into her eyes, a shiver runs through me.

Here is the full answer for what I'm seeing. Yes, Heidi had been trapped in the wilderness, unable to go home. Yes, the power she discovered was addictive. But that doesn't explain all of this. Madness does, and that is what I see in her eyes. Madness.

For years, the sheriffs of Rockton presumed the hostiles were simply people who'd reverted to a more primitive form. I'd dismissed that, but it is part of the answer. Heidi is not sane. She likely hasn't met the legal definition of that word in a very long time.

She lost something out here. Lost or surrendered it. Dr. Moreau on her island, creating creatures to serve her, descending into madness.

"You think I can go home?" she says. "After all this? Pick up where I left off? My friends and family have long forgotten me.

And look at me. *Look.* There is no going home."

"Yes, there is. I can —"

Heidi lunges at Émilie, and I pull my gun, but Heidi's rush is only a feint, cut short before Émilie can even stagger back. Heidi looks at my gun and instead of snarling at me to put it away, she smiles.

She smiles.

That wasn't a feint. She wanted me to pull my gun. She wanted her people to see that and think she is under attack.

Dalton scrambles from the plane, shouting, "Get the hell over here, Casey!"

But nothing moves in the forest, and barely a heartbeat passes before Anders shouts, "Clear!"

"All of them?" I yell back.

"The three archers are in cuffs. There was another woman with a knife. She bolted."

Heidi snarls, spinning on the forest. "Liar!"

"It's over, Heidi," Émilie says.

Heidi wheels on her, but Émilie raises Petra's little gun and says, "No."

"Fine," Heidi spits. "Let me go. I'll —"

"It is over." Émilie enunciates each word. "You are going home, whether you want to or not. Your people are going home, whether they want to or not."

"They'll want to," Maryanne says as she comes around the back of the plane. "Most will. Once their minds are clear. Even if they joined by choice, no one stayed by choice."

"You!" Heidi lunges at Maryanne, but I grab her as Dalton comes over to tie her hands.

Heidi pulls harder than I expect, and she breaks free, getting two steps before Maryanne yells, "No!," and I think she means Heidi. But then I see Maryanne running for the plane. The boy, Bennett, is out of the plane and aiming a gun at Heidi. Maryanne is running right into the line of fire.

"Maryanne!" I shout as I lunge her way.

But Bennett doesn't shoot. He just stands, frozen. Then Maryanne is there, taking the gun from him, and he lets her, his eyes glistening with tears as he rocks in place.

"She's — she's —" he says.

"She's nothing," Maryanne says to him as we cuff Heidi. "Not anymore."

He nods and falls against her shoulder as her arms go around him.

Thirty-Six

We don't linger after that. Victor is definitely dead, and he's taken any further answers with him. We need to find Edwin and Felicity. We know at least one hostile fled, possibly to warn those holding them captive. Following Bennett's directions, Dalton and I take off with Storm and leave the handcuffed hostiles with Petra and Anders.

It turns out there's no need for concern. Yes, the remaining hostile did run to the others, but only to warn them to flee. The three of them melted into the forest, leaving Felicity and Edwin, who are half out of their bindings by the time we arrive. They're unharmed. They were only pawns, grabbed by a madwoman because she'd been sane enough to know that if they'd been coming from Rockton, they could be valuable hostages.

As we're escorting Edwin and Felicity, we meet two of Edwin's men searching. We leave Edwin and Felicity with them after securing a promise that they'll send Sebastian home tomorrow.

Once they're on their way, we take a moment to breathe, just breathe. And then we head back to help Anders get the hostiles to Rockton.

Four captive hostiles. I don't include Bennett in that. He's been a prisoner for two months, and we won't treat him as one now. On the way to Rockton, we get his story. He's from a community nearly two days' walk from here. A couple of months ago, he'd been captured while hunting away from home. His family and community will certainly have been searching for him, but he hadn't told anyone where he was going — he'd left after a fight with his parents, needing time alone. He's eighteen, and the authorities may have written him off as a runaway. In northern communities, particularly Indigenous ones, that's often as far as an official "investigation" goes.

For Bennett, the last couple of months are a blur. He barely believes me when I tell him it's May — he'd presumed this must be a freakishly early thaw, because there's no way two months have passed. We'll need to have a long talk about what happened and what to tell his community, but he's a smart kid, and I trust he'll help us out with whatever spin we put on it.

We don't bring the hostiles into Rockton. That's unsafe on so many levels. We put them in the hangar. Émilie, Phil, and the council arrange a swift pickup.

Do we trust the council with this? I can't even begin to answer that. All I know is that our priority is Rockton and its residents, and I will grudgingly trust Émilie to oversee the hostiles' proper care and rehabilitation.

As for the small group still left in the forest, any action there has been put on hold. Rounding them up and shipping them south for reintegration smacks of some very ugly history, but in this case — knowing that most have been unwilling participants in an experiment — it's a move we must seriously consider.

Dalton and I are in the Roc. It's two in the morning. Going on forty-eight hours without sleep, and now that the hostiles are gone, we should be in bed. But Isabel wanted a celebratory drink, in honor of solving the hostile mystery, and the truth is that I'm not sure I could sleep just yet.

So we're in the Roc waiting for Isabel. A single candle lights the silent building. Storm sleeps nearby, a celebratory bone abandoned nearly untouched before she drifted off.

"You did it," Dalton says, his arms around me as I stand with my back to the wall.

He hugs me so tight I can't breathe. There are congratulations in that hug and there is pride and there is love, and there are all the things I desperately wanted from my family growing up and never got. I can wallow in self-pity about that, or I can accept that my family was unable to give what I needed. They *did* love me. They *were* proud of me. Whatever I lacked, I have it now, in this place, with this man, and my eyes flood with tears.

I look up at him and say, "Do you think it's enough? That this will fix things?"

He hesitates, and then his smile falters. It doesn't break or evaporate. One second of dismay, and it returns with a fierceness that sends pride and love coursing through *me.*

"It will be," he says. "We'll make sure it is."

"I fear it's not that easy, Eric," says a soft voice from the shadows.

We turn to see Isabel, bottle in hand as she closes the storeroom door.

"Rey Sol Añejo," she says as she lifts the tequila. "Bought specially for when you solved this mystery, Casey, because I knew you would." She sets the bottle down. "You solved all the mysteries. Dead tourists who weren't tourists at all. Dead settlers mistaken for hostiles. And the hostiles themselves — the biggest mystery of all. Solved in one fell swoop."

She pours a shot of tequila and holds it out.

As I take it, she says, "But now comes the big question. Does it matter? Yes, I know what's happening here. Phil told me your suspicions, and I think you're right. They are shutting us down. The hostiles were the apparent reason but . . ."

"They were an excuse," I say.

"Jury's still out on that one," says another voice, and I look to see the door open, Petra coming in, others following. Kenny and then April. Mathias and Anders. Phil bringing up the rear and shutting the door behind them.

"Surprise!" Petra says, throwing up her arms.

I chuckle, the sound a little ragged. "Not sure if this is a surprise party or an intervention."

"Party?" April says. "I was told it was a meeting to plan —"

"— to *discuss,*" Isabel says as she passes out shots. "A meeting to discuss our future as a town. Or for now, just to say that we're in."

"You're in . . . ?" I begin. "For your relocation plan," she says. "Yours and Eric's." Petra clears her throat. "Yes," Isabel says. "Some of us believe we're jumping the gun, and it will all work out fine, but I'm told you believe in planning ahead. Having contingencies, just in case."

"Who told . . . ?" I look at Dalton.

He shrugs. "I said everything would be okay. I didn't say *how* it would be."

Phil says, "Like Petra, I believe this is indeed jumping the gun. But I also agree with you, Casey, that contingency plans are never a waste of time. I'm not saying I'd join you if you relocated, but I believe I can be of assistance on the management side of preparations."

I look across their faces, and the tears well again.

April strides over, casting a cold look at the others. "Petra and Phil are correct. This discussion is premature, and it upsets Casey unnecessarily."

I smile at her and shake my head. "I'm not upset, April. Just . . ." I'm not sure how to articulate what this means to me, seeing all these people — our friends — here to support the idea of Rockton, to support us and our ability to make it happen. So I just take a deep breath and say, "Thank you. It — it means a lot."

"And hopefully will indeed be unnecessary," Isabel says. "But in case it isn't, I declare this the first meeting of the potential next Rockton. Drink up, and let's talk."

ABOUT THE AUTHOR

Kelley Armstrong graduated with a degree in psychology and then studied computer programming. Now, she is a full-time writer and parent, and she lives with her husband and three children in rural Ontario, Canada.

The employees of Thorndike Press hope you have enjoyed this Large Print book. All our Thorndike, Wheeler, and Kennebec Large Print titles are designed for easy reading, and all our books are made to last. Other Thorndike Press Large Print books are available at your library, through selected bookstores, or directly from us.

For information about titles, please call:
(800) 223-1244

or visit our website at:
gale.com/thorndike

To share your comments, please write:

Publisher
Thorndike Press
10 Water St., Suite 310
Waterville, ME 04901

